DEADLY OPPONENT

A shadow fell across hers, and Senea spun around, to stare into the face of a Heldan who had just come up behind her.

The enemy.

And she was alone.

She dove as he jumped for her. He hit her from behind, body to body, throwing her to the ground. Senea struggled under him, trying to throw him off.

"You're a little wild one, aren't you?" he said. Then the Heldan drew in a breath and shifted his weight on her. Senea was just able to glimpse a change in his eyes before his form was blurred by a dark aura that seemed to flow out of him.

A tingling sensation ran from his fingers through her skin and arm. The air became bitterly cold, as darkness came over her—it was something wrong . . . so hideously wrong that it was beyond her understanding . . .

THE HELDAN

Deborah Talmadge-Bickmore

A Del Rey Book
BALLANTINE BOOKS • NEW YORK

A Del Rey Book
Published by Ballantine Books

Copyright © 1994 by Deborah Talmadge-Bickmore

Library of Congress Catalog Card Number: 93-90864

ISBN 0-345-38243-9

Manufactured in the United States of America

First Edition: April 1994

10 9 8 7 6 5 4 3 2 1

Dedicated to:
Cory, Jaime, Lori-ann and Lowell.

Also
To my mother.
And to the memory of Charlee.

CHAPTER ONE

The door thudded open, echoing heavily against the wall. The objects on the mantel over the hearth shook with a sharp rattle. Melina broke in, short of breath from running. There was excitement on her face, and her red hair was in disarray.

The rag rested on the rough wooden table, Senea's hand clenched around it. Their mother looked up from the mending she was doing, and their father turned from the fire.

"Father," Melina said breathlessly, glancing at Senea with a strange expression in her green eyes. It was almost as if she suppressed a wild exultation. "There is news. A rumor going around. Aldived has called for held-law."

There was utter silence.

The rag sped from Senea's hand abruptly and struck the opposite wall, spattered the plaster with a wet spray, and fell to the floor.

Senea slammed the bucket of water on the table, sloshing water over the rim, and stalked out of the house, leaving shock in the room behind her.

Mother and father looked at each other, helpless in their distress.

And from the corner, where she had been sitting quietly, playing with a rag doll, Loran stirred and rose. She went to her mother, frightened from the sudden tension that gripped the room.

"What's held-law?" she asked.

"Shush, child," her mother said, and looked to her husband. "Tolen?"

He rose. "I'll go and find out the truth of this."

Melina went to the table and sat down on the bench, gath-

1

ering the folds of her loose-fitting dress into her lap. Tolen left, closing the door that Senea had left standing open.

"Senea will have to go to the Held." Hope was in Melina's voice.

"Be quiet, Melina. It may only be a rumor."

Loran looked from one to the other. "Is Senea going to be a heldan?"

"She is the oldest," Melina said. "And she is not wed. That makes her the one to go."

"We don't know anything for certain."

"Mother, don't you see what this means?" Melina asked, trying desperately to hold on to the elated hope that she felt. "Aldived will pay dowry, and then I can get married."

"Do you want Senea to go into the Held?" her mother asked angrily, upset at Melina's words.

"Why not? No one wants to marry her anymore. I don't want to become an old maid just because she turned down everyone who ever asked for her, and now she's so old nobody wants her."

"Melina, that is enough!"

"You know it's true!" Melina said. "Neither Loran nor I can get married if Senea doesn't. At least if she goes into the Held—"

"I said, that's enough!"

Melina glowered at her mother and fell into an angry silence.

"Mother?" Loran's frightened voice was almost a whisper. "Will Senea become a heldan witch?"

For the first time since Melina had come into the house their mother paled. She turned and looked squarely at Loren.

"That custom has been changed," she said firmly.

She looked to Melina and marked the new expression on her daughter's face. It spoke like a shout in the silent room.

Melina sat like a girl carved out of granite. Her eyes were suddenly cold and hard as marble. Only her hands moved, twisting and untwisting, and that was from anger and hatred. And the movements were in the ancient patterns for protection against evil.

A chill came on Senea's mother that had nothing to do with held-law and its taking of her firstborn. It was not so simple to say that customs had been changed. No one knew for certain what the helden did behind their walls.

* * *

There was a flatness in the world stretching as far as the eye could see in any direction. It was illusion only, though, for there were valleys, ravines, and canyons out there where few ventured. Out there helden watched, and protected, and kept the peace. They were silent, unseen guardians of the people, each held-tribe guarded by their own.

They were a caste of warriors, the helden, men and women alike, each taken by held-law, a law that was called for at the discretion of the Tribelord. The oldest unwed child from each family in the held-tribe by law became of the held-caste, entered the Held, and became a warrior, one of the protectors of the people.

The last time held-law had been called, Senea had been a young child, too young to be taken, and therefore had been spared. None of the family thought that the call would come again for many more years, and thus all daughters of Tolen would be safely within marriage when it did come. The last thing Senea had expected was for it to happen to her.

One could see most of the plain from where Senea sat in her solitary anger. She came here sometimes, to this rise of hill behind the valley where the held-tribe was located, to this place of aloneness where she could sit and let the quiet of the vast plain soothe her.

But this day Senea sat, brooding, on the crest of the hill, angrily ignoring the plain that lay in soft colors of apricot and gold. She was twenty-four years old, as the time was reckoned in the held-tribe, from wet season to wet season. It was long past the time when it was appropriate for her to have begun her own family and to have brought a dowry from the man she was to wed to her father. But none that had approached her had appealed to her, and there had never been anyone that she loved. And she would not marry out of duty. Then, finally, no one asked anymore.

A daughter who did not bring a dowry to her father's house was without value and a disappointment, one that Senea could easily see in her father's eyes. On her mother's face she only saw pain and sadness. Her two younger sisters had no hope, ever, of being wed until she did, and Melina, who was six years younger than she and of age, went out often to talk to a shy young man who loved her. They wanted to get married, but it was hopeless for them. Senea must wed first, and there was no one who showed interest anymore. She thought on this as she sat.

She had watched the pained anger in Melina's face slowly come over the past two seasons, then settle there permanently.

Senea flung a rock down-slope, which struck and rattled into some brush, out of sight.

Dowry.

And it would be on Aldived's terms. The Tribelord, by law, had to pay dowry for all females he took. And Aldived was Tribelord, and he had called for held-law, and held-law was irrevocable. And she was unwed. To refuse was unheard of, simply not done, even though it was a thing that she desperately wanted to do. She was no warrior, she thought angrily. Then fear raced through her. *She was no warrior.*

She ran a hand over the light hair that she wore clasped at the nape of her neck and tried to imagine herself as one of the helden that she had seen only twice in her life. She pictured herself being dressed as those two had been: breeches and sleeveless tunics, sandals laced up to the knees, with a quiver of arrows across the back, knife at hip, bow in hand, and a gold arm band on the upper arm.

She shivered. To be so brazen. She couldn't do it. She lowered her head to her knees and wept.

For long moments she stayed thus, enveloped in her grief and fear. She had been brought to this through her own foolishness. When she finally would have accepted *anyone* during the past couple of years, there had been no one to claim her, no one that had desired her. But she had always kept a hope secreted in her heart that someday one would come and take her to be his. Now this would never happen. And she was afraid. She did not want to become heldan. She did not want to become a part of the held-caste because then she would never marry.

She closed her eyes and let the thoughts whirl around inside her mind at a furious pace, unable and not caring to stop them. When she finally raised her head the sun was going down.

The plain stretched out in alternating bands of apricot, blue, gray, and purple. The sky overhead had become a sullen blue-green, orange and pink at the horizon. The nightly windshift, that which each evening attended the cooling of the land, picked up and tugged at the hem around her feet.

She thought about Melina, who would surely not grieve at

this turn of events. She had seen the pain and unhappiness in the younger girl's eyes too long for her not to know that this would be a way to free her. She also owed her father and the woman who had mothered her.

Dowry increased a family's standing in the held-tribe. The greater the dowry, the greater the standing. And Aldived, being Tribelord, would give a large dowry because of held-law. This would bring honor to the name of Tolen in the held-tribe.

She rose up of a sudden, her mind set with determination on the idea of bringing honor to her father and happiness to Melina. Her simple dress, a loose shift that fell from neckline to sandals, fluttered in the wind as she strode down the hill and down the wash into the wide gentle valley of her held-tribe.

The valley was edged on the south with a river and on the north with a high ridge of rock. She did not turn her head to look at the Held at the upper end of the valley. The gate there had never been open as long as she could remember.

The Held protected the entrance to the valley in which the village lay, and the helden that lived within its walls protected the rest of the lands all about, unseen and unheard.

She entered the door of her father's house quietly and looked about her, at her mother, at Loran and Melina, and finally at her father who stood looking into the fire. She closed the door and came into the room.

"I have come back," she said, not sure of what else to say. There were so many things that needed to be said, but she didn't want to broach any of them. So she stood, quietly waiting for someone else to speak.

There was silence, and Senea looked at each one of them again. Her mother was still mending as if she hadn't even moved in all that time, her head bowed, her fingers holding the shirt so tightly they were white. Loran huddled close by, her eyes wide with fear and confusion. Melina avoided her gaze, and her father still stood with his back to her, staring into the fire.

At last Tolen spoke. His voice was low, with words thick, as if he had difficulty saying them. "I have asked at the Held. Held-law is called for tomorrow morning. As soon as the sun rises."

Senea made a helpless gesture. "Then I have no choice. I must go."

Tolen bowed his head, unable to dispute her on it, and Senea simply bowed her head in turn and retreated into silence. She had nothing to say, shocked at her father's grief, touched by it as she had never been touched by anything. She almost went to him and put her arms around him, as a child would, and begged him to change it all so she wouldn't have to go. But she couldn't. There was held-law, and there was Melina.

She turned in dismay when sounds of weeping came from her mother's bowed head, bitter and quiet. Senea went to her and sank down on her heels. She put her hand over the mending and clasped her mother's fingers in her own.

"It's all right," she said. "I will be all right." She waited. The weeping stopped, but the head did not rise. "Honor will come to this house at my going," Senea continued at last. She tried to sound confident to ease some of the grief her parents were feeling. It was a confidence that she, herself, didn't have. "I have shamed you long enough."

Her mother reacted to that, took Senea's hand in her own, and pressed it to her lips.

"Mother, I will be all right. I am willing to go. Mother?" she pleaded, and waited until her mother looked up. "Melina will be free," Senea said. "It's for the best."

She turned her head, her eyes collided with Melina's, and she was astonished by the stony hatred she saw there. The girl looked up at her, unshed tears in her eyes—whether from anger or newly realized hope Senea did not know. But it was the other expression that she did not understand. She had expected that the accustomed expression of pain and anger on Melina's face would be gone. It was—but that it had been replaced by hatred puzzled her.

There was a protracted silence, then a hissing of a voice. "Heldan witch!"

And in that electric moment her world turned upside down. She shook her head. The words went right through her without touching. *Heldan witch!*

At first she had just been trying to live with the thought of becoming heldan, of leaving her family. She stared at Melina. She had heard what she had heard in her sister's voice—hatred of an ancient, feared evil. But there had not been that practice in hundreds of years. Everyone knew that.

Heldan witch!

The very idea made her feel ill, sicker even than the

thoughts of going into the Held. A sudden urge filled her to run from this place, to run straight for the plains and far away.

She rose slowly to her feet and looked down at her hands, then put them behind her to hide their sudden trembling. "I must get ready."

A cry went up. A small body impacted with hers and embraced her with a fierceness that startled her. Senea freed her hand and touched the dark head that rested against her heart.

Loran . . . her youngest sister. Senea felt the room begin to spin. For a moment, she just stared down at her.

"Don't go," Loran pleaded. "Don't go."

Senea tried to disengage Loran's arms, but the small hands were entangled in her dress and would not turn loose. Her heart was suddenly moved by the child who clung so tightly to her. She closed her eyes weakly. She had not expected this, had not expected that anyone would care that she was going to leave them and never call them family again. She had assumed that everyone would be relieved. Clearly Melina would be. She didn't want Senea here. She put her arms around the young girl and held her close.

"I'm not really going anywhere, Loran," she said. "I am going to be at the Held, that's all."

"You'll never come here again."

"But I will, sweetheart. I'll see you often." Her eyes sought her mother's, seeking understanding for the lie she had just told. "I promise." She laid a cheek on Loran's head and blinked back tears.

"You promise?" Loran echoed. Her hands did not unclench.

"Yes, dear. I promise." And Senea closed her eyes in painful guilt.

The hands relaxed and withdrew.

Senea put the child from her and forced a smile to further compound the lie. "Go play," she said. "Everything is going to be all right. You'll see." She looked at her father, who still had not turned around.

"I'll go get things ready now." And that was another untruth, for there was nothing for her to ready. She was not allowed to take anything to the Held. When Tolen did not turn around, she went uncertainly to the small room she shared with her sisters.

* * *

Senea felt her left hand aching, uncurled the clenched fingers, and looked at four bloody marks where fingernails had bitten her palm. She dropped the hand to her side. Despite herself, she felt a terrible despair engulfing her. Not only would she be lost to her family—but she would also be hated. It was some horrible joke being played.

She stood staring at the bedroom, then looked at the shelf next to the window that had her belongings neatly arranged on it. She wondered what would become of those things and doubted if she'd ever know. She looked at the bedstead that she had shared with her sisters from childhood and thought about how much less crowded it would be without her. It would be even less so after Melina was married. Loran would have the room for her own after that. She almost envied Loran that privacy. She sat down, blinked back the tears that had come unbidden, and took a deep breath to stop the sudden tremor that had come.

"I don't want to be heldan," she whispered.

CHAPTER
TWO

The dawn was showing in the east, and on any other day Senea would have been up preparing the morning meal and the tribute bread for the Held and doing the things that she used to do to make her continued presence in the house less of a burden.

But on this morning she watched the growing grayness on the horizon. Standing at the small window with her cheek against the roughness of plaster, she looked out on the quiet of the held-tribe. It was a village really, but more so, because it was far bigger than any other held-tribe, or so she had heard.

She wondered how many others were watching as she did, waiting for the sun to touch the distant hills that would signal that held-law was in force. To those to whom it applied, it would signal that they were no longer of the held-tribe, but were thereafter of the held-caste, a group apart, but vital to the safety of all the held-tribe.

She had stayed awake the long hours of the last night in her house. She tried to imagine what it would be like in held-hall, hating the waiting and yet glad for the waiting because it seemed to prolong the time until the sun began to show over the horizon. She had listened to Loran's and Melina's breathing, steady and rhythmic in their sleeping, and she knew that she would miss them desperately. She looked at their quiet faces in the darkness, deep shadows hiding most of what she longed to see.

Melina had come in earlier, silent and cold. She had readied herself for bed with her head bowed and her nostrils flaring. Senea watched her with numb patience, feeling nothing but a terrible emptiness. But it was all too clear. Melina had con-

9

trived this turn of hatred, Senea realized, out of a combination of guilt and fear—she had a personal motive for wanting Senea gone, but it was easier to hate because of a supposed superstition than to feel guilt at her sister's forced removal.

It had been hard for Senea to watch this while she was teetering on the edge of a chasm that had grown in her mind. Some deep part of her soul had longed to fall in and lose itself in that inner pit of darkness. At least the agony would have ended that way.

But slowly, inexorably, Senea's mind was propelling her toward a choice, and it was, she told herself, the only choice.

Anything was worth the happiness that she could purchase for Melina.

And there was the hope that perhaps, despite the separation from her family, she would find activity in the Held to make up for the loneliness that had become a constant companion by her side.

A thousand times that night she imagined that a knock would come to the door and someone would be there to say that it all had been a mistake, a joke of Aldived's while in one of his drunken humors. But no knock came, and no such knock would ever come.

She looked back out the window to see that the gray of the dawn now had a little pink in it. It was promising to be a morning of color. The very air seemed alive. Her heart beat strongly; her muscles were so taut that her ribs and stomach hurt as she realized how close the time was. Just a few more minutes. Not even an hour, and she'd no longer be of heldtribe. A fine sweat broke out on her face and on the palms of her hands.

In the growing light of the dawn, there was still no movement, a silence that was not usual at this time of day, when the people were usually beginning to stir about. But now, Senea could not even hear the cry of a baby, nor the bark of a dog. It was as if some dread thing hung over the whole held-tribe.

She had heard how in times past, for as long as there was memory within the tribe, the day of held-law was a day of mourning, that in the houses that gave a child to held-law there was a lamenting and weeping as if that child had died. And in truth, it was as if that child *had* died, for helden had no house, nor kinsmen. Even if they should see each other again, no acknowledgment or recognition could come between them.

A sense of wrongness grew in her, and she looked at Loren and wondered if she could ignore her sister if she ever saw her again.

Senea sat on the edge of the bed and clenched her limbs together, wrapped her arms about her legs, and watched Loran in the growing light. She was unwilling to leave without imprinting that face in her mind forever.

Of all people in the held-tribe that she was going to miss, she would feel the absence of Loran the most. Loran, who did not yet understand why having an older unwed sister was a thing of shame; Loran, who did not yet understand what was happening to that older sister because she was unwed.

Even in her own house, of the members of her father's family, she would miss Loran the most.

Of a sudden she realized that she couldn't go without saying good-bye to Loran at least one last time, desperately needing to hold her close—to tell her how much she was loved and to reassure her and tell her not to worry.

Senea could not go to the Held without doing at least that much more.

She reached over and touched the girl's hair, the dark curl that had tumbled over her brow. Senea slipped a finger under and lifted it away and smoothed the hair back gently so that she could see the sleeping face better.

The eyes opened, sleepily at first and then more clearly. "Senea?"

"Shh," Senea said, and pulled back the corner of the blanket. "Come here."

Loran went to her, and Senea gathered her up and held her close, feeling the warmth of sleep still clinging to the little body. She shut her eyes and tried to hold back the pain that suddenly came.

"What's the matter, Senea?" the sleepy voice asked.

"Nothing, dear. Just saying good-bye." She put her cheek against the curly head. "I love you, Loran."

"Me, too."

Senea tightened her arms briefly and then, to keep her grief from the little girl, said, "You love you, too?"

Loran laughed, a sleepy expel of air through her nostrils, then she said, "No, I love you, too."

"I know." Senea fell silent for a moment, listening to the

drowsy breathing close to her chest. "Loran," she said, "do you want my things?"

The little girl stirred. "You're not taking them?"

"No. I'm not going to need them."

The curly head nodded. Senea sighed inwardly. "You lay down and go back to sleep. I'll put them on your shelf."

Loran slipped back under the blanket without another word, asleep before Senea even turned away.

Senea went to her shelf, looked out the window, and saw that there was now blue in the sky. She gathered up her possessions: a comb given to her when she was ten; a throat chain that her mother had given her when she had turned old enough for the young men to properly take notice. She hadn't worn it in three years. There was her favorite rag doll that she had saved from childhood; a ring made of silver, a blue stone in the setting—this she would give to Melina, and she put it on her sister's shelf. There was a piece of silk, pale pink, a box of jeweled hairpins that she had never worn, and more that she gathered up and arranged on Loran's shelf. Then she left the room, closing the door behind her.

Her mother was there, and she looked up from the fire where she was preparing the breakfast that Senea usually cooked. Her eyes were red and swollen, and there was great pain in the way she stood, stricken to see her daughter come through the door. Senea swallowed hard and tore her eyes from her mother's face.

Tolen was standing, looking out the window by the table, just as she had been doing in the bedroom. Still he would not turn to look at her.

"It's time for me to go," she said huskily, the words constricting in her throat.

A sob shook her mother; Senea looked at her in pain, did not know what to do. There was nothing she could do. She looked back to her father, wishing that he'd turn around and face her.

There was a sudden wail from somewhere outside. The time had come. The sun had begun to show over the horizon, Senea didn't have to see it to know it. She went to her mother, took her hands, and held them tightly.

"Don't cry," she begged. "Please! For Loran. Don't cry. Spare her this."

Her mother stared at her for a long moment, eyes red and

swollen, then nodded. "You're right," she whispered. "Loran will not see any of it."

"Thank you." Senea leaned over and kissed her mother's cheek. "I love you." Then before she could be answered, before tears of her own came, she turned and went to her father.

She reached out and placed a hand on his arm. Words failed her; an ache came to her throat. Still, he did not turn. She pressed his arm to tell him the things that she could not say and stepped away.

He cried out then and pulled her to him in a grip that crushed the air out of her, then just as abruptly put her from him. He turned away and did not look back.

Senea took a faltering step backward, staring at his bowed head. Tears came that she could not stop. She looked at her mother one last time and saw that her face was wet, too. She saw then that Melina had come into the room and was watching her. Senea stared at her, suddenly bitter, a feeling that shamed her.

"Witch," Melina whispered, hate so thick around her it shivered the air like heat waves.

Pain struck Senea like a fist, and she stepped backward.

"That will be enough of that!" their mother snapped. "Melina, I'll hear no more of it!"

Still Melina glared at her, and Senea began to feel the first stirrings of panic. Tears fell down her face, feeling like hot coals on her skin.

Righteous indignation flared up in her.

"Stop *staring* at me," she said aloud, and then felt her heart crawl up into her throat. She had to get away from there. She turned without another word and flung herself through the door.

Stopping as the door closed behind her, she hastily wiped her face and tried to gain control of herself. Then she looked around.

Others had come out of the doorways even before she had; some she knew, many of them as young as Loran. She looked at the fear and uncertainty in their faces and tried to conceal her own. She went to them and fell into the group. Her heart beat painfully, sweat filmed her skin, and she wiped her face with a hand, then wiped it on her dress. Her lungs ached from the labor of trying to breathe normally. The tense mood of the group caught in her throat and made breathing difficult.

She was aware that the village would have been full of strange rumors; all the old stories would have been brought back to life. There was a tension and an ominous sense of suppressed hatred and anger in the narrow streets. It gave her a sharp feeling of apprehension and an awareness of impending evil. And the closer she got to the Held, the worse it was.

"Hai, hai!" a voice called out when they approached the gate, a meaningless word that made no sense, but the gate opened immediately upon the sounding of that voice. The children around her shied back from that gap. They had never seen it open before. Senea looked about her and saw that the group that stood at the gate was at least two hundred in number, maybe more. She was startled at that. She did not know that held-law would take so many.

Not all of them were children. The older ones that approached her age were mostly young men. There were a few girls, too young for marriage; an event that would never take place for them now. She felt pity for them, to have their hopes and dreams torn away so cruelly. A movement at the gate caught her attention, and she turned.

Six helden strode out and took up positions on either side of the gate, three to each side.

Senea saw with some interest that two of them were female, standing side by side, in dust-colored breeches and shirts and laced sandals, their long hair pulled back. Missing were the quivers and bows, but knives were strapped to their hips. They stood looking over the group with a measuring gaze, showing nothing on their faces.

"Enter," a heldan said, and no more.

The group moved forward, and Senea moved with them. She held herself silent, her heart constricted with panic as the walls rose up and over and behind as she walked through the gate. A dark tunnel made by the walls of two buildings led to a wide arena. Senea then saw that the two buildings were in reality only one long windowless structure that ran the entire perimeter of the Held, beginning and ending at the gate. Every few yards all along its length were doors that gave entrance to the building. Rising behind were the thick walls of the Held that separated them from the village.

There was a grating behind them. The gate closed heavily.

Senea looked over her shoulder as a heavy beam was lifted and placed across the gate, barring it until held-law would be called again. She stared at it, knowing with a finality that had not come before that she was now cut off forever from everything she had ever known.

She turned away, not wanting to look at that gate again.

Another movement drew her gaze, a long line emerging from a door in the building to her right.

Helden. The protectors of the held-tribe.

And in the growing light of morning the line came to them. They turned to meet it, and there were no words, a pall of silence coming over them.

The column stopped, a long line of warriors that stood shoulder to shoulder facing them. A pair of helden detached themselves and came forward.

"Welcome to the Held," one of them said in a loud voice. "This is your place now. Any other does not exist for you; forget where you've come from. You have no kinsmen there. This you must learn first. A heldan with kin-ties is a weak link in our defenses. I am Roskel, and I am second-in-command here. All disciplinary problems are referred to me—and know this: I have no mercy." He spun and a knife twanged into a pole a distance away. The vibration sounded harshly in the stunned silence. Senea blinked. She hadn't even seen his hand move. Roskel turned to face the group again.

"There are many codes by which you will live," he said. "And the first and foremost is that bringing harm to another of your held-caste is punishable by death. Absolute loyalty to the members of your Held is demanded. However, do not think that because of that I will not deal with you if you are brought to me. Take my word for it. Do not learn the hard way."

There was a moment's silence. Roskel's eyes swept over them, assessing and evaluating, then he inclined his head to his companion.

"This is Gellan. She is heldan over the heldien, those fourteen years of age and younger. Those of you who are heldien will be housed apart from the helden." He paused and looked at Gellan.

She stepped forward. "You are to separate into two groups. Those fourteen and under move off over there." She indicated to the far left. "The rest remain here."

For half a moment no one moved. The wind ran gently

around them, blowing a fine sifting off the arena floor. Gellan turned and walked to where she wanted the children to go. Then the group split in silence; the young people, some tall, some not, some not much more than children, and others approaching adulthood, followed the heldan that now controlled their lives. She waited for them, then led them across the wide stretch of arena.

There were less than a hundred left.

Roskel studied them critically.

"The rest of you have a much more rigorous training ahead of you than the heldien," he said. "Held-law was called to give us added numbers, both young and not. You, we need now. Other helden have been threatening our borders. An increase in our numbers will discourage them. What you have ahead of you is tough—tougher than anything you've had to do before. Make up your minds that you are going to hurt before you're through and accept it. Complainers are not tolerated here." He paused, then, "I want you to line up in rows of ten. One row behind the other and be quick about it!"

Senea looked about and took her place in the line that formed next to her, one among others, seven complete lines and three in another. Seventy-three of them. She saw, also, that the helden had fallen into the same arrangement, seven lines of ten, one of three. The other helden that did not join those ranks dispersed across the arena, as if they were not needed, and went about their own business. Senea stood still as her companions, as did the helden, and felt the stares that were fixed on them.

A figure dressed in black appeared in a doorway beyond the helden, along with a second figure, clothed in blue. They were joined by a tall heldan. The three of them strode past the helden lines and stopped beside Roskel. The heldan inclined his head and withdrew three paces.

Aldived. Tribelord. Not one of the held-caste, but commander of the Held, giving his orders through the Heldlan who was Heldlord. It had been Aldived's orders that had called for held-law.

His clothing was unrelieved black, from boots to tunic, his hand glittering with jeweled rings, his hair black, and his face bearing a small pointed beard. He had a sloppy way of standing, as if he were not used to standing at all. Senea had not noticed before, in all the times that she had seen him, at festival, and at the weddings he had performed, how his posture slouched, indolent and dull. He looked weak and soft compared to the lean hardness of the helden behind him.

Beside him stood a small man with a pinched face and restless eyes that did not linger long on anything. His skin, which was pallid, took on a blue light, reflecting the blue of his robe. Yunab. Aldived's counselor.

Senea shuddered inwardly as she looked on him, felt his eyes move over her face, and slide on to the young girl beside her and on again. He was more dangerous than any heldan there, ruthless, vengeful, powerful, and he had the ear of Aldived. Some said that he was the moving force behind Aldived, and Senea did not doubt it, not when she could see the malevolence on his face. Yunab was a man to be wary of, a man it would not be very wise to cross. Senea shivered as she thought on it.

"I am Aldived," the Tribelord spoke, his speech slow and apathetic. "I'm sure that many of you have reason to dislike me right now, maybe even hate me." He shrugged, an indifferent gesture.

"So be it." He raised a hand to tug at the small black beard on his chin; the morning sun flashed off the jewels on his fingers. He suddenly looked as if he had run out of things to say. He turned uncertainly to the heldan at his side.

Senea watched as *that* heldan turned his tawny head and spoke a few short words to Roskel, suddenly seeing him for the first time. He was taller by almost a head than anyone around him. His hair, which was the color of tanned leather, was tied loosely at the back of his neck. There was something about the way he stood that drew Senea's eyes and held them. It was something more than the hardness of lean muscle under tanned skin. There was something about him that the others did not have.

The ranks of helden behind him were clearly experienced, very good at what they did, honed to a proficiency that was evident in the way they stood and moved. There was a sleekness to their strength that was frightening.

But here, in this heldan, there was a difference, an intensity that was held under tight control, a power that flowed through even the slightest move, a strength that was more than sinew and bone.

Like an animal, thought Senea, excellent of his kind, dangerous and deadly.

He looked back around and ran his gaze across the lines. For a brief, shocking moment his eyes met hers.

He hesitated, then deliberately looked back, his eyes unmistakably on hers, and for an instant a chill curled through her from head to toes as she stared back. He turned his head slightly and spoke to Aldived, his eyes leaving her face momentarily, then returning. Aldived looked thoughtful at first, then pleased. He nodded.

The heldan turned then, inclined his head slightly to Aldived, and swept his hand to the right. He waited until the Tribelord started to move, and together they approached the group in which Senea stood. Inspection, Senea realized with a start, and apprehension came on her in a chilly wave.

They advanced along the first line and she watched them uneasily as they stopped and spoke to each new recruit. She could hear Aldived's languid voice as he questioned them in tones that lacked spirit. She could hear parts of the murmured answers. From time to time the heldan that accompanied him turned his gaze on her, analyzing and calculating and each time, when he looked away, she was shaking.

They started down the second row, sometimes questioning, sometimes not, coming to the end and stepping to the third row.

She was fourth from the end. She clenched her hands, suddenly wanting to run.

Aldived paused in front of a girl, second from the end, and asked, "What is your name?" in a dull, listless tone.

"Treyna," he was answered, the girl's voice thin and frightened. Aldived grunted politely in acknowledgment, stepped to the next girl, and looked her up and down.

He stepped in front of Senea.

His ice blue eyes frowned slightly, went beyond her, and came back again, disinterested. He nodded a slight greeting and moved on.

The heldan that was with him started past her without looking at her. She was just beginning a sigh of relief when he stopped and turned on her brown eyes that stopped just short of being black. Breath froze in her lungs.

"Your name?" he asked. His voice was quiet but slightly textured, like the running of a hand against the nap of velvet.

"Senea," she choked.

The heldan held her eyes a moment ... taking in her age, she thought. He would know what that meant. She blushed. Then he turned and stepped away.

Senea closed her eyes and almost sagged; what strength she had was suddenly gone. She found herself trembling in every muscle, her heart hammering loudly in her ears.

She could hear him speaking now and then, his voice a low murmur behind her, easily distinguishable from Aldived's as they continued down each row.

At last they returned to the front of the ranks and stopped beside Roskel. Quiet words were spoken, then Roskel stepped forward.

"We will now do the pairing," he said. "Each of you will be given a trainer who will instruct you in both the held skill and the heldcode. Your trainer has absolute say in your training, and as trainees, or heldii, you are to regard his or her word as law. But remember, if you become a problem you will be brought to me."

He turned his head and beckoned to another female heldan. She brought to him two baskets that were round with small holes in the tops.

"This is Reena. She will be assisting me." Roskel reached into one of the baskets and brought out a small white ball.

"Each trainee, or heldii, will take a ball; the helden will also take a ball. Those with matching colors are paired." He took the basket, dropped the ball back into it, then nodded to Reena.

She stepped back, keeping the second basket.

Roskel turned to Aldived and spoke to him at length. The Tribelord nodded, frowned, then nodded again and finally turned. He gestured to Yunab and together they left the arena, a departing of vibrant blue and black from a world of yellows, tans, and grays.

These were Held matters now.

The heldan who had asked Senea her name strode to where Reena stood.

Roskel followed him. "First lines come forward."

The heldan line moved first and came to rest where Roskel stood. And when the first row of Senea's group hesitated, he said, "Come forward, heldii." They then went forward and faced the line from which their trainers would be chosen.

Roskel offered the basket to the first heldan. He took it,

reached a hand in, and drew it out again. The basket was passed to the next heldan. Reena went to the trainees and started her basket there.

Silent moments passed while the baskets were handed down the lines. When they reached the ends of the rows, there was a brief confusion while pairs found each other and the balls were returned to the baskets.

"Second line," Roskel called, and the line in front of Senea stepped up. The baskets were passed again and soon more pairs moved off across the arena.

"Third line."

Senea's heart lurched and began to beat with a painful force against her ribs. Her hands were suddenly clammy, and she wiped them on her dress as her line went to that place where the others had stood. Nervous tension hung in the air so thick it was almost a visible thing. Senea looked up and saw that the heldan who had asked her name was watching her. She jerked her eyes away.

The line was coming toward them, and Senea regarded it, determined not to look again at the heldan who kept watching her. She forced herself to wonder which of the advancing would be her trainer; she wondered which one would have total control over her life.

A move caught her attention, and she turned her head.

The heldan who had asked her name strode to the advancing line and stopped it. He spoke briefly to the heldan who stood first in line there, took him out of line, then stepped into his place. Senea saw a wave of surprise pass from one heldan to the next, looked and saw surprise even on Roskel's face.

Roskel said something, a question that was answered curtly. Roskel hesitated a moment. Then he took a step backward and nodded for the line to move forward.

A heldan who was slightly shorter than Senea stepped up in front of her, looked at her expressionlessly, his eyes a pale green and hard. Senea avoided his stare and inadvertently met the gaze of the heldan who now stood at the beginning of that row. She looked away from him also. Nervous sweat started to trickle down her side.

Reena came to the heldii and offered the basket to the first in their row. A young girl who reached in took out a yellow ball and passed the basket to the girl next to her. That girl looked up, glanced nervously around, a frightened hunted look on her face. Senea realized that here was a girl almost as old as she. *Treyna*, Senea recalled. The name that Aldived had asked for.

Treyna put her hand into the basket and brought out a blue ball and closed her fingers over it in a tight white-knuckled grip. Senea felt pity for her.

The young girl next to her took the basket and drew out a white ball, then handed the basket to Senea.

Senea almost shrank from it as she held it in her hands. It was lighter than she had expected, the woven strands hard and smooth, not like the reed baskets she had made at her father's house. The opening was just large enough for a hand to fit through and was edged in an intricate braiding.

The air hurt her lungs as she reached inside and felt the smooth balls, indistinguishable by touch. She picked one and pulled it out. She passed the basket along, then became aware that she had been holding her breath. The pounding of her heart throbbed painfully in her head. She exhaled and stared at her closed hand, afraid to see what color she had.

Then she realized that all movement around her had stopped.

She looked up and saw several of the helden staring at her and she wondered in a sudden panic what she had done wrong. She looked about in confusion, saw some of them glancing at the beginning of the heldan line, then back to her. A chill premonition touched her and she turned.

The other basket had not even started down the opposite row, but was in the hands of the heldan who had asked her name. His head was turned and he was watching her, waiting.

For a moment she did not move, and it was possible to hear voices come from across the arena.

Then she began to understand that he waited for her to reveal the color of the ball she held. She very suddenly was frightened, even before she looked.

Trembling, she opened her hand.

Red.

Then to Senea's dismay, the heldan looked with unhurried deliberateness down into the basket that he held, put his hand in, pulled it out again, and gave the basket to the heldan next to him.

No one moved. There was silence.

Senea glanced nervously about her and saw that all eyes were on him and his closed hand. She forced her stare back.

He opened his fingers, turned his gaze on her. The ball was red.

For a time there was only the stirring of wind across the arena. Then came a murmur of astonishment from the helden, and a look of disbelief was on Roskel's face.

Senea stood still, stunned; stared at the heldan who had contrived to be her trainer and sensed that this was a thing not done. She wondered why no one spoke against it.

She did not know when the baskets had resumed their way down the rows, only became aware that the lines were breaking apart. She heard, then, the voices of the helden giving quiet instructions, heard the shuffle as they moved across the arena.

The heldan who was her trainer walked the short distance between them, looked down on her, and held out the hand that still had the red ball. Hesitantly, she laid hers beside it.

"I am Heldlan Vayhawk," he said. "Come with me." He turned and strode away without looking to see that she followed, but paused briefly to drop the balls in their separate baskets.

Senea stared at his retreating back and saw the sun shine off the gold band on his arm.

Heldlan! Heldlord!

He stopped and turned. Senea pulled herself out of her paralysis, went across the width of the arena to him, and heard Roskel call for the fourth lines to step forward.

CHAPTER THREE

Vayhawk came to a door in the building and waited for her, observing her with a level examination that brought heat to her face. She walked past him into the gloom. He swept his hand to the left, directing her down a hall that was lined with several doors, all on the right side of the hall. The left side was the outside wall.

These were living quarters, Senea saw, as she went by.

A musky smell hung in the air, a scent she didn't recognize, but one that was pleasant nonetheless. The only light in the place came from the doors that opened out onto the arena, three that she could see ahead at regular intervals, and the one behind that they had just come through.

Vayhawk stopped at the fourth door on the right-hand side of the hall and pushed it inward.

"Your bunkroom," he said.

Senea peered in at a narrow room that she suspected was identical to all the rest. There was nothing to distinguish it from any other. From where she stood, she could see that there were two sets of double bunks against opposite walls.

"It is ten doors down from that far corner." He indicated a turn in the continuing corridor. Then he said, "Go in."

Senea went forward, not wishing to and feeling her skin contract as she passed close-by him, almost touching. She stood in the center of the room. It was very narrow; she could have reached out and touched both top bunks at once. Vayhawk remained in the doorway watching her, an unreadable expression in his eyes.

"This is your permanent quarters," he said. "There will be

23

no changes made. If you have difficulties with your bunkmates
. . . resolve them."

Senea looked half-about at the narrow confines of the room.
It was slightly smaller than the room she had shared with her
sisters, and her skin prickled at his words. She could hear quiet
activity down the hall, other trainees being shown their living
quarters, and she wondered who her bunkmates would be. She
looked at Vayhawk with uncertainty.

There was silence for some few moments.

Then Vayhawk came into the room, an unhurried tread that
Senea stepped back from, suddenly afraid of him. It was a retreat that he saw, and for a terrible moment Senea felt trapped
as he regarded her with a close scrutiny.

With the room fully examined, Vayhawk motioned Senea toward the door. He waited until she had gone into the hall
ahead of him, then he pulled the door closed and led her down
the long hall, past the three doors that opened onto the arena.
She saw through those doors, which gave only brief glimpses
of the outside, that there still were five lines of trainees out on
the arena to be paired.

The hall made a sharp turn and stretched out into an even
longer dark corridor that was relieved at intervals by sunlight
coming in through open doors. It seemed that the living quarters of the helden traveled the entire perimeter of the Held. The
hall was so narrow that Senea had to walk behind Vayhawk so
that others could get by them. Two helden were standing and
talking in the doorway of a bunkroom, looked questions to
Vayhawk when they saw Senea; he ignored them.

Other rooms were open with helden and trainees in them
talking in low tones. A heldan and his trainee squeezed past,
going the opposite direction. It was eerie, Senea thought, this
quiet that hung over everybody as if held-law had affected
even the helden with a feeling of strangeness.

Senea glanced out a door she passed and saw that there
were more pairs coming across the arena.

Finally Vayhawk turned and entered a room that was
brightly lit from an opening in the ceiling; the walls were lined
with shelves and in those shelves were folded clothing, all in
the dusty yellows and yellow-greens and yellow-grays that the
helden wore.

A female heldan who had been leaning back leisurely

against the edge of a table stood up with surprise on her face—which was quickly hidden.

"Heldlan," she murmured, and inclined her head subtly in salute. Her eyes went to Senea, question there, then she looked back to Vayhawk.

"Find her something more appropriate to wear," he said. He looked sidelong at Senea, evaluating, measuring, and frowning at her dress.

"And get rid of that ghastly thing." He turned to the door and paused.

"Find someone to show her around and acquaint her with the way things are run here." He looked at Senea again and added, as if it were an afterthought, "Then have her sent to me." He strode out and disappeared down the corridor.

Senea stood still and suffered the questioning gaze of the female heldan. She ran her hand down the offending dress and stared back, not knowing what else to do.

"I am Layna," she was finally told, and then came the question that she knew was coming. "You are paired to Vayhawk?"

"Yes."

Layna shook her head in astonishment, then she said, "I would not want to be in your place."

Senea returned her gaze and dread descended on her as she wondered what had prompted those ominous words. She searched Layna's face but saw nothing.

Layna turned to the shelves, pulled out a few things, and laid them on the table.

"Your clothes," she said. "And anytime you feel you need more, come and take what you want. Most of us only have two or three sets, though. I will show you where you can put those on, then I'll find someone to show you around."

Senea picked up the clothing and shrank with dismay at the lightness of the bundle. Recognizable were the breeches and the shirt, and she could feel the sandals that had been wrapped in them. Following Layna down the corridor to another door, Senea found herself in a large bath.

The musky smell that she had noticed earlier hung thick in this humid place that was rich in brown woods. The only light came from overhead through a skylight and glistened on water that stood undisturbed in a large cisternlike tub, steam rising from it. Wooden benches lined the walls. There were female helden on one side, close to the door, waiting for their young trainee girls to exchange their clothing for heldan dress.

Layna indicated where Senea was to go and turned aside to talk to the helden.

Senea went to where she had been told to go, began to take off her dress, and felt the sudden stares of the helden on her. They had just been told about her pairing to their Heldlan. The heat of embarrassment rose to her face. She turned her back and stiffly continued to change her clothes.

She dressed carefully in what had been given her: yellow-gray breeches that were unfamiliar and uncomfortable and a dusty shirt that was collarless and sleeveless. It was such a drabness of color that she felt depressed just donning them. She put on the sandals, laced the leather ties up over her shins to pull the calf-guards tight against her legs, and tied them just below the knee. Last of all, she undid her hair, shook it out, and clasped it again at the nape of her neck.

She sat down and folded her dress, her hands smoothing out the blue material. It was the only thing she had brought into the Held with her and she was reluctant to give it up. An unaccountable attachment for it seized her, more for its color than for what it was, a last remaining piece of the life she had had before this day.

She raised her head when Layna came to her, accompanied by another heldan.

"This is Mara. She will show you around." Layna stooped to gather up the blue dress from Senea. "I will take this."

Senea's hands tightened on the dress and would not let it go. Layna looked at her with a frown. Senea stared back stubbornly. Then, knowing it was pointless, she yielded it up. Layna took it, turned on her heel, and left.

Senea looked after her, feeling desolate at the removal of the last link with her former life.

Mara put a hand on her shoulder, regarding her kindly.

"It won't be so bad," she said. "You'll get used to all of this and then it won't matter. For the next little while you're going to be too tired to think of anything except your bunk anyway. And once you get there . . . if you even get there . . . you'll be too sore to worry about anything but sleep."

Senea rose and followed her across the bath to a door at the side, not the one by which she had come in, and she found herself in a washroom. Large washing bins lined one wall. Racks draped with drying shirts and breeches were on the other.

"We take care of our own needs," Mara said. "There are none to serve us, and we do not wait on each other." She turned and held the door to the bath open again.

"We are responsible for our own meals, also. There are over four hundred of us here now. Twice as many as yesterday, and no one has time to do that much cooking. Only in heldien hall, where the children are, will the cooking be done on large scale. But you and I won't have to worry about that."

Mara led the way out of the bath, down the corridor and to a large room also lit by skylights, shutters pulled back by heavy chains. Here there were tables and fire hearths—five of them—and three ovens.

"This is where you prepare your meals when you are here. There's another one on the other side of the compound, but we use the one that's closest to our bunkrooms to cut down on congestion. It could get pretty crowded otherwise.

"You can come here anytime you're not on patrol. The middle of the night if you wish. Just make sure you leave it clean. Roskel is very particular about that kind of thing. And he can be very unpleasant about it, too." She grimaced. "But I'd rather have *him* unhappy with me than . . ." She stopped suddenly, mid-sentence, looked at Senea apologetically.

"I'm sorry."

Senea swallowed uneasily. She had caught what Mara had been about to say and did not finish . . . that she'd rather have Roskel angry with her than Vayhawk. She wondered wildly for a moment what manner of man this Vayhawk was that others were moved to sympathy for her. Then to compound her dread, Mara laid a hand on her arm and said, "I don't envy what you have before you, girl."

Senea stared at her.

"Vayhawk was ten years old when he came here last heldlaw. That was twenty-two years ago. He was good from the beginning. Learned very fast. You can only become Heldlord by being the very best. And Vayhawk is the very best; and he'll be tough on you. I hope you are up to it."

She led the way across the large room to a door that was beside the ovens. She opened it and waited for Senea to go in.

"This is where the donations from the village are kept. The vegetables are kept in the bins." She showed Senea the wooden bins along one wall. She lifted the lid on the nearest so that Senea could see the food inside.

"The bread is kept in the shelves over here." She went to the far wall. "We'll only accept the high-grain bread. The rest is like eating fluff."

Senea looked at the loaves of bread in the shelves, some already cut, and recalled the countless times that she had taken bread to the heldgate and put it through the small window.

Every day bread was made in her father's home and taken to the Held, just as every family in the village did—required donations of bread, vegetables, and fruit from the fields beyond the ridge, donations for the protection that the helden gave in return.

Senea stared at those loaves of bread and wondered which one came from her family. It would have been made by her mother's hands today, because she was no longer there to do it. She swallowed the ache that came to her throat and turned from the room.

Mara let the door swing shut behind them and led Senea across the eating hall, past the tables. "What is your name?"

"Senea."

"Well, Senea," she said, holding the door open, "I don't know if you realize what an unusual thing our Heldlan has done. Tradition keeps him free from the pairing. It has not been done as long as *I* know about, since even before I came here. Not everyone can do the job of Heldlord; it is very demanding. And to take this on as well? It is . . . well . . . surprising.

"I'll wager that there will be those who will not be pleased, and pressure will be put on him to turn you over to another. But he won't. He'll keep you, and he'll make you a better heldan than any of the rest of us. Either that, or break you in the trying. I wouldn't be in your place for anything."

Senea had been following Mara down the corridor not seeing where they passed, greatly disturbed at what she was hearing. She did not see the curious looks that some cast her way from those who had witnessed what had happened in the arena and recognized her.

"That's the one that Vayhawk got himself paired to," she finally heard someone say behind her back, and she kept her face ahead, pretending not to hear. She did not know if the speaker had intended for her to hear and did not want to know.

She was conscious that she had become a curiosity among the helden. She felt herself strangely exposed to them and felt their stares on her, the girl that Vayhawk had contrived to have paired to him.

And she saw the question on their faces, the same one that was occurring to her as well. Why?

Senea became aware that Mara had stopped talking as she led her down the right-hand side of the corridor, a wordlessness that seemed uncharacteristic, as if she also felt the weight of the stares that were cast their way. She looked over her shoulder and glanced sympathetically at Senea. Then she said, "It'll pass. Soon they'll all be too busy to care."

Senea took courage at that and hoped she was right.

Mara came to a door at the sharp corner of the hall, and Senea saw that the corridor that swung to the right was the same one in which her bunkroom was located. She stood with her back to the door and counted ten doors to her own while Mara knocked behind her.

Mara opened the door, and Senea turned around with sudden consternation. Then she felt Mara's hand on her shoulder gently urging her into the room. She hesitated and glanced at Mara, who smiled encouragingly and nodded for her to go ahead.

Senea stepped into the room and heard Mara close the door quietly behind her, leaving her.

Her heart beat in a lost, forlorn terror as she faced Vayhawk. He was leaning back leisurely in a chair with his legs propped up. He looked at her with shadowed eyes. Roskel sat in a chair that was inclined back against the wall between the table and the bunk, his arms folded across his chest, hands flat against his sides as he relaxed there.

Senea's eyes faltered before theirs, and she glanced nervously around.

The room was a bunkroom, and because it was in the corner of the Held, it was twice as large as any of the others that Senea had seen. A single lamp on the table against the wall cast a circle of light on the floor. Standing at a right angle from the table against the other wall was the bunk. There was a closeness and a warmth to the room that under any other circumstances would have been soothing, calming.

Vayhawk observed Senea, the lamplight shining on his hair

in soft tones of tan and beige, and after deliberation, he beckoned her to come forward.

She came hesitantly to where the light was stronger and waited while the Heldlan looked her over. He then turned his head expectantly to Roskel as if he awaited some kind of opinion. Roskel shrugged noncommittally and sat his chair down, exhaling through his nostrils.

"It's possible," he said in an apparent continuation of a discussion that she had interrupted. "But you are the only one who can be certain."

Vayhawk looked to Senea, leaned an elbow on the arm of the chair, and pulled thoughtfully at his lip.

Roskel regarded him with a frown. He looked at Senea, studying her for a long moment. He shrugged then, yielding up the misgivings that were in his eyes.

"Well, I'll leave it for you to decide," he said, rising to his feet. He inclined his head to Vayhawk in salute, looked then to Senea, and raised his eyebrows suggestively as he walked past her, going to the door and stepping out into the corridor.

Senea was dismayed by that silent sexual insinuation and stared at Vayhawk with a new fear.

He was still regarding her, his forefinger slowly rubbing his lower lip. He then took his hand away from his mouth and drew a couple of quick circles in the air and said, "Turn around." The light vibration of his voice rippled through the air to her.

She hesitated, then complied, embarrassed under that close observation. She came around again, unable to meet his gaze.

"Come here." He sat up, pulled the stool on which his feet had been resting toward him, and indicated for her to sit there. Senea did not move, suddenly loath to go near him. He looked up at her, waiting, and there was nothing but for her to go to the stool and sit.

That nearness to him was disturbing, and she found herself under that close scrutiny again.

He leaned back then, putting some distance between them.

"My second-in-command has been expressing his doubts," he said. His eyes surveyed her face, a slow, deliberate examination that seemed to take a very long time.

"Tell me about yourself," he said finally and, when he saw the hesitancy on her face, added, "your family. Tell me about your family."

Senea looked up at him uncertainly. She remembered Roskel's words, *Forget where you've come from. You have no kinsmen there.* She wondered why Vayhawk would have her now go against that, but when he did not look away and waited wordlessly for her to answer, she told him, "I have a mother and a father and two sisters."

A flicker of calculation went across his face and he asked, "How old are your sisters?"

Senea was reluctant to answer; it would reveal too much and he seemed to be probing for something that she wasn't so sure she wanted him to find.

"Melina's eighteen. Loran's seven."

"Your father?"

"He's a farmer." She lowered her eyes then and hoped desperately that he would not go on questioning her. Thoughts of her family just now were very painful.

"His name?"

"Tolen Daunle."

"You were on good terms with him?"

Senea's heart lurched at his use of the word *were*, as if her father or she were dead. She closed her eyes until she could make herself answer.

"We got along in most things."

"Except in the case of dowry?"

She jerked her head up and stared at him. He was walking too close to personal matters, rude and tactless. She regarded him with angry resentment.

It was several moments before Senea saw that his eyes were level on hers, taking in every action and reaction. She quieted herself with some effort and pushed away the anger that had flared and was uneasy thereafter.

Vayhawk sat forward and leaned his arms on his knees, his brown eyes on her so that she could not look away.

"Think on this," he said. "If I can make you angry, then I have gotten past your guard. If I can make you angry, then you are as good as dead. And your held-tribe is in danger."

He paused, then said, "Think of your family. Think of what they mean to you. Remember the things you did for them, the things they did for you, the things you did together. Remember the things that were said and the dreams that you shared and the marriages that are waiting for your sisters. Think hard on these things, heldii. And after this, you must forget. Your family's safety depends on your forgetting them. You may keep your name, but nothing more."

Stricken, Senea stared into Vayhawk's eyes, her mind involuntarily going back to a memory of a time when Melina was wading ankle-deep in the river that ran past the held-village. It was dry season and the water was low.

Sometimes, when the river was low enough, the fish could be seen swimming around with their backs high out of the water. On this particular day Melina saw a fish wiggling against the current and, wanting to take it home, chased it. After a few steps she plunged into a hidden hole that was very deep and very dangerous, for Melina could not swim.

Senea had saved Melina's life that day; she had jumped into the hole and pulled her out.

She had almost forgotten.

"Understand," Vayhawk said, "you are now in the Held. You will learn to be heldan, to live, think, and fight like a heldan. You will hurt before you are done, but you will also learn to live with it. And when you are through . . . if you make it through . . . then you'll be given a gold armband stamped with the symbols of your Held and your rank."

He sat back again and Senea looked at the band on his arm. The gold caught the light of the lamp in a soft glow, the markings there indistinguishable.

"One more matter before we begin." Vayhawk's voice brought her eyes back to his face. "Helden live by a code of loyalty and obedience. Within that code there are laws that have been as long as there has been a held-caste. Punishment for the disobedience of those laws is severe . . . death.

"As a heldan, your loyalty to your Held must be absolute. It is forbidden to inflict injury or death on others of your own Held. Punishment in this will be swift and without mercy. There can be no weapon ever drawn against another heldan of your own Held, except in the Games. There, injuries are inevitable, but you cannot kill. There is absolutely no communication with members of other Helds, even if Tribelords come together for bargaining. Instant, unquestioning obedience of a ranking heldan is demanded, and the Tribelord is always obeyed.

"Remember that we are the invisible defenders and protectors of the held-tribe. You will fight for it . . . and die for it if necessary."

He stopped talking then, sat watching her with unreadable eyes. Senea grew uneasy and looked down at her clasped hands.

"Have you eaten today?" he asked.

"No."

He looked her over with a critical, measuring gaze. "That's just as well."

Senea looked at him sharply, anger flaring again, but at the warning in his eyes, she recalled what he had said about allowing herself to become angry and fought it down.

He drew in a breath then, and rose to his feet, an easy unbending upward that seemed natural to him.

"Come," he said, gesturing to the door. "I will show you somewhat of the boundaries that our Held patrols."

CHAPTER FOUR

Senea felt the heat immediately upon stepping out into the early afternoon. Distant sounds of the village from the other side of the Held came to her, and she paused to listen. Vayhawk stopped beside her, listening as she did, but there was not the pain on his face that was in her ... new ... and aching.

"Come," he said at last, and walked away.

Senea looked after him for a long moment before she followed at a pace that soon caught her up to him.

He held in his hand a bow, strong and well polished. Across his back was a quiver filled with long white arrows—his identification color, he had told her. He had strapped across one hip and over the dusty yellow shirt a long knife, the sheath handmade, edged with milky stones that matched the white grip of the knife.

The wind sang softly over the yellow grasses where they walked. Senea listened to it and looked about her at the plain that stretched out endlessly in every direction. Here and there slight elevations of hills relieved the sameness of that great expanse, but what could not be seen there were the valleys and canyons that ran with rivers and wildlife. And, in some of those very distant valleys, other held-tribes with their own helden.

Senea thought about the times she had spent sitting on the upper edge of the valley where her held-tribe was, looking out over the fields to the plains beyond, wondering what it was like out there away from the village and the river and the fields. There one had to live by his or her own wits to survive. Never did she think that she would venture out there, let alone be one of the helden that watched there. And she looked at it now with a fear that came from the realization that she walked in a dream that had somehow become real and she knew that there would be no waking. And almost . . . almost she turned and fled.

But her fate was set, and there was no turning it aside. She forced herself to look with unyielding directness at what her life was to be like from now on, fighting the enemies of her held-tribe.

But . . . she no longer knew who her enemies were. What of Melina? What was she doing now? *She* had called her a heldan witch, tainted, a thing without honor, and would have driven her out as an enemy.

Senea realized that she had actually begun to consider seriously the possibility of this heldan power. But there had been, after all, nothing said, apparently nothing to fear—no lurking horrors, no witches, no sorcerers, except those the villagers had chosen to create.

Relief temporarily swept her recent antagonism for the villagers and Melina out of her mind. How could people be so stupid? And she was instantly ashamed of the thought. And then immediately had a second thought. *Unless there was something the helden weren't saying about it.*

A faint tingling sensation assailed the nape of her neck, and she shivered. She looked hard at Vayhawk. The implications of *that* were almost more than she could get her mind around. She pushed it away.

They came across the picked bones of an animal.

"Leave it alone," Vayhawk said, going around it. "There are scavengers here that you might miss, that may not miss you."

Senea looked at the bones uneasily and wondered what animal it had been. She did not ask because she was reluctant to show her ignorance. She trod carefully behind Vayhawk until they were well past the stripped carcass.

After a while a canyon opened up before them, and Vayhawk began to descend along a trackless way, leading Senea to the bottom of a barren, narrow place with nothing but rocks and sunburnt grasses. She followed behind him as he then began to climb the other side of the canyon. She wondered if he felt the silence the way she did.

Often in the climb she found that she had to pause and rest, coughing, and wait while the painful pounding of her heart slowed. Vayhawk did not stop to wait for her, but continued without looking back until he disappeared over the top. Senea pushed herself to catch up to him, laboring painfully up the side of the canyon. She was afraid that he'd leave her behind.

She made the crest at last and came to where the plain was flat again and bore no track, nor any other sign to indicate that helden had walked there.

Vayhawk stood a few steps away, considering the plain before him. He looked over his shoulder at her and waited for her to reach him, then pointed to a distant rise in the land.

"Our own helden," he said, and Senea looked, still breathing hard, but did not see anything.

For a long moment Vayhawk stood still, letting Senea catch her breath, waiting for her to spot the helden on the distant hill. It took her a little time to find them, and then only when she saw a movement.

She wondered in amazement that Vayhawk had seen them at all, for they blended with the sunburnt colors of the plain. There were two of them, barely discernible, the color of their clothing merging with the land around them. Senea glanced away, and when she looked back she could not find them again.

After that, Vayhawk went more slowly, and Senea was able to keep up with him, but even at that she found it difficult; the climb out of the canyon had tired her more than she had realized.

At long length, the color began to fade from the land as the sun lowered to the western rim of the horizon, a sandy-white elliptical sphere, huge and fantastic, seeming to fill half the sky in front of them.

A rise in the land came between, a dark hill against the sun, a small silhouette against huge whiteness.

Toward that featureless hill Vayhawk led as the sun turned from yellow-white to a warm orange ball that stretched from southern horizon to northern horizon, a flat-topped half-globe shape. He began to climb the hill taking hold of Senea's arm to guide her steps. Once at the top he stood looking out toward the plain that lay in bands of golds, browns, and grays under the sunset. The orange light rested on him like brass, his hair the color of russet and the tan of his arms deepening into the richness of bronze.

The windshift had begun, a nightly occurrence, and tugged gently at them as they looked out over the darkening plain.

"Over there, five more days' travel," Vayhawk said, pointing to the distant west, "is the boundary of the held-tribe Sojei. On the southwest is the Weija. And surrounding on the south, east, and north are Jauedi, Deijoi, Mao'aa, Jas'po and Wuepoah. Eight held-tribes in all. We are the Mon'ay. Some are content to leave us alone, some are not.

"And to the north, several days' journey, are the Ja'sid. A very dangerous people that are getting bolder all the time. They've been into Sojei lands west of us and in the Wuepoah lands to the north of us. They've been found in our lands as far as the held-tribe." His eyes rested on her with a soberness that touched her with a chill.

"They carry a power with them." He looked out at the plain again. Senea stared at him. It took heavy control not to betray her shock any more than that. She felt as if the breath had been knocked out of her. For a long time Vayhawk was silent. Then he continued in a low voice.

"They have a special caste within their Held, a separate caste of helden who dress in black and patrol in their own groups, or sometimes with other helden. These Black Ja'sid have a power that is not like anything you've ever seen before. It's a blackness that destroys. It sucks the life out of everything. With it they have destroyed every held-tribe they have come across.

"I have felt it. And you will, too. It's in their touch and their weapons. And there is almost no way to defeat them. The only way is to find them alone."

A cold seemed to settle over her, some of the brightness seemed suddenly stripped from the sunset. His shrewd, speculative eyes turned to fix intently on her. He regarded her in the strained silence, assessing her reaction. The moment stretched uneasily, and it took all of Senea's strength to control the sick sense of foreboding that gnawed at her vitals. She tried to look away, around at the horizon, but her eyes were glued to him. She couldn't seem to unfix them.

His stare was direct and challenging. And she was forced to believe him even if she found it difficult. She stared at his eyes.

"They live in the north desert now," he continued. "But they come from the very far north, beyond the desert mountains. If we don't stop them, they'll be in our lands." He looked at her. "That's why you're here."

Senea scanned the distant horizon, listening to Vayhawk with a growing unease. She shuddered involuntarily and silence draped like a shroud around them. The plain was deepening slowly into grays and purples and brown-golds. The sun sank inch by inch as she watched, the sky going from orange to purple and red, deep and glowing.

Vayhawk stood looking into the sunset, the windshift feathering through the hair that lay gathered between his shoulder blades. At last he turned his head and looked down on her, his eyes dark in the dying light, thoughtful and measuring. It seemed the look in his eyes reflected a power, a force to stop an army. A faith to move mountains, a borrowed power of the stars, the myths of magic that surrounded the helden like rubbish, all were there, focused in the shadow of his eyes. It was simple and dangerous but it'd been right in front of her all the time.

Imagination? Probably. But before she could probe it, he turned and started down the hill back the way that they had come.

Light failed them after a while, and they were traveling in the dark. Unsure of the terrain, Senea stayed close to him, his hand taking her arm at times to guide her around obstacles that only he could see. Unaccustomed hunger was an ache in her stomach, and pain dragged at her legs and feet. Twice Vayhawk stopped and let her rest, although he did not seem to need it, and each time it was harder to walk again. His hand came more frequently to her arm to steady her.

After what seemed like a very long time, they came to a black cleft at their feet that was the canyon they had crossed earlier. Vayhawk stopped and slung his bow across his back, the string passing across his chest from shoulder to hip.

He took Senea's arm and said, "Lean on me." Slipping his arm around her, he began the descent.

Senea clung to him, searched for footing, holding her breath in the fear that they'd go sliding uncontrollably down into that blackness. But Vayhawk was steady in his moving down, one level to the next, his strong arm holding her close so that her steps were guided by his.

They came to the bottom and started up the other side, a long stumbling climb over boulders and brush, rocks and pebbles that rattled away behind them. Just as they came to the lip of the canyon, Senea lost her footing and slipped, but

Vayhawk's arm pulled her up to her feet and brought her over the top.

He moved his hand to her arm and guided her on, and his voice came to her out of the dark.

"After this you will have to do the climbing on your own." He was silent a moment before he continued. "Lives will depend on your ability to cross these lands unaided."

Senea thought on that and wondered if she could ever do it. She had serious doubts, but left them unspoken and concentrated on keeping her feet moving. Even with Vayhawk's firm grip around her arm, she found it increasingly difficult to keep up the pace, slow as it was. She stopped trying to keep her bearings and watched the ground, looking for the snags and obstructions that caught at her feet. She wanted more than anything to stop and rest, but she didn't say anything, also wanting desperately to get back to the Held.

If she hadn't been so tired she would have laughed. The heldan Mara had said that she'd soon be so tired she would only have thoughts for her bunk and sleep. Senea hadn't realized how truly Mara had spoken.

She longed with every fiber of her sore body to stop and sleep. The dark, narrow room that she was to share with three others was the most desirable place she could think of just then. She held away thoughts of the room she had for years shared with her sisters, knowing with a self-preservation that was instinctive that thoughts like those would be her undoing as tired as she was.

She closed her eyes, stumbled and pitched forward, but Vayhawk pulled her up before she touched ground, a scrambling for footing that left her shaken and unsteady. Wordlessly, the Heldlan put his arm around her and kept her moving, not stopping to let her rest.

Senea thrust all thoughts from her mind and let her legs move of their own accord, taking their impetus from the strength of Vayhawk as he drew her on. Everything ceased to exist: the night, the plain, the Held ... everything except the exhausted pain of her legs and the relentless arm about her that forced her to keep walking.

When she faltered, the arm would only tighten to keep her on her feet, to keep the pace steady.

She must have drifted in empty thought for a time then, for she became aware of a voice hailing them. Vayhawk answered

an unintelligible word that she knew she should have understood. A light fell on her, and she blinked uncomprehendingly
into it, realizing slowly that it came from an open door.

Vayhawk put her from him, gently but firmly, and held her
at arm's length until her mind cleared and she knew where she
was. The door to the Held stood open and a soft light came
from it; a heldan standing just inside watched them with puzzlement on his face.

"You have to make it on your own now," Vayhawk said.

She looked up at him, not understanding what he meant.

"Come," he said, and propelled her gently but resolutely
through the door. He let go and waited for her to get her bearings.

She caught at the wall and fought the weakness in her
knees, understanding distantly that he wanted her to negotiate
the halls and find her bunkroom under her own power—with
a strength that she was afraid she didn't have. She forced herself to move, the thought coming to her that if she didn't, he'd
leave her to sleep or collapse where she was. She saw the certainty of it on his face, so she pushed herself from the wall and
walked down the corridor on trembling legs.

An eternity passed as she walked by an endless succession
of doors. Vayhawk had left her somewhere along the way . . .
at his own bunkroom, she thought. She found her own door,
stopped, and counted bunkroom doors to make certain. She
pushed it open and stepped inside.

Three bunks were occupied; the top one on the left was
empty. She looked at it in despair, did not think she could
climb into it, decided she would sleep on the floor instead,
then thought better of it and climbed slowly. She hesitated a
moment when her strength ebbed, then pulled herself into the
bunk. She was asleep instantly.

CHAPTER FIVE

Someone touched her shoulder; Senea drew a sudden breath and opened her eyes. They closed again. A hand then gently shook her. She forced her eyes open and looked around in slight panic.

The shadowed figure of Vayhawk withdrew a step from her bunk and waited for her to sit up. She pushed herself up, ran a hand through her hair that had somehow become unclasped, and sat staring sleepily at him, wondering what he was doing there.

"Come on, girl," he said low, the light texture in his voice very noticeable in the dark quiet. "Before you awaken someone."

Senea heard the slight impatience in his voice and shook off the sleep that clung to her. Hastily she slid from her bunk, landing as softly on her feet as she could.

The room was as dark as it had been when she had climbed into her bunk and she wondered how long she had been asleep. She knew it hadn't been long enough.

Vayhawk held the door open, and she walked out into the hall with him behind her. She looked at him questioningly, and he handed her a bundle of clothes.

"Go bathe," he said. "And meet me outside the Held."

Senea took the clothes and hesitated uncertainly. Vayhawk frowned slightly, his face alight in the dim torchlight that burned a short distance away.

"I will be waiting," he said, then turned and walked away. Senea held the clothes to her and stared after him.

* * *

41

She slid into the hot water and felt the heat seep into her muscles, relaxing and soothing. Sleep began to descend on her, and she shook it off. She found a cake of soap on the tub's side and washed herself and her hair thoroughly, and got out dripping. She found a large soft cloth and dried, then she dressed, sitting down to lace up her sandals.

Her limbs hurt from the walking that she had done the day before, and for a moment she sat still with her eyes closed and her head back against the wall. The silence and the warmth of the bath closed in around her, and she found it difficult to move.

The door opened and Senea's eyes flew open. She relaxed with a sigh when she saw it was Mara looking at her. She bent and laced her sandals.

"He has you up pretty early, doesn't he?" Mara said with sympathy. It was more a statement than a question, and Senea nodded, took a leather thong that had been with the clothes, and tied back her wet hair. She tried to clear the sleep from her head by breathing deeply.

Standing, she looked with dismay at her soiled clothes on the floor, not knowing what to do with them. She stooped to pick them up. Mara came to her and took the clothes from her hands.

"I'll put these in the washroom," she said. "They'll wait until you can get to them later. You better not keep Vayhawk waiting."

Senea looked at the heldan thankfully. She noticed in the dim light that Mara's eyes were as dark as her hair and her skin was deep with tan. "Why are you here so early?"

"It's not early for me. I'm just coming in from patrol. I'm going to take a bath and then sleep for a long time. All day if I can." She flashed a smile at Senea. "You better go."

Senea stood still a moment, lethargy rooting her to the spot.

"Go, go," Mara insisted. "Before the rest of the patrol gets in. I have a feeling that Vayhawk wants to get you away from here before the patrol changes."

Senea pulled herself out of the blankness that had started to come on her. "Why?"

Mara put a hand on Senea's back and took her to the door, propelling her firmly forward. "How should I know? Now go." She opened the door and gently pushed Senea into the hall. "Hurry." The door swung shut, and Senea was alone in the dimly lit corridor.

She stared at the door a moment before she could force herself to turn and walk down the corridor. She drew in several gulps of air trying to clear her head, feeling the dead weight of her arms and legs. She inhaled again, hoping that the air would give her the energy she didn't have.

She came to the door that seemed to be the only exit a person could use once entering the Held. Avoiding the intent gaze of the heldan who stood there, she waited for him to pull open the door, noticing that it could be barred by a heavy beam, locking anyone in or out.

Vayhawk was standing a few steps outside the door when she walked out into the beginning of dawn.

He handed her a small leather bag. "Your day's rations," he said, and showed her how to put her arm and head through a leather strap, so that the pouch hung at her hip. Then he turned his head and looked to the left, and Senea heard it the same time he did—soft voices a distance away.

There was no possibility yet of seeing clearly who was coming. Halflight tricked the eyes, made the land out to be flat when it was not, made figures to be identical when they were not.

Vayhawk took her arm wordlessly and led her away in the opposite direction, to the north, toward the river that ran past the village. When they had gone out of sight of the Held he let go, shifted his bow to that hand, walked at a steady pace to the river.

"Where are we going?" Senea ventured to ask when they came to the bank of the river, unsure whether she was even allowed to ask.

He looked sideways at her, and she thought for a moment that he was not going to answer, but his voice came to her, "North," a single word that did not really say anything. He slid the bow into the quiver on his back and led the way into the river.

Senea slowed as she entered the water, fighting current which rose about her knees, cold and strong. The water fell briefly as she passed the halfway mark, and she saw that Vayhawk was already coming out on the other side. As quickly as she could, she waded the rest of the way, struggling against the current which became even stronger before she climbed out onto the bank.

Vayhawk had gone on, disappearing through the tamarisks

to climb up the ridge that was behind them. Senea followed him at a much slower pace and finally came to the top of the ridge to find him waiting for her. When she reached him he turned and started walking again, not allowing her any time to rest.

Senea followed him for several minutes without being able to catch up, and finally, in irritation, she sprinted until she came up beside him. Clenching her teeth, she determined that she would keep up with him no matter what and said nothing when he looked sidelong at her.

"Am I going too fast?" he asked tauntingly.

Senea glared at him, then saw the mocking amusement in his eyes as he watched her, and it shook her to know that she had been so easily read. Remembering what he had warned about anger, she looked away and guiltily thrust it from her.

When she looked back, Vayhawk was still watching her, the early light of day making it easier to see his face. His gaze was speculative as he considered her, as if he were trying to decide what she was capable of. She flushed.

"Let's run," he said then, and took off at an easy lope that Senea soon caught up to. She was able to keep up with him for several minutes, but then she gradually fell behind. When he did not stop she tried to catch up to him again but an increasing ache in her side made it impossible. Finally she stopped and sank to her knees. Gulping at air, she pressed her hand against the throbbing of her side.

She saw Vayhawk stop and turn back at an easy stride. She closed her eyes and listened to the pounding of her heart, the rhythmic hiss of blood in her ears, and felt the warmth of the sun as its first light struck her.

Vayhawk's footsteps crunched softly on the sunburnt grass, and she squinted up at him in the bright light. He dropped to his heels, studied her for a long moment, then reached for the pouch he had given her and opened it one-handed. He took out a piece of dried meat, then eased to the ground to sit cross-legged in front of her.

"We'll rest," he said, and tore the meat in two and handed half to her. "Eat."

It was a lot like tough, salty leather, but at that moment it tasted better than anything she'd ever eaten. Vayhawk watched her with an amused glint in his eyes. She avoided his gaze and sat cross-legged to let the ache in her side fade. Vayhawk gave her his water pouch, and she drank, then handed it back.

The sunlight shone on the wind-burnt grass in a bright golden-yellow and the plain lay in gentle folds of yellow and bronze where the ground swells rose and dipped in succession to the horizon. A small flock of birds flitted from rise to rise, their chirping the only sound in the morning air.

Vayhawk drew out his knife. Sunlight flashed off the long blade as he thrust it into the ground in front of him. His dark eyes raised and regarded Senea as he took his hand away, the white handle of the knife becoming almost translucent in the bright light. Senea met his gaze. She swallowed at the meat she had been chewing and sat with her hands clasped tightly.

"Since I have undertaken your training," Vayhawk said, the texture in his voice vibrating across to her, "it will be my task to decide when you have become skilled enough to be on your own." He paused a moment, then continued.

"When you can reach my knife and pull it out of the ground before I do, then you will be free of me." He nodded toward the knife, his eyes steady on her face. "Try it."

Senea looked at the knife that had been driven to its hilt into the hard-baked soil, the sun shining on its handle in a white blaze. She'd never be able to do it.

She looked up and saw that Vayhawk was serious and was waiting for her to attempt it. She did not have any choice but to obey.

She shot her hand forward to snatch the knife out of the ground.

A steel hand clapped over her wrist and held it tight.

Senea gasped in startlement and tried to jerk her hand back out of his grasp. He was leaning forward, his face close to hers, his hand holding hers several inches from the knife. She realized, then, that she had only just begun to move when he had stopped her. Senea glanced down at his large, brown hand which gripped her lighter-colored arm, and she tried to hold down the sudden shaking that started inside her.

Vayhawk reached down with his other hand and pulled the knife out of the ground with a slight tug and slid it back into its sheath at his hip, the white handle flashing in the sun. For a moment longer he held her arm, his eyes smoldering into hers, his face still close, the brush of his breathing on her chin.

"It's in the eyes," he said. "The move is in the eyes first."

Senea stared at him, unable to look away, her heart pounding painfully against her ribs.

He sat back then, releasing her, turned his head to scan the plain. "I have received reports of Ja'sid helden in the north," he said.

Senea rubbed the numbness out of her wrist, and a chill touched her at his words.

"I cannot with leisure train you, Senea, as another would have done." It was the first time he had used her name, and it brought her eyes up, the sound of it on the vibrating timber of his voice a shock.

"With the Ja'sid helden crossing our borders and coming into our lands, I do not have the time. You will have to keep up. No matter how difficult."

He stood, unfolding upward, and waited for her to gather herself to her feet. Then without another word, he started walking toward the north. She followed at a pace behind.

Senea rolled aside on the bank of the small dried-up creekbed where Vayhawk had told her to stay and watched through the branches of a scrub brush as Vayhawk approached the two helden just beyond the crest of the rise. They greeted him with words that did not carry on the dead air; one raised an arm and pointed to the northeast.

The Ja'sid were out there somewhere.

Senea rested her forehead on her arm and closed her eyes, wanting to ignore the ache in her legs and back. The relentless blaze of the sun was hot in the trough where she lay, and her head hurt; the skin on her arms was red and painful. But for the moment she was content to lay there without moving, trying to sleep while she waited for Vayhawk to return.

Too soon she heard quiet footsteps coming her way, and she looked up, her vision momentarily blurred, the sun blinding her. Vayhawk settled down on his heels beside her and she no longer had to look directly into the sun to see him.

"They're farther on," he said.

Senea considered it, lay there unwilling to move.

"Much farther?" she asked.

"Some."

Senea lay still and thought what it meant, put her aching head to her arm again. "And then what? I cannot fight."

"It is as I have said," Vayhawk said. "Our first duty is to the held-tribe. We are to protect and defend and, if necessary, give our lives in the doing of it. If you are heldan for only one day, and die in the performance of that duty, then there is honor in it." He drew a short breath. "They do not know that they have been spotted. That can only be in our favor."

Senea was not reassured in that, though she knew he had meant for her to be. But she thought about the power that he had said these Ja'sid helden were capable of and was uneasy about it. She still was not certain she had understood him right. She drew in a breath, measuring slowly, trying to gain energy from it, finally gathered herself up off the hard ground and started moving.

Vayhawk swiftly overtook her.

"Don't overdo it," he said, taking her arm and slowing her pace. She winced, his touch unexpectedly painful. Vayhawk hastily withdrew his hand, and frowned at the redness of her skin. "That will have to be taken care of," he said, "before it gets worse."

He drew his knife out, strode to a low-growing plant on the side of the dried creek bed, and dug it up with two twisting thrusts of the blade. Then, as he came back to her, he removed the remaining clods of dirt from the bulbous root, cut the plant off with a quick swipe, and resheathed his knife. A clear gellike substance welled out from the root into his hand.

"This will help," he said, and began to spread the gel gently over her skin, the cool moisture drawing out the heat.

Senea stared at his hand, long-fingered, strong and confident, as he stroked the slick gel onto her forearm. His hand moved slowly up to her shoulder, down again, and stopped. She looked up as he raised his eyes to hers. A dark, challenging look came to his face as he studied her. A tremor shivered through her and she pulled away, suddenly wary.

One of the helden that Vayhawk had been talking to came over the rise to them, and Senea stepped back, putting distance between herself and the Heldlan. Vayhawk turned his head to the heldan.

"They are moving."

Vayhawk looked back to Senea, handed her the root, motioning for her to use it on her other arm. She took the root uncertainly.

"This is Landry," Vayhawk said, indicating the heldan with a slight nod of his head.

There was a moment's silence. Landry's eyes went to Senea, wondering at a presence that should not have been there; wondering, Senea thought, at questions that he would have asked had Vayhawk been another. She saw him look at her arm, bare of gold, and take in her condition: exhausted, sunburnt, unskilled . . . of little use to them, a danger to them because she was unskilled.

"Her name is Senea," Vayhawk said. His tone was impatient, almost challenging.

Landry said nothing.

He was shorter than Vayhawk, leaner, wiry, almost surly. Senea started rubbing the root's gel into her arm, using it as an excuse to break eye contact with him, shaken at the sudden tension. She recalled that Mara had said there would be some who would not be pleased that Vayhawk had taken her as heldii. And she wondered again why he had.

Vayhawk took her arm then, when she was finished, and kept her beside him as they followed Landry up the rise. His mouth was set in a firm line and his eyes glinted dangerously with a tightly controlled anger that was frightening to see. This kind of anger made him more dangerous, instead of careless, because he had it completely controlled. Senea strove to keep up with him, did not want that gaze directed at her, and felt him hold her back, keeping the pace slow.

"You'll need all your strength," he said quietly.

She glanced at him and saw that he was watching her with an unreadable expression. She looked away uneasily and concentrated on her feet.

Landry led them, making no great haste. He was cautious as he followed the rolls of the land, careful not to silhouette them on the horizon.

Senea stayed close to Vayhawk, worrying now at her part in the confrontation that was ahead of them, a confrontation that was inevitable, even being actively sought. She was certain that this day was going to be her last and was frightened at that. She wondered what Melina was doing and thought of her father, her mother, and Loran. Guilt touched her for thinking of them, but she was distressed that they would never know whether she lived or died in this day's doings.

By the time she spotted the five helden who had been trailing the Ja'sid, her stomach was knotted with tense fear.

Vayhawk lifted his bow off over his head, and with a silent

look at Senea to stay close by him, he crept to the scouts who were concealed on the side of a rise, crouching almost double as he approached them. Senea followed, stretched flat against the rise when he did, head down, heart pounding furiously.

Vayhawk inched forward, looked over the ridge in the direction the nearest heldan was pointing.

"How many?" he asked, a murmur.

"We count ten."

He turned and motioned with his hand for Senea to come up beside him, then directed her gaze toward one end of a shallow ravine.

There was a movement.

Helden were advancing along a narrow cut, a line that almost merged with the colors around them.

She exhaled slowly, a breath she had been holding, apprehension prickling along her spine. They appeared no different than their own.

Vayhawk's arm was against hers, a warm hardness of muscle pressing the band of gold sharply into her skin, painful on her burn. But she did not move to ease that discomfort, suddenly sensing that this was the only place of safety . . . next to the Heldlan who had, against tradition, and for reasons of his own, paired himself to her. She saw the way others looked to him for a decision, and for the first time she reckoned what it would be to be paired to another.

Vayhawk carefully weighed what lay before them, his eyes going from one concealing place to another, seeming to judge where the enemy could hide, then, turning, he sent four helden farther along the lip of the ravine toward the approaching Ja'sid. With a gesture in that direction, he then sent Landry and the other heldan who had met them earlier the other way. That left Vayhawk and Senea alone.

"Now we wait," he said quietly, and drew his bow around in front of him, resting his chin on the hand that gripped it.

A hot wind blew across the ridge, sent a fine dust into the ravine, fanned it, and scattered it before it touched ground. Senea raised her head to see where the Ja'sid were, but Vayhawk's hand came up over her head and gently restrained her. She lowered her head back to her arm.

Then a white arrow whispered from quiver and was put to the bow, its notch held against the string.

There was silence, save for the murmur of the wind.

Vayhawk's head went up, a slowness that was torture to watch; he lowered it again, his eyes on her, and waited.

Senea returned his gaze, held her breath, watched as he turned his head again, and looked down into the ravine. The bow came up slightly; the arrow was pulled back slowly until the sharp-barbed head was at the tensed bow, fingers wrapped around the string.

Then she heard a sound that had not been there before, one that was not movement of wind over ground. It was a measured tread that was not any louder than the wind, an almost-inaudible sound that she would have missed had she not been expecting it. She raised her head a fraction, a slow move that echoed what Vayhawk had done, one that he did not try to stop, his eyes on the helden below.

She peered through a sudden swirling of dust picked up by the wind and blinked through it when it was tossed into her face.

The Ja'sid helden were close now, threading their way along the bottom of the ravine, out and down among the rocks and outthrusts. Their course was a winding trail that would lead them past the ridge where she and Vayhawk waited. They were almost close enough to make out the individual differences between them. They were close enough to see that they all wore the same color of dusty yellow, no varying colors of green-yellows or gray-yellows among them. Nor was there anyone dressed in black, so the power that Vayhawk had talked about was not with them. Senea was relieved a little in that. She peered at them more closely.

They all carried bows and wore quivers across their backs. The heldan who led the column had a dark beard, one that was trimmed close to his face, an indulgence that Senea had not seen among the helden of her own Held. Beyond that she could not tell them apart, not from where she was.

Suddenly the arrow beside her hissed from the bow.

She flinched.

The bearded heldan below stopped mid-step, turned, seemed simply to be looking around; then he fell. The arrow had not seemed to touch him. But darkness spread over his side and ran to the dirt underneath him, a white shaft buried up to the feathers in his ribs.

Senea stared, horrified, and tasted bile. She had known that these helden from the northwest were going to be killed, that enemy helden were dealt with in that way, that the role of the Held was to do that very thing. But knowing it and seeing it were not the same.

A sick shudder took her.

She wanted to turn her eyes away but could only stare with mesmerized fascination at the lifeblood of the Ja'sid heldan that was leaking all over the ground.

Vayhawk's handiwork!

There was half a moment of stunned silence, time enough for Vayhawk to notch another arrow, pull it back, and release it whining after the first.

A second heldan stiffened, then fell.

Then a cry went up, and the Ja'sid scattered.

Vayhawk rose up on his elbow, sent another arrow whistling into the ravine. From the right and left on the ridge other arrows flew; one more Ja'sid went down.

A speeding shaft coming from the ravine sang swiftly through the air between Senea and Vayhawk, close enough that Senea felt the brush of wind on her ear. She ducked with a stifled cry, heard Vayhawk curse and scramble forward.

"Stay here," he said, and he disappeared over the edge.

An instant she stayed still, head down, heart hammering in reaction. The sun shone brightly on her back, hot now in the early dry season. Absurdly it distracted her, pulling her mind to the discomfort of her burnt arms and to the blistering and peeling that would follow in the days to come. She knew that there would be more of it even beyond that as Vayhawk taught her to be heldan. That is, if she lived through this day.

Anxiously she pushed herself forward, unable to keep her head down, and saw that Vayhawk was sliding down the steep slope on his heels, rocks rolling, dirt flying, dust rising from his descent. His bow was in hand; the sunlight shone on his bronze shoulders and arms, glaring yellow off the armband. He struck the bottom running, headed for cover. Arrows flew at him ... past him.

Senea stifled a cry of alarm ... and breathed in relief when he reached an outthrust of rock and ducked out of sight.

Then there was dust on both sides of her; helden jumping down from one protrusion to the next, abandoning concealment in their haste to follow Vayhawk to the ravine.

A cry of pain sounded to her right. An arrow had found its mark, and a heldan stumbled, lost his footing, slid uncontrollably through brush, hit a boulder hard, and rolled over and over to a stop. Rocks rattled past him and disappeared farther down the slope.

Shuddering, Senea watched for him to get up. He didn't. She tore her eyes from him, the knowledge that he was dead cold in her. She looked for Vayhawk.

The Heldian emerged from where he had been hiding, ran crouching across a dry creekbed, dodged an arrow, dove for another outthrust, and lost his bow. Hesitating only a split second, he left it.

Then his knife was in his hand and he was running, hunched over, toward where there was a Ja'sid heldan hidden behind a large stand of rocks.

Senea spied him. He could be easily seen from where she was on the ridge. He leaned against the side of the rock and launched an arrow at the helden coming down the slope. Almost instantly another arrow was at his bow, drawn and let fly.

He was relatively safe from attack where he was, even from Senea's position, and at the same time he could easily pick off those on the ridge. The only way he could be stopped was from behind. Vayhawk must have seen this before he had gone over the edge of the ridge.

Vayhawk skirted around some brush out of the Ja'sid's line of sight, sidled up to the rocks, then edged around, with his back to the stone. He eased up behind the Ja'sid, grabbed him in a swift move, pulled him back, his hand coming up before there was a struggle, a flash of blade across the throat.

Nausea rose in Senea as he dropped the body.

There was a sound, and Vayhawk spun to the right, hair flipping over his shoulder, feet wide apart, knees bent, knife ready.

A body struck his and he was down, grappling with a Ja'sid who had thrown himself around some brush. Sunlight reflected off metal, knives seeking vital organs, the struggle kicking up dust that blew away on the wind.

Senea cried out in terror for him, rose partially to her knees, her heart clutched with alarm, ready to jump over the ridge and scramble to his aid. She momentarily forgot that he had told her to stay where she was.

A shadow fell across hers, and she spun around, and stared up into the surprised face of a heldan who had just come up behind her.

She saw instantly that he was dressed completely in black and adorned with weapons that glittered and winked in the hot sun.

Black Ja'sid.

The enemy.

And she was alone. She froze where she was, weight on her hands, looking up at him.

He was older than most helden she had seen, his hair shorter. He had a hardened look about him, like one who had done a lot of killing. His bow was across his back, alongside his quiver of arrows. Apparently he hadn't known what was going on in the ravine, but seemed to have flanked the ridge unseen by Vayhawk's scouts.

Senea saw him look past her to the fighting below and quickly size up the situation. His blue eyes looked back to her, and took in the fact that she wore no gold and had no weapon. His surprise turned to anger, then to animal appraisal.

"Well, now . . ." he said. His voice sent chills crawling over her.

He grinned and looked her up and down with slow deliberation. It was not a look that had ever been used on her before, but she certainly understood it. A heated flush rose to her face. Anger followed.

Then she saw his knife. Black-handled. It was not yet drawn, but the sight of it turned her anger to fear. Sheathed, it was a knife. Just—a knife. But it reminded her of what Vayhawk had said about their power being in their weapons as well as in their touch. And she recalled how easily Vayhawk had just used his and she knew that this Ja'sid could do the same; could just as swiftly put the blade to her own throat. That breath would be her last, killed by a power she didn't understand.

His leering smile was triumphant. "There's nowhere for you to go," he said.

Senea backed up against the cliff, her legs shuddering under her. She looked past him and saw that he was right. There was no way around him.

He took a swaggering step up to her and raised a hand to touch her. She flinched, not wanting that touch on her skin. She wasn't sure what this power was that was supposed to be in the Black Ja'sid's touch, but she steeled herself against it.

He hesitated only a moment before his palm came against her cheek in a caressing move.

"What heldan would bring you out here and then leave you alone?" His smile was unpleasant.

Senea stared into blue eyes that glinted like hard iceflints, and she realized that she felt nothing unusual coming from his hand. Groping behind her she found a rock in the wall that was loose.

"He must not be much of a heldan to leave a pretty thing like you up here unprotected."

Senea worked frantically at the rock, trying her best to conceal what she was doing. She thought of Vayhawk again and wanted desperately to scream, to bring him scrambling up the slope to her. She imagined his knife jammed in the Ja'sid's side, blood dribbling all over him and onto the ground, wanted a white arrow buried in his back, his face in the dirt. Shocked by herself, she thought in panic again of screaming. But she couldn't scream. She just couldn't . . . she clamped her teeth together.

"I certainly wouldn't leave someone like you alone for the enemy to find." He moved his hand slowly down her jaw and neck, over her shoulder.

Senea glared at him, her fingers still working furiously at the rock. Sand dribbled over her hand and fell with a quiet rattle at her feet.

The Ja'sid stepped closer, pinned her to the cliff, and looked down on her in dark, vengeful greed.

Suddenly the rock was free. She struck him with it, catching him alongside the head, and wrenched herself free of him. Then she ran.

He cursed. She jumped down the slide. Dirt gave way under her, and she slid wildly to a level place, the Ja'sid close behind her.

She scrambled to her feet, jumped over a small lip of rock, and ran. Her legs were weak, the terror for what she had done hitting her. She had never struck anyone before in her life.

She jumped again and fell. Looking back, she saw that the heldan was almost on her.

There was a rhythmic sound in her ears. Rasping sounds that came over and over. Sobbing, terrified sounds that she realized were her own.

She got her feet under her and dove for the next slope as the Ja'sid jumped for her.

She hit, rolling, tumbled through brush that tore at her face, and came to a jarring stop that knocked the breath out of her.

Pain shot through her. She turned her head, gasped for air.

The Ja'sid was scrambling down the slope to her.

She had to get up ... couldn't ... had to anyway.

She rolled to her side, sobbing at the fire that lanced through her. She forced herself to her knees as rocks rattled down ahead of the Ja'sid.

She could hear his breathing now, panting grunts of animal pleasure, the hunter closing in on its prey. It terrified her. She sucked in a painful breath, tried to get to her feet, and made it.

She threw herself to the side, crying in pain, just as the Ja'sid lunged for her.

He landed where she had been, spun with a growl, and came after her.

She whirled to run but saw that the ledge had come to an end, a straight drop of several yards directly at her feet. It ran to the right of her and back past the Ja'sid. On the left rose a steep ridge, impossible to climb in haste. She had nowhere to go and wheeled to face the heldan.

Half a breath they stared at each other. Senea gasped for air, body heaving with the effort, lungs and side aching. She saw with satisfaction that she had left a jagged cut on the side of his face that ran from eye to ear. Blood was smeared across his cheek and still ran freely, dripping to his shirt. His eye was swelling.

"I've got you now," he said, his voice a hoarse whisper.

This time Senea would have screamed for help. But she didn't. Instinct told her that he'd rush her if she did.

Then she thought of his knife; she realized of a sudden that she should have gone for it before, that she could have killed him. As heldan she should have and knew that Vayhawk would have.

Memory of Vayhawk using his own knife came to her. She shuddered. She couldn't have done it.

She cast a quick look on both sides of her, reckoned between the jump and the climb.

The Ja'sid stepped forward. She stepped back, dangerously close to the edge. He stopped.

Senea saw that . . . she stepped to the very edge of the drop, desperately hoping it would stop him from rushing her. She could see that the thought was in his mind.

"We'll go off together if you try it," she said. Her throat was raw, her voice hoarse.

His eyes narrowed, and he looked past her to the drop. He raised his eyes to her face and straightened up. He held out his hands in surrender. "I won't come any closer." The tone was a placating one.

Senea did not move. His face did not have the look of surrender. She looked with uncertainty along the ledge, saw that there was a slope from the plain that rose to it several feet behind the Ja'sid. She had gone the wrong way.

If she could walk along the edge now and get past him, she might be able to reach it.

"We could stay like this until the wet season," the heldan said. "But you're going to get tired standing there."

Senea took a step, a sliding sidestep in the direction that would take her past the Ja'sid, staying as close to the edge as she could.

He started. She froze.

He wiped at the blood that ran down his face, smearing more across his cheek, and she could see that he was trying to figure a way to get her without throwing them both over. She thought, with a sudden fear, that he might just decide to push her off instead. She bit her lip and took another step. He did not come closer. She took another.

Then, slowly, one step after another, she edged past him. Her heart was beating furiously, and she was shaking so hard she was afraid that she'd go over the edge without him; but she was determined that she was not going to make it easy for him.

The heldan glared at her and glanced at the slope. He was clearly waiting for her to reach it. Senea realized suddenly that she had not thought what would happen once she reached the slope. He could attack her then without her pulling him off the ledge with her. Now she thought about it with sudden fear.

She turned and lunged, went down the slope in a plummeting slide, and hit the bottom, staggering at the impact.

The Ja'sid hit her from behind, body to body, throwing her to the ground, knocking the breath out of her.

She struggled to get to her knees, sobbing, air refusing to enter paralyzed lungs. Her fingers groped for rocks and brush as she tried to pull herself away from him.

She sucked in a ragged breath; she almost got her feet under her, but he seized her and dragged her down, screaming and fighting.

Over and over they struggled, a tangle of arms and legs.

His lips were pulled back, and he was snarling like a dog, his eyes blazing with fury, and she was afraid he'd tear her apart with his teeth.

She came up against a boulder with jarring impact and stopped.

Then she thought of his knife and realized that it could be in his hand in an instant, rammed into her, tearing and ripping and shredding, the blood gushing, hot and sticky over them both. She almost gagged with horror and fought him furiously, bare-handed, wild cries like an animal coming from her throat.

Her fingers came up and tore at his face where she had struck him with the rock, where the flesh was tender and bleeding, and his hand seized her wrist and slammed it hard to the ground.

The weight of his other arm went across her throat, his forearm snapping her head up with a crack of meeting teeth.

He stared down at her, panting, his body heaving at great gulps of air, the heat of his breath on her face. His legs straddled her, and his weight was on her stomach, his hand crushing around her wrist.

Senea struggled under him, trying to throw him off. He leaned weight onto his arm, a painful choking pressure that cut off her air. She fought him more furiously then, until she realized that he was not letting up, and that he could strangle her that way. She went limp, and he eased back.

"No more of that," he said, his voice a hoarse whisper.

She stared into his eyes, heart pounding, panic just barely under control, and thought about his knife again. Her free hand was just inches from it.

"You're a little wild one, aren't you?" he said.

Senea moved her hand, not sure whether to go for the knife fast or slow.

The heldan drew in a breath and shifted his weight on her.

His left hand moved slightly. She was just able to glimpse a change in his eyes before his form was blurred by a dark aura that seemed to flow out from him, swallowing them both.

A tingling sensation ran from his fingers through her skin and arm. A sense of wrongness grew in her, a weight in her stomach. It came in a great wave, like the building of a storm, like the sudden change in the wind . . . She felt suddenly dizzy, weak, strangely unsettled, and then time began to turn and dip crazily. The air turned bitterly cold.

His nails were digging into her arms like tiny brands, and she had the nightmarish feeling that her identity was slipping away. She gasped in mingled pain and fear as he bruised her flesh.

She became aware, at last, that her vision was darkening, and as the day deepened into twilight, the ground seemed to close in on her, as if trying to enfold her in a final embrace from which she would never wake. And the cold increased as the darkness came on.

Desperately, Senea's fingers closed around the Ja'sid's knife handle. She hesitated, afraid, stared into his darkening eyes trying to keep what she was doing out of her own.

The icy menace in his gaze, as dead as stones, somehow transferred itself into her heart. There was very little real movement for long moments as she struggled to keep her consciousness.

His blue eyes narrowed suddenly, almost startling her out of the trance-state, and she jerked the knife from the sheath just an instant before he snatched at her hand, her heart leaping in panic as she realized that she had seen that move in his eyes before he made it.

Then stabbing upward with all of her might, she tried to bury the knife into the heldan's side, but he lunged away, and she missed. Crying in frustration and fear she scrambled to her knees and backed to the boulder where they had been struggling. She was shaking so violently she was afraid she'd drop the knife, so she held it with both hands in front of her ready to fend the Ja'sid off if he should come at her.

Awareness, reality, and then sheer mounting panic swam into her as she understood what had happened to her. This was the Ja'sid power. Senea felt as if she was trying to fight her way out of a maze. That flood of power had taken her over totally, but now expended in a single moment, it had gone, leaving only a hideous aftertaste.

The Ja'sid rose slowly from the ground, crouching, looked warily from the knife to her face.

"Stay back," she said desperately. She caught her breath. Her chest hurt.

"Give me the knife." His voice was almost a growl.

"I mean it," she said.

He took a step toward her.

"I'll kill you. So help me, I'll kill you."

He looked at the knife, raised his eyes again, shrugged, a disbelieving gesture. "You couldn't do it." He took another step.

Senea's breath caught in her throat with a sob. "I will."

"Give me the knife."

She didn't answer, but clutched the knife tighter and gasped at air that did not seem to want to enter her lungs. She thought disconnectedly of her father and what he'd think if he could see her right now, with her back against a boulder, prepared to take a man's life.

"How long have you been heldii, huh?" The heldan was trying to distract her now. Senea stared at him, determined not to waver a moment.

"Long enough to know how to use that thing?" He was taunting her. "How long? Two months?" And when she didn't answer, "Longer?"

She still didn't answer and he raised his eyebrows. "Less? One month? Less than that?"

Then he was coming at her, a sudden rush that took her by surprise. She thrust the knife up with both hands, caught him in the belly, his momentum driving the knife up to the hilt.

But he didn't stop; he didn't even seem to feel the blade jammed into his vitals and was on her with a murderous rage, thrusting her to the ground. The knife was pulled from him, her hands still grasping it.

Then she was grappling with him, knife between them, struggling to keep it from him. Over and over they went, kicking up dust, slick blood on their hands, on their arms, soaking into their clothes, the knife becoming slippery with it.

He grabbed her wrist in a viselike grip and twisted hard, pushing the knife toward her with relentless strength. Senea saw with horror that he was going to shove it into her, with her hand still on it.

She tried to pull away from him, but his weight was on her, bruising, crushing, his hand still twisting her arm until she thought it would break.

Then the knife slammed against her, shoved savagely, and hit her ribs. It felt as if the knife ripped clear through her. Something snapped. She lost her grip on the knife, feeling pain like she'd never known.

His eyes shot up to lock on hers, abrupt and invasive. Senea felt herself turn cold inside as the darkness that had come over her before sprang awake yet again. Something wrong . . . so hideously wrong that it was beyond her understanding . . . The Ja'sid power!

A shock like a bolt of pure energy shot through her, filling her body until she felt her bones would shatter with the sheer force of it, and though she tried to scream, not the smallest sound came from her throat. She felt as if she had been kicked in the stomach; agony flooded her and the whole world was a single dark vortex of torture, twisting and tumbling around her.

A shadow rose over her, blotting out what light was left, and in the dark recess of her mind was the half awareness of strength being sucked out of her. A strange disembodied sensation came over her. Her life was running out of her with her blood. No—it was being sucked out of her where the edge of the knife blade drank into her blood. She was shivering convulsively; it was so cold that her limbs were numb.

An unholy bonding was forming which she was powerless to deflect. She discovered this fact on the verge of madness. She was becoming part of the Ja'sid—body, mind, and soul— the pressure was building, building; she couldn't fight it . . .

Some unseen force took ahold of the both of them, and he would use their combined strength to do his bidding like a servant, and with it he would pull the life-force out of her.

Fighting her way out of the nightmare, she knew she must rally her mind to survival or she'd snuff out like a candle flame in the wind. She fought back to the surface, came back to her own body, and fixed her eyes on the eyes of the Ja'sid. Her throat was raw from the screaming inside her trapped body.

Disbelief registered on the Ja'sid's features.

The blade was wrenched from her, and she saw that this

time he was going to ram it into her all the way. She knew she was going to die, and she tried to stop him with her hands, but he was too strong.

Then she felt two sensations almost simultaneously. They were the sharpest, most exquisitely painful feelings she had ever experienced. Her consciousness whirled as something slammed into her. A wave of nauseating darkness rose; she felt her life giving way—

She resisted.

She took the force that was in her and pushed it away. Unexpectedly she felt a flaring of power within her so devoid of light it seemed inordinately heavy. It pressed on her chest like a fist.

She heard the startled intake of breath from the Ja'sid and saw a look of the most profound horror transfigure his face. He reeled back violently, as if he had been struck by a monstrous, invisible hand.

Senea stared at him, her thoughts moving rapidly down an astonishing path. It had been a decided effort to break away from the bonding with this black-clad heldan. But she was free of him now, and there was the faintest whisper of knowledge within her soul, the realization of a power she had never thought she might have, and it astounded her.

The Ja'sid then raised his hand, to thrust the knife at her one last time.

In desperation she reached up and bit him, forced her teeth into the big muscle that was part of his palm. She bit hard, tasting blood, thick and salty.

The heldan yelped in pain, and his right hand came crashing against her head and tore her hold loose, momentarily dazing her.

Then she saw that he had also knocked the knife out of his hand. It lay a short distance away. She lunged for it at the same moment that he did.

The heldan seized it, his stretch longer than hers, and he hit the ground with an abrupt burst of expelled air. Senea scrambled for the knife, sobbing hysterically, snatched it from his fingers, and turned on him before he could get up.

The pain in her side was like fire and a black fuzziness was getting into her eyes. She blinked again and again, trying to keep her vision clear, waiting for him to rise, but did not realize immediately that he was not moving.

Then she saw the shaft of an arrow buried in his back. For a moment she didn't understand what that meant.

Dead. He was dead.

Senea stumbled back a step, staring at him, still expecting him to strike at her with his hand as if he were a snake. Blood was running down her side and hip, soaking into her shirt and breeches. She raised a hand to the wound and tried to stop the flow, still keeping her eyes on the Ja'sid.

A movement above her brought her head up. Two helden were jumping and sliding down the slopes of the ridge toward her.

A strangled sob caught her throat, and she backed against the boulder, knife held out in front of her, knowing she could never fight two of them.

CHAPTER
SIX

Senea gasped breath and tried to stay steady on her feet, leaned against the boulder for support, and watched through a darkening haze as the helden reached the bottom of the ridge. One went to the dead Ja'sid and turned him over. The other came at her.

She flung the knife up, low, striking at him, unable to put much strength behind it. A hand seized her arm, shadow and hand came around her arm.

Vayhawk.

She gasped breath, struggled for mental balance, then in sudden release sagged to her knees, put her hand to her side, and brought it away wet with blood.

She heard Vayhawk murmur an exclamation and drop to one knee beside her. Then she was crying shaming, uncontrollable tears in total, eerie silence. Vayhawk held her until she stopped, then bent over and lifted her shirt away from the congealing and oozing blood on her side. He examined lightly with his fingers where the knife had ripped into her.

"Heldlan."

Vayhawk turned.

Landry was bending over the dead Ja'sid. "You better see this."

Vayhawk looked back to Senea, his eyes grave as if he were deciding whether she'd be all right if he left her. "I'll be right back," he said. He rose and went to Landry.

Senea leaned against the boulder, the dark haze almost completely obscuring her vision now. A numb dullness was beginning to come over her. Through the lacy blackness over her vision she saw Landry show Vayhawk the wounds on the Ja'sid:

the knife wound in the stomach, the wounds on the side of the head, and even where she had bit the Ja'sid's hand. The Heldlan looked at the body for several moments before he lowered himself to his heels beside Landry. He looked over at her with an expression that she could not read and turned back. Then he spoke to Landry in tones that she could not hear, reached down and unbuckled the knife belt on the Ja'sid, and pulled it free. He cleaned the Ja'sid's knife with a handful of dirt, slid it into the sheath, then handed the belt to Landry.

Just before darkness came completely over her, Senea saw Vayhawk roll the Ja'sid over and cut a large piece of material from the back of the shirt.

The next thing Senea was aware of was a hand at her chin turning her head gently.

"How is she?" It was Landry's voice.

"She'll live," a lightly textured voice answered.

She struggled to open her eyes and saw Vayhawk sitting on his heels regarding her closely.

"Will she be able to make it back to the Held?"

"She'll make it."

Senea turned her head slightly and found Landry standing next to her, looking down on her. "You should be proud, heldii," he said. "You got him solid. He would have been dead in a couple of more minutes, even without the Heldlan's arrow." There was a tone in his voice that dismayed her, a veiled threat that she didn't understand.

"When you get to the Held," Vayhawk said sharply, "tell Roskel to send a double patrol out here." And when Landry hesitated, he added, "I'll bring her in."

Landry looked from Senea to Vayhawk as if he were about to object, then nodded imperceptibly, slung the dead Ja'sid's belt over his shoulder, and strode away.

Senea looked back to Vayhawk and found him regarding her with a measuring approval.

"You did well, Senea," he said. He folded the material he had cut from the Ja'sid's shirt into a small, thick pad, then, "Let's get you back to the Held."

He stood and gently lifted her to her feet. Senea cried out as pain shot through her ribs and side, radiating out from where the Ja'sid's knife had struck bone.

"I'm sorry," Vayhawk said, and thereafter moved more slowly as he took her left arm and put it across his back so he could grasp her hand at his right hip. The bow on his back rested lightly on her elbow. Then he slipped his left arm around her and put the pad of material under her shirt, over the wound on her right side. He held it in place with his hand, the pressure of that hold pulling her tightly against him.

The pain immediately lessened under the pressure of his hand, making it easier for Senea to breathe. But still, she could only take shallow breaths, each intake of air a searing flame that pushed against her ribs. She leaned against Vayhawk, unable to do anything else.

Then walking slowly at first, and gradually increasing the pace, he began to take her back to the Held.

Time stopped for Senea. Her world became narrowed to the agony in her side, the fire that accompanied each breath, the strength of Vayhawk holding her close, and the little bit of plain about them. She reckoned she might last until night.

She struggled to keep Vayhawk's pace, his long strides carrying her forward, keeping her moving down a gentle roll of the land and into an ill dream of pain and long moments of empty thought. She came to herself and saw that the sun had set and a gray twilight was on them. Still Vayhawk moved her forward steadily, the pace never faltering. His hand was always at her side holding the material in place, pulling her close, his warmth keeping back the chill that kept trying to take her.

She drifted a time again, and when she came to they were in darkness.

"Where are we?" she forced herself to ask.

"We're almost there." His voice was quiet. "Lean your head on my arm. Sleep."

She didn't argue with him and did what he said. She dozed until she found herself splashing through water. She stumbled, and Vayhawk's arm tightened around her, guided her across the river, and pulled her up the bank.

Then they were in the Held. She had lapsed into unconsciousness in spite of her best efforts and came to as they entered the light. She heard voices, words that were unintelligible, until she felt other hands on her and a voice angry with shock. "What have you done to her?"

Senea looked up and saw Mara glaring angrily at Vayhawk.

"Are you on patrol tonight?" he asked curtly.

"Yes."

"You're relieved," he said. "Take care of her. Then bring her to me."

"Bring her to you?" Mara echoed in protest. "She needs sleep!"

"She'll get sleep."

"Vayhawk, she can't do any more today."

A trace of anger was in the Heldlan's dark eyes for just a second. "Heldan, have you forgotten what it is to be heldii?"

"No. But . . ."

"Bring her to me," he said, and his arm slipped away from around Senea. A lance of intense pain jarred her ribs at the movement, and she caught her breath on a gasp for air.

Senea felt the smaller frame of Mara take her weight, the change of hands causing new pain to shoot through her, and felt an unaccountable coldness come over her at the departure of Vayhawk. Even in the agony of the moment she almost wished that he hadn't gone.

Then she was in the bath, lying on a bench. How she got there she couldn't remember. A great lethargy was on her. Her eyes rested on Mara, who was kneeling beside her, a bowl of aromatic water in her hands.

"Sit up, Senea," she said. "I have to clean your side."

Senea tried, earnestly, but there was a burning pain in her ribs and the effort was beyond her strength. A blur came over her eyes, making focusing too difficult. The darkness began to come back over her, and that was easier and more comfortable. She felt a touch on her, a knife cutting away the blood-encrusted shirt—Mara, she remembered.

Mara began to wash the clotted blood from the knife wound. She worked carefully and deliberately. Then Senea felt herself lifted. She cried out at the stabbing pain. A vessel's rim touched her lips. She drank, finding something cool that she did not recognize, and swallowed several times. It began to wake her; some kind of stimulant. And a painkiller. Within a couple of minutes she was able to stand with Mara's assistance.

"Let's get you cleaned up before I bandage that," Mara said.

Somehow Senea's clothes were removed, and she was helped into the hot water. Then she was fully awake, because the heat of the water was painful on her burnt skin and lanced into her wound like liquid fire. But it was immediately dulled, and she washed the best she could. Mara helped her out of the tub, wrapped her in a soft cloth, and set her on a bench. She then dressed Senea's wound with a stinging bitter-scented ointment and finally bound it with a clean cloth that wrapped around the ribs.

"You look terrible," Mara said.

Senea managed a smile, watched Mara pick up the bloodied clothes that were on the floor and toss them in a basket. Senea shuddered. The blood had been hers and the Ja'sid heldan's. It shocked her to see how much there had been; she understood now Mara's shocked anger at Vayhawk. She remembered Vayhawk's question to Mara, *Have you forgotten what it is to be heldii?* She wondered what he had meant.

"Mara, how long is a person usually heldii?"

"Sometimes until they earn their gold at the Games, although they still have much to learn even beyond that. Most of the time, however, it's until their heldan determines that the heldii is good enough to be assigned by Roskel."

"There is no other test?"

"Not usually. The Games are no easy thing. Usually, that's enough." She looked at Senea with a frown. "Why?"

"Today ..." Senea stopped. It was hard to talk, the effort painful. The breath it took was a fire in her side. "Today, Vayhawk took his knife ... stabbed it into the ground ... said that when I could get to it and pull it out before he could I would be free of him."

Mara made a sudden sound in her throat, a sort of laugh, or an expel of air that expressed pity, or anger, or surprise that was not really surprise.

"Girl," Mara said, "he's got you tied to him tighter than a heldan is tied to the Held. You'll never get to that knife before he does. The reason he's Heldlan is because no one can do anything faster or better than he can. You'll stay heldii to him forever if that's the test he's given you."

This perplexed Senea—frightened her.

"A person stays heldii as long as their trainer says," Mara explained. "The pairing then is changed by Roskel. By then he'll be able to tell what pairs would work best together. Who would work best with whom. Whose skills will complement another's. That sort of thing. Then the pairing is permanent ... until one gets killed, that is."

Mara patted Senea's hand. "Don't worry. I'm sure Vayhawk

has his reasons for what he did." She stood. "I better go get you some clothes to wear."

Senea watched Mara stride from the room and then she leaned back against the warm wooden wall. She pulled the large cloth tighter, felt the pain in her side which had subsided somewhat to a dull ache. She recalled what Vayhawk had said, *You will hurt before you are done, but you will also learn to live with it.* Roskel had said pretty much the same thing. She wondered if she would ever become that hardened. She flexed her hands, trying their strength, and found the numbness that had blanked her mind and weakened her limbs was retreating. The stimulant in the drink that Mara had given her was rousing her senses, making them increasingly clear.

Mara returned after a couple of minutes, and in her hands she bore a yellow-green bundle that she laid on the bench beside Senea.

"Your clothes," Mara said. "If you will let me, I will help you."

And Mara did so, carefully, gently, helping her to pull on the shirt when Senea's senses spun and went gray, then helped with the breeches and the lacing up of the sandals.

Mara stood beside her, waiting until she had her breath again. "Vayhawk is in the eating hall. It's not too far to walk. Do you think you can make it?"

Senea nodded uncertainly. "I will try."

She put her hand on Mara's arm and used it to steady herself so that she could stand. Then she walked the few steps to the door, leaning on Mara who moved with her, but stopped against the wall, legs trembling so that she thought that she could not go on. For a while she stood still, breathing hard, close to being ill; Mara was watching her closely, worry on her face. It was a few moments before Senea could even push herself away from the wall, leaning heavily on Mara.

They negotiated the hall together, but at the eating-hall door Mara hesitated and removed Senea's hold. "From here you should try to go on your own strength."

Senea looked at her uncomprehendingly.

"You're the Heldlan's heldii," Mara explained carefully. "You have to understand . . . he can never look less than what he is. You have become a part of that image because he chose to be paired to you. He has enemies who would grasp any chance at all to discredit him and will use you to that end. That is why he wants you to be seen before you can go to your bunkroom. You have to appear strong in spite of what has happened to you. Others will be seeing you as a vulnerable spot in the Held because the Heldlan has been paired to you. You will have to show them that they are wrong, even if it kills you to do it."

Senea stared at Mara, a chill coming on her. She understood suddenly why Vayhawk had insisted that she find her bunkroom on her own the night before.

"Then why did he pair himself to me?" Senea asked. "If this is all true?"

"I don't know."

For a moment Senea returned Mara's concerned gaze. She saw again in her mind the moment when Vayhawk had looked deliberately down into the basket he held to find the ball that matched hers. Surely he had known all of this when he had done it . . . yet, still . . . he did it.

"Go on," Mara said. "I'll be right behind you if you need me."

Senea looked at the door, a new fear in her. She heard the words that Mara had not said, *Please, try very hard not to need me,* not that she didn't want to help, but that she knew that Senea had to do this on her own. Senea suddenly was very loath to go into that room.

For another moment she stood still, staring at the door, gathering the dregs of her strength.

Then she put out her hand and pushed the door inward and walked stiffly into the room, her hands clenched tightly at her sides to keep herself from trembling. With relief she saw that Vayhawk was sitting fairly close to the door, not at the table nearest the door, but not so far into the room that she couldn't make it to him.

He was leaning casually back in his chair, talking to Roskel, his feet on a nearby chair. Senea walked toward them, forcing herself to walk steadily, and saw that there were others in the room, eating and talking. Roskel saw her and sat up. "Heldlan."

Vayhawk looked up and saw her. He took his feet down, but remained leaning back, shifting only very slightly. His eyes watched her closely as she went around the table and sat down in the chair where his feet had been. She saw that he had bathed also. His hair was wet and he had changed his clothes.

"Are you all right?" His voice was low.

She nodded, not daring to say anything for fear she'd betray a tremor in her voice. She glanced at Roskel and saw that he, also, watched her closely. Mara sat down next to Senea, and Vayhawk turned his eyes on her.

"The wound is not serious," she said. "It should heal quickly. The rib is broken." She looked at Senea and back to Vayhawk. "She has had drugweed . . . it is all that is keeping her on her feet." Then Mara leaned forward and fixed Vayhawk with a fierce stare. "She should be in her bunk, Heldlan."

"Your concern is noted, heldan," Vayhawk said tonelessly.

Mara looked at Senea and sighed imperceptibly, and Senea understood that the heldan had done all that she could.

"Mara," Roskel said. "Go get the heldii something to eat."

Mara inclined her head and stood, pushing back her chair, a scraping of legs across the floor.

Senea shifted uncomfortably in her chair as Mara went behind her across the room to fetch something from the fires. She took the moment to catch her breath, and she had settled so that her side was not hurting so much by the time Mara returned. Her hand shook when she began to feed herself.

There was roasted meat, which did not appeal to her, even though it had been cooked in the way she most liked. She was afraid that she would not be able to keep it down. There was a grain bread, thick and satisfying, some fresh fruit, and cool water. She ate slowly, feeling the strength that had gotten her into the room slipping away from her. A fine sweat broke out on her skin, and she drew in quiet breaths of air to keep back the dark that hovered around the edges of her vision.

She heard Vayhawk and Roskel talking in low tones, but only caught snatches of what was said. She concentrated, instead, on keeping her mind clear. She shut her eyes to ease their tired aching, hearing activity and the murmur of voices around her, felt sleep descend on her, and forced her eyes open. She met Vayhawk's dark eyes which were watching her with an intentness that drove all sleep from her.

Then his eyes swung to a movement beside Mara.

Landry. With another heldan. And Treyna.

Senea saw that the girl did not look any more at ease than she had at the pairing the day before. The hunted, frightened look was still there.

The heldan who had come with Landry settled down in the remaining chair and looked at Senea with veiled curiosity. She looked away and kept her eyes to the table, concentrating on keeping her hands steady.

Mara touched her arm.

Senea looked up and met the steady gaze of Landry, who stood slightly behind the seated heldan.

"Heldii," he said, a greeting that had no feeling of a greeting. He put a knife belt on the table. Senea saw with surprise that it was the one Vayhawk had taken from the dead Ja'sid. "It is yours," Landry said. "It has been cleaned and sharpened, as is the custom."

Senea looked up from it to Mara, questioningly.

"It is the custom," Mara said. "If a heldii kills an enemy, that heldii is given that enemy's knife. It is an honor paid. And you choose your own colors."

"Colors?"

"By which you will be identified."

Senea looked from Mara to the others around the table. Roskel, Vayhawk, Landry, Treyna . . . and the unnamed heldan who watched her with an expressionless face that seemed to hide a threat behind it.

"I don't know what colors already belong to others," she protested.

"Perhaps your heldan would suggest something," the un-identified heldan said, the threat that she sensed from him barely disguised in his voice.

Silent glances went from one to the other, and Senea followed these exchanges with anxiety.

"What do you wish, heldii?" Landry asked.

Senea perceived that there was something going on here that she didn't understand, something in which she was an unwilling participant. Vayhawk's enemies, she recalled of a sudden. Landry and this heldan, whose name she didn't know, enemies who would use her against Vayhawk. She was helpless in this and looked to Vayhawk, aware that the others did, also.

His eyes were on her, steady and unperturbed, and for a slow breath it was as if they were alone, the Heldlan holding her stare captive with his black-brown gaze. Then, without taking his eyes off her, he said in a quiet, but distinct voice, "Red and white."

An instant lapsed before Senea understood what he meant.

She had almost forgotten to what he had spoken . . . the problem of her identification colors. Then a cold went across her back, like a chill wind suddenly brushing past; she realized what the colors he had chosen stood for; red for the color that paired them together, white for the color that was his own.

She stared at him, and he looked back with a challenge, daring her to object, to refuse them.

She cast a look around the table, seeing that Roskel and the unnamed heldan had understood Vayhawk's choice, also. They were looking at her to see her reaction: Roskel, with a silent analyzing watchfulness that came from being Held-second, the other heldan's like a predator waiting, his narrowed eyes making her suddenly cautious. She almost rose to walk away from them all, but a grip on her arm advised her otherwise before she could make the move. She looked at Mara, whose hand lay on her arm. Senea saw that Mara hadn't caught what had happened, but she was sensitive to the sudden tension that had come over the table. Treyna, standing beside Landry, was looking bewildered and frightened.

The unnamed heldan sat back in his chair with a smile that was less than friendly. "Perhaps the heldii has less wit than luck."

Senea felt Mara bristle and saw the dark eyes of Vayhawk on the heldan, studying him.

"No offense meant," the heldan said, letting a false smile on his lips.

"None taken," Vayhawk replied.

"It's just that I couldn't help but wonder." The heldan affected a shrug that managed to be insulting.

"What couldn't you help but wonder, Sky!" Mara said, in spite of the look of warning Roskel gave her.

Senea looked at the heldan. So, his name was Sky.

Sky looked at Senea with a cold, calculating gaze. "I can't help but wonder if the heldii was just lucky; that if my heldii had been in the same situation she could have done the same thing."

"I doubt it," Mara snorted in derision.

Sky frowned at her and looked back to Vayhawk.

Senea contemplated Treyna, who was listening with open dismay on her face, a feeling that Senea shared. The affront was so clear in Sky's voice. But Senea hoped that her feelings did not show on her own face as plainly as they were on

Treyna's. She tried to imagine Treyna grappling with the Ja'sid and encountering that blackness as she had done and could only see her lying dead on the ground. And yet, she knew that luck had been with her, that the Ja'sid would have killed her if Vayhawk and Landry hadn't gotten there when they did. She and the Ja'sid would have died together in a withering of mutual power. It was true that she hadn't survived because of wit, and she knew that no one would know that better than Vayhawk. But this was something that she could not voice.

Instinct told her to remain silent, that her survival was not really the issue.

Sky touched the knife on the table and turned it so that the black handle was within his grasp. "This could have gone to my heldii just as easily as it went to yours."

"Easily!" Mara said angrily. "That was a *Black* Ja'sid! Senea was nearly killed."

Sky shrugged that off. "But she wasn't." He turned his eyes on Vayhawk. "What do you say? Care to make a wager?"

"What kind of wager?" Mara demanded of him.

Sky frowned at her again. "Who is this heldii paired with, you or the Heldlan?"

"Mara is being protective," Roskel said, and turned a look on her that was meant to silence her. Mara clamped her lips together and leaned back in her chair, crossing her arms.

"What kind of wager are you talking about?" Vayhawk asked.

"Your heldii against mine."

"The stakes?"

Sky shrugged again. "How about the knife? If my heldii wins . . . the knife is hers."

Vayhawk was silent a long minute, studying Treyna with a long, scrutinizing examination that left her shaken. He then swung his gaze over to Senea, obviously compairing.

"Done," he said, turning his eyes back to Sky.

The heldan leaned back on the rear legs of his chair in satisfaction, pursed his lips together smugly.

"Only . . . if your heldii loses," Vayhawk said quietly, "you drop two levels in rank."

"Wha . . ." Sky's chair came down with a thud. He stared at Vayhawk in a sudden rage.

The Heldlan looked at him in mock surprise. "Do you wish to withdraw?"

Sky glared at him. "No!"

"Well?"

Sky faced Vayhawk with a fury, and Senea thought that the heldan was going to attack. Apparently, so did others, for Roskel and Mara were suddenly alert, and Landry put a restraining hand on Sky's shoulder. For a frightening moment Senea thought that Sky was going to defy them all and fling himself across the table at Vayhawk. But there was heldcode and it stayed him.

Sky visibly brought himself under control, looked at Senea with thinly disguised malice, raked her face with his eyes, and let his gaze rest on her lips a long, lingering moment before he looked up to her eyes. A slow smile moved across his mouth, unpleasant, and chilling. "I'll accept," he said finally, keeping his eyes on her. "But if your heldii loses, she's mine."

There was a sharp intake of air . . . from Mara, Senea realized. Sky had openly insulted Vayhawk. Senea realized this also, although she didn't understand the nature of the insult. She stared at Sky, unable to pull her eyes away from his. Her heart thudded painfully until he looked away.

"Well?" he asked Vayhawk. "Shall we make this contest interesting?"

Senea scanned from face to face, suddenly realizing they were talking about a fight between Treyna and herself. A coldness settled in her stomach, and she looked around in disbelief, betraying it. She met Vayhawk's scrutiny, saw that he was seriously considering Sky's challenge, and felt a sudden fear. She looked to Mara, then to Roskel, wanting someone to point out that it was against heldcode. But there was no help. All eyes were on Vayhawk, and his were on her. She turned back to him and knew his decision before he spoke.

"Accepted." His voice was soft.

Senea glanced down rather than show her dismay at this, reckoning silence the best course.

"Good," Sky said, and stood, his chair rattling across the floor. "You better train her well, Heldlan, because I will enjoy taking her from you."

Senea looked at Vayhawk from under her eyelashes. His lips were pressed in a tight line, and there was a dangerous glint in his almost-black eyes.

Landry leaned over to take the knife. "I will change the handle," he said.

"No." Vayhawk's hand went over the knife belt.

Landry straightened up, quickly hiding the anger that had shown on his face. "Whatever you wish, Heldlan." He turned and strode away.

Sky inclined his head to Vayhawk, flashed Senea an insolent smile, and followed Landry, taking Treyna with him. And in the long silence that followed that departure, Senea gathered up the utensils that she had used when she had eaten. She started to rise to take them across the room, wincing at the pain in her side. Vayhawk's hand came over her wrist.

"Go get some sleep," he said; looked at Mara. "Take her to her bunkroom."

Mara rose, took Senea's arm, and waited for her to stand. Senea tried and failed.

"Oh, for pity's sake, help her," Vayhawk said wearily.

Mara slipped an arm around Senea's back and helped her to her feet. "Heldlan . . . Roskel," she murmured in departing salute before she led Senea to the door.

CHAPTER
SEVEN

Senea awakened to a dull pain, the source of which she could not pinpoint. A warm twilight was around her. She turned her head and saw Mara sitting beside her on the bunk. For some reason she was in a lower bunk instead of her own top one. Senea grew confused.

Mara reached forth a hand and laid it on her arm. "How do you feel?" she was asked. "Can you sit up?"

She tried, but her pain prevented it and she gave up. Closing her eyes, she let the sleep start to come over her again.

"Senea, wake up."

She felt a touch on her head, a soft touch that moved to her face, disturbing, keeping the peace of sleep from her. She moved her head, trying to dislodge that touch, wanting it to go away.

"Senea, you need to eat. Please try to sit up."

She was lifted, then let back on a raised cushion, and the elevation of her head dizzied her for a moment. Then the pain centralized to her side, throbbing in alternating beats of stabbing torment and dull discomfort. In her nostrils was the sharp, pungent smell of food, unpleasant on the warm air.

She opened her eyes and saw that Mara was still there. She tried to move, wincing at the spasm in her side. Past and present finally began to return in her mind.

She remembered the plain and a fight and a Ja'sid heldan who—she remembered clearly—had tried to kill her with some kind of power.

And she remembered Landry and a heldan named Sky, and a wager made.

She tried to rise and succeeded in sitting up for an instant

76

before her arms began to shake uncontrollably. Mara caught her and laid her gently back to the cushion.

Thereafter, it was easy to let the sleep drift over her where there was no remembrance at all, but Mara would not let it. The heldan lifted Senea's head and poured broth between her unwilling lips. Awareness came back to her.

"Where's Vayhawk?" she asked weakly.

"I don't know. He left early this morning and has been gone all day."

And as Senea thought on that, Mara added, "It's not unusual. He's always at the borders."

After that Senea drifted for a time and came back to find herself propped half-sitting. A movement in the dark brought her head around. A black figure rose from the adjacent bunk, came to her, and knelt. "Do you need anything?" A voice that she did not know.

"Who are you?"

"Treyna."

Treyna. Sky's heldii.

Senea was confused. "What are you doing here?"

"I'm one of your bunkmates."

Memory crossed Senea's mind of Sky's eyes on her, cold and plotting. She shivered and stared at Treyna's shadowed face.

"Mara?" she asked, trying to keep her mind focused, and heard the quiet breathing of others sleeping.

Treyna rose and sat by her, touched her arm, a gentle touch that reminded Senea of her mother.

"She's sleeping. She was up with you all night and the whole of the day. You were in fever. When you passed the danger she asked me to watch you."

Senea let go a carefully controlled breath. "It's been an entire night and day?"

"Yes. And it is almost morning again."

Senea took that in.

"I will go get some food," Treyna said. "Mara wants you to eat as soon as you are able."

"Yes," Senea agreed. She moved up carefully against the cushions as Treyna went quietly to the door and left.

Senea slipped a hand within the coverings where a binding crossed her ribs. She shuddered at the knowledge that she

could have died—would have died if Vayhawk hadn't found
her when he did.

She thrust the memory of that away and another memory
took its place: Vayhawk and Sky making a wager on the outcome of a fight between Treyna and herself. This she could not
understand. Both Roskel and Vayhawk had talked about
heldcode and the penalty of taking up arms against another
heldan of one's own Held. None of it made any sense. But
what perplexed her even more was that Roskel and Mara had
not objected to any of it.

By the time that Treyna returned she had determined that
she wasn't going to have anything to do with it.

Treyna set a tray on the bunk, and Senea saw in the dim
light that she had brought a bowl of stew and some grain
bread. Her hand shook when she picked up the bowl. She set
it down again before she dropped it.

"I can't," she said.

"I'll help you."

"No." Senea stopped the hand that was already reaching for
the spoon. Then she looked at Treyna in the dim light. "I'm
sorry about what happened earlier. I want you to know that I'm
not going to fight you."

"But you have to."

Senea heard that with surprise. "What do you mean I have
to? Fighting each other is against heldcode. Didn't Sky tell you
that?" She saw Treyna shake her head and was bewildered by it.

"Not in the Games," Treyna said. "That is how it is done.
Ranking is decided at the Games."

"Games?" A vague memory stirred. Mara had said something about the Games.

"And bets are made." Treyna looked down unhappily at her
hands that held the tray. "Especially on the heldii."

"They were betting on Games?" Senea felt suddenly foolish
and was glad that she hadn't objected before. "Not on a fight?"

"It'll be a fight," Treyna told her. "At the Games it's accepted." Then she added in a frightened voice, "Sky is determined that I'm going to win."

Senea picked up the bowl again and began to eat in spite of
her trembling hands. She thought about what Treyna was saying.

"I don't want to fight," Treyna said. Her voice broke, but

she brought it under control. "I don't want to be here. I want to go home."

Senea did not answer. There was nothing to say. No remedy could be made. She set down the bowl and took Treyna's hand. The girl returned the clasp almost with desperation, then she loosened the hold and slipped her hand away.

"You better finish eating that or Mara will be angry with both of us. She's threatened to make us both pay if you don't eat something."

"All right," Senea said, and picked up the bowl again. She finished the stew, then ate the bread, watching Treyna, who had moved away to sit on her own bunk, eyes averted. Then Senea leaned back and eased the tray to the edge of the bunk.

Treyna came to her at her movement and took the tray. "Sleep awhile," she said. "Mara won't be here for some time so you might as well rest."

Senea gave no response, and Treyna left, leaving the door open. An illumination came from the corridor outside. Senea shut her eyes and rested, hearing quiet activity down the hall: the murmur of voices, helden coming from or going on patrol, perhaps taking heldii with them. Somewhere someone laughed.

She slept, woke briefly when her bunkmates left, then slept again.

She woke and knew she was alone. Her side hurt, but the throbbing had stopped. For a moment she lay still in the darkness, staring out into the lighted corridor.

Then she rose and walked stiffly to the door. She rested a moment against the wall. When she caught her breath she looked out and walked out into the corridor, pulling the robe she had on about her. She caught at the wall and leaned there as a helden shouldered past, looking at her curiously. Senea returned his gaze a brief second before she remembered that she needed to be taking her clothes with her. She went back into the bunkroom, found them in the niche next to her bunk, then she returned to the hall.

It was a long walk. Several times she stopped and leaned against the wall until she could go on. At length she came to the bath and went inside.

The door to the washroom was open, voices coming from inside. There were several helden dressing, and there was one in the tub. She hesitated, then went to the far wall and removed the robe. She couldn't bathe because of the binding on her wound, but she washed her face in a basin, freshening up the best she could. Then she dressed, took the robe into the wash-room, and hung it to dry on a rack. She didn't know where it had come from, but figured that it would remain there un-til she found out. She went into the corridor again, realizing that she hadn't even noticed if anyone had stared at her this time. She shrugged it off. It didn't matter anyway.

She stood in the corridor a moment trying to decide whether to go back to her bunkroom or look for Mara. A heldan edged past her, and she backed up to the wall, murmured an apology after him, looked up and saw Vayhawk coming toward her.

She thrust herself away from the wall and waited for him.

He stopped in front of her, his dark eyes looking her over, a slight frown lining his brow. She returned his gaze as stead-ily as she could, expecting him to order her back to her bunk. Instead he took her arm and propelled her gently ahead of him until they came to his door. He opened it, waited for her to en-ter, and stepped in behind her.

"Sit down," he said.

Senea went to the nearest chair by the table and sat, bending slowly because of the stiff pain in her side. Vayhawk closed the door, putting them into darkness, then moved across the room and lit the table lamp. He pulled it close so that it shone brightly on his skin, throwing the rest of the room into dark shadows. He looked down on her.

"You are well?"

Senea hesitated before answering. "I'm mending."

"Enough to be walking the halls?"

Senea shrugged. "I grew tired of sleeping."

There was silence for some few moments while he scanned her face. Then he turned and went into the darkness of the room.

He came back and settled down on the stool facing her. "You will learn, then," he said. He held out a sheathed knife. She took it uncertainly, knowing it to be the Ja'sid's without having to be told. The handle was no longer black, but was milk-white, almost transparent with delicate veins of red curl-ing around it, meeting in a cobweb fineness on the back where the grip would fit into her palm. A lot of time and care had gone into the making of it, and Senea knew that it was Vayhawk's work. It came easily from the sheath, the lamplight reflecting off the blade. She turned it over in her hand, unable to say anything; she was unexpectedly touched. It was beautiful.

She looked up and met Vayhawk's dark eyes, but still could not find anything to say. He leaned forward and showed her how to hold it so that the sharpened edge of the blade was held forward from the thumb. His hand closed over hers as he gently wrapped her fingers around the handle.

"There are two ways to hold a knife," he said, his eyes coming up to hers. "This way is the most accurate until you become more skilled." With his hand over hers, he showed her how maneuverable the knife was in that grasp, how easy thrusts and twisting moves were. "You must practice these moves over and over again, until you can do them without thinking about them. If you have to think about what you're doing, then you will not live long."

His hand left hers in a slow caressing motion, his gaze level on her. A tremor went through her, and she looked down nervously to return the knife to its sheath. The hairlike threads of red on and deep within the handle were the color of blood in the golden lamplight.

"It is made from milkstone," Vayhawk said. "The same as mine. I knew where there was a piece with red in it." He paused, and Senea glanced up at him and saw that he was still watching her, probing and assessing. "It seemed fitting," he added, challenge in his voice.

The tone in his words brought her head up, and she met his dark gaze, knowing full well what he meant. She recalled of a sudden what Mara had said to her: *He's got you tied to him tighter than a heldan is tied to the Held.* And this knife with its colors of red and white and its grip made out of the same stone that his was made from was another band that tightened that tie. She saw that he knew it, had been deliberate in it, and now he dared her to protest.

She didn't.

She, after a dogged fashion, flung his dare back at him by accepting without comment his choice of colors, as well as his choice of stone and the implied binding that he meant by it. She looked at him squarely, almost with insolence, daring him to take it back.

Comprehension passed over his face, and a dark smoldering came to his eyes, an acknowledgment that she had accepted his terms. He leaned closer. "I have to report to Aldived. Then we begin."

There was a stillness in Vayhawk's voice that chilled. Senea did not try to answer. She looked away to where her hand lay curled around the sheath of the knife that now belonged to her.

A knock sounded at the door.

For half a breath Senea thought Vayhawk was going to ignore it and just let whomever was there go away. She felt a sudden panic, as if some rescuer was going to pass by and not see that she was in trouble.

A second knock sounded.

"Come," Vayhawk said without turning his head.

The door opened. It was Mara.

"There you are," she said. Relief was clear in her voice. "I've been looking everywhere for you, girl. You had me worried." She came toward them. "What are you doing out of bed anyway?"

"I found her wandering the halls," Vayhawk said.

Senea could not pull her eyes away from his. She seemed to be falling into them; she felt the dark midnight-brown closing about her.

"And you didn't send her back to bed?" Mara was indignant.

Vayhawk looked at Mara.

"She *is* heldan, Mara. Not a child."

Mara clamped her lips together and glared at the Heldlan. He stood, a smooth unfolding upward.

"But since you are so concerned," he continued, "you will assist me in her training. When I am out at the borders, yours will be the responsibility to work with her here. For a while, at least."

"For a while?"

"Until she has recovered enough to go with me."

"And who will decide that?"

"You will, if you want."

Mara glanced at Senea with a frown, then looked back to Vayhawk. "All right," she said.

"You agree?" There was mock surprise in his voice.

Mara's frown deepened. "Yes."

"Good." He went to the door and opened it. "Tell Roskel that you are to be relieved of other assignments when I ask for you."

Mara hesitated, looked uncertainly to Senea, then inclined her head to Vayhawk and strode out into the corridor, her footsteps blending into the other noises of the Held.

The Heldlan slowly pushed the door closed and stood in the dark looking at Senea. There was silence. Senea let go her breath and felt the tension return to the atmosphere of the room. She clasped the knife in her lap until her hand hurt, looking warily at him as he came back into the light.

He stopped at the table, looking down on her with a dark and fathomless gaze. Then he undid the buckle of his knife belt and slowly pulled the strap out of the metal loop. The knife handle shone with a translucent glow as he wrapped the strap around the sheath and laid it on the table.

Senea watched his hands with a hypnotic fascination, her breath stilled so that her throat hurt. Her heart was beating with slow, jarring strokes; the deliberate, unhurried movements of his hands sent shivers through her.

He leaned over to her, his face only a few inches from hers, his eyes burning with a fire that alarmed her. She shrank away from him against the back of the chair. His fingers touched her hand and slid around with a slowness that was like pain to take the knife out of her grasp.

"We don't go to Aldived with weapons," he said softly. His eyes looked down, grazed across her mouth, raised again, and scanned her eyes. After several moments he straightened and placed her knife next to his on the table, held out his hand to her. "Let's go."

Senea hesitated uneasily before she took his hand and pushed herself out of the chair. She gasped at the lancing pain that shot through her and clutched at his arm for support until the sudden spasm left her. Then she stepped away from him, his nearness disturbing her. An amused gleam went across his face, then was gone. He bent and blew out the lamp, throwing them into total darkness.

Senea ran her hands up her arms nervously.

"Remember," Vayhawk's voice came so close to her ear it startled her, "that you are only heldii. When we are with Aldived do not speak unless you are spoken to first." She flinched when his fingers went around her arm. "Stay close to me and do exactly as I tell you."

Senea could feel him close behind her, a radiating of body heat instead of an actual touching, and she almost let that warmth pull her back against him. But she held herself apart until he took her to the door and led her out into the hall.

She stood slightly behind and to one side of Vayhawk so that she was near him and yet was not an obtrusive presence. The antechamber in which they waited was smaller than what Senea had expected. Where Aldived lived had always seemed so large when she had looked at it from the ridge behind the village, standing close to the Held, being one with the village and yet accessible to the Held. She had always assumed that the rooms inside were large and spacious. This was not.

It was ornate, but small.

Aldived came, dressed in black as was his wont, his bejeweled fingers laced together. Yunab was following behind. They entered the antechamber, and Vayhawk stepped back a half step in deference and inclined his head respectfully. Aldived's blue eyes swept over him, then centered on Senea, a faint frown on his face. She remembered suddenly to pay him her respect; she bowed her head slightly and looked up to find him still watching her.

Then Aldived turned to Vayhawk and waved an indolent hand at a chair.

"I will sit," he said, his voice dull; and he settled himself on the edge of the reclined chair as if it were a throne. He leaned to the side, resting on the only arm the chair had, his jeweled hand at his mouth. Yunab moved to stand behind him, his dark glittering gaze looking from Vayhawk to Senea, then back again.

Senea looked on them both: in her mind she saw a reversal of roles, Yunab as the true leader of the held-tribe, and Aldived doing as Yunab told him. Yunab gazed at her directly, and in his eyes she saw a dangerous ruthlessness that sent chills through her.

"I had been told," Aldived said, "that you had taken a heldii."

"Yes. I have."

"And did more than go against custom to do it, I hear."

Vayhawk did not answer. Aldived frowned at Senea.

"I seem to vaguely recall this one. What's your family?" he asked her.

Senea caught a warning glance from Vayhawk, and she remembered to think of herself as heldan. "I have no family, Tribelord," she said.

The frown eased from Aldived's face. "She answered well. You are able to do this? You have the time?"

"I have the time," Vayhawk said.

Aldived studied the Heldlan for a moment, then nodded. "Yes, I believe that you do—even if you don't." He looked back to Senea and surprised her with a sharp and aware twinkle in his eyes. "You'd make time." Then he straightened up. "Enough of this. Tell me what you have discovered."

"It is as we have suspected, Tribelord. There is increased movement to the north and to the west. The Ja'sid have made contact with the Sojei and the Weija."

Aldived chewed his lip a moment, then leaned against the arm of the chair again. "What of the Jauedi?"

"There were none with the scout patrol we intercepted."

"That does not say that the Ja'sid have not made contact with them."

"Agreed."

Aldived tapped a fingernail lightly against his teeth. "And the Ja'sid are still coming into our borders?"

"For the time being."

"You have patrols watching them?"

"Yes. Double."

"And to the west?"

"Double patrols."

"How long before the heldii will be of some use to us?"

"A little while yet."

"There's no way to use them now?"

"All the trainers have been instructed to take their heldii with them on patrol."

"Good." Aldived nodded. "Then, at least, we have the additional eyes. What about the Wuepoah on the north?"

"There is no movement along those borders yet."

"I see."

"The Wuepoah has been the least aggressive held-tribe in the past," Vayhawk said. "But if the Ja'sid make a move against them, it won't be long before we will be threatened from even that direction."

"You have assigned double patrols there also?"

"I have. But that has left our defenses weak on the east."

Aldived leaned his chin on his jeweled fist, his elbow on the arm of the chair, and frowned at the floor. For a fleeting moment, Senea had the impression that he was hiding a very keen intellect behind that facade of indolent dullness, that he was far more in control of what was going on than he led others to believe. She stared at him, trying to see more behind the listless expression, but saw nothing.

Yunab shifted, a whisper of movement on the back of Aldived's chair. Senea did not like how the counselor was watching and listening to Aldived and Vayhawk. She had a sense of being scrutinized and analyzed and of being added to plans and schemes already in motion. His presence unsettled her, and she wanted very much to be allowed to leave. She didn't understand why Vayhawk had wanted her there.

"Perhaps you can more evenly distribute your patrols now that you have heldii going out with your helden," Aldived suggested.

"I'd prefer to wait until the heldii have had a little more training. They've only been in the Held four days. A few more days would give them skills that they do not yet have. Until then I do not feel comfortable counting them as regular patrol."

Aldived pursed his lips together, then nodded. "All right. Do whatever you think is best."

"Tribelord," Yunab put forth, "the matter we discussed?" His voice was low, but it cut into the conversation like a weapon. Senea saw Vayhawk's back stiffen, an imperceptible tensing of dislike that Aldived and his counselor did not see.

The Tribelord looked half-around with a puzzled frown. Then comprehension came to his face, and he turned back to Vayhawk. "Oh, yes . . . A thing that we have been giving consideration to . . ."

"Tribelord," Yunab broke in again. "Perhaps the heldii should not remain."

Silence.

Then Aldived looked at Vayhawk expectantly, his eyebrows raised. The Heldlan nodded once, very stiffly, and turned his head to Senea. "Wait for me in the corridor." His eyes were dark with a tightly controlled irritation. Instinct told Senea to obey instantly and without any word. She bowed her head to Aldived and left, moving so as to control the extreme pain she was beginning to feel.

She went out to the dimly lit hall, pulled the door closed behind her, paused, and looked about her at the ornate elegance that still astonished her. Never before this day had she seen anything of the like: gleaming latticework of gold, sheer and shining fabrics, rich woods and marble floor, even here in the hall. Then, needing to sit, she went to a low wall that separated the hall from another partially enclosed antechamber. She carefully settled herself on it and leaned back against the sidewall, closed her eyes, and wished that she were back in her bunk.

Time passed, quiet and slow, and she was able to relax as the pain in her side eased to a dull throbbing. The silence was soothing, and she dozed.

Suddenly a light step sounded beside her, and Senea opened her eyes, startled. Yunab was looking at her in the dim light, malice thinly veiled in his eyes. She slid to her feet and glanced down to show her respect, then met his stare directly, shuddering inside.

"Heldii," he said in greeting. His black eyes looked her over critically. "You are not well?"

"I am all right," Senea said.

Yunab answered nothing for a moment, only stared at her.

"I am just tired," she added, caution keeping her from saying anything further.

His lips tightened. "To lie is to show disrespect, heldii."

Anger came on her; but again caution dictated that she smother it. She averted her eyes a second time to the floor and realized that someone must have told him about her encounter with the Ja'sid. "Forgive me," she said softly.

"Forgiven," he said. "Come, sit down."

The tone was suddenly kindly; it threw her off balance, and for an instant she stared at him. He moved to the wall, expecting her to settle back where he had found her. "Please. Sit down," he said, and Senea eased back onto the low wall, watching him closely. Suspicion prickled at her.

"The Heldan will be a while yet," Yunab said. "We might as well get to know each other."

The suggestion struck her as confusing. Enmity was still on his face, although it was not in his voice. She shrugged, tried to figure why he'd want to talk to her, and could not. "I don't know what I could tell you."

A cool smile that did not reach his eyes touched his mouth. He leaned forward and laid a hand on her arm, his fingers pressing lightly. "I'd like to be your friend."

Senea looked into the counselor's black eyes, but could not see behind the concealing screen that was there. She did not trust him. "I don't know what I could do for you."

"It's more what I could do for you," he said. "I could make your life in the Held very rewarding. I'm sure that you already know how hazardous it is to be heldan." His eyes went meaningfully to her side, then rose back to her face. "There is very little comfort in that kind of life. But I can offer compensations that others have found desirable."

"I don't know what you mean."

"Power, prestige, a swift rise in rank."

His fingers still pressed her arm, an intimacy that she did not like. She would have pulled away but thought better of it and bore his touch with great self-control.

"I can see that these things happen for you."

"How?"

"A word in the right place, in return for other words in the right place."

Breath failed her an instant. "What kind of words?"

"Nothing much," he said with a shrug. "Where the Heldlan goes ... maybe who he sees, who he talks to. That kind of thing." His cool fingers slipped to hers and took her hand. "Just keep me informed."

It chilled. Senea stared at him, realized with astonishment that he was playing on her emotions. He had taken in her age and reckoned that he could flatter her by his kindness and attention, thus persuading her to spy for him. Astonishment became anger. This time she could not hold it down.

She gathered herself to her feet and pulled her hand from his. "You forget that there is heldcode," she said tightly. "Loyalty to the Held."

"You would not be betraying that loyalty," Yunab said.

"There is also loyalty to the helden."

"The helden are not the Held."

"And I am only heldii."

"I can take care of that."

"I will not spy on Vayhawk."

Yunab drew in a slow breath, his eyes suddenly full of malice. "I see." His hand came up to take her chin, and he looked at her with an insulting intentness. She jerked away from his grasp. "I suppose that's understandable," he said. "If I were the Heldlan, I'd take steps to see that my heldii remained loyal also. Especially if I defied custom to ensure I got the one I wanted."

Senea stared at him in stunned silence.

"Just remember," he said with a suggestive smile, "helden are not to have kin-ties. Not even among themselves."

She would have struck him but for the opening of the door across the hall. She fought for control and stepped away from him, but could not pull her stare from him. Indignation at his insinuations stung fiercely, and she was appalled and enraged by the malevolence in his eyes. She clenched her hands until her fingernails dug into her palms. There was a soft footstep behind her, and a gentle hand went around her arm.

"Senea." Vayhawk's voice was quiet and admonishing.

She tore her eyes from Yunab and looked half-about at Vayhawk.

"Let's go," he said.

She nodded stiffly, realizing that she had given Yunab a weapon to use against Vayhawk; that by her anger—which she should have controlled—she had given him exactly what he had wanted. It didn't matter that it wasn't true; Yunab would use it anyway. The guilt on her face was enough to convict her . . . and Vayhawk.

She let Vayhawk lead her along the hall and out into the evening air, greatly disturbed by what had happened. She could not shake the cold that had settled on her. They were walking to the Held when Vayhawk broke the silence.

"Did you accept?"

"What?" She looked up at him in shock.

"Did you accept Yunab's offer?"

Senea stared at him in surprise. "How do you know about that?"

"It's my job to know. Did you accept?"

"No," and then she added, "I hate him."

"Now, Senea . . ." His voice was quiet. "You should show respect at all times, no matter what the provocation. This is the dignity of the Held."

Senea looked at him with a frown.

"Even if it's Yunab." Vayhawk cast an unreadable glance at her. "I'm afraid you've made an enemy tonight."

She shook her head. "No. I've made you an enemy."

A brief smile touched the corner of his mouth. "Yunab was already my enemy." He fell silent then, his thoughts obviously on some other thing that troubled him, something that he brought from his interview with Aldived. Senea walked beside him silently, not wanting to disturb him.

Windshift moved across the ground, and the very last of the sun sank, an edge of faded orange in muted contrast to the black horizon in the distance. The sky overhead lost the last hint of orange and yellow before turning purple and gray. But Vayhawk did not seem to notice. His face was lined with a deep frown, and his thoughts were far away.

Senea put her hand to her side to ease the pain and drew in a breath. "Yunab will use me against you." A thought that troubled her.

Vayhawk came out of his thoughts, looked up, and centered on her face, reading her for a moment. Then he said, "He's already tried."

Senea returned his gaze. "He'll turn Aldived against you."

He shook his head. "No. Aldived is not turned easily. There's more to him than he shows." He stopped her with a hand on her shoulder. "You're in pain."

She nodded wordlessly and closed her eyes in sudden weariness. His arm went around her. "Let's get you back to the Held. Mara's going to be upset with me again."

Senea managed a weak smile at that. "It really wasn't your fault."

"Mara's not going to see it that way."

Senea laughed weakly, winced at the pain. "Don't tell me you're afraid of her."

"Only of her wrath."

"Maybe she should be Heldlord, then," Senea said, and sagged against him, the strength suddenly gone from her legs.

Vayhawk cursed, picked her up easily in his arms, and carried her to the Held.

CHAPTER
EIGHT

She awoke in her bunk, finding Mara sitting beside her with a steaming bowl of soup in her hand. The rich aroma filled the bunkroom, but instead of stirring Senea's appetite it sickened her, and made her stomach want to revolt.

"I'm not hungry," she said reluctantly, pushing herself up to sit against the wall.

"Vayhawk's orders." Mara handed her the bowl. "He wants you well fed. And well rested."

"He's gone?"

"The Ja'sid have penetrated inside our borders again. He's gone with a large patrol to stop them."

Senea forced herself to sip a spoonful of the soup and thought about that. She was glad that Vayhawk had not taken her with him. "The Ja'sid are to the north and west of us?" she asked, still trying to get the neighboring held-tribes straight in her mind.

Mara nodded. "They've been trying to take land from us for quite a while now."

"Why?"

"We have better valleys than they do. More game, more fresh water, fish." She shrugged. "They're a warlike Held."

"And we're not?"

Mara frowned at her. "We defend our held-tribe. Nothing more. And you know what it is that we defend against." Mara's expression sobered.

Senea fell silent and stared at the bowl in her hands. Even the most casual reference to that phenomenon evoked a cold, mocking sense of menace within her. Ja'sid power. She tried to make herself drink another spoonful of the soup and could not.

"When you feel well enough, Vayhawk wants you to practice the knife routine he gave you."

Senea looked up at her. "I don't know if I can remember it."

"I will help you. We all have to learn it in the beginning."

Senea set the bowl down on her lap and rested her head back against the wall. The unbidden memory of her sisters came to her: Melina with her young man, probably planning her wedding now, Loran . . . her heart lurched painfully at the thought of Loran. Sweet Loran. She closed her eyes and expelled a breath of air. She still felt very tired.

Mara took the bowl. "You have to eat," she said. "I don't want Vayhawk blaming me if you don't start getting well. And he *will* blame me, Senea."

Senea opened her eyes and saw the somber expression on Mara's face. She pushed back the blankets and slid to the edge of the bunk. "All right."

Mara handed the bowl back to her, and Senea forced herself to eat the entire contents. At last she gave the bowl to Mara.

Mara took it, laid it aside, then handed Senea a goblet fashioned out of a roughly finished gourd. "Drink this," she said.

"What is it?" Senea eyed it with a frown. A vague suspicion began in her mind, but she was not certain what she had to be wary of.

"Drink. Then I'll answer questions."

Senea took the gourd, sensing that Mara was not going to answer until she did. Raising it to her lips she downed the contents with a single swallow. Gasping at the unexpected burning in her mouth and throat she thrust the gourd back at Mara. "What is it?"

"A tea made from a desert plant. The old Held'len call it Maiden's eye." Mara's gaze flicked over her face. "It's given to every heldii who enters the Held."

"Why?" Senea asked, suspicion growing ever stronger in her. "What is it?"

"It prevents the birth of children. Forever."

Senea stared at her. "I don't understand."

Mara's eyes were unwavering of a sudden. "Ours is a society of strictness," she said. "You know this. We are paired from the very beginning. And later, when we are no longer heldii, Roskel pairs us again with whomever he decides will be our best partner. This pairing lasts until death. This is our patrol partner.

"But there are times when helden become more than partners. When male and female seek each other out as they sometimes do. Those who do this can never be paired. Ever. Even if they should stop seeing each other in that way. They still can never be paired. This is a tradition that has been handed down as long as there is memory within the Held. Even longer."

Senea sat still as cold ran down her back. She was not sure what Mara was saying.

"A heldan who is pregnant cannot defend the held-tribe. And there is no place for babies here. There are no kin-ties, and these relationships come and go. Few are permanent. In fact I don't know of any."

"So you gave me this drink in case I ever . . ." Senea couldn't even bring herself to finish it.

Mara smiled grimly. "It's given to everyone who enters the Held. Its part of being heldan."

Senea stared at her, thinking on what she was saying, and realized what had just been taken away from her. Any future she had ever had as being a mother was suddenly, permanently lost—without any forewarning—without any discussion, without her agreement. Suddenly she was angry. These people just took what they wanted. They had taken her future, they had taken her from her family, and now they had taken her children. She felt anger like a pain in her chest. They would keep taking and keep taking until they had taken even her life. And she felt like striking out, physically, forcefully, angrily. But she could not. Nor could she sit still.

"I'll get up now!"

"I think you should get more sleep."

Senea shook her head emphatically. If she stopped now she'd lose her impetus. "I'll get up." She thrust herself up to stand on shuddering legs. "Help me to the bath."

Silently Mara rose, her eyes gravely taking in Senea's anger. She took her arm and helped her to walk, providing her an anchor that made it possible to move. Senea forced her senses into order and determinedly bathed. She would not let Mara touch her, and she bandaged herself, then she dressed. Finally she was walking stiffly on her own. "Where is my knife?"

"Probably in Vayhawk's room."

"Good," Senea said, and pushed through the door to the corridor. She knew that Mara was following her but she didn't turn to see. Through an open door to the arena she saw that there were several helden and heldii practicing, some with the bow, some with the knife, and some learning body holds.

She did not pause to watch but went on slowly to Vayhawk's room.

She found her knife on the table where the Heldlan had left it. He was gone. She lit the lamp and sat down with the knife in her hand, breathing heavily just from the walk from the bath.

The room felt strange without Vayhawk's presence, as if it were empty even though Mara and she were there. She turned the knife over in her hand, looking at the almost-transparent handle.

"Senea, you should go back to bed," Mara said, frowning at her from the door. "You'll never get well at this rate."

Senea shook her head, although her body cried out for her to comply. "Would you go back to bed?"

It was a moment before the heldan answered. "No. But I'm used to it."

"How does one get used to it?" she asked angrily. And she meant that two ways. How did one get used to such an assault on the body except through endurance and resistance, that is, if one ever got used to it. Mara sighed and came to her. "Vayhawk wants you well."

"I will practice first." She put the sheath on the table, held the knife in her hand the way Vayhawk had shown her, and looked expectantly to Mara.

Mara expelled a breath of air again and drew out her own knife, green-handled and long. She sank easily to her knees and sat back on her heels. "Normally we'd do this standing. But for your sake we will not today. Come beside me so that you can see what I am doing."

Senea moved, trying not to show Mara how much pain she had. But she could tell by the heldan's sober eyes that she wasn't fooled. Senea knelt stiffly and sat back on her heels. She returned Mara's gaze stubbornly and waited for her to begin.

"I'm doing this at your insistence," Mara said. "If Vayhawk is displeased, the responsibility is yours."

Senea nodded. "I understand."

Mara showed her each move in the routine, the thrusts and twists that were to become second nature as she practiced them again and again. This was just the first of many such routines and was the simplest to learn. Each routine became increasingly difficult until they were so complex that only a few helden had been able to master them. Vayhawk and Roskel were the best, ranking one and two. Mara was ranked seventy-nine.

Senea did the routine over and over until Mara made her stop. "Go to bed," she said, grasping Senea's wrist. "Go to bed."

Senea stared at her. Her hand was trembling so hard she could not control it. She dropped the knife to the floor and nodded. "All right." Mara helped her to her feet, then took her back to her bunkroom.

Senea wasn't even aware of when the heldan had left.

Senea stood looking out on the compound. She had just come from the eating hall and was on her way back to her bunkroom where she was going to rest and practice the knife routine. She had spent three days sleeping off the effects of the Maiden's eye and now she was restless and bored. She stopped to watch the helden and heldii that were practicing in the light of the early evening.

She saw with dismay that many of the heldii were advancing far beyond anything that she could do. There were several who were becoming quite proficient with the bow, and she had not even had one in her hand yet. She also saw that most had gone beyond the simple knife routine that she had been learning. But it was the body wrestling that caused her the most concern, a sort of hand-to-hand fighting that was unlike anything that she had ever seen.

She watched the helden and heldii practicing body holds and throws, and she put a hand to her side.

She was still stiff and sore, but she was healing and was no longer in a torment of pain. But, although she could move more freely than she had been able to, she knew she would not be able to do what she saw out in the arena . . . not for a long time.

She watched the wrestling with foreboding.

A sharp, angry voice brought her head around, and she saw Treyna and Sky a short distance away. Sky was speaking angrily in a voice loud enough to cause others to turn and look at him with frowns. He snatched a bow out of Treyna's hands and threw it to the ground. Treyna flinched from him and put a trembling hand to her mouth. She had a stricken, frightened look that seemed to have become a permanent part of her. She bent to pick up the bow, but Sky forestalled her, picking it up himself, and thrust it into her hands. He was still talking to her with angry gestures to her hands and the target that was several yards away.

Treyna gripped the bow nervously and tried to fit an arrow to the string. The arrow fell to the ground. She picked it up, glancing with fear to Sky's glowering face. Again she tried to put the arrow to the string and again she dropped it. Sky exploded in an angry tirade of words and grabbed the bow from her. He fitted an arrow and sent it to the target . . . dead center. He pushed the bow into her hands again, still speaking angrily.

Senea couldn't hear anything of what he was saying, but saw enough to make a good guess and saw the mortification on Treyna's face when the girl realized that others were watching. Senea felt pity for her. But for Sky she felt only rage and contempt. She clenched her hands as she watched Treyna's fumbling attempts to control the bow and wanted more than anything to go out there and stop it.

There was a movement behind her, and the soft roughness of Vayhawk's voice sounded in her ear. "She'll never be able to do it." His hand gently took her arm and moved slowly, almost caressingly, up to her shoulder.

Senea looked around at him and saw that he, also, was watching Treyna. She looked back to the arena. "As long as that boor is her trainer, she'll never learn anything."

"Respect," Vayhawk admonished, the faint vibration in his voice sending a shiver over her skin. "Respect."

"Can't you stop it?"

"It really is none of our affair."

"How can you say that?" Senea turned around, pulling away from his hand that had rested on her shoulder. "You're Heldlord. Can't you stop what he's doing?"

"No." His dark eyes regarded her soberly. "It is not our place."

"Not our place?" she said angrily. "What he's doing is cruel."

"That may be, but we cannot step in."

"And he can do anything he wants?"

"No. There is heldcode."

Senea stared angrily at him, then turned around in time to

see Sky grab the bow from Treyna and stalk away from her without looking back. The heldii glanced about her, stricken, standing helplessly where Sky had left her. "Heldcode is not enough!" Senea said.

She could feel Vayhawk behind her, his breath soft on her hair, the heat from him warming her back, and she knew that she just had to lean back slightly—only a fraction of an inch—to touch him, so close was he. But she was too angry to let that attraction affect her. She pushed away from him without turning her head and said, "I'm tired."

She strode down the corridor feeling his eyes on her back, but did not dare stop or look back at him.

She went to her bunkroom and entered its gloom, anger and regret mingling together inside her.

She stretched out on her bunk but could not sleep. The memory of Sky and Treyna hung before her, sharp and crystalline. No matter how she tried she could not make it go away and could see over and over the expression on Treyna's face, frightened and mortified. Resentment and anger filled Senea until she thought that she was going to explode with it. She thrust herself back against the wall and gripped her arms around her knees and glowered angrily at the dark wall at the foot of her bunk, resting her chin on her knees.

For a long time she sat thus, waiting for Treyna to come.

Her other two bunkmates came in, first one and then, after an hour or so, the other, each falling to sleep almost the instant they climbed into their bunks. And still Treyna did not come.

Senea took her knife from the niche in the wall and impatiently slipped it in and out of the sheath.

More time passed.

Absently she ran her thumb over the smooth knife handle that Vayhawk had made, recalling the warmth of him behind her, his hand moving up her arm and resting on her shoulder. Imagination that she could not stop came to her of leaning back so that she rested against him, if only for a moment, his hand on her arm, his breath on her hair and brow.

She thrust the image away with an angry snap of the knife into the sheath and thought instead of his fingers moving over her hand, slow and cold as ice, taking the knife from her, his eyes just inches from hers. She forced that image away also, jerked the knife free of its sheath, and ran through the routine at a furious pace, sitting cross-legged with her back against the wall. But when she finally slid the knife back into the leather the images still had not stopped.

She thrust herself to her feet and went out into the dimly lit corridor, hoping that movement would stop the whirling thoughts.

She went to the nearest outside door and looked out onto the dark compound. It was silent and empty and strangely inviting. She went out into the darkness, folding her arms tightly against her, and gripped the knife in her hand. She looked at the stars in the blackness of the sky and felt a serenity in their silent shimmering. Slowly the tension left her and the tightness in her back and legs eased.

A figure separated from the darkness and came toward her, the quiet footsteps the only sound in the compound. She was not surprised that it was Vayhawk, and she looked up into his dark face when he stopped in front of her. Even in the darkness she could feel the force of his gaze and stepped back from it. Suddenly she feared as she had never feared before that he would reach out and touch her.

"You are tired of sleeping?" The light rasp of his voice was always more noticeable in the dark . . . and the amusement in his tone shook her.

"I was waiting for Treyna."

"Sky has taken her on patrol."

Senea did not answer, unwilling to get into a discussion about them again. She ran a hand up her arm, feeling cold when she hadn't before. She gripped the knife as if it were a weapon against the onslaught of his shadowed gaze.

"I spoke to Sky," Vayhawk said. "I suggested that he ease up on Treyna."

"Suggested?"

"That was all I could do."

"What did he say?"

"He and I have a wager," Vayhawk told her. "What do you think he said?"

Senea didn't answer. She could guess.

"He thinks I have interfered . . . and rightly so."

Senea turned away. "I'm sorry."

"Helden have to be strong, Senea. From the beginning. If they are not . . ."

"I know," Senea said. "They won't survive."

"Treyna is going to have to become stronger. As she is, she is useless to us."

Senea looked to him sharply, anger and resentment coming to her again.

He stepped to her and grasped her arms in his hands, turning her to face him fully. "There is no room for compassion here," he said. "Lives depend on each heldan being able to face difficulties alone. Their own lives depend on it. The Held depends on it. No one will be able to stop and worry about a single heldan who is not able to do what needs to be done. Treyna could not have done what you did."

"Please," Senea said, shaking her head, her voice almost a whisper, the nearness of him throwing her into a turmoil that she could not fight. "I did nothing. I ran."

"I know," he said. "But when you were cornered, you fought. Even with your teeth."

"I was afraid."

"Yes." His grip loosened and he slid his hands up, then down, her arms. "I know you were." His fingers released her for a moment although his palms did not quite leave her arms. Then he drew in a breath and closed his hands again, moved them slowly up to her shoulders. "Are you well enough to go with me now?"

Senea looked up at him, tried to stop the sudden quavering inside that was caused by the touch of his hands on her skin.

"I don't know. You'll have to ask Mara."

"Forget Mara," he said with a faint impatience, the coarse timbre of his voice husky. His grip on her tightened imperceptibly, making her tremble so that it was impossible for her to answer.

Finally he dropped one hand away, said, "Come on," and led her with unrelenting firmness to a door close to the eating hall. He took her down the corridor to a room that was much like the clothing room. But here, in shelves and in earthen recepticles, were arrows and bows, all unmarked, all plain of identifying colors. There were also knives in shelves, some with handles, some not. Three benches were against the wall with arrows and knives in various stages of construction.

"Everyone is assigned duty here to keep our weapons supply up," Vayhawk said. He went to a nearby shelf and selected a bow. Fitting the string in the notch, he pulled back hard on it and let it go with a loud *thup*. "One week out of the year." He unstrung the bow, put it back on the shelf, picked up another one, and tested it in the same way. He turned then and found a quiver and went to a drawer in one of the workbenches. He pulled out a bundle of arrows that had been painted white with four bands of red encircling the shafts, one at the notch of each arrow, one where the barbed heads were attached and two in the center, each band of color measured meticulously so that each arrow was identical to the next. He slipped the arrows into the quiver and came to Senea. "We paint our own."

He handed the bow and quiver to her, and she took them hesitantly, staring at the arrows, knowing that it was he who had painted them.

With the colors he had chosen.

And the pattern he had chosen.

The white foremost.

She looked up and met his challenging gaze. She had known it would be there, but again accepted what he had done without comment.

"The belt for your knife is in my room," he said, his dark eyes looking down into hers, probing and analyzing.

For a moment neither one of them moved.

Then he took her arm and turned her around and showed her how to put the quiver over her head so that it rested on her back, the strap passing from the shoulder to hip. Stepping around her, he unstrung the bow and handed it back to her. "It will lose its spring if you leave it that way too long. Either carry it or put it in your quiver."

Then he went to the door and held it open. "Let's go get that belt."

CHAPTER NINE

The sun had come up gold and pink in a morning mist, one of the last of such in the advancing dry season. They came, soon after that, to a valley in which a river murmured softly as it crossed their northward path and flowed slowly to the west—a valley filled with trees that could not be seen from the plain until they stood on the crest of the slope and looked down into it. It stretched east and west as far as the eye could see.

With a sigh Senea sank down on the soft sand where shade from the trees gave some relief from the heat of the sun. She wrapped her arms around her knees, bent her head to them, and closed her eyes. The pain in her side lanced through her so that she almost could not breathe, and she concentrated on taking slow, careful gulps of air until the pain eased somewhat. There was an angry twitter of birds in the branches overhead, a flurry of wings, and then silence.

She heard Vayhawk return from the river and drop an armload of wood onto the sand. She looked up at him. He came to her and knelt to one knee. "Are you all right?"

She nodded, seeing no point in admitting that she hurt as much as she had that first day when he had brought her back to the Held. They were far from there now and nothing could be done.

He gave her some water from a small leather pouch. After she drank and he received it back from her he said, "We'll rest here awhile." Then he looked at her with a frown. "You're in pain."

"I'm fine," she forced herself to say.

He studied her a moment longer before he stood up. "You stay here. I'll be right back."

She nodded again, and he strode away into the trees.

Silence closed in around her then and the exhaustion she had held back came down like a flood. She had not slept at all the night before, having been disturbed about Treyna, and now it was all she could do to keep her senses clear. Easing herself to a nearby tree, she leaned against it and closed her eyes. The tightness in her muscles released in small rhythmic jerks, and the pain in her side subsided to a tolerable ache.

The shade under the trees was cool and soothing and she sank into the comfort of it, drifted into a timelessness that was empty of thought and sensation.

"Senea," a quiet voice came to disturb that peace. Fingers caressed her cheek with an intimate sensual touch that she thought she dreamed. A hand took her chin and gently shook her, pulling her out of the oblivion. "Senea." She opened her eyes with an effort and saw Vayhawk bending over her. He sat back on his heels and regarded her with a contemplating frown.

She moved; the pain that had been in her side was almost gone. She must have slept quite a while, for she saw through the leaves that the sun was directly overhead. She had been asleep for at least two hours, maybe more.

"Come," Vayhawk said. "I will show you how to prepare waterfowl."

Senea got to her feet, wincing only slightly, and followed him to where he had left the firewood. A dead water bird with orange and gray feathers lay on the sand. Its orange head was bent at an unnatural angle. She could not see any wound on it, so she decided that its neck had been broken. She grimaced at the thought of having to do that for herself sometime.

Vayhawk squatted and indicated for Senea to do the same. She sat on the sand next to him, crossing her legs, still not strong enough to sit on her heels the way that he did. She watched as he first gutted the bird and then quickly scooped out a deep hole in the sand. He put the entrails of the bird in the hole and buried them, only just slightly, leaving the hole still quite deep.

"We will make a bed of hot coals," he said, putting a small pile of sticks and twigs into the hole. He drew out a flint and some soft bark from the pouch on his hip. He struck a spark and blew a flame into being, then thrust the knife into the sand while he tended the small flame into a large one.

Senea watched him as he bent over the flame to add more wood. The sunlight filtering through the trees rested on him like burnt gold. His hair was in varying colors of beige and brown, and the bronze of his arms and shoulders glowed with a richness of deep tan. She looked at his hands with a mesmerized fascination and seemed to recall the feel of them on her face, just as she had awakened, slow moving, caressing and intimate. A trembling quiver moved through her and settled in her stomach.

She pulled her eyes away from what he was doing and found herself looking at the knife that he had thrust into the sand beside him. The handle glowed with an iridescent play of sunlight, the white milkstone skimmed with an almost-invisible dusting of rainbow colors that was only a trick of light. She stared at it a moment before she realized that she could have it in her hand before Vayhawk turned around. She looked up at the Heldlan and saw that his attention was still on the fire that was now burning strongly in the hole. Holding her breath, she inched her hand toward the knife, watching him closely. He sat back a moment, and she froze, but he did not look around and she moved her hand toward the knife again, keeping her eyes on his profile.

Suddenly his hand slapped around her wrist, strong and unyielding, and dark amused eyes turned to her. She stared at him in startlement, a rush of cold pouring over her. A wry smile touched his mouth, and his eyes sparked with mischief. He had deliberately baited her, had left his knife in the sand to tempt her into trying for it. She tried to jerk her hand back, but his grip held, and he tightened his fingers so that she winced. He gently moved her arm in a way that suggested that he might pull it a good deal harder if he chose. He leaned forward so that his breath was on her mouth, and his eyes simmered with an inner fire. Senea was seized with panic. Then he smiled. "We need some mud."

Senea blinked. "What?"

"For the bird. We need some mud."

"Mud?"

Vayhawk sat back, releasing her. He pulled his knife from the sand and resheathed it. "We'll let the fire burn down while we get what we need." He stood and waited for Senea to do the same.

She rose, looking at him in puzzlement. "What do we need mud for?"

"To cook the bird in." He turned and strode away toward the river without looking back.

Senea followed him incredulously, trying to imagine how one cooked a bird in mud. At the river she helped him scoop up what he wanted, thick and gelatinous, and took it back to the fire in her hands. They went back for more, and he showed her how to encase the bird, feathers and all, in the mud and bury it in the glowing white and yellow coals.

"When the bird is cooked the mud will be hard," he explained, "and will pull off the feathers. The feathers keep the mud away from the meat." Then he looked at her with that probing gaze. "Do you know the knife routine?"

Senea nodded hesitantly, taken aback by the change in subject.

"Show me."

She hesitated, then cleaned off her hands with sand, as he had done. She drew out her knife, not wanting to do the routine while he watched. Slowly and carefully she went through the moves and breathed a sigh of relief when she was finished, looking up at him with fearful anticipation. He drew out his own knife and went through the routine with a speed that was difficult to follow. Then tossing the knife to his other hand he did the routine again in a swift mirrored pattern. Senea blinked, dismayed at his skill.

"Try it," he said. "The other hand."

Senea took the knife in her left hand. It felt awkward and she was less sure about the moves, several times forgetting to do the routine in a mirrored image of the first. Patiently Vayhawk watched and silently corrected her when she made mistakes, his hand coming over hers and gently guiding it in the way it should go. Finally he took the knife from her and slid it into her sheath.

"Enough," he said. "We will do it every day, until you know it by instinct. But for now, you will start on the bow." He drew his bow out of the quiver on his back and strung it, bending it to do so.

Senea took hers out of her own quiver and strung it with a little difficulty, then assumed carefully the stance that Vayhawk held, feet slightly apart, turned at an angle from the dead tree that he indicated was their target. He showed her the grip he had on the bow with his left hand. She copied it.

"There are three ways to hold the arrow," he said. "One with the thumb and finger." He showed her how to put the arrow to the string with his thumb and curled index finger holding it in place.

"The disadvantage to this grip is that you are pulling back the arrow instead of the string. It's harder to do, and if you're not very skilled at it, it's not very accurate. A few helden use it because it's faster. You don't have to take time to set the arrow in place.

"The second way is to hold the arrow between your index and middle fingers." He changed his grip on the arrow, his fingers wrapped around the string.

"This way you are pulling back the string and the arrow just rides along. Much easier to do. But it doesn't have the speed of the first way. You have to take time to notch the arrow before you can aim. In a fight it could slow you down.

"The third way is a combination of the two. You hold the arrow to the string with your thumb and knuckle, and the other fingers pull back the string." He showed her how his fingers were slightly around the string and even how the end of his index finger was at the string also.

"This has the best of both methods, is only slightly slower than the first, but is much faster than the second. We have helden using each method. It's all personal preference." He lowered the bow. "You try."

Senea took one of her arrows out with uncertainty, had visions of being as clumsy as Treyna, and didn't even want to try.

"Try each one and see which feels the best."

It was difficult. It was exceedingly difficult. Senea's unskilled hands fumbled with each hold and struggled to get them right. She found the second way, with all the fingers wrapped around the string, a little easier, but was unwilling to settle for that one. She wanted to be able to use the last that combined the first two. She tried several times to keep the arrow next to the bow and not pointing off in some other direction. Finally, she lowered the bow in exasperation.

"This is impossible!"

"It takes patience," Vayhawk said, and he put his bow over

his head, the string passing across his chest as he moved around behind her. Then with his arms around her, he showed her how to hold the arrow and bow, his hands over her. Guiding her, they drew back the arrow and let it go. It buried itself deep into the trunk of the dead barkless tree.

Senea was suddenly very aware of the lean hardness behind her, the warmth of flesh on her arms, and of the slight movement against her back when he drew out one of his own arrows to put to her bow. "Let's try it again," he said, his voice vibrating softly in her ear. His hand moved over her fingers and helped her hold the arrow in place, then fell away as he let her draw it back on her own.

"Your line of sight should be below your target," he said, "or your arrow will go too high. Look at the base of the tree."

Senea nodded, distracted by the solid muscle of him pressed against her. Concentration was difficult, and her heart jarred with each stroke. Holding her breath, she released the string and saw the arrow fly to the tree, strike a branch, and fall to the ground. She let go her breath and lowered the bow.

"Again," Vayhawk said.

And again.

And again.

Soon he was no longer helping her, for she could put the arrow to the string with some success although her aim was still haphazard. She went through all of the arrows twice and Vayhawk went to gather them up a third time. He came back to her, slowly separating his arrows from hers. Senea watched him and thought how alike the arrows seemed when they were together in his hands. The difference between hers and his was almost nonexistent, the white shafts merging together into one bundle. And she wondered, not for the first time, what Vayhawk was trying to accomplish by choosing to be paired to her. She thought of Yunab's accusations, *If I were Heldlan, I'd take steps to ensure that my heldii stayed loyal,* and shrank back when Vayhawk handed her the arrows.

He looked at her with a puzzled frown, his dark eyes searching her face. Then he reached out and took the bow from her.

"I think we can eat now." He replaced his own bow in his quiver that was sitting upright in the sand and stuck her bow beside it. He turned and went to where he had covered the coals with sand to keep the heat close around the cooking bird.

Senea watched as he carefully removed the sand and dug the

large ball of baked mud out of the coals with his knife. He cracked it open and pulled off large chunks of baked mud and feathers, it all coming away easily. He looked over his shoulder at her. Swallowing her apprehensions, she went to him.

As they were eating, he leaning against one tree, she leaning against another, she asked a question that had been in her mind the whole day.

"Vayhawk, why don't the other helden talk about this Ja'sid power?" She forced her voice to remain even, knowing he would pick up any untoward nuance.

"What do you mean?"

"It's just that they . . . they don't . . ."

He waited for her to complete the sentence. When she only clenched a fist and glanced at the ground, he offered, "The subject is taboo with them."

Senea looked at him with slowly dawning comprehension. "It is with the villagers, also," she said, and her voice was sick. "I had hoped that it wouldn't be true."

Vayhawk nodded in perfect understanding.

"It's a potential lever for us." His eyes blazed with a dark light. "We are going to need every weapon we can find to bring down these Ja'sid—these barbarians who think they can gobble us up."

"What do you mean?" Senea asked weakly. "Surely you can't mean . . . we use . . ."

"We have to do what we must to survive. There aren't many choices. Not until the butchers stop hunting us or are driven from our land."

She hesitated, staring at him. A point of awe, this heldan, his name carried a sense of overcoming the insurmountable. To a strong people with a stony will, there could come a point where they would break instead of springing back. This warrior had no such limit. Taboos did not encumber him. And she wondered if she would manage as well.

"It draws you, doesn't it?" she said, and the reading of his next thought was nearly uncanny.

"Yes. It does."

A silence fell between them.

Vayhawk broke it. "They may win anyway," he said, meditatively.

She looked at him, really afraid for the first time in her life.

* * *

By late afternoon, two days later, the sky was veiled with a thin covering of clouds. The blue of the sky could still be seen through the layer, and there was not any noticeable relief from the heat. The valley and the river were far behind Senea and Vayhawk as they were still heading north—for the borders, Senea finally figured out.

She followed Vayhawk, and for a long time there was no need to talk. The terrain was easy to traverse, the gentle rolls and swells of the hills unbroken for long distances. In the side of one gentle rise was a large opening, a round entrance to a deep burrow. Vayhawk saw it before they had descended into the depression. Touching Senea on the arm, he bent and picked up a round rock. He hurled it far, far out toward the hole.

It erupted, a snarl of gray and orange fur that was twice the length of a man, a cloud of dust bursting from the burrow behind it as it tore across the hollow toward them.

Vayhawk's bow was in his hand, the arrow already gone before Senea even knew that he had moved. Another arrow was in place and was flying after the first. A third was in his hand and at the bow before she could even draw a breath. But he did not pull it back because the animal had fallen and was still.

He took a couple of cautious steps down the slope toward it, then looked up at Senea. The beginning of windshift blew a loosened strand of hair across his brow. He turned and went to the animal. She followed him, half expecting the creature to jump up and tear them apart.

Vayhawk turned its head up with his foot. Senea gasped with mingled horror and awe. The snout was long and fangs overlapped each other along the full length of the muzzle. Three-inch claws extended from the feet. The two white arrows were buried almost to the feathers in its chest, a silent testimony to the strength of Vayhawk's draw on his bow.

"I have shown you," Vayhawk said, "so that you will understand that a heldan without knowledge of this land can fall victim to it. This wolfhound has been here a long time. We usually leave them alone. Make great detours around their lairs. But first take a good look. They are one of the most dangerous animals you'll come across out here."

"I believe you," Senea said.

They walked quietly thereafter. Senea said nothing, but looked uneasily from rise to rise, searching for more signs of burrows. She looked once backward over her shoulder to where the windshift was brushing across the dried grasses, almost expecting to see the wolfhound that they had left dead following them.

The sun sank so that long shadows of the rises lay across their path. And their own shadows stretched across the plain to the east in long, moving lines of darkness. The windshift was a cool relief from the fervent blaze of the afternoon sun. Senea's eyes rested several times on Vayhawk's back where his tan-colored hair lay gathered between his shoulder blades. The quiver of arrows on his back was almost the same color. He had not replaced his bow, but was carrying it in his hand. And he kept it strung.

The sun touched the western horizon and stretched into a larger yellow globe that reached from south to north, magnified a thousand times by the dry season air. And as they walked, it sank so that they were in early twilight.

Finally Vayhawk stopped before a rise that was topped with a ridge of rock. Senea looked to him, suddenly wondering if this was the border and if he intended to go beyond. But he looked upward at the rock to a deep crevice that she had not seen until she followed the direction of his gaze. He took her by the arm and guided her up the ridge to the cleft in the rock. He looked inside, then satisfied that it was empty, he put her inside and gently pushed her down to the uneven floor, her back against the rock.

"Stay here," he said, dropping to his heels in front of her. "There is something that I have to do, and I can't take you with me." He reached in and drew out her knife and put it in her hand.

"Don't move from here. There will be eyes to see if you do." He looked at her steadily, the dark shadow hiding the expression on his face.

"And whatever eyes see you, if you leave here, will not be friendly." His hand took her wrist meaningfully. "I'll be back."

Then there was a movement, and he was gone.

Silence closed in around her, thick and frightening. She clutched the knife in her hand and looked around at the dark rock, but could not see much in the deepening nightfall. She strained to hear. There was no sound of Vayhawk going back down the ridge. Maybe he went up and over. She sat stiffly, listening for a while, but the silence seemed to extend all

around the ridge. Nothing seemed to be moving. She relaxed
and rested against the rock. She suddenly realized that she was
very tired.

She closed her eyes and slept.

Voices.

Senea's eyes flew open.

A stone rattled over rock above her. Her breath stilled in her
throat and she clenched the knife tightly.

She couldn't tell how long she had slept. The dark was so
thick she could just barely make out the opening in front of
her. If she hadn't known it was there she wouldn't have even
seen it.

There was a scrape of boots on rock. Somewhere. A murmur of voices drifted down to her from overhead.

Her heart hammered loudly in her ears, and she wiped at
sweat that was suddenly on her face.

She had no way of knowing whether it was an enemy patrol
or one from her own Held. But she suspected that Vayhawk
had taken her right up to the border, if not beyond. She held
her breath as she listened to the voices come closer until the
words were almost distinguishable. There was a quiet laugh,
distinctly female. Then nothing.

Senea waited, long, dragging minutes.

The sounds did not recur, and Senea wondered if she had
been discovered. But nothing stirred. No one came at her, not
from overhead, nor from in front of her. Then just as she was
beginning to relax again, there was a movement in front of the
opening, a darker shadow in the night. Panic froze her where
she was.

"Senea?" a half-whispering voice came to her.

"Vayhawk?" Relief rushed through her.

A figure that was no more than a suggestion in the darkness
stepped to the opening. "Come on." His whisper was urgent.

Senea scrambled to him, slipping her knife into its sheath,
and gasped when his arm went unexpectedly around her, its
strength also urgent.

She caught her breath. She felt something . . . no more than
a shadow . . . a subtle change in the environment coming from
the touch of Vayhawk's arm around her . . . an intimation of
strength filling her body. For an instant she felt the pounding
of her own heart.

Then it was gone as Vayhawk hurried her down the slope. Releasing her, he led at a pace that was difficult for her to keep up with.

"Vayhawk," she gasped. "What's wrong?"

"A patrol," he said. "I led them away from you, then circled back."

Senea took that in silently, then realized that they were running, a thing she would never have expected of Vayhawk. And then she knew what she had only suspected before. They were well inside another Held's boundaries.

Wordlessly she followed the Heldlan until he slowed to a more leisurely pace, and she knew they were back in their own lands. And part of her mind wanted to think about the implications of the hint of power she had felt in Vayhawk's touch when he had pulled her out of the cleft; but another, stronger part reacted instinctively against the idea.

CHAPTER
TEN

Senea paused on the crest of the rise before following Vayhawk down into the shaded valley. The heat of the dry season was advancing; the days were becoming longer and hotter. Everything seemed withered in the heat, blasted and shrunken under the unrelenting sun. Across the plain, heat waves flowed upward from the expanses of sand and bare rock, shimmering like transparent veils. Objects appeared distorted, bent, waving as if they were underwater.

Senea turned away from the golden-white of the plain and made her way down the slope to where Vayhawk was waiting for her, standing in the cool of the shade watching her.

When she reached him, he turned and lifted his quiver off over his head. He dropped it and his bow to the sand and began to take off his knife belt.

Senea watched him with surprise. He had never taken off his knife belt outside the Held that she had ever seen. She eyed him now with a foreboding that she could not explain. He came to her, tossing the belt to where his quiver lay on the sand. His dark eyes evaluated her critically in that frank appraisal that reminded her uneasily of that first day when he had asked her name.

"Today," he said, "we will begin on the hand-to-hand skills." He made a slight gesture with his head. "Put your things over there."

Hesitantly Senea did as she was told. She looked at him with a shrinking inside that was a sudden reluctance she was loath to identify. She had watched others at the Held teaching their heldii the body holds and the hand defenses that she knew Vayhawk would eventually have to show her. She had deliberately kept the thoughts of that eventuality away and secretly hoped it wouldn't ever come.

"There will be times," he was saying, "when you'll be facing an enemy with only your knife and your hands. However, if you are sufficiently skilled this will be enough."

He moved toward her with a swiftness that startled her, swiped her feet out from under her with his foot, and thrust her back to the sand with a single push of his hand.

She gasped, the breath knocked out of her, pain lancing through her lungs and side. It was a moment before she could move and try to sit up. Vayhawk leaned over and, taking her hand, helped her to her feet.

Senea straightened up slowly and sucked air into tight lungs.

"I will show you," Vayhawk said, and he carefully demonstrated how he had thrown her off balance while taking her off her feet with his foot. His hand on her arm kept her from falling back again.

Then he showed her that it could be done from the other side as well. He released her and stepped back.

"Now you try."

Senea stared at him, the source of her reluctance suddenly becoming very plain. Vivid pictures of heldan and heldii grappling together in body holds assaulted her, scenes of bodies struggling in the dust, physical violence that had nothing to do with enmity, a violence that could easily become something else. And suddenly she was thinking that this was what the Maiden's-eye tea had been given to her for. She stared at Vayhawk, shaken to the core at the direction her thoughts were taking her. She stepped back away from him, instinctively putting some distance between them, and drew in a trembling breath. He frowned at her in puzzlement.

Then his eyes narrowed in comprehension.

He drew in a tight breath, his face becoming closed and distant. "Would you rather Mara teach you?"

Senea was taken aback, the sudden anger in his voice surprising her, and before she could answer, he said, "I can very easily arrange it."

"No," she said weakly, appalled at how he could throw her completely off balance.

He scrutinized her for a long, unbearable moment, then the hardness on his face eased. "This is not a game we are playing here," he said, the tone of his voice unreadable. Senea waited, returning his look, trying to decide how he had meant that. She was not sure whether he was talking about the training, or about something else between them.

He stepped to her, his hand going around her arm, starting an uneasy trembling inside her.

"Let's try again."

Once more he demonstrated how the foot went around the ankle to pull the opponent off his feet. His hand pushed her back, but his hold on her arm kept her upright.

"Now you try." He stepped back.

Senea hestitated, still loath to touch him, and slowly exhaled a breath she had been holding. A slight breeze stirred the air, fluttering through the leaves overhead, and a momentary flash of sun reflected off Vayhawk's arm band. The shimmering light through the trees moved across him like gold, the dark tan of his shoulders a deep richness of bronze.

She was suddenly afraid of him. But she stepped forward and cautiously attempted to do as he bade nonetheless.

Vayhawk's hands reached, gently adjusted her stance, then withdrew. His eyes were level on her.

"Now try."

Senea moved. Hand. Foot.

Nothing happened. Vayhawk remained on his feet.

She stepped back uncertainly, but the expression on his face told her that he wanted her to do it again.

She came back to him and with her foot tried to hook his ankle. It was an awkward move, and she hesitated again.

"Do it fast," Vayhawk said.

She nodded and tried once more. Suddenly her foot made contact, and she thrust back with her hand. To her surprise Vayhawk landed hard on his back in the sand. She stepped back appalled and a little exultant.

Vayhawk got up and nodded approval, then motioned for her to do it again. His hand touched her arm while he corrected her stance again. "All right," he said, and Senea thrust him back to the sand, the movement much easier this time.

And once again.

And again.

Then he stopped her, taking her arm with his hand. "Now . . . I want you to attack me."

"What?"

"Attack me."

She frowned at him in confusion, not understanding what he meant.

"Pretend I'm a Ja'sid."

She looked at the Heldlan's face and thought he was mocking her. She sought some trace of humor in his eyes. She found none.

"Attack me, Senea," he said slowly. "I'm your enemy."

She looked at him, a chill abruptly shaking her as she understood what he wanted her to do. The memory of the Ja'sid who had attacked her came at her, like new, as if it had happened only that morning. She recalled how their bodies tangled together while they fought, the memory of it vivid in her mind. She saw that Vayhawk was becoming impatient, and there was nothing for her to do but to do as he said. She made a half-hearted attempt, going at him uncertainly with arms upthrust, shrinking from touching him.

He easily sidestepped her and struck a sharp blow across her back that sent her reeling uncontrollably into a stand of underbrush.

She spun on him furiously. His dark eyes were blazing at her.

"You've got to mean it," he said, "because even if you don't, your enemy certainly will."

"I don't know what you want."

He regarded her and drew in a carefully controlled breath. "I want you to attack me, Senea," he said tightly. "Just as if I were a Ja'sid from across the border. I want you to think like a heldan."

Then he moved with a suddenness that caught her by surprise. She was just barely able to leap out of his reach with a little laugh of triumph. But she wasn't prepared for his next lunge.

His body collided with hers, tearing a cry from her throat.

She struck the ground. Hard. His face was close to hers, his left hand tight around her outstretched wrist. She stared up into dark eyes that smoldered into hers.

She fought to pull a breath into her lungs, the weight of him on her making it almost impossible. His breath was ragged on her mouth.

For several moments he did not move. Another small breeze came and lifted the stray hairs on his forehead.

Then he said in a voice so low she almost didn't hear, "You're dead."

And his right hand touched her side where the Ja'sid had wounded her before, then slid upward to show how vulnerable she was. Had a knife been in his intentions . . . She drew in another painful breath.

"This is no game, Senea." The flutter of his words shivered across her skin, its touch more disturbing than the thoughts of another knife in her side.

Another several moments his eyes held hers.

Then his hand on her outstretched wrist loosened its grip and moved out over her palm, a slow, deliberate tracing that made her tremble. His fingers laced through hers, clasping her hand tightly. Senea watched his gaze drop to trail over her mouth and come back up again to her eyes.

All at once, she sensed the air around her as if it were a breathing, living entity: she became slightly aware of the deep bass thrum of a heartbeat that seemed to pass from Vayhawk to her. She could not immediately say what it was but it sent a shiver over her skin, a suspicion of understanding that this bodily contact was more than it appeared.

She met his look—and knew the reality of her fears coming true and she froze.

He knew it.

And on his face was grave acknowledgment of her fear.

He released her and used his hands to push himself up from her, a slow moving that she had to close her eyes against. For a long moment she lay still, trembling, and let the silence surround her.

"Are you all right?" the husky coarseness of his voice came to her.

She opened her eyes and saw that he was sitting close to her. She nodded, afraid yet to speak, afraid she'd reveal too much with her voice.

She began to sit up and he reached out and helped her.

"You are certain you are all right?"

"I was not hurt," Senea said, knowing that was not the question he was asking her.

"The feeling leaves when the touch is broken," he said softly.

She looked up at him, and the blood that had resumed somewhat its normal circulation drained a second time, for the

Heldlan's black-brown eyes regarded her soberly, reading her from trembling hands to her face. "Perhaps it would be better if Mara taught you."

Senea returned his gaze, hiding her dismay. She looked down to her hands, then asked, "What about Sky?"

"What about him?"

"You have a bet."

Vayhawk shrugged, a movement she did not see, but one that she sensed. "Mara is very good. You can learn a great deal from her."

Senea looked up. "But will I win?"

He regarded her thoughtfully, then answered frankly. "Probably not."

"I do not want to be heldii to Sky."

Vayhawk's eyes were steady for a long time, contemplative and considering. Then he said, "Very well. But . . ." he leaned forward, "there will be no more timidity. You're heldan now, Senea. You must learn to think like one. Learn to fight like one. You have to be aggressive. And . . ." he paused, looked at her mouth meaningfully, looked back up to her eyes, "there'll be no more distractions."

Senea saw the certainty of it on his face and felt a sudden regret at his words. She knew they were final. She nodded, determined that she would not disappoint him again.

"Good." Vayhawk stood. "I will show you what I meant for you to do."

CHAPTER
ELEVEN

Senea lowered herself stiffly to her bunk and closed her eyes wearily for a moment. The dark quiet of the Held was around her like warm water and, slowly, she let out a soft sigh, trying to relax. She could hear the even breathing of her bunkmates, and she envied them.

How long had it been since she'd had a full night's sleep? She couldn't even remember.

She ached everywhere; she felt battered from head to foot. She had not known that a body could take so much punishment and still be able to move. Vayhawk had been merciless with her, and she was beginning to understand Mara's pity for her in the beginning. She tried to breathe carefully to ease the pain in her side, but it did not seem to help.

Even her eyes hurt.

A long while she lay thus, trying to find comfort in the oblivion of sleep.

But it did not come.

She opened her eyes and stared into the darkness. There would be no sleep for her this night. The soreness of her muscles was too great.

There was a movement in the bunk across from her and another sound that she couldn't readily identify.

For a long moment she listened, then realized it was Treyna.

Again there was a sound from Treyna's bunk, a silent weeping that was being choked back.

"Treyna?" she whispered.

There was no answer.

Senea pushed herself up, ignoring the painful protest of her body. "Treyna, what's the matter?"

118

Still, no answer.

Senea stood and went to Treyna's bunk. She put out her hand and touched the girl's shoulder.

"Treyna?"

The shoulder moved, a slight yielding. Senea sat back down beside her. "Are you all right?"

"Go away," the trembling voice whispered to her.

Senea was taken aback and wasn't certain she had heard right. "What's the matter? Is there anything I can do?"

"No." The voice was adamant. "I cannot talk to you."

"What has happened?" She looked at the dark figure on the bunk, her face impossible to see, and Senea felt an unsettling sense of dread. "Is it Sky? What has he done?"

"He would be very angry with me if I talked to you."

"Why? That's ridiculous." Senea tried to keep the irritation out of her voice. "We're bunkmates. He can't expect you to totally ignore me."

"He has threatened me." Treyna's whispered words were pleading, almost begging for Senea to go away.

But Senea stubbornly remained. "How's he to know if no one tells him?"

"He'll find out. He has ways." Her voice raised for a moment, then quickly fell back into a frightened whisper. She pushed herself up against the bunk, pulled out of Senea's reach.

Senea shook her head, a move that she did not expect Treyna to see.

"I don't understand. Why doesn't he want you talking to me?"

"The bet!" Treyna's voice was suddenly bitter. "Always the bet!"

"The bet?" Senea echoed.

"All he can talk about is the bet; how I can't do anything right, how I'll never win, and how he'll make me sorry if I lose."

Senea was surprised at the anger in Treyna's voice. In the silence that followed she drew in a breath and finally asked, "Is there anything I can do?"

"Do?" Treyna laughed bitterly. "There's nothing anybody can do."

Senea put out her hand and laid it on Treyna's arm. "I'll talk to Vayhawk, have him call off the bet."

"Oh, no!" Treyna's voice changed instantly to fear. "You can't do that! Sky will know I've said something to you . . ." Her voice trailed off. Then she said in a whisper, "He scares me. He's always so angry. I'm afraid he's going to send me to Roskel."

"There must be *something* I can do," Senea protested.

"No. Don't do anything. It'll only get worse if you do."

Senea did not answer, reluctant to give in.

"Please," Treyna begged.

Senea sighed. "All right. But I don't like it."

"Do nothing."

"I could teach you what Vayhawk teaches me."

"No. I can't let you do that."

"I'd be glad to."

"You don't understand," Treyna whispered angrily. "I am forbidden to talk to you! Sky will take me to Roskel if he ever finds me with you!"

Senea was silenced with dismay.

Heldcode.

The heldan's word was law. She had forgotten. And Sky had forbidden.

"I'm sorry," she said.

"Please, go away," Treyna insisted. "Please! I have enough trouble."

"All right," and again, Senea said, "I'm sorry."

She hesitated a moment, but there was no reply from Treyna, so she went back to her bunk and lay wide-eyed and angry for the rest of the night. Forgotten were the muscles that ached and the side that throbbed.

Long before dawn she heard Treyna get up and leave.

She couldn't find Vayhawk, so she stood in the doorway that was closest to her bunkroom watching the heldii practicing out in the compound. Treyna and Sky were nowhere to be seen, and Senea decided they had probably gone out on patrol. She chewed on her lip, anger at the things that Treyna had said burning into her mind. She felt a loathing for Sky that she had never felt for anyone. She crossed her arms tightly in front of her and expelled an angry breath.

"Do you want to tell me about it?"

Senea looked around and saw Mara regarding her with a sober gaze. It had been several days since she had met Mara in the corridor, their goings seeming always to be in different directions. Senea had suspected that Vayhawk had kept them apart a time, taking her out of the Held before Mara thought appropriate and resuming her training sooner than Mara would have agreed. But, then, Vayhawk was Heldlord. He could do anything he wanted.

Senea drew in a breath now and attempted to hide what Mara had already seen on her face. "I didn't know you were there."

"Your thoughts were elsewhere."

Senea looked back out onto the compound, watching a heldii that was close-by wrestle his heldan to the ground with a head grip.

"Where is Vayhawk?" Mara asked.

"I don't know."

Mara looked at her for another moment, then moved closer and looked out on the compound, her eyes grave.

"There is something troubling you," and when Senea did not answer she continued, "Vayhawk would want me to answer any questions that you have."

Senea dropped her hands to her sides and turned away from the door. "It is nothing that you can help with."

"I see," Mara said. Then, "Shall we walk?"

Senea really did not wish to. She was still sore from the day before, but she nodded and waited for Mara to lead the way. But the heldan shook her head and indicated that they were to walk together. Wordlessly, Senea went with her along the narrow corridor. She found herself remembering the first day that she had followed Vayhawk through this hall, frightened and bewildered. And she remembered Mara—a source of strength and sympathy that day.

Now they walked, she of the heldii, Mara of the helden, weighted by training and responsibility, governed by heldcode that this moment felt like shackles. When they reached the cooking hall she waited while Mara entered first, then followed to a table close to a firehearth.

Senea sat watching the fire die, a blaze that some other heldan had built to cook upon. It was now a small flame spread upon orange coals and soon would be gone.

"Why did you bring me here?" she asked of Mara at last.

"So that we may talk."

The soft glow of firelight was on Mara's face. Senea looked

at her, frowning. For a moment it was as if Senea were seeing her for the first time. She suddenly wished that she could run out of the Held to her father's house and forget that any of this had happened to her.

"How is your side?" Mara asked.

"It's fine."

"Vayhawk is not pushing you too hard?"

Senea shook her head. Mara looked over at her, her eyes searching and skeptical. Her hand resting on the table reached forward, took hold of Senea's wrist.

"You tell me if he is. Vayhawk can be very tough."

"I can handle it," Senea said.

Mara studied her longer, then sat back. "You wouldn't tell me anyway . . . if you couldn't."

"There *is* heldcode," Senea said, not really sure what Mara was trying to get at.

Mara nodded slowly, her eyes still intent on Senea. "And . . . something else."

Senea looked at her with a slight frown. "Remember that I'm only heldii."

"And heldii are to obey without question. But there is wisdom in all things, Senea."

Senea shifted in her chair and turned slightly away from Mara so that she faced the firehearth more directly. Mara's words stirred something in her that was far from comfortable. The fire was gone now, the orange glow of the coals deepening to a bloodred. She did not know what Mara was trying to say, but for some reason she felt threatened. She looked sidelong at the heldan. Mara was looking at her evenly, watching and judging her reactions. Senea drew in a breath and folded her arms across her ribs, an unconscious defensive move.

"There is nothing for you to be concerned about," she said.

A smile touched Mara's mouth, but did not reach her eyes. "You are beginning to sound like a heldan."

Senea did not answer.

"Is it the bet?"

Her voice was quiet, but it stunned. Senea's eyes went to Mara's with a guilty start.

"Ah," Mara breathed as she realized that she had guessed right. "What is it? You are afraid?"

"No."

"No?" Mara was puzzled.

"There is nothing to fear from Treyna," Senea murmured.

Mara studied her a long moment before she nodded. "I agree. So what is the problem?"

Senea shook her head.

"Treyna," Mara guessed. The sudden knowledge was in her voice.

Senea gave a single bitter expel of breath and saw a frown leap into the heldan's eyes. She met Mara's gaze, read the questions there that she could not answer, and she turned her face away to stare at the coals that were turning white around the edges. Then in the silence that hung heavily on them she said, "She will not last long here."

"This is a hard place. Only the strong survive."

"She should not be here."

Mara sighed. "Held-law was called."

Senea looked at her angrily. "Have you watched her?"

"Yes."

"She'll never learn anything as long as Sky has her."

Mara shrugged, a gesture that somehow did not convey indifference. "There is nothing anybody can do. She will have to get tough."

"I don't think she can."

Mara spread her hands then. "She doesn't have much of a future here, then."

Senea's back stiffened. "Aren't you being a little cold?"

Mara's gaze did not waver. "A heldan has to be cold. There is no room for sentiment, not with the kind of life we lead."

Senea glared at her, but could not answer. She knew that Mara was right. Every heldan had to be able to stand alone whenever necessary. That had been demonstrated to her very forcefully. Even within the Held, each heldan was alone. She stood, pushing the chair back.

"What are you going to do?"

"There's nothing I *can* do," Senea answered, and when Mara did not reply, she added, "There is heldcode between us."

"Between you and Treyna?"

"Yes."

"Vayhawk did this?"

"No."

Mara drew in a soft breath. "I see." And the only other name was Sky. Treyna's trainer. Vayhawk's enemy.

Senea turned and caught her breath. She stared in horror at Sky. He was standing too close to not have heard what had been said. Cold crept over her as she stared into his hard eyes and saw the rage in the tightness of his mouth.

"Sky." She said his name weakly, as if to convince herself that he was really there.

His eyes narrowed as he examined her face, then he turned on his heel and strode for the door.

"No," Senea gasped, knowing that he was going after Treyna. She pulled herself out of her numbed daze, leapt after him in desperation. She caught hold of his arm as he pushed open the door.

"Sky! Don't!"

He turned on her, jerked his arm from her grasp.

"She didn't mean to tell me," Senea pleaded. "I wouldn't leave her alone. She had to tell me to make me go away."

Sky looked at her, the muscles of his jaw working as if he had his teeth clenched together. The eyes that he had leveled on her were filled with intense hatred and something else that she had never seen before. She stepped back in sudden fear.

"Heldii," he said in a low voice that sent chills over her. "You would be well advised to remember your place." His eyes traveled slowly over her face and went back to her eyes.

"You need to be taught proper manners. But that's not surprising, considering the source of your training." His smile was slow and malicious. His voice was edged, cruel, and it shocked, like a blow.

For a slow moment Senea took the meaning of his words and the shock turned to anger.

"I wouldn't say that your heldii is being trained properly either!"

The instant the words were out of her mouth she knew that she had made a mistake. He lashed out and gripped her arm with fingers that dug into her flesh. He pulled her close so that his face was only inches from hers and his fury-darkened eyes bored into her.

"Girl, you are treading dangerous ground!" His whisper was almost a growl. Senea tried to pull her arm out of his grasp, but his fingers tightened painfully.

"What I do with my heldii is my business and is no concern of yours. That is until you lose the bet and *you* become my heldii."

"Lose?" Senea choked, appalled that her voice failed of sound. She forced herself to laugh, a shaky expel of air. "I don't think that I would lose even against you." The words were out before she could stop them.

Hard fingers took hold of her other arm and pulled her even closer.

"That sounds like a challenge!"

"If that's the way you want it."

His eyes went to her mouth with deliberation and he smiled a slow, chilling smile. "I accept." And his darkened eyes looked back up to her. "It will be a pleasure."

Senea was transfixed, unable to move. His voice seemed to come from far away. It was a whisper that seemed a shout to her. Blood rushed uncontrollably in her ears and the beating of her heart was painful. She felt she was going to be sick.

She could see what was coming but was powerless to stop it.

Enlightenment flared in her mind. She dammed the sudden realization of her power and looked at him, met his eyes and felt a stillness. The stillness spread over all the room and into her bones. Tears gathered in the corners of her eyes. She trembled with the enormous force of this thing that she could feel gathering between them. The breath left her lungs.

It was like two polarities of one powerful force. It gathered whenever two helden came together. And she knew that Sky would be quick enough to feel it. She thought distant, angry thoughts that this would come upon them now.

She was right . . . Sky's eyes widened slightly, and he stared at her with thinly disguised astonishment and a newly dawning interest. And it came leaping into her mind in one fatal rush that given enough time he would realize what it was and figure out how to use it. A premonition perhaps.

But now his eyes had gone oddly piercing as he looked at her, his thoughts concentrating wholly on her, and she realized her escape lay open before her.

She inhaled the rich scent of smoldering coals and lingering food aromas mingling with some strange spice. She resisted the force that was pulling the two of them together, determinedly pulled herself out of it.

It had as well been a blow. Sky stepped backward a pace as if struck by an invisible hand. His eyes opened wide and his lips parted. In the next instant he regained his composure. His lips twitched slightly, contemptuously.

He pushed her hard against the wall and released her. Abruptly he turned away and with that movement an invisible but tangible barrier crashed between them. He turned a threatening look on Mara, who was coming up swiftly on him with her hand at her knife. Mara stopped, but before she could say anything, Sky shouldered through the door and strode down the corridor.

Senea looked helplessly to Mara a long, tense moment before she could think of anything to say.

"What did I challenge him to?" was what she could finally get out.

Mara's voice held little sympathy. "You challenged him to the Games."

Senea leaned her head against the wall. She could feel a slight breeze on her cheek from a hidden crack somewhere. She glanced at her hand and saw it, as if it belonged to a stranger—the long fingers, shapely despite the broken nails, delicately boned.

Mara moved to her and put a hand on her arm. "You thought with your emotions, not with your head."

"I was stupid," then, "Please, don't tell Vayhawk."

Mara frowned. "You should not ask that of me."

Senea closed her eyes and nodded. "He'd find out anyway."

"Yes, he would."

Senea sighed then and pulled away from Mara's hand. A terrible fear had taken hold of her reason and was growing with every moment—she was safe from Sky now, but she didn't feel safe.

"I'm sorry," she said. "Forget I asked." And not waiting for an answer she pushed through the door to the corridor.

CHAPTER
TWELVE

Helden gathered around the perimeter of the compound, leaving an area in the center where Roskel stood. Helden, but not all helden: heldii also hovered around the doors looking on in curiosity. All were required to attend; only those on patrol were not there. Senea moved to a pole in their midst, wanting the strength it would give her to stand. She was distressed at the ordeal that was to come, for it was of her doing.

She cast a glance to where Treyna stood at the edge of the cleared space. Her head was bowed, every line of her body showing fear and shame. Sky stood next to her, his hand mercilessly gripping her arm. And as Senea looked, Sky raised his eyes and met her stare with vengeful malevolence.

Defiance!

Senea realized it with a start.

He was doing this to Treyna in defiance of her. And of Vayhawk.

The early morning wind whipped across the compound, kicked up some dust, and flung it aloft.

Senea tore her eyes from Sky's and crossed her arms, searched the compound once again for Vayhawk. Somehow she had to put a stop to this. All night she had waited for Treyna to return to the bunkroom. She did not come. Nor did Vayhawk return to the Held. Anxiously Senea scanned the faces of the helden, but he was not among them. Without him she was helpless to do anything for Treyna.

Suddenly she met Yunab's cold stare, and she stiffened as if she had been struck. Involuntarily she glanced toward the place in the arena where Treyna stood.

Eveything was just as it had been. So why had the flesh of her face and hands begun to creep, and why had the hair along the back of her neck begun to stand up, as if the flesh back there had suddenly tightened?

She squinted back to Yunab. He caught her gaze again and for a moment his eyes narrowed. Yes, there was something different.

She forced herself to show no reaction.

But her stomach contracted, curiosity mixing with suspicion, and she stood motionlessly against the pole, unable to pull her stare from his. She wondered what he was doing here, and thought that he was waiting for something to happen out of this thing that Sky was doing. Then she was frightened. She knew the wild violence that could explode out of this kind of moment.

She tore her gaze from him and looked anxiously back to Treyna.

Silence fell in the compound. The waiting helden stood, with the wind pulling gently at them and blowing a fine dust across the hardpacked arena. Senea clenched her fingers tightly, felt nails dig into palm, did not care.

Roskel nodded to Sky.

The helden around the edge of the space posed themselves, arms folded, and waited.

But when Sky stepped forward with Treyna there was a movement behind the ranks. Heads turned and a way was opened. And through their midst came Vayhawk, taller by almost a head than anyone around him.

He strode across the cleared space to Roskel and spoke to him while silence hung heavily on the Held. There was a murmur of words that Senea could not distinguish as Roskel turned aside and talked to Vayhawk at length. Finally, the Heldlan turned, looked first at Treyna and then at Sky. He bent his head to Roskel and asked a question that was answered with a few short words. Vayhawk gave him a brief nod and went back to the ranks of helden.

A hand on his arm stopped him at the first row before he could shoulder through.

Mara.

Senea watched as Vayhawk bowed his head to the heldan to listen. Her hands sought the pole behind her for support while her heart beat a cold, hard rhythm. Out of the corner of her eye she could see Yunab watching all of them, and she knew that this was going to give him what he needed to tear apart the Held.

"Heldan," Roskel began then, "you have a charge to make."

"I do," Sky answered.

"Make it."

"Held-second," Sky said aloud as if he were repeating some set formula, "I have given my heldii orders that she has disobeyed. I bring her to you for discipline."

Senea glanced from Vayhawk to Treyna's pale face and saw that there was a tremor on her lips. She looked back to Vayhawk, her attention torn because of worry about what Mara was telling him. She could not see him clearly but she saw well enough to note the frown that lined his face.

"Heldii," Roskel said to Treyna. "Do you acknowledge the truthfulness of this charge?"

"Yes." Treyna's voice barely carried to where Senea stood.

Just beyond Sky and Treyna, Vayhawk's eyes raised from Mara's face and searched the compound until he found Senea, and she knew that he had been told everything. She crossed her arms in front of her again, staring at the displeasure on his face, and leaned helplessly against the pole.

"Heldii, do you understand the seriousness of this charge against you? You have gone against heldcode and have broken trust with the helden."

Treyna nodded.

Vayhawk turned away into the crowd, and Senea quickly lost sight of him, found Yunab's gaze instead. He was still watching her closely.

Her eyes were then drawn forcefully to Roskel as he went on.

"When you first came to this place you were told that all disciplinary problems would be brought to me and that I would not be merciful. I also warned you not to find this out for yourself. Would you repeat for me, and for all the Held to hear, the heldcode?"

Senea bit her lip as she watched the horror come over Treyna's face. No one moved. No one spoke. A misery crept into Senea's taut legs, and a chill grew at her back where the wind blew. Then Treyna inclined her head to Roskel and began to speak in a thin, frightened voice that was carried away on the wind.

"It is forbidden to bring harm to others of our own Held . . . there is no communication with members of other Helds . . . no weapon can be drawn against another heldan of our own Held except in the Games—and then, no one can kill . . . instant, unquestioning obedience of a ranking heldan . . . we will give our lives for our held-tribe if necessary."

Roskel's face betrayed nothing, but Sky, at his side, was watching Treyna with sadistic satisfaction. When she was finished there was a glistening of tears in her eyes.

"That is correct," Roskel said. "Would you now tell us which of these codes you disobeyed?"

Treyna's head bowed, and it was a long wait before she got the self-possession to speak.

"Unquestioning obedience of a ranking heldan."

Senea watched Sky with a rising fury. He was so blatant in his enjoyment of Treyna's humiliation that it was all Senea could do to hold herself still. She wanted to strike him, to make him swallow that mocking sneer.

"A Held has to be a place of strict discipline," Roskel said. "Each heldan has to be able to rely on the other. Lives hang in the balance. And if there is one who does not have the discipline and cannot be depended on, then the Held and the held-tribe are jeopardized. When the heldcode is ignored it affects every heldan in the Held. For this reason are they here today." He paused and looked at her. His eyes were expressionless.

"Are there any extenuating circumstances that you wish to present before we go any further?"

Senea waited for Treyna's answer, knowing even as she did that Treyna would say nothing about what had happened. Nothing would be said about Senea's insistence that Treyna talk to her. Nothing would be said of her own disregard of heldcode. Nothing would be said, unless she said it herself. And as she watched Treyna shake her head negatively she knew that she couldn't let this go on any longer. She could put it all to a stop with just a few words.

She pushed herself away from the pole and began to weave her way through the crowd toward the front lines of helden at the edge of the clearing. A sudden hand around her wrist prevented her from stepping out into the clearing. She spun around with a start.

The night color of Vayhawk's eyes bored down into hers.

"Come," he said, and pulled her through the standing helden to a place against the wall of the Held.

"Vayhawk, you've got to stop this," she said in a low, anxious voice.

He turned a dark gaze on her and shook his head firmly. "Turn around and watch."

"But this is my fault. It's got to be stopped."

"Senea . . ." His hands took her shoulders and turned her bodily so that she faced the compound. "Do as I say."

"But . . ." she began in protest, wincing when his fingers tightened painfully on her arms.

She was not as close as she had been before, and from her vantage point Senea had difficulty getting a clear view of what was going on. But she could hear Roskel clear enough.

"Heldii, because what you have done reflects on the Held as a whole and the effectiveness of our job here, you will apologize publically now for the dishonor you have brought on us. And thereafter you will no longer be called heldii, but will be less than that, until such time as I judge that you may be restored to status as heldii. You may not speak unless spoken to. The heldii will have more rank than you, and obedience to them will be required of you."

Senea listened with appalled silence and then she saw the stricken, ashen gray face of Treyna.

"Vayhawk, you can't let them do this to her!" she pleaded in a whisper so that others around them would not hear.

It was a moment before he spoke. "It is already done." The coarse vibration of his voice was close to her ear.

"But it's my fault!"

"Nevertheless, you will do nothing."

Senea turned half-around to face him, a chill running over her. "What are you saying?"

Vayhawk's hands faced her forward again. "Watch . . . and learn."

Treyna stood with her head bowed. The wind whipped at the compound, a whisper of sand ran along the ground. And Senea realized that Treyna was weeping, and guilt at the girl's mortification stung her. Sudden tears stung her eyes and she had to blink furiously to clear them.

"Poor Treyna," she whispered. And as she listened to

Treyna's halting and trembling apology to the Held, Senea felt deep shame for her part in the whole thing.

"Heldcode is the foundation by which we live," Vayhawk said to her. "It cannot be taken lightly."

"But I'm just as guilty as she is," Senea insisted.

"And you will have to watch her humiliation, but you will do nothing."

"Why?" Senea asked in sudden anger. "To protect your reputation? Is that why you will not let me stop them from doing this?"

She drew in a hiss of breath when Vayhawk pulled her suddenly back against him, his hands tightening into an iron grip on her arms.

"For you, heldii, punishment is to do and say nothing that will release Treyna from her judgment," he spoke huskily into her ear, an edge of steel in his voice.

"Consequences, Senea. You need to learn consequences: to think before you speak, and above all ... to keep your word."

"To keep my word?" she echoed, and in the next instant understood. Vayhawk was talking about her promise to Treyna, to keep their conversation confidential. She was surprised and shocked; she hadn't realized that Mara had understood so much. She opened her mouth, then closed it, for there was nothing she could say.

"What you have done, and have done so thoughtlessly, is to undermine the loyalty that helden are to have for one another. This is the heldcode. Loyalty. And the damage may never be repaired."

"What about Sky?" Senea asked hesitantly.

"Sky walks close to the edge, and he will be dealt with in time. But that is my concern. Just as you are. And because you are, all eyes are on us. You have to think everything through, see all sides, and consider the Held before you do or say anything."

Senea listened to the softly spoken words and felt the flutter of his breath on her hair, the painful grip of his fingers on her arms, and her heart beat in hard, measured strokes that took strength from her and left her leaning weakly against him. Before her, she could see all of the Held, all of the helden, and for the first time she reckoned the responsibility that was

Vayhawk's. Heldlan of Held and held-tribe, Heldlord of all the lands that surrounded them, and responsible for the safety and peace of all. A heavier burden than what even Aldived bore. And she suddenly understood that that burden rested partly on her as well. What she did reflected on him, just as what Treyna did reflected on Sky and the entire Held. The gravity of what she had done became clear to her.

There was a movement and the helden began to step aside. Senea saw that Sky and Treyna were coming through the crowd toward where she and Vayhawk were standing. She stiffened and tried to pull from Vayhawk's grasp. But he held her firmly, would not let her retreat.

"Do nothing," he said in a low voice.

Sky pushed through the remaining helden and stopped when he saw Senea. She met his look directly and watched as a mocking smile moved across his mouth. She held herself still and was grateful that Vayhawk stood behind her and that his hands had not left where they had been holding her. But then she looked to Treyna and met the shock of utter hatred where she had not expected it.

Senea stared at her, unable to believe what she was seeing. The frightened look that had become the accustomed expression of Treyna's face was gone, and in its place was the most intense hatred that Senea had ever seen. And it was directed at her. Cold iciness ran through her as she met that look, unable to pull her eyes away.

Sky spoke a single word to Treyna that Senea did not hear, and they moved on, going through the door into the Held. Senea stared after them. Then when she turned her head she found herself impaled with the hard, amused glare of Yunab, who had been watching all of this with great pleasure. For a long moment she could only look back at him. Then he turned and was also gone.

It was several moments before she realized that Vayhawk's grip on her had loosened and that she was still leaning against him.

His hands moved down her arms and his fingers brushed lightly over hers.

"Let's get out of here," he said, and his hand closed around hers.

She nodded, trembling violently inside, hearing in his voice that he really did want to leave. He wanted to get away from the Held just as much as she did. Gratefully, she followed him across the compound, ignoring the curious looks that were cast her way.

Once outside, his hand fell away from hers and he led the way out onto the plain.

CHAPTER THIRTEEN

The night came quietly, with only the sounds of the windshift blowing across the hill. Senea sat against a boulder and watched the last of the color leave the sky in the west. The peace of the plain had taken a long time to replace the troubled turmoil that had been in her mind. Thoughts of Treyna and Sky did not leave her, not for long agonizing hours. But gradually the quiet, and the relief that the windshift brought to the furnace of the plain, lent calm to her, and she relaxed.

Vayhawk came to her and settled on the sand at her side, a darker shadow in the night. He had lingered near as she had sat so, watching the sunset, not disturbing her but staying within calling distance. He seemed to have sensed her need to be alone and was willing to give her that time. Now he sat beside her, a warmth in the cool of the night, a presence that seemed to have more right to be there than the rocks and the sky. Senea contemplated him as she rested against the boulder trying to put a name to that aura about him that gave him that right. She could not find it.

"Are you feeling better?" he asked of her.

"Yes."

His answer was comfortable silence.

Senea put her arms around her knees and clasped them close. "I should apologize," she offered. "I have not been taking any of this seriously enough."

Vayhawk did not answer, and Senea felt his gaze turn on her, contemplative and attentive.

"I spoke out of turn," she added. "I should not have said anything to Mara or Sky."

"An important thing to learn," Vayhawk said. "To think before you speak."

Senea looked out over the darkness that was the plain. "What of my challenge with Sky?"

"What of it?"

"Does it stand?"

"It stands."

Senea nodded, an acknowledgment that was lost in the dark.

"The responsibility of that is yours. I cannot step in to undo it."

"Consequences," Senea murmured.

"Consequences," he confirmed.

Senea sighed and laid her cheek on her arm, looking at a star that hung close to the horizon. It blinked from red, to white, to blue, and back again, a shimmering caused by the movement of the air over the cooling plain.

"Can I beat him?" she asked.

Vayhawk was slow to answer as he gave careful consideration. "Sky is very good," he said. "He's seventh in rank. And he's ruthless. He will not hold his hand against you."

Senea closed her eyes and reckoned what she had done. "I have no chance," she finally said.

"There's always a chance."

Senea raised her head and looked at him.

"Sky does not hold his anger well. He loses his head easily."

Senea considered that, thought she understood what he was telling her, and knew something else that she would not have known earlier.

"I think," she said to him, "that there will be blood between us: you, Sky, and me. In spite of heldcode."

A gentle breeze from the fading windshift ran around and between them as Vayhawk turned his head and looked out into the night. Senea crossed her arms behind her drawn-up knees and inhaled in an uncertain breath. After a long space he spoke in a low voice, "Sky has become obsessed with some dark thing, and he will divide the Held if he is not stopped."

A chill went down Senea's back. "And you have to stop him?"

"I *am* Heldlan."

He said nothing further. That said it all.

Then Senea voiced the thought that came to her. "I am being used against you."

Vayhawk turned his head to her and raised his fingers to touch her face. "Of course. That is to be expected." His hand fell away then.

"But, with caution, nothing will come of it. Your caution." And those words placed the responsibility directly on her.

Senea stared at the dark figure of him, a dread coming on her that had not been there before. His shadowed face showed no feature that she could read; she felt his gaze on her but could not see his eyes. The gravity of his voice echoed through her head, and she shivered at the burden that he placed on her.

"Vayhawk . . ." and the words that held the question seemed to come of their own accord. "Why did you take me as heldii? Surely you knew all of this was going to happen."

The silence that followed became a weight that was as tangible as the ground underneath her. Her heart thudded in frightened jolts, and she berated herself severely for asking.

Vayhawk finally drew in a breath through his nostrils. "I thought it might. But it was a thing I dreamed, and I had to follow it."

"A dream?" she echoed, not certain what he meant. When he said nothing further, Senea realized that that was the only answer she was going to get.

"You are to stay here tonight," he said then, gathering himself to his feet. "I will be back for you at dawn."

"Where are you going?"

"We watch for the Ja'sid here," he continued, ignoring her question. "Their land is out there three or four days' travel, and there will be patrols. But what you have to watch for is the heldan that comes alone. You will not hear him before he's on you, so you will have to be alert. No sleeping."

"Where are you going?" She was suddenly afraid and she stood, dropping her voice at once to half-whisper, for she was just as suddenly aware that they could be discovered by their speech. "Why are you leaving me here?"

"This is what patrol is."

"But the Ja'sid . . ." she was about to protest.

"Have taken many of our helden and could just as easily find you."

"But I'm not ready," she said fearfully. She knew it when she spoke these words that they were against heldcode, and she cancelled them with a shake of her head. "No, I will do as you say."

A breath of time lapsed before he spoke again. "Stay alert. Listen to every sound; listen to every silence; pay attention to every change. That heldan is out there, and he will find you if you give him anything to follow. So, not only do you have to be aware of everything around you, but you have to avoid giving your position away. No sound, no movement, nothing that will tell him where you are."

Senea looked out into the darkness and crossed her arms tightly to ward off the cold.

"Where will you be?"

"On an errand."

She looked up into his dark face and recalled the night when he had left her alone, sitting frightened in the cavity of a rock in another Held's borders.

"The same errand as the last time?" she asked then, and for half a space she thought he was not going to answer.

Then, "Heldii," he said softly, "you ask too many questions."

Senea shrugged, self-conscious in the close scrutiny that she knew was turned on her. She did not know if he was angry with her or not.

"I suppose," he said at last, "that a Heldlan's heldii would learn things that no other heldii or heldan would. But remember, the wrong knowledge could be dangerous. What you learn of Heldlan business you keep to yourself."

This she understood after this day's harsh lessons, and she nodded, "I will." She frowned then and wondered what confidences she was agreeing to keep. She knew nothing—nothing, except that Vayhawk kept going somewhere and leaving her alone. And this he did not want known. She looked at his shadowed face. Where did he go when he left her?

"Are you ready?" he asked.

Senea drew in a breath and pulled her thoughts back to the night ahead. "Yes, I guess so."

"All right," he said. "Find yourself a place and stay there. A place that will give you a good vantage point. The purpose of patrol is to watch the borders."

"What do I do if I see someone?"

"What would a heldan do?" A question that needed no answer.

She considered and knew what he meant. Defend her held-tribe. Even if . . .

She shuddered and did not complete the thought.

"I'll be back at dawn," he said as he turned away, and Senea suddenly wanted to stop him, to beg him to stay with her or take her with him. But she held her silence and watched him disappear down the slope into the night. She could not hear any sound of his going, and she marveled that he could move across the land so soundlessly. It was an ability that she had not yet mastered.

The night breeze stirred and lifted a strand of hair that had escaped its thong. She shivered and looked about her to find a place to wait out the night. She could see nothing except shapeless shadows, and she knew that to find a hiding place would mean groping around the rocks and boulders blindly. Deciding against moving at all she sank down to sit cross-legged right where she was. After all, it was where she had been sitting as she watched the sun disappear behind the horizon. What better vantage could she find? But as she sat staring out into the dark, she grew afraid and she drew out her knife to grasp tightly in her hand.

The night grew long into the hours, each hour longer than the last. Pain entered muscles that had not moved, sank into the bones, and her legs grew numb. Senea fought the need to change position, fought the need to sleep. She remembered that she had not slept well the two previous nights for worry about Treyna.

The night was quiet, close and concealing. Her head nodded; her eyes became heavy. Twice she caught herself dozing, only to drift toward sleep again.

Then to keep herself awake she began to straighten her legs, one agonizing inch at a time, taking so long to make each move that new pains lanced up and down her thighs.

One leg was out in front of her when she heard it. Or, rather, when she didn't hear it. A silence that wasn't there before, an empty silence devoid of insects that were usually not noticed until they were absent.

She froze, her breath dying in her lungs, and she listened intently. There was nothing. No movement. No sound at all.

And she could not tell if the threat was in front of her or was coming from behind.

Slowly she drew her leg back, taking care not to roll a loose pebble or to snap an unseen twig. She eased up to her knees and moved back against the boulder she had been leaning against.

Silence.

She waited.

Nothing.

A faint touch of leaded gray showed in the east.

More time passed. The gray lightened.

Still Senea did not hear anything. The insects had resumed the chirping and buzzing sounds that were a part of the night, but Senea did not relax. Something or someone had been out there and could still be. Instinct told her that she was still in danger.

The gray in the east became a deep purple-blue, the horizon edged in green and pink. The plain stretched out in grays and blacks. But there was no movement.

A bird warbled sleepily from somewhere in the rocks to the left. Through the gentle haze in the air, Senea watched valleys and canyons that had not been visible the day before slowly come into being. The land grew and extended toward the horizon, developing new limits as the dawn grew.

Still there was no movement.

Senea rested her cheek against the boulder as she searched the plain with her eyes. Weariness ached in every part of her body. She eased to the ground to sit and get the weight off her knees. She looked at the sun coming up over the eastern hills throwing long shafts of light into the haze on the plain and wondered where Vayhawk was. It was another worry . . . that something had happened to him, and he would not be coming back.

A pebble rolling across stone brought her head up.

It had been behind her.

Holding her breath, she listened for another sound but could not hear beyond the thudding of her heart.

She gripped her knife and tried to look behind her without making noise or sudden movement that could be seen.

A figure appeared from behind a low bush and, ducking, came quickly toward her. For a half breath Senea prepared to fight, then she saw that it was Vayhawk. He reached her, took hold of her arm, and pulled her almost forcefully behind the boulder into the branches of a dried scrub brush. She stifled a surprised cry and huddled down behind the boulder. She met his shadowed gaze.

"What . . ."

His hand came up, covered her lips with his fingers. "Sh." It was a sound that was no sound. He turned his head and peered over the top of the boulder.

Senea moved close to him. "There's someone out there," she whispered.

He nodded and looked back at her. "That's why I let you know I was coming," and at Senea's confused frown he added in a voice barely above a whisper, "How did you know I was there?"

"There was a noise. A pebble. I thought . . ." She stopped. Of course. A signal. She should have known.

Vayhawk's eyes lit with approval and something else that left her shaken when he turned to look back over the boulder. She edged up next to him and scanned the plain.

The sun was completely above the horizon now, and the valleys and canyons were crisp cuts of blue and apricot in the plain that shone gold with the morning light. Two birds whizzed overhead, chirruping shrilly, then disappeared down over the slope of the hill. The dry branches of the bush needled painfully into her arm and back, but she did not move.

"Over there," Vayhawk murmured, pointed to the right at a small rise a short distance from the base of the hill.

Senea saw them then, three figures moving cautiously around the rocks and bushes, threading their way toward the hill.

Ja'sid.

And she knew before she turned that Vayhawk was watching her and knew without being told what was to come next. She stared at him as a sick feeling slid to her stomach and lay there. His dark eyes studied her face with a close examination, a slow searching that made her shiver.

"Are you ready?" he asked in a low voice that vibrated like a whisper of wind through tall golden grass.

She swallowed, nodded slightly and said, "Yes," a word that was lost because it lacked sound.

His eyes lingered a moment on her face, dark and fathomless, impossible to read, then he turned his head.

"You go around that way." He indicated the slope of the hill to the right. "I'll go the other way. We'll catch them in the middle." He looked back to her.

"Can you do it?"

Senea nodded, not daring to say anything, lest she betray her fear.

"All right," Vayhawk said then. "Let's go." He turned on his heels, ducked his head, and disappeared around the boulder.

Senea inched forward, feeling that she was in a suspension of time; languor crept into all of her limbs, fear overwhelming her with immobility. Her lungs hurt, and she realized that she was holding her breath. She sucked in air and forced herself to slip out from behind the boulder.

She paused half a step to survey the hill and the slope before her. She could not see Vayhawk but knew he was well on his way down the hill. She stepped into the shadows behind the rocks and bushes and moved quickly down the slope, keeping as well as she could to the shadows.

She reached an open space and bolted across for a low scrub brush, startled and shocked when she heard a cry go up. She gasped for air and leapt for cover, changed directions, darted around the bending of a stand of rocks, and ran along its cover, trying to keep to the sand to muffle her steps.

After a minute she stopped to peer around the rocks, smothered a cough, and pressed her hand to her aching side. She tried to keep her breathing normal and silent as she listened for any sound other than her own. There was nothing.

She gathered herself up and started to move, hearing at the same time a rapid sound of footsteps coming up the slope toward her. She dove back for cover behind the rocks, but saw at once that she had been discovered.

Half a breath they faced each other, heldii and Ja'sid; and in that half breath Senea snatched out her knife. And in the next instant the Ja'sid was coming at her, and she had a terrible sense of having gone through this before. The Ja'sid hit her just as she flung herself aside, and with a twist of body she drove her knife into his belly, and a knee to his head toppled him writhing to the sand. Another blow to the neck with her foot ended his struggles.

A sob of horror choked her at what she had done, and she stared at the unmoving body as she backed up to the stand of rocks. Suddenly her stomach threatened to be ill, and she had to force herself to move away.

Moving slowly at first and then running she made for a cluster of low-growing trees. She stopped behind a twisted tree to scan the area below. Seeing nothing, she scrambled forward, ducking under a branch, slid down a slope of hard sand and hit bottom.

She heard it then, a scuffle somewhere ahead in the rocks. Creeping forward she edged around until she could see beyond.

Vayhawk had encountered the other two Ja'sid and was fighting the two of them for his life.

The one that was behind him came up and struck a sharp blow to his side that staggered him. Then he was seized in a body hold and was struck again from in front.

Vayhawk kicked upward and contacted hard, wrenched himself around and grappled with the one that had held him pinned.

The first Ja'sid fell gasping to his knees.

Without thinking about it, Senea sprinted forward and lunged at him and struck him bodily to the ground. There was the crack of dry branches as they rolled over a dead scrub.

The Ja'sid's knife bounced away.

Senea scrambled for her feet, but the Ja'sid seized her and yanked her back to the ground. She grabbed for her own knife and at the same time tasted the grit of dirt in her mouth.

The Ja'sid snatched at her hand and wrenched her arm savagely, his grip tightening ruthlessly, the heat of his breath on her face.

Numbed fingers dropped the knife. Desperately, she clawed at his face with her free hand.

He cursed and struck a brutal blow.

She sagged. Then they were locked on the ground, dried grass crushing under their straining bodies, fingers grasping wrists, elbows against sternums.

Senea saw her knife just inches away and forced herself to grab for it. The Ja'sid stopped her with a wrench of his arms.

Then his hands were around her throat, tightening viciously. His black eyes seethed murderously into hers, the weight of him heavy on her.

She gagged, surprised at the sudden pain. Both of her hands came up to yank helplessly at his larger, stronger ones. She could not breathe.

She struck at him, fought him desperately, heard the choking sounds that were her own, and heard the kicking of feet on hard, rocky ground.

Suddenly a titanic flash of bloodred light blasted against her eyes, radiating out from the Ja'sid's hands. Her body shook with uncontrollable spasms. Pain flooded her body; her chest throbbed sharply, red mist swirled before her eyes. It built up swiftly until she felt her head must burst. Then the red flashes began to turn black.

Consciousness began to slip from her and absurdly she became acutely aware of the hardness of the Ja'sid's body and the heaving of his gasps and her surprise at the maleness of him. And somehow this awareness was a part of the power of him.

She was half-conscious, close to the borders of an uncertain nightmare, but she had to find the strength to pull free, before the world of blackness stole the chance away.

Then, suddenly, he was torn from her, and she convulsed in dry, racking coughs that would not stop and would not let air into her screaming lungs. Dust and tears stung her eyes, and she blinked furiously, the black gone, her hand to her throat.

She coughed again and again and again.

Finally, she was able to gulp for air, and coughed spasmatically at the pain that that breath caused.

Through her tears she saw Vayhawk grab the Ja'sid, drag him to his feet, and smash him in the face with his fist. Then the Heldlan's knife was in his hand, his eyes ablaze with a rage that Senea had never seen in them before. He leaned forward to pull the Ja'sid to his feet again and his leg came against Senea's.

A force of energy flared from that contact, glowing white-hot between them. It came and it came, lashing at them solidly. Senea had never felt anything like it. And she knew that Vayhawk was going to kill the Ja'sid with it. She knew it as surely as she knew the sun would rise.

Vayhawk's motion was slowly timed, beautifully fluid, but seeming so slow Senea could follow everything he did minutely.

He grabbed the Ja'sid by the hair of the head, pulled him to his feet, and swung. She could not watch. She closed her eyes before the knife found its mark.

She felt the strength being pulled from her in a rush that was like the wind being knocked out of her. She felt the knife slice through flesh, felt the taste of blood through every fiber of her body. They were one, Vayhawk, the knife, and herself. What they felt, she felt, what they tasted, she tasted, and as the knife drank the life from the Ja'sid's blood, she drank the life from him also. And with it, his pain.

She cried out from the depths of her spirit until she was absolutely numb. She heard the body fall to the ground. And her contact with Vayhawk was broken.

Suddenly the shock of what had just happened overtook her. She drew a long, sobbing breath and shut her eyes again in a desperate and futile attempt to blot it out. She tried to rise, but fell, and clutched at a boulder to hold herself.

Another spasm of coughing shook her, and she couldn't get her breath. Again, she tried to get up, but her body had stopped functioning. Her brain struggled, but her muscles would not respond. She panicked, fighting for air.

Gentle hands took her and pulled her close. "Relax," he said. "Don't fight it. It'll come."

Senea clutched at him and gasped.

"Relax," he said, his voice close to her ear, and his arms went around her, drawing her against him.

Then she was crying, hoarse sobs that hurt just as much as the coughing had, and shamed her as well. His hand came up and gently pressed her cheek to his chest.

"You're all right, Senea. It just hurts. It'll go away in a little while."

Senea closed her eyes and forced herself to relax and let her lungs work naturally. She concentrated on the heartbeat that was thudding loudly in her ear, and soon she found it easier to breathe, even though the pain was still in her throat. The smell of sweat and woodsmoke surrounded her along with the smell of dust. The strength and warmth of Vayhawk's arms enclosed her, and she rested against him, face next to his fever-heat, her hand on his chest, his breath on her forehead.

Long silent minutes passed, long moments in which neither one of them moved. His arms were tight about her; his cheek against her brow; and he was the only thing that was real to her, a world apart from everything else. She closed her eyes and abandoned herself to that world.

Then, too soon, he stirred and his hands moved to her shoulders.

"I have to take care of the bodies and gather up the weapons."

But Senea stopped him. "Wait," she said, forcing her voice past the pain in her throat. "What was that that happened?"

He drew in a breath and took a long time to reply. "What do you think happened?"

"I don't know." Memories came flooding back. She swallowed with difficulty.

"I can't explain—it was a feeling, a fear—" And suddenly the words were out before she could stop them. "I could taste it, his life, his blood." She stopped with revulsion. "But that's impossible."

He shook his head. "No. That seems to be part of it."

An uneasy chill came up Senea's spine. "Part of it?" she echoed.

His dark eyes bore into hers. "It's important. It's proof that we're facing a power we don't know how to combat." With that he gently put her from him and rose to his feet.

"In the Held there are tales from long ago, mostly told by our elder helden. Rumors of things that were once done and then rejected. Almost everyone within the Held discounts them. Tales grow, and dark tales always grow the faster and the stronger. It's hard to tell what parts are true and what parts are not. And legends always have their special weapons. But if they are true the past will come looking for us, and if we are not prepared they will destroy us." He turned to look at her.

"It could be immeasurably dangerous. We have to find how to control it. I had only suspected the possibility that what happened here could be done."

"What did happen?" Senea asked with no more than a whisper.

"I used it to draw the life out of the Ja'sid."

Involuntarily Senea's eyes were pulled to the dead heldan. Somewhere at the depth of her she was shocked, even though she had already known it.

"No," she murmured, arguing with him in the silence. "No. It's ridiculous. It couldn't possibly happen like that . . . not that way. It was your knife cutting open his throat. It *couldn't* . . ."

"You don't believe it?" He looked at her soberly. "You know it happened. You felt it."

She could only return his stare. It was impossible, but true. She knew it, and he knew it.

"It's not impossible," he continued. "It's very possible. It happens when two come together—when they are close and have been together a while, and know how to direct it. And when blood and knife blade and hand come together, when the blood spills over the knife and the hand . . . that is when the power is the strongest."

"How do you know all of this?" she asked, the chill of his words causing her to shiver.

Vayhawk sank to his heels in front of her and took her hand in both of his. "I dreamed it . . . that it would be this way. And I had to play it through. I had to find out if there was any truth in it. If it was what these Black Ja'sid use against their victims, then we, too, must learn how to use it. It is the only way our Held and our held-tribe is going to survive.

"These Ja'sid always travel in pairs. Rarely are they ever found alone. Sometimes there are more than two, but almost never alone. We have been able to kill Black Ja'sid, but only after losing some of our own, and only after separating them. This is the first time that none of our own helden have been lost."

Senea looked sideways at the dead Ja'sid again.

"I have to take care of things," Vayhawk said.

She nodded. She continued to look at the body of the Ja'sid and recalled how Vayhawk had killed him in such anger. She had felt that anger in him. It had coursed clear through her, and she recalled it now of a sudden. She looked up as the Heldlan rose to his feet and strode to the dead body and stooped to pick it up. The morning sun blazed off the gold on his arm band.

Senea looked from it to him and wondered what had caused that terrible rage in him. She shivered.

CHAPTER FOURTEEN

She was asleep when she heard him come into the bunkroom; she rose and went with him, taking her weapons. She was concerned, for he did not come for her very often anymore, but waited outside the Held after sending for her.

She followed him now and in her heart there was misgiving. He took her arm and brought her up to walk beside him, and she looked up at his midnight-brown eyes and felt an unspoken something pass between them.

This silent feeling between them was happening a lot more often lately.

"Vayhawk," she whispered. "Is there anything wrong?"

"No," the Heldlan said. "We go to Roskel for assignment."

"Assignment?"

"This is the life of the Held," he answered.

It struck her with uncertainty.

The Held was quiet, the coming and going of the patrol change not yet beginning. There was a murmur of voices behind one door, a smell of cooking from the eating hall, and the muffled echo of their own footsteps in the corridor.

Roskel's bunkroom was at this end of the corridor, close to the exit, directly opposite Vayhawk's across the width of the Held. Inside it was the same, one bunk, a table, the room twice the size of the regular bunkrooms. On the table was spread a map, studded with small pieces of painted wood, arranged in groups and singly.

Roskel looked up from the parchment he was reading, bent his head slightly to Vayhawk, his eyes going expressionlessly to Senea, then back again. The Heldlan held out his hand palm up, revealing two more markers for the map: one white, one red and white. Roskel raised his eyebrows in surprise.

"You will take assignment, also?"

"For now," Vayhawk said.

Roskel looked once again at Senea as he evaluated her and calculated where to send them. She withstood the examination, knowing that he had been watching her closely from the day she entered the Held. He knew where her weaknesses and strengths were. At last, he nodded with an intake of air, took the markers from Vayhawk, and turned to the map.

"I'll send you northeast," he said. "We are weak on the Jas'po borders." He placed the two markers on the upper right-hand corner of the map, side by side. There were other markers there, maybe about twenty. Senea did not recognize any of the colors.

Roskel met the eyes of the Heldlan, and Vayhawk nodded, satisfied; but then Roskel's glance went to Senea.

"It is a long watch, heldii. A two days' journey there, if you don't sleep. Four if you do. A one-week watch at the border, back again to report, then do it again. Can you do this?"

Senea looked to Vayhawk and saw that he was watching her with the same intentness that Roskel did. She nodded and swung her eyes back to Roskel.

"I can do it."

Roskel nodded in acknowledgment. "I think that maybe you can." He stood.

"I will send runners to you," he said to Vayhawk, "to keep you informed. Any word to Aldived?"

"No. I have already talked to him."

"Very well." Roskel's eyes passed over Senea again. She felt his scrutiny, the assessing of her value to the Held, and she met his gaze directly. He nodded slightly to her, a gesture of respect that surprised her. She looked to Vayhawk and saw that he, too, had seen it.

"Heldii," Roskel said. "Bear yourself well. Yours is a double burden." And he inclined his head to Vayhawk in salute, and a look passed between them that Senea did not understand.

Vayhawk put a hand to Senea's back and directed her to the door. She stepped out into the corridor, almost fearing the eyes of him who was Heldlord, who had witnessed the honor that had been paid her. But the gaze that she found on her when she turned was warm with pride. She flushed and looked away.

Then stopped and stepped back unconsciously into the protection of Vayhawk's closeness.

Sky and Treyna came to a halt in the corridor, having just come in from patrol. The heldan put his hand to Treyna's arm and moved her to the other side of him so that he stood in between. His eyes flicked over Senea's face, took in how close she was standing to Vayhawk, then looked to Vayhawk with a mocking smile.

"Heldlan," he said in false salute.

"Sky," Vayhawk returned. "Treyna."

Treyna stiffened, then inclined her head to Vayhawk, her jaw tight and lips in an angry line. She glanced with animosity to Senea, then directed her attention back to Vayhawk.

The Heldlan said nothing further, but lightly touched Senea's back to propel her forward. She complied, feeling Treyna's eyes boring into her, and her skin contracted at that silent attack.

Another movement drew her attention, and she saw Yunab advance out of the shadows. His bright eyes flicked over her and Vayhawk, then he turned away before anything could be said to him and joined Sky and Treyna as they went down the corridor. Sky's hand went up and touched Treyna, drawing her closer to him, before they rounded the corner.

Several moments later, when they were outside the Held, Vayhawk said to her, "I think we have a problem there."

Senea eyed him questioningly. But he didn't elaborate, and she had to be content with that.

With a silent intake of air she followed him, saw in the dim light of early dawn the dark shadows of helden coming in from patrol; but on this day there was a difference, for she was almost one of them. She wasn't going with Vayhawk on Heldlan business, but was going instead as heldan on heldan business. And Vayhawk also becoming, for a time at least, one of them.

The unease the confrontation with Sky and Treyna had left in her stayed the while she walked behind Vayhawk as he led her toward the north. They skirted around the fields of the held-tribe. She smelled the air and felt the now-familiar early crispness of it, like some living thing.

She found herself looking toward the familiar places that she had seen and known all her life, knowing they were there someplace beyond in the dim light of dawn. She knew, also, that Vayhawk would not take her so close that she would be able to see them. There was excitement in her heart and an uncertainty in her stomach from the thoughts of spending at least two weeks away from the Held. Her senses, for some reason, were alive to the whole plain, the scents of the grasses, dry and sweet, the feel of the plain under her feet, hard in places, soft sand in other places.

The land of the Held, where she walked free. Unlike those of held-tribe.

She walked swiftly behind Vayhawk in the growing light of dawn along the bed of a dried-up stream, the rise of the bank on the left, a rocky ridge on the right. The stream was a natural path of stone, washed clean of dirt and sand from countless wet seasons, now baked hard from the hot days of the dry season. It was the habit of helden to walk in the depressions of the land.

She could forget about the Held out here, where there was only Vayhawk and herself. She could forget about Sky and Treyna, could forget about the Games, and could forget about what had happened between Treyna and herself. She could even forget for a time heldcode, because there was only Vayhawk and the land, and she was learning the ways of both.

The gold on Vayhawk's arm glared in the early morning sun. Its markings proclaimed him Heldlan, Heldlord of all the lands they crossed. Senea climbed behind him through a cleft on the left where the swell of land had been riven by years of floodwaters rushing to the stream below. She slid down the opposite side in a white powdering of dust and crossed the long slope of the upper land in his footsteps.

The day advanced, hot and sweltering. And toward midday there was a cluster of reeds growing like a mirage at the base of a cliff, pale green shafts with segments as long as a finger and as big around.

"Here is water," Vayhawk told her. "We will rest awhile."

He took his knife and with it cut a stem of reed from the cluster and handed it to Senea, then cut another.

He strode away from the reeds a good distance and waited for her while he broke a segment from the reed. Then he showed her how to twist it, breaking the outer shell, and put it to his mouth to suck away the moisture.

He settled to the ground in the shade with his back against the smooth stone of the cliff and motioned for her to sit also.

"Where there is water," he said, "there are predators. We will wait here and get more reeds when we leave."

Senea sat, looking warily for signs of waiting creatures. She could not see any, but she knew that did not mean they weren't there. The sweet moisture from the reed soothed her throat, and she leaned her head back and closed her eyes.

The silence of the sun-scorched plain, the oppressive heat, made her sleepy, and she dozed.

"Senea . . ."

The sound of her name on the soft roughness of Vayhawk's voice brought her eyes open.

The afternoon sun was lower in the sky and shone brightly in her face. She moved painfully. The heat had sapped the strength from her. Vayhawk dropped to his heels beside her. In his hand he held several reeds, moisture beading at the cut ends.

"We have to move," he said, the twilight shadows of his eyes looking soberly at her.

Senea nodded and tried to get to her feet. When she couldn't, Vayhawk rose and helped her to stand with a strong hand around her arm. He handed her a couple of reeds.

"Use them both," he said. "We'll get more." He strode away then, went to where the cluster of reeds stood and cut the rest of the slender stalks from the plant.

Senea followed slowly after him, sucking at the twisted reeds. He handed her more. Then she went with him along the base of the cliff and back up onto the open plain again.

It was a long walk. The afternoon lengthened. The sun sank to the horizon and grew to a fantastic size that filled half the sky behind them, yellow and warm. Windshift sprang up, moaned through an unseen gorge somewhere to the left, and ran along the ground tugging at the yellow grass that crunched underfoot.

And that night, and all the next day, and the next, they traveled northeast.

The windshift sprang up. Gusts of sand swirled before where Senea lay, stinging her face. There were patterns in the sand, tracks of tiger lizards, birds, desert rats, and sand beetles. Circles and semicircles of white sand where the wind whipped the grasses back and forth, halfway around and back again.

From the crest of the dune flew a constant spray of fine sand. Senea, on her belly on the edge of the dune, her back to the wind, peered at the world before her.

Steeply sloping ledges extended far away into the distances as precarious steps between successive cliff faces. Canyon after canyon after canyon, all merging together, opened up on each other in a great maze that did not seem to have an end. Senea looked for a long time at that tremendous expanse of rock sculpture, wind and dust and emptiness.

The sun touched the skyline behind her, merged with it for a moment in a final explosive blaze of light and heat, and sank out of sight. The gray shadows of the canyon walls advanced across the canyon floors, moved up to muffle everything. A wave of cooling relief apart from the windshift that was like a separate movement of air washed across the dune where Senea was. Each flurry of wind shrouded her in coarse and sandy dust that stung and swirled grittily in her face. The canyons no longer looked gray, but blue-gray with the softness of evening.

There was a movement at her side as Vayhawk edged up next to her. He scanned the shadowed canyons, taking a long breath and then exhaling softly.

"What do you think?" he asked, casting her a sidelong glance.

Senea shook her head, unable to put into words her awe of that vastness.

"The Jas'po hold it all as far as the eye can see in any direction. They rarely seem to have reason to leave it."

"I can see why," Senea murmured, thinking of all the game and water that would be in abundance there.

"This is the easiest watch that we have."

Senea looked at him with a sudden suspicion, and she didn't like what she was thinking, that Roskel had sent them to the easiest watch because she was heldii to the Heldlan. Suddenly it all seemed like political favoritism.

Vayhawk returned her gaze steadily and watched the expressions on her face with practiced closeness, and she wasn't surprised when he turned his head to look over the darkening canyons and began to speak.

"Roskel is the Held's second. It is his to run the Held, to make the assignments, to do the disciplining, to see that all is running smoothly and efficiently. Then, I am freed to go where

I am most needed." He looked at her again, his eyes dark like twilight.

"I could not do what I do without him."

Senea looked back at him, felt the closeness of him, both in his words and in proximity. The *Heldlan*—it came to her again—to whom she was paired. Almost like a marriage, that pairing. He had taken her, taught her, and for the past several weeks had been her constant companion, except for those times when he left on his errand that was still as mysterious as it had been at the beginning. And since that time when he had promised that there would be no more distractions between them, and especially after their run-in with the Ja'sid who had nearly strangled her, he had held himself slightly distant, a desert warmth that circled around her yet was held away, never approaching too near.

She looked at him now and felt his arm against hers, the band of gold pressed lightly into her skin, and she felt the magnetic lure of him. His presence was like a white-hot heat fanning her, and she was acutely aware of him. And she felt it like before, an energy force created by the touching of flesh, a something that slithered forward in a blur and wrapped itself around them although there was no sound and no movement. The Ja'sid power.

"If Roskel sent us here, it is because he needs us here." Vayhawk's voice broke through her thoughts and brought her back to the present.

He rose to his feet, and the power that had surrounded them broke apart in a silent fizzle. "Come. Let's see if you remember what you've been taught."

Senea got up slowly and eyed him warily.

"Go on," Vayhawk said. "I'm just going to watch."

And Senea reluctantly waded back through the soft sand toward the rocks. Looking quickly around in the swiftly gathering dusk, she found a place where the rocks jutted up and over a sandy impression. She went to it and inspected it quickly for signs of the yellow snake that liked to lair in such places. Finding the sand smooth and unmarked, she began to gather weeds from the sun-dried scrubs that grow around in the cracks and fissures of the rocks. Shortly she had a small fire burning, hidden in a small hole and behind a screen of boulders.

She looked up expectantly then and Vayhawk came to her

and sank to his heels, put out a hand to the fire. His eyes centered on her.

"Food?" he asked, his expression saying, *Where is it?*

Senea blinked. She only knew how to hunt waterfowl.

Vayhawk reached out a hand and turned over a flat stone that was at the base of the wall that rose up and over them. With his knife he gently probed the sand where the stone had been. There was a tiny burst of sand, and a slurry of a many-legged creature slightly larger than Vayhawk's thumb. With a deft move the Heldlan killed it, his knife flashing forward, severing the forebody from the back. The legs, all coming from a single point on the front half, vibrated in death-spasm. Two deadly pincerlike claws fell open, and lay limp on the sand.

Senea stared at the glistening yellow creature with revulsion. It was a spider like none she'd ever seen before. Vayhawk picked up the front half and tossed it in the fire.

"I think you will find more," he said, an amused lift at one corner of his mouth. "It is best to find them all anyway. Their sting is venomous. You clear this place of them, and I'll be right back."

"Where you are going?"

"To find the rest of supper."

And he chuckled good-naturedly at her open horror, then stood up in a fluid motion to stride away into the dark. Senea stared after him a moment before she could make herself move.

She looked around the place she had chosen as shelter with distaste, seeing now the rocks, large and small, that she had not noticed before. Shuddering, she picked one up. She didn't even have to probe with her knife, because a yellow cluster of legs darted toward her knees. She choked on a half-stifled cry and stopped the creature with her knife, severing the body into halves—more clumsily than Vayhawk had—but she did it. With the blade of the knife she flicked the legs into the fire, and grimaced. It was another long moment before she could pick up another rock. By the time Vayhawk had returned she had found four more.

He squatted and tossed a dead yellow snake to the sand in front of her. "Clean this, and I'll show you how to cook it."

Senea looked up at him. He was watching her with an amused gleam in his eyes. She looked down again at the snake, a rope of golds and yellows shining softly in the dim firelight, beautiful, but deadly.

She drew in a breath; well, this was better than spiders.

Quickly, she cut along the snake's underside and slipped out the entrails, put them aside to bury, then sat back and watched as Vayhawk put the spider bodies inside the cavity she had just cleaned, lining them up side by side. He then draped the snake over the two forked sticks that he had pushed into the sand on either side of the fire.

"Now we wait," he said, moving to lean against a boulder, his shadowed eyes regarding her across the fire, then motioning with his hand. "It's your watch."

Senea hesitated before she inclined her head and went out into the night. She climbed the dune and sat on its crest, hugging her knees to her. She watched the moon come up, a slice of silver giving little light. The windshift had died away, leaving a warm night that was close and enveloping. Senea stared into the blackness that was the canyon maze of the Jas'po and wondered what good she was doing on the top of a cliff when the Jas'po were so far below.

Leaning her chin on her knee she listened to the distant howl of a wolfhound and was glad that it was not close. It died away to silence, the night chirping of the sand beetles the only sound. She was content thereafter to watch the stars in the sky and the moon that rose. After a time there was a whisper of sand behind her, and Vayhawk came to sit beside her.

He handed her a chunk of cooked meat off the end of his knife, cleaned the knife in the sand, and slid it back into its sheath.

Senea tasted a small nibble, expecting the snake to be horrible, but it was surprisingly good, and she ate it hungrily, tossing the small rib bones over the cliff when she was finished. She cleaned her hand in the sand, glanced at the dark figure of Vayhawk, and found him watching her, his face shadowed and featureless.

She also *felt* him. The force of his personality reached out across the gulf between them and touched her like a phantom hand. She suddenly felt more naked than naked, as if she had been caught in the middle of some treacherous thought. She turned her head abruptly and looked away from him. The miles and the desert canyons stretched on forever.

"It is beautiful, is it not? The emptiness of it, the silence."

Irony was totally absent from his voice. He had seen her admiration of the landscape; there was not much that ever passed his notice.

"Yes," she said. Then, to change the subject, she asked, "Why did Aldived let you come out here on patrol? Aren't you needed more watching the Ja'sid?"

"Roskel will send a runner if there's anything that I should know. And Aldived agreed with my reasons for doing this."

Senea looked at him in surprise. "You talked him into this?"

Vayhawk shifted so that he was more directly facing her. "Aldived knows everything that is going on. We discussed this side trip and the reasons for it. We both decided that the time was right for it to be done.

"Do not be taken in by Aldived's act of indifference, Senea. He sees a lot more than he seems to. There is a lot more to him than there appears to be. And when he makes his move there will be many helden who are going to be caught unaware. Several will discover that they have made a terrible mistake in underestimating him."

Senea studied his face in the moonlight. For some reason her whole being was awake, totally sensitive and aware of him, just a few inches away from her. Her mind caught hold of something that he said and focused intently on it.

"Why are we here?" she asked. "What is the time right for?"

"We thought it was time to explore just what can be done with this power thing."

That sounded like a question. She realized the drift of his thoughts. Vayhawk looked up, and she felt the shock of his gaze hit her like a live coal.

She felt as if the ground were falling away beneath her. "A test—?" She tried to gather something to say, but words were beyond her. For a moment the world about her had turned dark, without any moon or stars, and the dune and sky seemed to sway. When they steadied again she became aware that Vayhawk was still talking, though at first the words were no more than a jumble of meaningless sounds.

"Do you want to find out why heldcode exists?" he was saying. "At least some of it?"

Senea turned her head and stared down into the canyons at the silver shadows, the blue-black shadows, the vibrations of dust motes in the air across the lip of the dune. Her mind was filled suddenly with feline prudence. She was certain that he already knew what was going to happen, that he was using this to put another tie around her and bind her even tighter to him. And she felt the need to protest.

"This power, won't it harm us if we don't know what we're doing?"

"Harm? Well . . ." There was an odd emotion in his voice. "Not harm, no. Not in any usual sense. It just means that we have to learn how to be much more aware of each other than we have been. We have to learn what the boundaries are. Learn what can be done and what cannot be done, the precautions we'll have to take."

"This thing seems to happen just from two bodies touching. Why haven't the helden known about it before now? Why haven't the villagers?"

"They did, a long time ago."

Senea looked at him with surprise. "The tales you were talking about?"

He nodded. "Many generations ago, our helden had this power and knew how to use it. Then they rejected it and set out to destroy it."

"But why? If without it we are not as strong?"

"The honest answer is I don't know. But I think I can guess. It's not too difficult to understand. It's extremely hard to control. Once you've learned how to tap into it, it just comes and then you have to direct it. And it's extremely difficult just being a heldan. I think they found it easier to keep the two separate and not try for both at one time. Then somehow heldcode kept the power away until it was forgotten, and no one knew anything more than tales. But the Ja'sid never forgot. That we know for certain. And they set some of their helden apart to become very proficient with it. The Black Ja'sid."

Senea clenched her hands together. The past rose up like a haunted demon inexplicably to confront her.

"Well, shall we find out why they said that lovers could not be paired on patrol?" His voice was low.

She looked up at him with a startled shock. "What?"

He laughed softly, and moved, forsaking the shadows like a wraith, pulled her to him with a strong hand.

"Relax," he instructed, an undertone of amusement in his voice. "Let it take control."

He leaned over her and his hand brushed her face. Suddenly

she felt he was smothering her; she was becoming engulfed in the warmth of him, still herself but also part of him. It was as if he didn't just touch her skin, but touched her deep inside, deep in her mind, deep in herself. He owned her every nerve, every heartbeat. She couldn't resist him. It was a sudden flash of recognition, of absolute knowing, a spark that exploded through her, a burst of heat. There was a force that was created when the two of them came together. It was the combining of their strength to create something even stronger, and it reached out and would have pulled any other strength that it found into itself. It had the potential to grow within itself until it completely consumed them.

Then suddenly the contact she had with Vayhawk was gone. The force shattered, tearing through her, and fled in shock waves that gradually gentled, rippled, and faded to the corners of the canyons and were absorbed by the air.

And when Vayhawk moved away, she was left with only the deep gaze of his dark eyes. She was too weak to move.

"That's why there are no kin-ties," Vayhawk said in a quiet voice. "Strong emotions make the force more powerful. I'm guessing that originally heldcode was meant to stop marriages among the helden. The power created by such pairings was too difficult to control. But through the generations, heldcode grew until it became what we have today."

She heard what he said: strong emotions made the power stronger. She met his gaze and knew he meant that the emotions between the two of them had become strong enough for him to make the attempt. He had been waiting until the time was right. Aldived had been waiting. They had calculated this from the very beginning. At least Vayhawk had. And Aldived had agreed to it.

She saw that he had followed her thoughts as they crossed her face, and challenge darkened his already moon-shadowed eyes. He was daring her to protest his use of her in this method. She stared back, feeling a little sick, but mostly angry, and flung his dare back at him. Whatever he dealt to her, she could take, and without comment.

He smiled and then his face was a mask, closed to her; she could read nothing.

"How did you know it would be this way?"

"I dreamed it. About the Ja'sid, about the power . . . and about you."

But that was all he was going to tell her. She waited for him to say something more, but he didn't. Her hands clenched unconsciously at her sides until the nails became painful in her palms.

Like a steel band, his hand closed about her wrist and tightened very slightly . . . But it was not a remonstration . . . It was a silent request for understanding. Senea slowly reached out her own hand and touched the back of his wrist. Her anger disappeared, totally, between one breath and the next.

"I will watch for a while," he said. "You go get some sleep."

Senea drew in an unwilling breath, suddenly wanting to stay where it was so peaceful, but she murmured assent and rose to her feet. She stood a moment looking out over the blackness that was a void beginning a short distance from her feet and stretching out into forever.

"Senea . . ." His hand went gently around the calf of her leg, and she looked down with a start. "Go get some sleep. It will be here later." The faint rasp of his voice came to her like the whisper of sand running across desert stone. She stepped back away from him, wondering that he had been so sensitive to her mood. Turning away, she left the dune, going to where the fire was only a bed of coals. The remainder of the snake still hung on a stick nearby.

She settled down where the sand had not been packed, placed her bow and quiver where they were in easy reach. She lay back then, with a hand behind her head, and looked at the points of lights in the dark sky.

There was a touch on her arm that moved up to her shoulder, a light brush becoming more substantial as it gently shook her awake. The dark figure of Vayhawk looked down on her.

"Your watch."

Senea stirred, took up her bow and quiver, and went out again to the dune. There she sat trying to banish the sleep that clung to her. The crescent moon was riding low in the west now, the night chill well advanced past midnight. Vayhawk had apparently let her sleep half the night, if not longer. She flexed her leg muscles, trying to take the languor out of them, sat cross-legged, and yawned.

An unexpected sound brought her head round, straining to hear beyond the sand beetles. After a moment she heard it again, a faint scraping on stone. The signal of her Held. She rose, sleep forgotten, looked in the dark toward the sound, back past where Vayhawk was, and to the left. Taking her knife in her hand, she moved silently down the dune and around the rocks, and stopped to listen. She saw it before she heard it, a movement of black shadow merging into another. She froze and hissed at the shadow a warning as it fronted her and became a figure that she could not see clearly.

"Messenger for Vayhawk," a voice she did not recognize said.

"Who sent you?" she asked, suddenly realizing that if there was a password, she didn't know it.

"Roskel."

"Very well. Wait here," she said, making the only decision she could. She turned and slipped quietly away and went around the rocks, looking quickly behind her to see if the shadow had followed. She saw nothing. After waiting a moment longer to make certain he hadn't followed, she stole into the seclusion of the temporary camp, went to Vayhawk, and put a hesitant hand on his arm, feeling the warmth of his skin and the hardness of smooth muscle.

"Vayhawk," she murmured.

He sat up at once, his hand taking hold of her arm.

"There is someone here. He says he's a messenger."

Vayhawk looked past her to the opening in the rocks, an intense glance that she sensed even though she could not see it.

"Where?"

"I left him on the other side of the rocks. I did not know him."

Vayhawk stood, picking up his bow and quiver. "Go back to the dune. I'll find him."

Senea nodded and followed him out of the rocks, then walked up the soft sand of the dune to sit and clasp her arms around her knees while she worried about what was going on. The morning sun was sending up shafts of light from behind the horizon when Vayhawk finally returned.

He came up the sand dune to sit beside her and looked out over the canyons that were purple depths of shadow. His thoughts were very far away. Absently, he gathered up a handful of sand and let it run through his fingers. Senea watched him apprehensively and knew before he spoke that he was going to leave her alone again for his mysterious errand. She knew the signs very well by now.

"The report was not good," he said. "The Ja'sid are moving in force—west and north. We're going to have a fight on our hands turning them back." He looked at her with a frown. "I cannot stay."

"Should I go with you?"

"No." He shook his head. "I'll be back for you."

She was about to protest, but the expression on his face stopped her.

"You stay here. You are on patrol assignment . . . until Roskel says otherwise. I cannot overrule that." He raised a hand and touched her face lightly, then drawing in a breath through his nostrils, he lowered it again. "I will be back."

His brown-black eyes lingered on hers and set her heart to beating painfully. He rose then and went down the dune, went quickly around the rocks, and out of sight.

Senea sat a short time looking at where Vayhawk had disappeared around the stand of rocks, indecision and impulse warring within her. She thought about the force of power that had been created between them when he had touched her and knew that he would need her.

Then she was on her feet, going to the temporary camp, impulsiveness becoming purpose. She took the snake that still hung on the forked stick, stuffed it into her side pouch, kicked sand over the cold fire coals, and started after Vayhawk.

Anxiously as she walked she scanned the plain ahead of her and found the faint traces that led due west. Wherever he was going, it was in the same area where he had left her that first time. She walked steadily—though keeping her pace slower so she would not catch up to him. She was disobeying him and knew that it could mean discipline in front of the Held, and reduced status. She stopped for a few minutes, fighting indecision again.

She should turn back.

But she bit her lip, determinedly feeling a slight surge of quickening power within her just at the thought of him, and she went on.

It was madness, what she was doing; she could not hope to go undiscovered. Vayhawk would eventually become aware of her; yet still, she did not turn back. She was driven by something that she did not understand. She kept to his trail, following along the dried streams where she could see the long, hurried stretch of his stride.

Each time that she had to cross over a ridge between the troughs of the plain she scanned ahead fearfully, expecting to see him, but never did. Then, eventually she became confident that she would not catch up to him, that his pace greatly outdistanced hers, and she was relatively safe from discovery.

She rested in snatches whenever she could go no farther, sleeping at times when she did stop. Once she found a cluster of reeds and added them to her pouch. When night came, she kept due west, knowing that Vayhawk would not stop. She followed the stars that he had taught her to go by, reckoning their turning in the sky as the night passed. Sometime the following day she noticed that Vayhawk's pace slackened, the strides shortened. She slowed up and continued thereon with caution. The farther she went the more stealthy and cautious she saw that the Heldan had become, and she followed suit.

Then in the very late afternoon she heard low voices. She stopped, dropped down to a crouch, and edged up to the top of the crest, finally inching forward on her stomach. She raised her head slowly and peered through a low-growing scrub, looking down into a depression between two hills.

Vayhawk was with a group of six helden. He sat on his heels, with his knife in hand, scratching something into the hard soil. He spoke in a voice that did not carry very far, his words unintelligible. His hand moved and included all of them in a gesture that then pointed briefly in the direction of the Ja'sid lands. Another heldan spoke, his voice raised in anger; a third motioned him to silence. The third heldan then spoke to Vayhawk, in slow measured tones that Vayhawk listened to closely.

Suddenly Senea ceased to try to make out the words and stared at the clothing that the helden around Vayhawk wore.

Dark brown! Not dusty green or yellow.

And arm bands of silver! Helden of another held-tribe!

It stunned, and Senea stared, disbelieving her own eyes, because Vayhawk would not do what she was watching him do. He would never break heldcode. Never. Never. Never!

Suddenly grief and disappointment overwhelmed her, and she stifled a sob with her arm and hid her face against the ground. For long, painful minutes she lay thus, reckoning with what she had witnessed, trying, but not succeeding in understanding what he was doing. There was an explanation, she knew, but could not think of it. She could only think of the consequences of what he was doing. Death. Death. *Death!*

She looked up at last, wiped the tears from her face, and watched as Vayhawk stood and shook hands with a heldan in dark brown. The sun winked silver off that heldan's arm.

Another glare of reflected sun caught her eyes.

Yellow gold! Across the depression on the opposite hill!

Senea raised up to look over the low scrub behind which she lay; her heart constricted in sudden alarm. Someone else watched. There was a movement, and a face raised to look at her across that way.

Sky. It was Sky! She stared at him in horror and knew at once what he was going to do.

He raised a hand to his brow, in mock acknowledgment, then turned and disappeared over the ridge.

Senea leapt to her feet with a cry.

Froze.

She saw the helden below turn.

Saw Vayhawk look up at her in surprise. And she saw that surprise turn to anger.

"Oh, no," she whimpered, fear of him and fear for him mixing together in an all-consuming emotion she could not face. She stepped back, staring at his angry face.

Then she turned and ran.

His voice brought her eyes around.

Then he was running up the hill after her.

Crying out with fear and something else she couldn't identify, she leapt over a boulder and slid down the other side of the hill.

She darted around a small cliff and ran along a dry, dusty streambed that was strewn with white rocks.

But she knew she'd never be able to outrun him.

Coming up short, she came to a dead end, where the ancient stream had carved out a waterfall. It was a ledge of rock and hard desert mud-mortar baked together by the heat.

She whirled and cast around frantically for a way out. She was boxed in, ridges riding on both sides of the streambed.

Vayhawk came to a skidding stop around the small cliff.

"Senea!"

In desperation she tried to run past him. He caught her. She pulled away.

"No," she sobbed, whirled and ran; she couldn't believe she was running from him.

He swore and sprung after her. He caught her again and brought her to her knees. She tore herself loose, scrambling for her feet.

He brought her down again and threw his body over hers, pinning her to the ground.

Sobbing hysterically she struggled against him; she struck at him.

His hands grabbed at her wrists and jerked them outward. His eyes blazed into hers, and his breathing was hard.

"What are you doing here?" His voice was a low growl. "I told you to stay where you were!"

Senea looked up at him, at his eyes that were black with fury. She was unable to answer . . . what could she answer?

There was a lingering space; then Vayhawk swore softly and bent his head so that his cheek was against hers: touching, almost caressing.

"Senea," he whispered, her name shivering along her jaw. "Do you know what you've done? I wanted to keep you out of this." His hand moved out over hers and clasped it, brought it to his chest, and held it there.

Senea closed her eyes. "Why?"

Her voice trembled. It was barely more than a whisper. Unconsciously she turned her face to him, the corner of her mouth against his skin.

He exhaled, a breath of air on her neck that caressed, and his face moved against hers, slow, intimate, and began to turn to her. But then he released her and pushed himself up to his feet.

"Come." He reached down for her hand. "You're going back to the Held."

"You're taking me to Roskel?" She asked in sudden fear.

"No. I can't do that. This meeting must remain secret."

"Then what are you going to do?"

"I'm turning you over to Mara."

"No!" She snatched her hand back.

His eyes flashed and he bent, taking her hand, and forcefully pulled her to her feet. "I'm trying to stop a war, and I can't be worried about you getting into trouble. You broke heldcode, girl. Do you know that?"

"Yes."

"I can't take you to Roskel, because I'm under secret orders from Aldived. But I can't let this go, you know I can't."

Senea looked up with a start at his words. "Aldived sent you here?" And she thought back about what he had said about the Tribelord, that Aldived knew everything that was going on.

Vayhawk frowned. "Yes."

"Oh, no," she whispered. Suddenly she saw Yunab's hand in this though she didn't know where the suspicion came from.

"What is it?"

"Sky was there. I saw him. Watching you, on the other side."

Vayhawk's eyes narrowed. "You are certain? It was Sky?"

"Yes. He saw me, too."

Vayhawk stepped away from her with a curse and stood regarding her with a dark gaze that froze the breath in her lungs.

Then he came back to her and took her shoulders tightly in his hands.

"Go back to the Held. Keep an eye on him." Then he continued, with an urgency that shook her.

"Make time for me, Senea. I must complete what I am doing. The safety of our held-tribe is at stake. If I have to face charges because of it later, then so be it. But I need time to finish what I have started. Can you do that for me?" He looked at her, searching her face. "Will you?"

Senea stared at him in fear. "Yes, of course . . ."

"Good." His hands slid quickly down her arms and took her fingers in his. "Go quickly."

He turned then and strode away, and she heard him start to run once he rounded the bend of the stream.

She drew in a sudden breath and ran her hands up her arms, shuddering in reaction.

It had happened so fast.

One moment she was running out of terror from him, the next she was in collusion with him.

She raised a hand to where his face had been against hers,

recalling the warmth of him. Then she remembered the surge of power that had happened between them when they had struggled against each other, and the growing heat of energy that held them as they laid in the dirt together. The cords that bound her to him were becoming so strong they'd never be broken.

CHAPTER
FIFTEEN

Senea entered the Held in late afternoon.

Her first stop was Roskel's room.

Noting the surprise on his face when he opened the door to her knock she said, "Vayhawk sent me back . . . with a special assignment." She had rehearsed that speech for the whole of the journey as she came in so that she would not have to say overly much.

Roskel considered her a moment, then stepped back to let her in. She went hesitantly to the table and glanced at the map, then turned to face him as he closed the door.

"Is it something I should know about?" he asked as he crossed the room to his chair. He sat and leaned back on two legs regarding her.

The question took her aback, and her eyes faltered guiltily before his. Quickly she made herself look up again. "Vayhawk did not say."

Roskel watched her with that analyzing gaze of his, reading her sudden nervousness and her reluctance to answer. She flushed and swallowed uncomfortably. He knew that she was concealing something.

She sensed that there was very little he did not pick up on, and what got past him did so because he let it.

"Do you have anything to report about the Jas'po?"

"No."

She did not add that neither Vayhawk nor she stayed at the border long enough to have seen anything.

He nodded then, and reaching over took up her marker from the map. Vayhawk's had already been removed. He eyed her as he rolled the marker back and forth in his fingers. And Senea thought that he would ask more. She prepared herself to make what evasions she could, thinking that it would be best if Vayhawk gave the answers.

But he put the marker down with an imperceptible sigh. "Very well, heldii. You're dismissed."

An instant it did not register, then she inclined her head to him, murmured something that did not make sense, turned on her heel, and went to the door.

"Heldii . . ."

Senea stopped, her hand on the latch, and looked over her shoulder at him.

"Vayhawk will probably be gone for several days. If you need anything, I am here."

Senea returned his gaze with surprise. "Thank you."

He nodded to her, then, "Good day, heldii."

She returned the gesture and murmured, "Good day."

Going out into the hall, she stood a moment wondering what he had meant by that and wondered if Sky had said anything to him. But she dismissed that thought. After three days by herself, while coming into the Held, she had come up with her own suspicions of who Sky would be reporting to. And when she found him a short time later in the eating hall with Yunab she wasn't a bit surprised.

They looked up the moment she came through the door, and it was too late to retreat. Drawing in a quick breath she walked around the tables to the firehearth, trying to appear casual, thinking that her best course would be to bluff it out.

She was far from being hungry, but since she had come into the eating hall, she had to play the game. She went into the room behind the ovens, picked up a partially cut loaf of meal-bread, and returned to a table close to the hearth. As she tore the loaf in half, she saw that both Sky and Yunab were coming toward her. Keeping the fear off her face, she nodded in deference as they sat down, murmured, "Heldan, Counselor."

"Heldii," Yunab said in return.

Senea met his gaze with what she hoped was a mild curiosity, seeing the undisguised menace in his eyes.

"You are recovered, heldii?" he asked, the tone of his voice mocking. "Your wound has healed? Your rib?"

"Yes, thank you. It does not trouble me much anymore."

Yunab's eyes swung to Sky. "That would explain it, Heldan."

"Yes, indeed it would," Sky replied, and he smiled with open malice.

Senea looked at them and met their accusing gazes with misgivings that she did not allow to her face. "What would it explain?" she asked as calmly as she could.

"Your swift trip back to the Held," Sky said. "I had not thought you capable of it. I mean . . . your rib, and all." He leaned back in his chair and crossed his arms across his chest. "But then, you had a reason for haste. Too bad it was for nothing. You are too late."

Senea stared at him and felt the familiar anger begin to stir, but she held it down forcefully. This was not the time for emotions; this was the time for clear thinking. Vayhawk's life depended on it. Her life depended on it.

She had to stall for more time. Vayhawk depended on her to get it for him.

"Heldii," Yunab said, "you say nothing."

She looked at him perforce and met the open threat on his pallid face and forced herself to answer. "I'm afraid that I do not know what he means."

Silent glances went between them, and Senea watched with apprehension.

"You have been wise," Yunab said, "to always keep to the Heldlan's side. But this time it may cost you. If you do not report what you and Sky both saw, you will be held responsible along with Vayhawk. I don't think loyalty means jeopardizing your life for a traitor."

"Traitor?" She stared at him and was barely able to keep the horror off her face.

"Any heldan who meets with enemy helden is a traitor. It is heldcode, which you should be very familiar with by now. But if you don't report what you saw . . . what Sky saw . . . that our Heldlan has been engaged in this very thing of collaboration with the enemy, and make the two witnesses, then you, too, are culpable."

"Make the two witnesses?" Senea asked, her interest suddenly caught.

"It takes two witnesses to accuse the Heldlan," Sky said, and added almost as an afterthought, "heldcode."

He watched her as she realized what he had said—that without her corroboration he could make no accusation. Triumphant relief raced through her, and she hesitated only a moment when she saw amusement on his face.

Turning to Yunab, she said, "Forgive me, Counselor. I don't know what you're talking about. I did see Sky but he was alone, and I was alone. Vayhawk wasn't there. And I certainly didn't see any helden from another held-tribe. If I had, I would have reported it to Roskel." She looked at Sky, held her gaze steady. "I made no such report."

There was a slow smile that came across the heldan's mouth, and he nodded to her in acknowledgment of defeat. But then he asked, "Are you calling me a liar?"

Senea shrugged, feigning casual indifference. "I had not used the word."

"No," Sky replied. "But that is what you meant."

"Did I? That was very rash of me."

"Very."

Senea eyed him warily, not understanding his apparent lack of concern, wondered what sort of trap she had fallen into.

Yunab stood up, his black eyes seething. "Heldii." His voice was deathly quiet. "I'd reconsider if I were you, or your career is going to be very short. The Heldlan's days are numbered, and you, my dear, could suffer the same end that will be his if you are not more prudent." He paused then and looked at her with insulting closeness.

"But then, I don't expect you to be so wise. I'm sure that being heldii to the Heldlan has its compensations that you might consider worth the risk." He leaned forward in the attitude of sharing a confidence. "Might I suggest that you take another look at Sky? He, too, can be . . . exciting." His voice purred with insinuation.

Senea stared at him, going cold all over. She glanced at Sky involuntarily, expecting to see a leering grin, but was met with a dark look of fire that alarmed her. She stared at him, her breast heaving with her struggle for breath. His smoldering look grazed over her mouth and rose to her eyes. She watched that graze with a chill.

The door across the room swung open and closed again.

"Yunab," Roskel's voice broke the silence that had descended around the table, thick, heavy and black. "I had not been informed that you were here."

Senea sensed that Yunab turned and moved toward the Held-second. But she could not pull her eyes away from Sky;

she felt the heat of his gaze and sweat trickled down her side. Then she was flung back to herself with a shock when he looked away.

"My apologies," Yunab said silkily. "I did not send word to you. My business was with this heldan, here."

Sky rose and strode to Yunab's side.

Senea closed her eyes and sank back in the chair.

"Is there something I can help you with?"

"It is all taken care of," Yunab said. "But if I do need further assistance, I'll call you."

There was a silence that Senea barely noticed and then movement as they left. She put her face to her hands, leaning on the table. Again and again she heard in her mind Yunab's words, saw the dark look on Sky's face, and felt her own horror at what she saw.

"Senea."

She looked up with a start, then relaxed when she saw that it was Roskel.

"What has been going on here?" He sat down in the chair next to her, his light brown gaze serious. "What did Yunab want?"

"I don't know," she choked, not wanting to tell him any of the encounter.

"He was threatening you?"

She nodded. "I think so." She pushed back a loose strand of hair and knew that she could not say very much that would give Roskel any clues about what was going on.

He watched her with a frown. "This has something to do with why Vayhawk sent you back?"

Senea nervously took up a chunk of the bread that was on the table and tore it in half.

"It involves Sky and Yunab," Roskel continued. He did not ask her to confirm it. "If you're in trouble, Senea, I can help. Yunab is a dangerous man to deal with alone." His voice was grave. "Can you tell me anything?"

"No." She shook her head and looked up.

He regarded her a moment, then nodded. "All right. But know this, I am on Vayhawk's side . . . always. I can be trusted."

Senea returned his gaze and wondered how much he had guessed—what it was that he was suspecting. He rose then and held her eyes for a breath before he turned and strode away.

Senea sat still awhile in the silence and gathered her composure. Then rising, she discarded the bread, and went out to find Sky again.

She found him out in the compound where he was teaching Treyna wrestling moves. Senea stopped in the shadow of a doorway where she couldn't be seen and she watched. After a few minutes she leaned against the wall and hugged her arms to herself, running a hand up to her shoulder.

There was a change in Treyna. It was very evident.

No longer the timid, frightened girl that she had once been, Treyna now applied herself to the training with a determination that bordered on ferocity. There was anger in every move that she made. And Sky seemed to be feeding it, whether with coaxing or badgering, Senea could not tell. But it was plain that they were becoming a team that no one would want to come up against.

It was just as plain that they had become more than trainer and heldii. It was in the looks that passed between them and in the familiarity of their touching each other. Senea wondered at it as she recalled the way that Sky had looked at her and knew that there was going to be trouble because of it.

She watched them through the last long hours of the day as the sun lowered to the horizon, set, and dusk deepened.

Twice she looked around and saw Roskel watching her from the door of his bunkroom. She stared back at him the first time, unsure why he watched her. He nodded to her and turned away into his room. The second time, as she returned his gaze, two helden came in between and when they had passed her, his door was closed.

Later she followed Sky and Treyna to the eating hall and sat across the room while they ate. She listened with half an ear to the helden at the next table talk about the Ja'sid and speculate on whether they would come across the borders in force or not.

The talk caused her thoughts to turn to Vayhawk, out on the Ja'sid borders. No word had reached the Held yet about what was happening out there. She was worried about what Vayhawk was doing that she had to make time for. It was something that Sky could ruin, even yet. She felt it with a prescience of forewarning—that he could yet bring about catastrophe for them all.

She watched as Sky leaned forward and raised a hand to
Treyna's face. Whatever game he was playing . . . Senea could
not finish the thought. He sat back again and took a bite of
grain-bread. Whatever game he was playing, Treyna was
firmly entrenched in it. He reached out across the table and
took her hand, his fingers going between hers.

Whatever game he was playing, it boded ill for Vayhawk.

Senea watched as Treyna smiled. Suddenly, not able to
watch it anymore, Senea got up and left to wait in the hall.

It was only a short time before they came.

The laughter died out of Treyna's face, and her eyes fixed
on Senea as if they would swallow her, or bore through her.
There was a long pause while she stared back into Treyna's
eyes. This was definitely not the frightened girl that had come
into the Held several weeks ago. In her place was a young
woman whose icy stillness and control were almost frightening.

Sky put an arm around Treyna. "Come. We don't need to
concern ourselves with traitors."

Something flickered in Treyna's eyes, and she turned, looking away, affecting not to be interested any further by Senea's
presence, and she went with Sky down the dimly lit corridor.

The word *traitors* hung in the air like a tangible thing, and
Senea considered it with slowly rising anger. She did not know
what Vayhawk was doing, but she did know that he was not a
traitor. His only concern was the safety of the Held and the
held-tribe. And he was sacrificing himself to ensure that safety.

She stared out onto the dark compound through the door she
had waited by. Suddenly she felt the need to tell someone, to
make them understand what Vayhawk was doing. She thought
of Roskel, but did not know what his reaction would be. For
a fraction of a second she stood uncertain. Then she made herself discard the impulse. It was impulse that had put her where
she was now, and she could not succumb to it again. Turning
with determination she followed at a distance as Sky and
Treyna continued along the corridor.

A few minutes later she was sitting where she could watch
the door to Sky's bunkroom unobtrusively and without it being
obvious which door she was watching. She rested her aching
head against the frame of a door that opened up onto the compound, hoping the breeze would enter enough to cool her. The
heat of the well-advanced dry season had turned the corridor

into an oven, and she only now realized how wearing it had been on her. Ignoring the curious stares of two female helden she didn't know, she drew her knees up and wrapped her arms around them, prepared to stay a long time.

The night was half gone when she heard quiet footsteps coming toward her. Roskel settled beside her and leaned back against the wall with a weary sigh. Then he turned his head to look at her.

"You have been here a long time, heldii. Do you want me to watch for a while?"

Senea met his gaze with surprise, but did not know what to say.

"Night watch is always the hardest," he added softly. "And impossible without sleep." He shrugged then. "You can't watch him alone. He'll get by you."

Senea drew a deep breath and looked away. Roskel waited for her to answer.

At last she released her breath in a long sigh and made a half gesture of uncertainty. Her eyes met his, and she nodded her agreement.

"Good," he said quietly, "go get some sleep."

With a mixture of reluctance and relief she went away, first to bathe more than a week's dirt and sweat off, and then to her bunkroom.

She sat for a long, long while on her bunk, leaning wearily against the wall with her eyes closed. Finally she lay down, but she could not sleep, partly because of the heat and partly because the intentions of Sky and Yunab haunted her. Something was very wrong. If Vayhawk was following Aldived's orders, then Yunab knew those orders existed, may have even authored them! If that was so, then there was a trap being set for Vayhawk he would not be able to escape. A cold chill shivered over her skin. Try as she might, she could not think of anything to do to help him other than what he had asked. Make time for him and keep an eye on Sky.

There was muffled movement beside her bunk.

Senea's eyes snapped open.

The bunkroom was still in blackness, but a darker shadow crouched before her in the dark.

"Senea," Roskel's murmur came to her.

Senea rolled her head, easing the pain in her neck, and realized that she had been asleep.

"It is almost dawn."

Senea pushed herself up, stifling a groan at muscles that protested with pain. She wanted nothing more than to sleep for an entire day—longer, if she could. She couldn't even remember when she last had a full night's sleep. Moving stiffly, and trying to be quiet so as to avoid waking up her bunkmates, she followed Roskel out into the corridor.

"There is nothing to report," Roskel said as he turned to walk down the hall with Senea beside him. His clear eyes rested on her and somehow it did not seem right that he should be saying those words to her. She was only heldii. Embarrassed, Senea nodded mutely.

"I don't want Sky to see me at his door," Roskel continued, "so I will leave you now."

She nodded again and stood uncertainly as he walked away. After a few moments she heard his door close, and she turned to look out at the sky that was not yet light, but was not far from showing the first traces of dawn.

When Sky came out of his room, he only glared at Senea, then strode away. She followed him to breakfast, then out onto the compound where she sat watching him go through the knife routines. There was no point in concealing what she was doing. He knew she watched.

At midmorning, when the heat became too much for her, Senea moved inside the corridor and found Roskel waiting for her.

"I just received word from Vayhawk," he said, moving to her side. "The Ja'sid have joined with the Sojei to our west. Vayhawk wants all available helden to be sent to him." He stopped then and turned his gaze on her. "What do you think, heldii. Do I send Sky?"

Senea thought with sudden anxiety of all the possible things Sky could do out there at the borders. She clasped her hands together in a brief, uncertain gesture, then let them drop. The damage he could do . . . it would be better if he stayed in the Held until Vayhawk got back. But it was not her place to say. She was only heldii. And yet . . . she had been asked. There was nothing for it but to answer.

"No. Don't send him," she said, and looked up at Roskel.

He turned his head to watch as Treyna crossed the compound to Sky.

"Would it help if I suspended him from patrol for a while?"

Senea stared at him in surprise and puzzlement. "You can do that?"

"I can do whatever I think is best for the Held." He looked sidelong at her. "Would it be best for the Held, Senea?"

Senea studied his face and tried to see behind the expressionless eyes, could not see anything to tell her what he was thinking. But she knew that whatever she said, he would do.

"Suspend him," she said, and crossed her arms tightly in front of her. Her face set into an icy calm that covered her uneasiness, and she slid her eyes over to where Sky and Treyna were, then looked back to Roskel.

The Held, after that, became almost empty, except for the few helden that came in from patrol from the rest of the borders. These, Roskel allowed to remain on patrol duty, to eat, sleep, and return to the borders. Sky was suspended from duty of any kind and the glares he turned on Senea were dark and angry.

Senea felt more at ease now that he was confined to the Held, except for the two times Yunab showed up to talk to him. Both times the counselor left giving Senea a smile that sent chills running through her.

She watched Sky all the time, never certain that he wouldn't give her the slip even though he'd be breaking heldcode to do it. She didn't think that he would, but she wasn't quite sure. Treyna completely ignored her, never looking at her, never acknowledging her presence in any way. Senea couldn't help thinking that this was far from the way things were supposed to be in the Held.

Roskel sometimes came to sit with her when she ate, never saying very much, always looking at her with a gaze that she could not read. He watched Sky's room part of each night, saying only that if Vayhawk wanted Sky watched, someone was going to have to help. She couldn't do it by herself. She let him because what he said was true, and because he was Held-second.

He didn't ask any more questions, and for that she was grateful.

On the fifteenth night after Roskel had sent all the available helden to Vayhawk, while Senea sat alone in the corridor, she was startled by the banging sound of the Held door being flung open. She rose to her feet, saw Roskel come out of his room and disappear in that direction. The sounds of voices came around the corner.

Senea watched them come in—the helden from the Ja'sid borders, many of them wounded. She stood pressed against the wall in the confusion. The sounds, the raised voices, the groans of pain, the smells of dirt and sweat and blood, the crowding in the corridor held her transfixed and staring.

Suddenly Vayhawk was by her side, and he swept her ahead of him, gripping her arm and guiding her through the commotion toward his room. Once inside he closed the door, led her across the darkness to the table, and lit the lamp.

The golden light fell on him, and Senea gasped in dismay at the sight. She raised a hand to touch trembling fingers to a long, deep wound on his upper arm. Vayhawk reached across with his left hand and took her wrist, holding it tightly. He bowed his head, fatigue lining his face in deep creases of shadow. The moments seemed to crawl into hours while she waited for him to look at her. A bead of sweat ran down his temple.

"Tell me what has been happening," he said at last. His voice was soft, but clear.

Senea's breath trickled out in a long sigh, making her conscious that she had been holding it. Slowly she drew in another breath and began to tell him everything, starting from the moment she had walked into the Held and until the helden had returned with the wounded. Vayhawk turned his full attention on her as she spoke, but she did not flinch under that searching stare, even though she felt herself growing cold. She fell silent then and looked into his eyes, feeling she could fall into those wells of brown-black twilight and be lost forever.

"Vayhawk," she found herself saying, "what are you going to do with me?"

He stood in frigid silence, his eyes sweeping across her face. "What do you want me to do, Senea?"

"I don't know."

"You broke heldcode."

"I know."

His grip tightened fiercely on her wrist. Senea winced, stifling a cry of pain.

"I should turn you over to Roskel."

Senea paled. "When—" she faltered.

He drew her closer, watching her face.

"You know I cannot do that."

"Then what are you going to do?"

"What can I do, Senea?" His eyes intent on her.

Heat stole up her throat as she realized that he really meant for her to answer that, that he would stand there and wait forever, no matter how tired he was, until she gave him an answer. Quite abruptly she looked down at her wrist, where his hand was clasped around so tightly that his knuckles showed white. She tried to moisten her lips, but her mouth was dry as ashes. There was a long silence while she looked at their hands. Then she lifted her head slowly, as if his intent gaze was forcing speech from her.

"I don't know."

"Anything I do will jeopardize my mission," Vayhawk said. "And I can't do that. Not until the Ja'sid have been stopped." He bent his head so that his face was only inches from hers. "You've put me in a very difficult position, Senea."

She swallowed; she found herself numb. "Forgive me," she whispered, dismayed that there was no strength to her voice.

He tightened his grip on her wrist, and this time she did wince. A cold numbness shot to her fingers.

"We're co-conspirators now," he said to her. "Traitors. If I go down, you go down." He closed his eyes for a moment, fatigue showing heavily around his mouth.

Senea was silent, and tears unconsciously slid down her face.

Vayhawk's expression softened as he looked at her. "I'm sorry, Senea." His grip on her arm loosened, releasing a painful rush of blood back into her hand. And as he looked at her a silent something passed between them that left her breathless. Senea stared at him, feeling the nearness of him like never before. He raised a hand to her face, lay his palm there a long moment, then his thumb moved, slowly tracing over her lips in a caress that sent a tremor down the full length of her. He looked up at her eyes and straightened, his face ashen-gray with fatigue.

He swayed suddenly, and Senea caught him, found herself just as suddenly with the weight of him heavy on her, her arms tight about him.

"Senea . . ." his voice faded, the faint timbre in her ear.

She struggled to keep him on his feet and somehow got him to the bunk where he collapsed, dragging her down with him.

She disentangled herself and stood up just as a knocking sounded at the door.

"Come in," she cried, and looked up with relief when Roskel came in. "He's hurt."

Roskel strode across the room and sank to his heels beside the bunk. Senea watched anxiously as he examined the Heldlan.

"He'll be all right," he said after a moment. "But you'll have to tend to the arm." He rose and moved to stand beside the table, his eyes on Senea, sober, seeming to see into her thoughts. When he spoke again his words were quiet, measured and probing. "A runner has come in. A large band of Ja'sid was stopped at the north border by the Wuepoah."

Senea stared at him with a chill breath. How much had he guessed about Vayhawk's meeting with the Wuepoah? "You shouldn't be telling me this."

"Shouldn't I?"

"I'm only heldii."

He looked at her a long moment, and the concentration of those light brown eyes seemed to harrow her soul. "No," he said. "I think something more."

She did not know what he meant by that, so she gave him the only other answer she could. "I am not Heldlan."

"But you can give him the message."

Senea was taken aback. "Yes."

"Good." He turned to leave, paused, and looked at her again. "A Heldlan's heldii would be much more . . . of necessity. And Vayhawk's heldii . . . even more than that." He went to the door and looked at her a moment before he left.

Senea stared at the door as it closed behind him, certain now that he knew, or at least suspected what was going on. But his words were a puzzlement to her.

Later, when the light of morning lit the corridor, she gave Vayhawk Roskel's message.

CHAPTER
SIXTEEN

There was chaos in the Held; it was the full length of the corridor as Senea pushed her way toward the bath. Everywhere the helden were getting ready.

Senea stopped with uncertainty just within the door of the bath, listening to the loud, noisy excitement. Most of the helden were laughing and joking as they bathed and dressed. There were a few who were withdrawn in sober, preoccupied silence, but mostly everyone was happy and eager.

Because the Wuepoah Held was patrolling the northern borders, the Ja'sid retreated back into the desert. And because there was a respite from the fighting, the helden voted to hold the Games and rank the heldii. Then they could be sent out on patrol on their own.

In the meantime, Roskel sent triple the patrols to watch the borders at the desert. He felt that the quiet would not last very long, and then the Ja'sid would come back in force. Vayhawk agreed.

As Senea watched the helden in the bath, a sudden reluctance seized her and held her motionless.

Two days of Games. One day to face Treyna. The next day to face Sky. And afterward. . . . She'd either be heldii to Vayhawk, or heldii to Sky.

She spotted Mara in a far corner, and the heldan motioned for her to come over. Senea did not obey at once, an unconscious effort to hold away that which was to come. Then she threaded her way toward where Mara waited and sat down on a bench against the wall.

Mara smiled sympathetically when she saw Senea's troubled face. "Don't worry so much. It won't be so bad." She looked at Senea soberly. "You better hurry. The Games start at dawn. You haven't much time."

Mara didn't sound worried, which was encouraging, but it didn't ease Senea's apprehension any; Mara wasn't participating.

Senea pulled herself out of her thoughts and did as Mara bade, bathed quickly, dressed, and combed her wet hair, putting it back into a braid.

She followed Mara out into the corridor where they were met by three other helden.

"These are my bunkmates," Mara said to Senea. "Cora, Elene, and Kariana."

Senea nodded absently to them, murmured hello, and went with them out onto the compound.

The leaded gray color of dawn was beginning to show in the sky, the first trace of light that would begin the Games. As soon as it was light enough to see clearly, they would start.

Senea leaned back against the wall by the door where Mara and her bunkmates had stopped to talk to another group of helden. She listened absently to their jokes and tried to calm the nervousness in her stomach, forcing herself to relax against the wooden wall until she realized that she wasn't relaxing at all.

The compound was already crowded with the dark figures of helden, standing and sitting around the perimeter, leaving the center empty just as it had been when Treyna had faced Sky's charges. Senea forcefully shut out that memory and turned her eyes to search through the growing light for Vayhawk.

Unexpectedly her eyes fell on Roskel a short distance away where the light from the corridor shone on him. He stood leaning against a pole with arms crossed looking at her as if he were weighing up her strength and courage. Senea looked straight at him, and he pushed away from the pole and wove his way to her.

"You are ready, heldii?" His voice was soft and did not carry beyond the two of them.

"No," she said. "I'd rather be on patrol."

"Yes," he said. "But Vayhawk has bet on you." He voiced it without malice, even without sympathy.

Senea looked at the Held-second. He was not so tall as Vayhawk, did not possess the dangerous edge that was

Vayhawk's, but he was lean and hard, and in every way was a heldan. She had watched how the others acted around him, how they admired him for his total self-control and absolute professionalism, and how even the highest ranking of them was scared stiff of him. He looked at her now, his expression unreadable.

There was a movement at her side, and she saw that Mara had turned, her bunkmates moving away into the crowd.

"Roskel," Mara said in salute.

He nodded to her. "Mara." His eyes slid back to Senea. "Others have bet, also."

Senea looked at him and took in his meaning, that there would be much interest in her bout today. The muscles of her stomach tensed painfully.

"Aldived has even bet," he went on, watching her face in that way of his, reading every line, knowing exactly how his words were affecting her. "He sent word that he will be here to watch the Games today."

"What are you trying to do?" Mara spoke up, her eyes flashing angrily. "Scare her?"

Roskel glanced sharply at her, but said nothing. She went quiet at that and her angry expression faded to one of concerned worry.

Senea found that Roskel was now looking at her, studying her, appraising her narrowly.

"Do not worry," he said. "Aldived's bet was not large."

There was a movement at her side, and a hand went gently around her arm. It was Vayhawk, and he inclined his head to Mara and Roskel, then drew Senea away with him a few paces. His eyes studied her, shadowed and midnight dark.

"Are you ready?" he asked.

She looked up at him, the soft roughness of his voice brushing over her like a night breeze.

"Yes," she said. "I think so."

"Good." His hand slid up her arm to her shoulder, a caressing move.

"But, if I don't win . . ."

"Don't worry. You'll do fine."

"But, if I don't win . . ." she said again, thinking that she could be Sky's heldii by the end of the day, and that thought suddenly frightened her.

"Vayhawk," Roskel's voice came in between them. "Aldived is here."

Vayhawk turned, then stopped. He looked back to Senea. He reached his hand out to her face, then dropped it without actually touching her.

"Wait here."

He strode away with Roskel then, going through the helden that moved aside slightly as he passed. Senea watched him go, until it was difficult to see because of the crowd.

She turned and the blood in her drained, cold.

Sky stood a short distance away, watching her closely. He raised a hand to his brow in greeting, a slow gesture that managed to be insolent. Senea stared at him, thinking what it would mean to be Sky's heldii. It would be different for her than it had been for Treyna, for Sky wanted revenge.

She turned and tried to ignore him, but every time she looked back he was watching her. She crossed her arms, wiped a hand across her upper lip, and drew in a long breath.

Mara leaned toward her. "What is it ... What's wrong?" She turned her head and saw Sky looking at them. "Ignore him!" she said, taking Senea's arm to pull her away into the crowd.

Just then, Sky stepped clear of the group that surrounded him and came toward them. Senea watched him, wary, every sense alert. He stopped just short of them and smiled.

"Ready for the Games?" he asked, his eyes going to Senea and staying there.

"Go back to your heldii!" Mara said. "You're not welcome here."

"That's not very friendly, Mara."

"I'm not a very friendly person."

"I only came to wish Senea luck."

Mara snorted in derision. "The day you wish anybody luck will be the last day the sun comes up."

Senea tried to look away; she felt far from comfortable under the stare of those keen eyes. But his gaze held her captive.

"What do you say, heldii?" Sky's voice purred darkly. "Will you wish me luck in return? All in the spirit of the Games?" The grin vanished, and so did the casual tone, menace now on his lips. "I hope you're good, heldii. Because if you're not . . ." He let it trail off. "What Treyna doesn't do to you, I will."

"That's enough!" Mara said sharply. "Come, Senea. We don't need to stay here." Her hand went back around Senea's arm and pulled her away.

"Such a good friend—always protecting you," Sky said after them, a glint of steel in his voice. "Have you told her our secret, heldii?"

Senea turned with alarm and stared at him. Mara turned, also. And she sounded angrier than usual. "If you've got something to say, say it and be done with it."

An icy chill ran over Senea, and she searched frantically for some way to stop him, to keep him from revealing what he and she had seen together. She had lived in fear of this for days, and now that it was facing her, she could think of nothing that would stop him. She watched as Sky looked from Mara back to her. He smiled, a hard, mirthless smile.

"What do you suppose they do out there all alone, this heldii and Vayhawk?" His voice was low. "The days and nights that they are gone together. The rest of us are assigned to patrols that constantly change in number so that we and our paired partner are never alone. But not for these two. They are always alone." He stepped closer so that he looked down on her. His voice grew even quieter. "What do you do out there, heldii? Are you breaking heldcode?"

Senea stared at him in surprise. This was not what she had expected, and it was a moment before she even knew what he was talking about. Then surprise became anger, and she spoke softly, with unwise words better left unsaid.

"What we do is none of your business. And you can believe whatever you like, but I wouldn't be as quick to speak if I were you. I've seen you and Treyna together. Who knows what sort of things you have forced *her* to."

There was a moment of stunned silence, and Senea eyed him defiantly.

Sky turned red, fixed his suddenly blazing eyes on her, and moved forward another step. Senea shrank back only one step, defiance turning white-hot in her.

"Girl," his voice was so low that only she and Mara could hear him, "after I am through with you tomorrow, you will know exactly what I can force a heldii to."

Senea stared at him. A swift glance showed her that Mara was furious.

"And neither Vayhawk, nor this one, will be able to help you," he added with a slow smile when he saw Senea's glance.

Undaunted, Senea was about to reply when Mara's angry eyes caught her own, sending her back into silence.

Sky laughed, a low deep-throated sound that sent angry chills over Senea's skin. He stepped closer so that she came up against the wall, and he looked down on her while the laughter faded from his face. He put up a hand to the wall and leaned forward, his face coming very close to hers.

"Back off, Sky!" Mara said, grabbing his arm.

"Treyna!" Sky's voice raised a fraction.

There was a movement behind him. Senea looked past him in surprise. She had not known that Treyna was there.

"Do something about this heldan," Sky said. "I have more to say to Vayhawk's heldii."

"Yes, Sky." And she was starting to when a hand slammed to the wall between them. Treyna turned with a startled gasp.

Vayhawk was glaring down at her with fury-blackened eyes.

"Move away," another voice said to her, Roskel coming up on the other side of Sky to stand next to Senea. His light brown eyes settled on Treyna, emotionless and unreadable. Treyna's stare went from Vayhawk to Roskel. She shook with mingled fear and rage, but she raised her hands in surrender and stepped away.

Vayhawk turned to Sky. "Touch her and you'll face more charges than you'll know what to do with."

A corner of Sky's mouth lifted mockingly. "Anything you say, Heldlan." He stepped back. "I wouldn't want her until she was mine anyway." He looked at Senea, then to Roskel, then he turned that mocking smile back to Vayhawk. "But after today you will have no more say." He looked back at Senea with insulting frankness.

Senea drew in a furious breath and was about to strike him when Roskel laid a hand gently on her arm.

From behind Vayhawk, Treyna laughed. The Heldlan turned, and Senea did not need to see his face to judge its expression because Treyna paled and stepped back. He remained utterly still, wrapped in menace and in anger, for a full minute before he turned his eyes away from her.

Senea watched, knowing how it was to feel the full intensity of his stare. And to her surprise she found that she pitied the girl. But Treyna lifted her head defiantly and looked past him to Senea.

"I will have to win, of course." The comment came off sounding like a challenge. And she moved deliberately to stand next to Sky in a show of united force.

Anger fired briefly in Vayhawk's eyes, but by the time he replied it was gone. "Might I suggest that you save your hostilities for the Games, then? You would not want to forfeit because of a breach in conduct. There are rules that must be followed, or has Sky been remiss in acquainting you with them?"

"No, Heldlan. He has not been," Treyna said. Her face and voice were calm, her hands steady, but Senea did not miss the pale lips and cheeks.

A smile icy-chill, less cheering than a frown, curved Vayhawk's lips. "That is good. But perhaps you should rehearse them to Sky again in case *he* has forgotten, especially the part about intimidation." He stopped and looked pointedly at her.

"Yes, Heldlan . . . except . . ."

"Except?"

Treyna looked helplessly to Sky, took a breath to say something, but did not. Vayhawk put a hand to Senea's back and guided her firmly around Sky.

"Heldlan," Treyna said behind him.

He turned to her again.

"I still intend to win."

"Of course, heldii. But you realize, don't you, that if you win and Senea becomes Sky's heldii, that you will become mine?"

Treyna was too stunned to answer. She looked to Sky for a denial but did not find it. He was looking at her with a silent warning to refrain from saying anything further. She glared at Vayhawk and then back to Sky. His eyes still warned, and though Treyna flushed red and then grew pale as alabaster, she was silent.

Before that moment, she had not known that her relationship with Sky was not a permanent thing. Senea could see the pain of that realization on her face.

"Perhaps your heldii will not wish so much to win, now," Vayhawk said to Sky.

For some reason this caused Sky to turn and stare sharply at the Heldlan, when his other comments had produced no real response. For a while their eyes locked, strong-willed and challenging. Senea moved to try to stop it but she saw Roskel raise his hand in warning, and she withheld herself, looking anxiously at Mara.

Then Sky stepped back, his jaw working with anger. "Someday, Heldlan, your arrogance is going to be your undoing."

Senea noted the vicious undertone in his voice. It had an edge, a slight chilling undertone, that had not been there before. She realized suddenly that Sky was the most chillingly dangerous man that she had ever met, even more so than Yunab. She didn't doubt for a second that he meant his words as a threat, nor his ability to make good on that threat. She stared with foreboding at him as he turned and stalked away.

"Roskel," Vayhawk said softly.

"Heldlan?"

"Start the Games."

Senea did not need to see the salute to know that Roskel gave it and admired him for it. She heard him move away into the crowd.

"Senea." Vayhawk's voice sounded close to her.

She looked up at him. The dark shadow of his eyes was soberly searching her face.

"I'm all right," she said, forced a smile at him, but saw that it did not fool him.

His hand touched her arm, trailed lightly down to her elbow, back up again. "It's all a part of the Games," he said. "Tensions and emotions run high. Some get out of hand."

The stillness of his voice sent shivers over her skin. She heard Roskel call the helden to order and saw out of the corner of her eyes that the Held as a whole inclined their heads to him while silence settled on the compound. Vayhawk's hand moved slowly up to her shoulder, and his eyes lingered on hers.

Then he drew in a breath. "Come with me," he murmured, and his hand closed around her arm, drew her with him as he shouldered through the helden.

"Good morning," Roskel's voice sounded from the center of the compound. "It is time for the Games to begin."

Senea jumped when cheering exploded from the helden, the suddenness of it startling. Vayhawk looked at her with a half smile, a good-natured teasing that brought a flush to her face. He put his arm around her then, with an affectionate squeeze.

"The rules are simple," Roskel continued when the last of the shouts and whistles had died away. "All challenges should have been lodged with me before today. No new challenges will be accepted." There was some good-natured booing and a few quiet chuckles and a solitary shout to shut up.

"All fights are until someone surrenders or cannot continue. All fighting is to be hand-to-hand. If knives are drawn, there is to be no killing. Heldcode will be in immediate force if there is a death. The heldii challenges will be first, followed by the ranking bouts. That's it. Have fun. And good luck!"

A second cheer went up that was louder than the first and took longer to die.

By that time Vayhawk had led Senea to the edge of the clearing where they approached Aldived, who was slouched back in an ornamented chair watching Roskel with a slightly bored frown. His clothing, from boots to tunic, was an unaccustomed tan color, to ward off heat, Senea thought, and she was surprised at seeing him in something other than black.

He turned his head to them as they drew near, and Vayhawk inclined his head in respectful greeting. Aldived's eyes slid to Senea in uncharacteristic interest for a moment, then went back again to Vayhawk.

"This is necessary? All this shouting?" His glittering hand waved vaguely at the compound.

"This is a time for relaxing, Tribelord."

Aldived's hand went to his mouth as he leaned on his elbow, his fingers pulling absently at his lower lip. "It seems so . . . unrestrained."

"It is," Vayhawk agreed. "But it's good for the helden to enjoy themselves once in a while."

"Well, when does this fight of your heldii's begin?"

Vayhawk shrugged. "That's up to Roskel."

Quite unexpectedly Aldived's eyes were focused on Senea. He dropped his hand to his side and shifted so that he sat more upright. His eyes flickered to Vayhawk then back to her.

"Heldii," he greeted with a slight nod of his head.

Senea inclined her head to him uneasily. "Tribelord."

"It's Senea . . . Am I right?"

"Yes."

"Good." He nodded again, and it was as if he couldn't think

of anything else to say. But then, "I hope you are good, heldii. I have bet five gold pieces on you."

"I will try my best, Tribelord."

"And I'm glad to have this chance to thank you personally."

"Thank me?" Senea looked at Vayhawk uncertainly.

"The Heldlan and I have discussed this power of the Black Ja'sid's. It is his opinion that we, too, could use this power if we knew how to control it. It seems that because of our forebears we have lost that knowledge. Perhaps it is possible that we can learn it again. I have encouraged Vayhawk to pursue it and see if it's possible.

"I understand that he has taken you out onto the plains to test his theories out, but you didn't get the chance to try. Held duties got in the way." His eyes centered on her with an intentness that was also uncharacteristic of him.

"What do you think, heldii? Can it be done? Can our helden find a way to use this power and turn the Ja'sid aside?"

She looked at him with a frown.

The corner of his mouth quirked with barely concealed humor at her discomfiture. He moved his right hand, a flippant gesture that was a satire of himself. The rings flashed in the light even though the sun had not yet come over the Held wall. There was a gleam in his eye that was gone the instant he shifted his gaze to look at the jewels on his fingers.

"I really want to know how you feel about all of this." His words and his tone of voice were in sharp contrast to the look of bored indifference on his face. "What do you think?"

Senea hesitated. She didn't know how to answer him. She didn't even know why he was asking her. She was only heldii, and she felt decidedly uncomfortable that his attention was on her.

She glanced at Vayhawk, hoping that he would intervene. But he was watching her with a half smile, waiting for her to say something. Swallowing, knowing that she was on her own, she turned back to Aldived.

"I don't know." It was an evasion and she knew it.

Aldived looked doubtfully at her, then produced a brief pained smile.

"You mean it?" His voice was low, its usual listless edge missing. "Do you anticipate a problem or are you just unsure? I wouldn't think the worse of you for it if you didn't think it would work. Vayhawk has told me of your experiences with the Ja'sid, and as one who has encountered the Black Ja'sid, you know more of this power of theirs than I do. I very much would like to know your feelings."

For a few seconds Senea merely stared at him in consternation, then she saw the cold common sense of what he had said.

"It's there," she said slowly. "The Ja'sid aren't the only ones who have it. But the power seems to be very strong. I don't think that it's easily controlled. I think it'll control you if you're not strong enough."

Aldived put out his hand and Senea took it without flinching—his eyes were unreadable. "Keep trying," he said.

She found herself looking into eyes that were measuring her with a gaze that seemed to bore to the very center of her. She met his direct gaze remembering the things that Vayhawk had said about him and knew that he had been right. There was a lot more to the Tribelord than he let on. When he finally made his move, there were going to be a lot of surprised helden. And some of them were going to find out that they had seriously underestimated him.

She was chewing these thoughts over when Vayhawk stirred beside her and muttered something unintelligible. She glanced his way and saw a cold look come into his face. Aldived turned, his eyes narrowing. Senea could feel the sudden tension in the air.

She looked up. Yunab was glowering down at her from over his nose. His eyes were black and flinty.

"Heldii," he greeted.

She nodded to him. "Counselor."

He practically ignored Vayhawk's presence, turning his eyes on the Heldlan for a very short moment, saying, "Heldlord."

Vayhawk inclined his head wordlessly.

Yunab turned his attention immediately back to Senea and smiled a smile that did not reach his eyes.

"Things are going well? You are ready for today?"

Senea rocked back on her heels. She glared up at him with displeasure. Vayhawk laid a hand gently on her arm, admonishing her to prudence. She glanced at him with a frown. She managed to assume a languid pose and turned her eyes back on the counselor.

"I'm prepared to do my best," she said.

"I hope your best is good enough."

"So do I."

"But if it is not, I think you'll find being heldii to Sky interesting."

Senea stared at him sharply for a moment and felt the convulsive movement of her throat as she swallowed. She found in herself indignant rage—an emotion tempered by awareness of the immediate closeness of Aldived and Vayhawk.

She glanced in their direction and saw that they were still and watchful.

Forcing the anger under control, she put her hands together and concentrated on the counselor, shaking her head.

"I don't think so. Sky is only a lackey, following your orders."

Yunab's face darkened with a rush of blood.

"Senea . . ." Vayhawk's voice came softly. "Senea, respect."

She was unable to comprehend how she could have uttered such a challenge, but was not sorry that she had returned Yunab's stare unwaveringly. She would dearly have loved to tell him more of what she thought of him and Sky, but wariness made her hold her tongue.

Yunab's eyes gleamed dangerously, and his mouth tightened. He stepped around Aldived toward her and said silkily, "That may be true, heldii. But he'll teach you agony. Remember *that* as you fight. You'll have agony such as will make the Ja'sid a happy memory by comparison. I know Sky, and he's got his eye on you, and he'll sheath his knife in your blood."

He stopped, but Senea made no move to answer. Instead, Aldived spoke up.

"Is all this threatening necessary? I thought there were heldcodes against this kind of thing." The mask of boredom and lethargy had descended once again over him. It was in his voice, a dull, listless tone that almost bordered on indifference.

Senea was surprised to see it after he had shown such vitality a few moments before. Even his eyes had taken on a hooded disinterested dullness.

Senea turned her stare from him and studied Yunab closely to see if he had seen the change come over the Tribelord. But he was not watching Aldived. His gaze was still intent on her.

"The heldii knows that it's all in the spirit of the Games," he said, and a swift smile changed his face, lighting it up and softening it, but there was no change in his eyes.

"Besides, I'm not bound by heldcode. Isn't that right, heldii?"

Senea, sitting motionless in the sun, stared at him. "No. But Sky is," she countered.

Yunab hesitated. "Yes. He is." He bowed slightly, mockingly polite, as if paying a compliment, and Senea knew that she had somehow been defeated.

She looked to Vayhawk and saw his grim expression.

"This should be an interesting day," Yunab added challengingly, bringing Senea's head back around. The counselor looked at her, and his smile widened. Then to her surprise and relief he turned and moved around to stand on the opposite side of Aldived without waiting for an answer. She held down a shudder of revulsion.

Vayhawk's hand touched her back and descended to her waist to bring her attention back around to him.

"It takes a great deal of courage to watch moments like this slide by," he said softly. "But it is best not to let him provoke you. Remember who and what you are."

"That's hard to do sometimes."

"Yes. But part of being heldan."

Senea looked up at him. His answer was always the same. And he meant for her to always keep it in mind. She thought on it as Roskel's voice called out the names of the first challenge fight. The crowd cheered and parted to let two heldii out onto the clearing.

The cheering died away, and there was silence, save for a whisper of wind high above the Held walls.

It was then that Senea saw the heldien across the clearing, the young ones that had come when she had into the Held on that first day. They were no longer frightened children, but had the look of the Held on them, proficient, confident, and skilled; so unlike the children of the held-tribe that they once had been. Senea shivered unexpectedly and felt a touch of pity for them, and sorrow for the innocence they had lost.

Then her gaze fell on a small group of elderly men and women seated on the ground next to the heldien, dressed in heldan dress, weapons at their sides.

"Our elders," Vayhawk said before she could ask. "The Held'len. They live in honor with the heldien, training them and teaching them. I, myself, was taught by such a one."

Senea looked at him, hearing the reverence in his voice with surprise. She had never wondered about the heldan he had

been heldii to. She wondered now at the one who taught him
to be what he was.

He met her gaze for a long moment, and his hand was at her
side holding her against him. The desert warmth of him came
to a rest, settling on her like the stillness of night. She blinked
at the change that came to his eyes; and time, and the Held,
and the Games, ceased to be.

For several slow heartbeats he held her pressed to his side,
the span of his fingers on her waist, a touch that caressed even
though it never moved. Then he stepped away, a single step to
the side that left her suddenly cold even as the sun came over
the Held wall, flaring like a white scream, its hot breath burning into the compound.

Vayhawk's hand left her side in a slow move, and he
directed her attention to the clearing.

In the center of the compound the two heldii that Roskel had
called forth had taken up their positions facing one another.
They eyed each other, circled, and exchanged places.

A second pass and it was over.

One heldii had the other down and pinned in a single move
that was final. Had he had a knife that heldii certainly would
have been dead.

An appreciative cheer met him when he stood up.

Senea applauded, looked around, and saw Aldived watching
the events with dull boredom; there was no interest on his face
at all. Then her eyes were drawn to Yunab, who was watching
her with such an intentness she could do nothing but stare in
return. Her heart chilled a beat, and it was a moment before
she was aware that Vayhawk was talking to her.

"Sit down, Senea," he said. "It's going to be a long day."

He touched her elbow and settled on the hard ground among
some helden, who eased aside to make room for him and
waited for her to sit by him.

She sank down to him trying to ignore Yunab's stare, but
she felt his eyes on her nonetheless. The skin between her
shoulders shrank from that gaze, followed by irritation that he
could affect her in this way.

Vayhawk rested easily, with his knees drawn up and his
arms folded over them, the sun shining on the red jagged scar
that ran from shoulder to elbow. Senea found herself looking
at it, recalling how she had taken care of it, cleaning and dressing the wound while he had lain unconscious on his bunk.

Senea drew up her knees and clasped her hands tightly around them and thought about what he had said that terrible night. *We're co-conspirators now. Traitors. If I go down, you go down.* How long ago had that been? Three weeks? Four? It was as vivid in her memory as if it had been last night.

She put her forehead to her knees and heard two more names being called from somewhere at the side of the clearing. When she looked up, Vayhawk was watching her.

"Are you all right?" he asked, his voice quiet so that only she could hear.

She nodded, then cancelled it with a shrug of her shoulders.

Vayhawk didn't reply, but continued to stare speculatively at her. Sitting tensely, she rubbed her bare arms.

"Is there any way to call this off?" she murmured, suddenly wanting to get out of the Held and out onto the plain where the loneliness and silence would be a relief from the tension.

Vayhawk shook his head faintly.

She had known it before she asked.

Just then Roskel caught her attention and motioned for her to come, signaling that her bout with Treyna was next. Senea held herself still at his gesture. Still she did not move, even when he strode to the cleared center to announce her name.

Vayhawk touched her arm, and she looked at him and almost held her breath.

It was irrevocable; there was no way to retreat.

Vayhawk rose to his feet and held out his hand to help her up. She had no chioce, but she stood without his assistance, feigning a confidence that she did not feel.

"This way," the Heldlan whispered, taking her by the arm and turning her to the clearing. "Remember the eyes."

His hand left her arm, and she felt suddenly alone. She saw all of the Held watching her; she wanted to turn and walk the other way. She forced herself to go forward, surprised at how far away the center of the clearing seemed.

The sun shone down white onto the compound, edging everything with a vividness and a hardness that she had not noticed before. Everything stood out separate, itself. The arena was cut off from the wind that whispered overhead, and the air was still and stuffy.

Roskel took her by the elbow and drew her to one side of the clearing, then left her as Treyna came out and took up her stance a short distance away. Silence fell on the compound, as still and heavy as the air.

Senea squinted at the girl.

Treyna stood defiant, looking at her with contempt.

This was not going to be easy.

Several moments they faced each other. A muscle in Senea's calf jumped like a sand beetle, hurting her. She ignored it.

The seconds dragged out long and silent while she worked life into her hands, clenching and flexing her fingers by turn.

Vayhawk was standing motionless at the clearing edge just within her vision, feet apart and arms folded. Roskel was behind Treyna where Senea could see him clearly, but she did not dare take her eyes off Treyna to look at him or at the Heldlan.

Suddenly Treyna was coming at her. Fast.

Senea moved to meet her, struck her an openhanded blow to the face. Her other hand grabbed Treyna by the hair and pulled her forward and down. She came up hard with her knee and contacted with Treyna's chin, snapping her head back.

The impact jarred, and pain lanced up Senea's leg. She stepped back with a wincing grimace.

Treyna fell to the ground and lay still.

Two heartbeats, and it had happened. Senea drew in a breath, blank for the instant, knowing what she had done. Treyna's attack, her own reflex—both too quick to unravel.

She stepped to Treyna, leaned over the prostrate form, put out a hand to probe for life, and found it. She sighed in relief.

Only then did she become conscious of the hot sun on her back and sweat soaking through her clothes. She wiped moisture from her upper lip and tried to calm the beating of her heart.

It was almost as hot as a human being could stand there on the hard arena, yet Senea felt a sudden chill as she turned and walked away from Treyna and met a roar of cheering. She walked past Sky without looking at him.

She was vaguely aware of smiling faces—one of them was Mara—of hands clapping her back and shoulders, of Aldived smiling, and of Yunab standing somewhere in the background. But her eyes centered on Vayhawk. His brown gaze was on her, long and warm, so that all else on the compound receded and they were left alone.

It was several moments before she realized that Mara was trying to get her attention. She turned and her eyes fell on the clearing that was now empty, except for the limp form of Treyna sprawled on the ground. Senea shivered and looked up to find Roskel watching her with a sober appraising expression. She knew that he was determining what assignment he was going to give her when the Games were over.

She stared at him a moment before she turned to Mara.

CHAPTER
SEVENTEEN

The sun hung, swollen and bloody, just above the western wall of the Held when Roskel called an end of the Games for the day. Senea heard the helden disperse across the compound, heard the noise of their voices as if they and she were in different places. Her legs ached from standing all day at the back of the compound where she had finally retreated after her bout with Treyna.

She had accepted congratulations as long as she could stand it and then escaped to the privacy behind the crowd. There she remained, paying little attention to the Games, leaning against the wall lost in the trouble of her own thoughts.

Now she followed the general flow of the crowd to the eating hall and settled at an empty table even though she wasn't at all hungry. Vayhawk had disappeared sometime earlier, and she did not see Mara anywhere, so she sat absently turning her knife over and over with her fingers, feeling out of place but lacking the volition to get up and leave.

Gradually she became aware of eyes on her, and she looked up and saw Sky watching her from the next table. Beside him sat Landry, of whom she had seen very little since the night he had presented her with her knife.

Landry's glance warned, said nothing, but remained watchful and cold.

Sky stood, moved with deliberateness to Senea's table, and sat down. Landry came to sit across from Sky, his eyes resting expressionlessly on Senea's face.

Sky looked at the knife that she clasped tightly now in her hand. He looked up at her, a faint smile on his mouth. The eyes that he leveled on her were dark with an inner something that she did not want to decipher.

"It seems you were lucky again," he said finally.

She met his gaze squarely. "Lucky?" She did not even attempt to hide the contempt in her voice.

"You would call it something else?" His eyes were on her questioningly. Carefully hidden was the malice that she knew was there. The very air seemed to be alive with the tension, volatile and dangerous.

Senea returned his look steadily, sensing that ill was going to come of this. She flicked her eyes to Landry and saw the confirmation of it on his face. But intuitively she knew she had nothing to fear from him. His role in this confrontation was only as a witness. She looked back to Sky then down at the knife in her hand. The spiderwebbed threads of red lay against the white like rivulets of dead blood. Lifting her eyes she looked at Sky.

"I was faster," she said.

His eyes narrowed. For a space he said nothing. Then, "You may be right." His eyes traveled slowly over her face. "It's just as well. You will be stronger for tomorrow." His smile was slow and deliberate. "It will make our contest more interesting. Well worth the loss of two levels in rank."

Senea took in his meaning. He had lost two levels in rank when she had beat Treyna. There was a veiled hint in his words, a promise that had not been spoken, a whisper of suggestion that told her that he planned to do to her more than violence—much more than violence.

Heat rushed to her face. This man was far more dangerous than enemy helden, far more frightening.

She stared at him, her imagination already doing to her what he meant to do during the Games.

With her hand on the table to steady herself, she rose, her breath painful in her lungs, the violence of the images making her ill.

She opened her mouth, then closed it again.

The only thing she had power to do was to turn on her heel and walk out of the eating hall, ignoring the amused eyes of Landry, who had watched in silence. Her face burned, and her breath was short as she exited the stuffy corridor and walked out onto the compound. There the windshift was beginning to stir the air.

To her relief the arena was empty. She stood still for a long time, watching as the western sky became striped with colors of purple, gold, and red above the Held wall. Gradually the tightness in her lungs receded, leaving a numbness that was cold within her.

She had followed right where Sky's words had led her. With a naïveté that was astonishing she had fallen for his trap. He had watched with satisfaction her shock when she suddenly understood what he had meant. There had been a slight mocking smile about his lips; the memory caused her to flush, and she found it difficult to hold the anger of it away.

A step sounded in the shadows to her left.

For an instant she ignored it. Then she turned, knowing before she looked who had followed her.

Turning her head to face him, she remained perfectly still otherwise, not even breathing.

Deadly, she thought. Viperous. Treacherous. Spiteful and deadly.

Her tongue touched her lips. "What do you want?"

"A last word," Sky said, stepping forward. "A warning, if you will."

"I think I know what you intend," she said tightly, and turned to leave.

"Do you?"

Ignoring him, she continued across the compound.

"You know," his voice followed after her, "there are ways of getting around heldcode."

Senea hesitated only briefly, but she determinedly went on. Then his next words brought her up short.

"But should you tell Roskel about Vayhawk's disregard of heldcode . . ." Senea turned sharply to face him just at the door that led into her section of the Held. "I could be persuaded to go easy on you tomorrow."

He was walking toward her. By the time he reached her she was clenching her hands, trying to control her temper.

"It would be in your best interests." He looked down on her, his face shadowed so that she could barely see it in the deepening twilight. "I'm no heldii that can easily be defeated."

Senea found no words to answer.

"Heldcode may prevent my killing you," he added. His fingers touched her face. Senea steeled herself against it, determined not to show her revulsion. "But it cannot stop other things. Painful things." His voice dropped to a throaty murmur that chilled her beyond belief. His hand moved slowly and intimately down the curve of her jaw. "But then . . . maybe you would like that."

"I am not afraid of you!" Senea flared. And she jerked away from his touch and stepped backward until she was against the wall, planning her escape into the Held.

Sky stepped forward, grabbed her suddenly, and pulled her off her feet into the dark, closed doorway. She tried to twist away, but she was helpless in his grip.

"I'm tempted to tear you apart right now," he said.

He spoke in a low, almost inaudible growl, and there was in his tone an edge of danger. He meant something far more terrible than death, something much more devastating—more personal, more intimate.

Her voice came out in a gasp. "Let me go!"

His hand came over her mouth, the weight of his arm against her ear. "I'd be quiet if I were you, heldii." His voice was hoarse and his body leaned close to her. "You wouldn't want to draw any attention to us right now. Someone might get the wrong impression."

Senea struggled against him, attempted to tear herself loose. His grip tightened. "Stop it!"

She fought harder until his hold on her became so painful she was forced to quit. She stared at the blackness of his face, hating him.

He knew it and laughed softly. Then a drawn blade gleamed, as if a chill light had been unsheathed, and came up between them, its tip coming to a rest at the base of her throat.

"It would be so easy," he whispered. "A slight pressure. A quick push." The blade of the knife moved, just barely pierced the skin. Senea winced, but tried not to. "But I don't need to tell you about knives," Sky continued. "You know all about them."

The blade moved up her throat, the sharp end pressing but not cutting, then the flat of it slid cool along her jawline. His hand came away from her mouth and touched the spot where the knife had pricked her.

"Let go of me!" Senea whispered, not able in her anger to raise her voice.

"But I can't do that. Not yet." He made a helpless gesture that she felt against her. The knife caressed her skin and moved up to her cheek. "I have plans for you, girl." His hand closed around her throat, tightening slightly. "I had hoped that after today . . ." His voice trailed off and he shrugged. "Well . . . plans change."

"Let me go, Sky. You're breaking heldcode."

"Am I?" His hand moved up so that the spread of his fingers reached from ear to ear. "You mean the one that says 'there can be no weapon ever drawn against another heldan of your own Held, except in the Games'?" He shrugged again.

"Well, there's also one that says 'there is absolutely no communication with members of other Helds, even if Tribelords come together for bargaining.'" The knife trailed over to her mouth and over her lips. His breath fluttered softly across her face.

"So you see, you really are in no position to object, heldii. But as long as we are quoting heldcode, how about the one that says, 'instant, unquestioning obedience of a ranking heldan is demanded'? I outrank you, girl, by some two hundred levels, even at the reduction of two."

Senea heard the edge come into his voice.

"I did not make the bet," she said.

"No. But you won the bet." His face came so close, his breath was hot on her mouth. He pressed her hard against the door-casing, his hand around her throat cutting off her breath. "And I still outrank you."

Senea's hands came up, clutching at his fingers, knowing that he intended to strangle her right then and there, fully believing that he would in spite of heldcode.

"I can do to you whatever I want," he said, and his grip on her throat increased savagely, his words dark and quiet.

Senea tried furiously to pull away from him, but he held her firmly, his body trapping her in the doorway.

"I'm going to enjoy it." He brought the knife down and pressed the full length of its edge across her throat. "I'm going to enjoy every moment of it."

And Senea thought she was dead.

Then, suddenly, he released her, and she gasped painfully at the air that rushed in.

"You think about that," he said, his body still holding her prisoner. "Think about it and dream about it. When you lie awake tonight imagine what it's going to be like. I'm going to be just like a Ja'sid."

And with that he turned on his heel and stalked off in the direction from which he had come, a black figure that vanished into the night. Senea stood frozen where she was while his footsteps retreated across the compound. Somewhere in the dark a door closed, and she was alone.

When she reached her bunkroom her hands were shaking so that it was difficult to remove her knife belt. She stuffed it into its niche in the wall, then sank down on her bunk.

"I hope that you are prepared for tomorrow."

She looked up and saw that Treyna was not asleep.

"Sky is not going to be as easy to beat as I was," she said from the shadow of her bunk, her voice hard.

"I can take care of myself," Senea said, and hoped that her voice sounded as confident as her words had. But she saw in the dim light from the corridor the skeptical doubt on Treyna's face, and when she thought of what Sky had said, she doubted it herself.

The sun was almost over the wall of the Held when Senea came out onto the compound the next morning. She stood just outside the door looking at the compound that was alive with helden. Excitement was everywhere, noisy and happy. But Senea did not share in it. She had spent a long, sleepless night in which Sky had been a dominant focus of her thoughts and imagination.

She saw Vayhawk to one side of the clearing and worked her way through the crowd to him. He looked at her long and hard for several moments before he reached out and touched a hand to where Sky had drawn blood with his knife.

"What is this?"

"I don't know," she lied. Her hand went up and felt the small wound at the base of her throat. She knew instinctively that she had better not tell Vayhawk anything about what had happened. He would confront Sky about it.

Vayhawk frowned at her, clearly not believing her. But he said nothing further and took her arm to lead her back to the wall of the Held. She went with him wordlessly, sat where he indicated, and was glad when he settled beside her. The warmth of him pulled at her stronger than ever. His arm was against hers, and when he drew up his knees to wrap his arms loosely around them, the metal of his gold band pressed into her skin.

Almost she leaned her weight against him and felt an unexpected compulsion to rest her head against his shoulder. But she held herself away and wished that they were out on the plain and away from this place.

It was in the hottest part of the day when her name was called. She looked at Vayhawk in a silent plea that she knew he could do nothing about. Then she rose to her feet and went toward the clearing without looking at him. She was afraid that if she hesitated even that much, she would lose her nerve and beg for the whole thing to be called off. And that would be shaming for her and for Vayhawk. So she strode quickly out onto the clearing, determined to get the whole thing over with.

She turned and waited for Sky to step out from the crowd; she watched him as he walked over to her. Perspiration beaded and rolled down her back.

He smiled slightly, but there was no humor in that upturning of lips. "Did you sleep well?" His quiet voice did not carry past her on the hot, sweltering air.

Something clenched in the pit of Senea's stomach, and she tried to conceal it. But he had seen it and knew that she had thought about him all night. He looked at her with a mocking glint in his eyes.

"How were your dreams?" he asked, taking a leisurely step to the right, beginning to circle around her. "Were they interesting?"

She held her tongue as he took another step, his left leg crossing in front, his head turned to look sidelong at her.

The images that had kept her awake for most of the night came flooding back, in force, the kind that grew in the dark, in those too-long hours of sleeplessness. Stark visions of Sky tearing the life from her with his hands. Ripping and rending. Savage. Brutal. And other things that had nothing to do with the Games.

He took another step.

Suddenly changed direction and lunged at her.

She bolted, ducking just beneath his clutching fingers. She spun to face him.

He laughed, a low-throated sound. "Come on, girl. You can do better than that." He circled slowly around her; she turned to face him, squinting in the harsh sunlight. "We've got to make this interesting for those who are watching." The smile on his face was dark and sinister.

Senea did not answer.

Every muscle in her body was tensed, ready to throw herself out of his reach at the first sign of movement toward her. Sweat was seeping into her eyes, persistent. The salt stung, and she had to wipe it away.

Vayhawk was standing at the edge of her vision, with arms folded, but she did not dare look at him, knowing that if she let her attention wander to him for even a moment it would be enough of a distraction to give Sky the opening he was looking for.

Suddenly, Sky stopped, his hand coming to rest negligently on the hilt of his knife. His eyes glinted with a mischievous light. "Let's raise the stakes."

Senea eyed him suspiciously. "What do you mean?"

"I'll put up more than my rank should you win."

Senea looked to his hand that was wrapped loosely around the handle of his knife, raised her eyes to his, and almost flinched. He was looking at her with open animosity.

"I'll put up what I saw at the northern border," he said. Then he smiled in a way that was both taunting and insulting. "What will you wager, heldii?"

Senea stared at him, heard a restless, impatient noise start in the crowd around them. She flicked her eyes over the compound and saw Roskel watching her from the clearing with uneasy concern on his face.

She looked back to Sky. "I have nothing to bet."

"Oh, but that's not true, heldii. You have a great deal to bet." When she didn't answer, he continued, "You have what *you* saw at the northern border."

Senea felt a coldness come over her.

"It's an even wager. Are you heldan enough to take it? Or do you need Vayhawk's permission first?"

A heated flush rose to her face. It was followed by anger. "I can take your bet!"

His smile was slow. "It is done, then?"

"Done!" she said angrily.

"Good."

Suddenly he lunged at her. She scrambled away, surprised—too late. He struck her, his hands clutching her.

She tore herself from him with a cry of anger and dove desperately to retreat, vain hope in that narrow space. She slid into a spin and ran, Sky close behind her.

She cursed herself for being a fool.

Think like the enemy, Vayhawk had tried to teach her. *Use it, flow with it; be the enemy.*

She should have seen what Sky had been up to—distracting her, putting her off guard. But she had fallen for his ploy like a novice.

She came up hard against the crowd, dove to the right, and felt a hand graze across her shoulder as she rolled away—Sky's.

He cursed.

Think ahead, Vayhawk had said. *Never fight by blind instinct. Nor let fear rule your head.*

She came to her feet as Sky hit her from behind.

She spun on one foot to keep upright, and barely managed to keep her balance.

A movement caught her attention—Sky swinging out with a strong looping left. It slammed into her jaw, sent her reeling.

Brutal hands grabbed her, yanked her against a hard body, jarring the breath out of her, his fingers digging into the flesh of her arms. She winced, saw his hand go to the knife at his belt and hesitate there.

"No," he murmured, his voice a hoarse whisper. "This is too easy."

His hand slid slow and hard, a sensual but brutal caress back up her arm to a painful grip that made her draw a sharp intake of air.

"I really expected more from you, girl."

For a moment neither moved, and silence was suddenly on the compound.

Senea found herself staring at the dark of his eyes.

They were green, a deep moss green, like that along the banks of a stream in the middle of wet season. For several heartbeats she sank into them, staring in mesmerized fascination, and was startled at how attractive they were to her, at how she was pulled irresistibly into their depths.

Then she came to herself with a jolt. She saw that he was laughing at her, a silent lift at the corner of his mouth.

And suddenly all the anger and contempt she felt for him flared in her and went deadly cold.

She reached down and freed her knife with a quick bend of her wrist. Swinging with all her might, she struck him alongside the head with the butt of the handle, flung her weight at him, throwing him to the ground.

He hit hard, rolled with impossible resilience . . . and caught hold of her leg just above the ankle, dragging her down, fighting and gasping.

The knife bounced away.

He seized her shoulders and flung her around hard to her back, his weight landing on her. She cried out at the impact, fought him furiously, her teeth bared, trying to dig her fingernails into his face.

His hands grabbed her wrists, wrenched them violently back and up over her head, and slammed them to the ground.

His eyes smoldered down into hers, his breath hot on her mouth. She glared at him, but he laughed, a shivering of breath on her skin.

"That was more like it," he said huskily.

She struggled under him and tried to pull her hands out of his grasp. His grip on her wrists tightened, fingers crushing— the tendons standing out in his arms.

"That will do you no good," he said. His weight shifted on her, the full length of his body pinning her to the ground. "You've lost the bet."

"I've lost nothing!" Her voice was breathless.

"But you have." He raised up on his elbows and smiled down at her. "I've been waiting a long time to see you like this."

She strained at his hands until she realized that his eyes had grown black with a dangerous fire. The smile left his face, and he looked down on her with vehement hatred.

"The things I'm going to do to you, girl . . ." he whispered, sending chills over her. His eyes raked her face. "You'll wish that you were dead."

"There's heldcode!" she spat at him. Her throat was raw, her voice hoarse.

"These are the Games, heldii. Anything goes . . . except a death. And I'm not going to kill you." He smiled then, a slow deliberate smile. "But you're going to beg me to."

Senea tore her eyes from his and looked to the crowd of helden a short distance away. Vayhawk was nowhere to be seen. She looked back to Sky, hearing the occasional shout of encouragement that broke the deathly silence that had fallen on the compound.

She thought about the things that he could do to her and suddenly knew that the visions that had kept her awake for most of the night were nothing compared with what he was planning.

He would hurt her. That was nothing. It was the look in his eyes. The stare. The scorn.

Her wits began to work. She threw herself at him in determination, fighting him furiously.

He snarled, wrenching her arms, twisting savagely so that they felt close to breaking.

She cried out in pain and spat into his face.

He swore, released one hand from her wrists, and raised that fist to strike her.

Without knowing it, she was on her feet, tearing her arms from his grasp, the strength of pent-up fury filling her body. Pain shot up her back but she ignored it as she turned on him to fling herself at him.

He was already standing, threat in his stance, wariness in the way he smiled at her. His arm band flared in the sunlight as he launched himself straight at her. Dust rose from the ground where he had been standing.

Senea danced back and let him go past, feeling the brush of his fingers on her arm as she pulled out of his reach.

He spun, snarling, his knife suddenly in his hand, and he was coming at her.

This time, she could not jump out of the way, but managed to knock the attacking knife hand aside, and she grappled with him. Instantly they were locked, each gripping the other's wrist, straining against each other.

Sky fell backward abruptly, pulling her with him. Senea lost her breath with a gasp when she hit the ground. Hard ropelike arms encircled her in a crushing hold.

Somehow the knife was gone.

She twisted and struck when she had a moment's leverage, over and over again—she almost flung herself up, but a wrench at her hair jerked her hard onto her back and he had her pinned. She saw the corded muscles in his neck, and the sun glaring in the sky; she felt the ground slip under her as they strained against each other.

Sky was looming over her. She reached down, picked up a handful of dust from the ground, and threw it at his face. He coughed and pulled back, rubbing his eyes while she fought to get to her feet. She heard a roar behind her, but did not know if it was the shouting of the watching helden or the sound of blood in her ears.

Without even realizing it, she was turning toward the sound. She heard someone shouting at her; a hand reached to stop her, but she evaded it and half stumbled, half fell into the crowd.

Suddenly she was driven down by a hard body from behind, throwing her violently forward into the crowd. Thankfully, there were hands waiting to catch her as she pitched forward.

She struggled to get to her knees, her fingers groping for a hold among sprawled bodies, grabbed at clothing and hair as she tried to pull herself away from him. She tried to turn about to meet the attack from the rear—a heavy hand descended on her shoulder and twisted it so savagely that she cried out with pain.

Turning, Senea brought her elbow back in a blow that caught Sky just under the ear.

Pain lanced through her arm.

Incredibly, he managed to twist with some incomprehensible acrobatic finesse, avoiding the sharpest brunt of the blow.

Ignoring the pain, Senea swung again and smashed her elbow back into his mouth. This time he did not turn aside soon enough, and she felt the flesh give and split. She hit him yet another time, a blow to the side of the head that toppled him to the ground.

Senea tottered back, fighting for balance as she stared at Sky's sprawled body. She had won. The knowledge circled around on the edge of her consciousness, not yet allowing her to feel the elation of victory.

She wanted to collapse. But stunned watchers stood staring at her.

She forced herself to stand up. She took a step and found that she could walk. She turned, looking for her knife.

Something was amiss. She knew it.

And heard a quiet laugh behind her.

That laugh had been such a small sound, but no heldan worthy of the name could have missed it. She had not won anything yet.

Sky had started to rise as soon as she began to move.

Laughing, Sky darted at her. He had found his knife again

and it whistled and buried its point in a pole that was behind her.

She did not wait to see it strike. He had another knife in his hand with the point turned slightly up. Senea had no idea where he had gotten it.

Desperately she looked around for her own weapon. It lay a dozen feet away behind several helden. Diving for it she scattered the helden every which way, but a firm grip on her brought her down.

Her hand just barely closed over the knife. Bringing it up blindly, she stabbed, feeling it sink into Sky's flesh. Then she saw that she had hit only the shoulder.

His hand came up and grabbed hold of her where her fingers and the knife were wet with his welling blood.

At that moment, a wall of darkness rushed out of nowhere. A blackness of spirit washed over her.

It was going to happen, even as she struggled to break Sky's hold. She could feel it building within her, coming from the contact of Sky's hand on her blood-wet flesh and the knife. This time it was so strong she might not be able to stop it. And if she couldn't, Sky was going to die. And if she managed to turn it aside, it would be forced in some other direction.

She tried to speak—to warn him—but failed.

Barely about to keep herself from being swept away in the grip of the force that was swirling around and through her, Senea thrust out rejection at the oncoming power. She hoped she could direct it away from Sky.

Something dark and strong coiled around her, pulling her into a swirling vortex of black pain. For a few frightening seconds it threatened to overcome her. She fought against it, pushed it away, repelled it, and sent it crashing against Sky. She could not stop it from rushing at him. He gasped in astonishment and pain as the force began to pull the life out of him. Senea tried to wrench her hand out of his.

His head jerked as if her shadowed gaze had struck him a blow, but he held on to her, persisting with an effort that was manifest throughout his body.

Senea felt the sudden understanding when it came to him. Abruptly his hand released her, and she gasped. She felt him return to himself with a snap when the contact between them was broken. His intake of air had the sound of surprise and triumph.

He stared at her a moment, then he bent close, lowered his voice almost to a whisper. "Now I've got you."

She could not answer. He had it figured out. She had known that he would. From that moment when she had challenged him in front of Mara and had felt the strong force that built up between them, she had known that he would figure it out.

He was going to kill her, and then he was going to kill Vaykawk. He was saying it, she realized, in a whisper that was barely more than a breath of sound.

"I'm going to tear you apart. Bit by bit. Piece by piece."

Anger flared. It poured out of her forcefully, cleanly. "Let's join the issue, then! You snared me, now get rid of me if you can!"

The anger gave her added speed and power. Mumbling something to herself, unaware that she had spoken, she got her feet under her and lunged forward. Pulling free and scrabbling over helden who were picking themselves up from the ground, she forced her way through the crowd with a speed and agility that took them by surprise. She dove for the doors of the Held. Out in the open like this, she didn't have a chance; she needed to get to the Held.

A voice called out from the crowd. Moving fast, Senea ignored the noise and voices and plunged into the dark of the corridor and dove across the eating hall.

The skylight shutters were pulled up, and only a thin shaft of light was falling through the darkness.

She was about to dash across the Hall itself when she realized she had permitted her anger to destroy her self-discipline. Halting, she deliberately took a deep breath. She drew a few more deep breaths to accustom herself to the taint of the air and felt less confined at once.

Crouching, she ran along the wall, ready to dive under a table the instant the door behind her gave hint of opening, and headed for the back wall where the cooking ovens were and back into a dark corner.

There she stood watching the door, trying to make her breathing slow and silent. Nothing could be seen in the darkness, and there was not a sound in the still air.

Then as she watched, the door opened. A single squeak of hinges.

A figure framed by light looked into the room.

Senea pressed against the wall feeling her stomach muscles tightening in anticipation.

Slowly the door closed again. Another squeak of hinges.

Senea held her breath and listened intently. There was nothing. No movement. No sound. Nothing.

She leaned her head against the wall and closed her eyes and dared to hope that he had not come into the hall but had gone down the corridor.

Cautiously she leaned forward and searched the shadows.

Still saw nothing. She stepped away from the wall.

"It does you no good to hide," a voice from the right said.

Senea spun.

"I'll just find you."

Involuntarily, she stepped back into the shadow, and he laughed. His form, darker than the blackness, moved along the wall.

It was as if a wolfhound had come padding into the eating hall, and the impression was so strong that Senea could almost have sworn that the heldan gave off a special scent: an animal smell, rank and menacing.

He came forward and stepped where the dim light from the skylight fell on him. Senea looked to the door and wondered why no one had followed them.

She turned her eyes back to Sky. The light color of his hair was the only thing she could see. His face was in deep shadow.

"I underestimated you, heldii." His voice was quiet, sounded close in the silence of the hall. "That's a mistake I don't often make."

She could not see the expression of his eyes, but she could hear it in his voice. Cold and deadly.

Her heart was beating so hard with anticipation that her chest hurt. She forced herself to exhale. Then she took a step to the side, her back to the wall.

"I don't make any mistake twice," he said. "Of course . . . there is a way to put an end to all of this."

She took another step.

"If you will admit defeat, this will end right here."

Another step. He turned to face her.

"Concede, heldii. You'll never get away from me again."

"It will do you no good to threaten me," she finally said. "I'm not afraid of you."

He shrugged. "You should be. I know your secret now. I'm certain you could tell."

Senea's hand fell against a chair, and she moved it between them, continuing to back along the wall.

"I wish that we could come to some kind of agreement," Sky said as he moved closer. "It would be a shame to put scars on that pretty face of yours. It would be even more of a shame to use the Ja'sid power against you. That's what it is, isn't it? The power of the Ja'sid."

He took a threatening step toward her. She thrust the chair at him.

He stopped short.

"What do you say, heldii? Do we call an end to this?"

"No!"

Suddenly the door flew open with a crash, and the chain was pulled to let the skylight shutters drop. Light flooded down on them.

Senea turned and saw Vayhawk standing at the door with his hand on the chain, helden crowding in around him. Relief almost overwhelmed her to see him, and she knew that it was plain to see on her face.

The growing crowd of helden was encircling them; several deep along the walls and climbing on the tables and chairs.

She tore her eyes from Vayhawk, and it was only then she saw that Sky had his knife.

He came at her with a growl.

She crashed into a table as she threw herself aside. He dove, lashing out with his knife.

Senea caught the blade on her arm; blood whipped from it in a crimson curtain and fell across her elbow. A portion of strength was ripped from her in the same instant.

Sky came after her and struck again, the blade held low, stabbing for the soft parts of her body.

She warded it off, getting a thin red scratch across her wrist. Then they went down crashing into a tangle of chairs, wood cracking and splitting with a tremendous racket.

A blow smashed across her jaw, half stunning her, and before she could recover her wits Sky had raised his hand. The edge of the blade flickered in the light.

Senea suddenly found herself countered, the knife coming at her throat. She blocked upward on Sky's wrist, seizing and twisting, but unable to stop it.

Relentlessly, a fraction of an inch at a time, the blade moved down. The blade slowly drove toward her throat. She tried with all her might to resist but wasn't strong enough. Slowly, slowly the knife descended and whenever Senea gathered the strength to push it back an inch or two, she reached her limit. The blade kept coming.

His muscles must have been used to this slow-motion combat. He had a stranglehold around the knife and refused to let go, and their bodily contact brought the force around them. Darkness descended over Senea, airless and chill. She didn't stand a chance if she didn't resist it.

Her next image of Sky was of narrowed eyes locked with hers.

She made a brief mental gesture, and a force like a hammer blow hurled at Sky. He jerked spasmodically, and the power came back at her like a knife blade. The blow smashed across her, for a moment absorbing all her wit, a deep black moment without organization; she knew that Sky was coming at her again with the knife.

She forced her mind to the surface, fighting the power with all of her strength.

Suddenly there was another presence. Vayhawk. He caught Sky's knife arm with his right hand, swung him up off Senea into a bear hug, and twisted the blade out of his hand.

"No more knives," Vayhawk said, his voice tight with rage.

He thrust Sky forward away from him and the heldan spun to face him.

"You're a dead man!" Sky spat.

For an instant Senea thought that Sky was going to attack him, but Roskel moved up beside Vayhawk, his hand on his own knife.

"I'd rethink that, if I were you, Sky. This competition can come to an end very quickly if you want it that way."

Sky glared at the two of them, the muscles in his jaw working with fury. Then he backed off, a single step back, and held out his hands in surrender.

"Whatever you say." Then he flung himself at Senea and hit her hard.

The impact of his body threw her against the wall, chairs flying in every direction. His hands went around her throat in a murderous rage; they tightened savagely. His teeth were bared, and his eyes dark with hatred.

The pain was instant—enormous.

Her fingers clawed at his hands, but for all the effect she had, those gripping fingers might as well have been bands of steel.

And she knew with a finality that surprised her that she was going to die.

She looked up into those moss green eyes that were blackened with murder-lust and wondered belatedly what had turned his enmity for Vayhawk into open hostility toward her. She wondered at the obsession for vengeance against her. There was a curious intimacy about it, even now.

She could feel it even as her life was being taken from her.

There was an intimacy in the way his breath was on her skin, the way he pinned her to the floor, the way his body was on hers. Very masculine. Very enticing.

She had never, before this, suspected that a man of his self-confidence and attraction could harbor such hateful feelings. And there had been something else about him, too, something that played around the corners of her mind like a face or name one should be able to place and couldn't.

Then thought swam on her head and broke apart like water on a stone. An eternity passed in which there was oblivion. There was a strange noise in her ears, and she found herself listening to it. A black mist kept getting into her eyes, and she tried to wipe it away, but could not reach that far.

Then somehow, there was the broken leg of a chair in her hand.

She thought about that a moment and wondered how it had gotten there.

Slowly she forced her eyes to open so that she could see Sky's face.

She lifted the chair leg so that it caught his attention. She allowed him a good look, then brought it down as hard as she could on the top of his head. There was a sickening thud as it hit him. He stared at her dazedly. His hands lost their grip.

Burning air rushed into her lungs, and there was a sharp taste of blood.

She hesitated; then she gritted her teeth and hit him again, contacting hard. The chair leg bounced away.

Then Sky was gone, sliding away as if he were not real at all.

Another eternity passed in which she coughed, fitful, wrenching coughs.

Then the mist began to fade from her eyes, and she became aware that Sky was sprawled across her body.

Shaking uncontrollably, she struggled out from under him, trying to gain her feet. She grabbed a table to pull herself up, but failed.

Sagging against the table for support, trying to give her rubbery legs some badly needed assistance, she fought to gather her strength for another try.

Her body hurt. Her head hurt. She was gulping air rather than inhaling it. Then she was sliding slowly down the leg of the table. At that instant, Vayhawk appeared.

Strong hands caught her.

Her last thoughts were of how intoxicatingly sweet the air was and how utter the silence was.

CHAPTER EIGHTEEN

"Senea."

Gentle hands touched her, bringing her out of a sleep that she was reluctant to leave.

"Senea, wake up." There was a shifting of weight beside her that disturbed her. She hurt, discovered this fact when an icy smear was put over her arm and slowly worked into the slice of pain that had been sending an aching fire down her elbow. For an instant it was relief, and she began to slip back into the comfort of darkness. But suddenly a more intense pain lanced down her arm. She flinched and tried to pull away.

"Senea?" a voice asked. "Are you awake?"

It was Mara.

Senea was hurting too much to be dead, so she forced herself to open her eyes, and focused on the heldan who was beginning a binding around her arm. Cold numbness spread from the wound. A bitter odor told her that an ointment had been used.

She looked past Mara and saw that she was in Vayhawk's room. She was lying on his bunk. It puzzled her for a moment. Then memory came back to her of Vayhawk catching her and picking her up.

Then she thought about Sky. He had meant to kill her. In spite of heldcode. In spite of the entire Held watching.

He had meant to kill her.

The memory of Vayhawk tearing the knife out of Sky's grasp came to her with a vividness that did not go away. She thought on it a time, realizing that if he hadn't stepped in when he had, she could very well be dead. He must have broken some kind of Game rule to do it.

But Roskel had backed him up.

Mara finished the binding on her arm, tied it. "How do you feel?"

"Terrible," she answered.

Mara smiled briefly. "I'm not surprised." Then her face sobered. "You were very lucky." She stood and picked up a bowl from the table.

Senea sat up slowly, putting her legs over the edge of the bunk, and grimaced at the pain that shot down her arm. She felt weaker than she had expected.

"I don't feel lucky," she said.

Mara watched her gravely. "You could have been killed."

That was the chilling truth.

"I know that," Senea said. Then, with a twist of her mouth she added, "But I wasn't." She knew as well as Mara did that Sky could have killed her, and it wasn't skill that had stopped him. It had been luck.

And Vayhawk.

And—she recalled—a chair leg.

"How's Sky?" she forced herself to ask, and didn't know which answer she wanted to hear . . . that he was alive or that he was dead.

"He's all right," Mara said, turning to put first aid supplies into a basket that was sitting on the table. "Though I'd give several of my ranks to see him otherwise." She looked over her shoulder at Senea, an angry glint in her eyes, her hand gripping a roll of binding.

"He's going to get away with it, you know, because it was the Games. He could have done anything, and no one would have been able to stop him. No one." She thrust the binding into the basket. "He has to be stopped."

Memory that Senea did not want came to her, of Sky's whisper. *The things I'm going to do to you, girl . . .* She could still feel his breath on her face, recalled how his body had pinned hers to the ground. *You'll wish that you were dead.*

It was not over. She knew that with every instinct that she possessed. He would yet have her in his power where no one would be able to help her. Someday.

"There's going to be blood because of him," Mara said. "And it's going to be bad blood."

Her own blood, Senea thought, and saw the same thought on

Mara's face. *You're going to beg me,* he had said. *Beg me for death.* And she knew that he'd make certain that she did.

She thrust that thought away and did not let herself think of what would happen when that day came. The things that he could do to her in that eventuality, when she let her imagination take her, made her blood run cold.

Mara put the bowl on top of the first aid supplies in the basket. "Come," she said, turning. "I will help you outside."

She picked up the basket and stood waiting, until Senea pushed herself to her feet. Then Mara's hand took her arm, lending support as she walked slowly to the door. There she stopped, leaned against the wall, and closed her eyes. Her head was swimming, and a sick trembling came over her. For one instant she thought she might faint, but she took a deep breath and forced the feeling away. For some reason her legs ached.

Mara waited until she had opened her eyes again. "Are you able to go on?"

Senea nodded, although she wasn't thoroughly convinced of it. "I don't understand why I'm so weak."

"It's the ointment," Mara said. "Desert weed. It numbs you a little. But you have to fight it."

Senea looked at her, heard an undertone in her voice that had not been there before. "Why?"

"Vayhawk has been challenged."

Senea stared at her, understanding with a chill what Mara was saying to her, that Vayhawk had been challenged for his position as Heldlan, that he had to fight to keep it. And if by some terrible stroke he lost, he would be reduced to second rank. He would be Held-second instead of Heldlord. The thought stunned her.

"Come," Mara said. She reached around and opened the door. "It has already started."

The heat hit Senea like a wall when she stepped out onto the compound, the ache in her legs forgotten, the dizziness in her head gone. There was an eerie stillness on the crowd of helden that she didn't like. The tension was so thick she could feel it, like a heavy hand. She stood still, her heart pounding. Not able to see through the press of the crowd, she looked around until she saw Roskel, a glimpse of chestnut hair to the left of the clearing.

She wove her way to him, with Mara close behind, and found his light brown eyes watching her when she reached him, studying her in that way of his, reading her every move. The habit of Held-second, to know at a glance the measure of a heldan, to see weakness and strength and weigh them constantly against the Held. His hand touched her waist and fell away as he directed her attention to the clearing, where she was loath to look.

She turned and saw Vayhawk hit a heldan, body to body, dust rising from the scrambling of feet. The heldan dove, rolling, came up to his feet, and lunged. But he fell motionless to the ground as Vayhawk spun and landed a solid blow to his midsection with an elbow.

There was a movement behind him, and Vayhawk whirled, face to face with another heldan; he grinned, thin as a knife blade. The sweat that filmed his skin quickly dried as the sun-scorched air stole it. A short distance away a third heldan was coming up from a crumpled heap.

"What's going on?" Senea asked in an anxious whisper. "Why are there three of them?"

"Hush," Mara said beside her. "This is the way it's done."

"One wouldn't be match enough," Roskel added in a low tone. "Vayhawk's too good."

Senea looked up at Roskel, but he was watching the fight, standing with his feet apart, his arms crossed on his chest. His face was expressionless. She looked back to Vayhawk, her blood pounding so hard in her throat that she felt strangled.

There was a sudden movement, and the second heldan had a knife.

Vayhawk stood there a moment. He drew a breath and just held out his hand.

To Senea's surprise the heldan tossed it to him, reacting by instinct to the authority of that silent command. Vayhawk caught the knife, walked forward, and swung it up, butt first. The heldan blocked, startled. Vayhawk swung again, thrust it up, under the jaw, and contacted hard, snapping the heldan's head back. Then he whipped around, ready for the third heldan.

Landry.

Senea's breath died in her throat.

Landry . . . whose cold, watchful silence had always been a real threat that had been overshadowed by Sky's more violent nature. Landry was easily overlooked, easily discounted and forgotten. But she could see by Vayhawk's sudden caution that he had not made the same mistake that she had. He was very much aware of the danger behind that quietness. And he looked at Landry with a dark wariness that boded ill.

Yunab's hand was in this, Senea thought with anger.

Where Sky failed, Landry might succeed.

With a slow deliberateness for the whole Held to see, Landry reached down and drew his knife. A humorless smile crossed his face, daring Vayhawk to try to take it, almost insolent in his stance. *Come and get it*, his body said . . . in the way he took a swaggering step . . . in the way he turned his back to grin at that crowd. He looked back over his shoulder at Vayhawk, but the Heldlan hadn't moved. He frowned and faced Vayhawk again. He brandished the knife defiantly, then spread his hands in mock confusion.

There was a breath of stillness. Then Vayhawk tossed away the knife he held and began to take off his knife belt.

A murmur moved through the crowd.

"What's he doing?" Senea whispered. A touch from Roskel's hand silenced her, his fingers closing lightly around her arm. She bit her lip and watched as Vayhawk slowly wrapped the belt around the sheath of the knife. He turned and tossed it to Roskel. The Held-second caught it with one hand. And for a brief, shocking moment Vayhawk's eyes found her, leaving her trembling when he glanced back to Roskel with a look that she could not read. Roskel drew her closer, and his hand moved to her waist.

Vayhawk turned then, an unhurried move, and faced Landry. He inclined his head in a formal bow and spread his hands to show that they were empty, a mocking smile on his lips. It was an insult, arrogant and disdainful, a declaration of superior ability. It was a gesture that flung Landry's dare right back at him.

"Do your best," Vayhawk said, his tone clearly meaning that Landry would never be able to touch him. "You can keep your knife . . . " he said.

Landry stood there drawing deep breaths, one after the other, his fingers working over the handle of his knife.

". . . if you think you need it," Vayhawk added. He moved deliberately to the left and kicked the other heldan's knife toward Landry. "Use this one, too."

Suddenly Landry flung himself forward with a yell, his knife flashing in the sunlight.

Vayhawk sprang out of the way, skidding to a halt against a pole. The crowd scrambled back as he crashed through them.

Landry rounded on him, his face flushed with rage.

Vayhawk dove, hit him, and drove him twisting to the ground. Vayhawk's arm went around Landry's throat and jerked back. His weight pinned Landry to the ground.

The heldan struggled. He tried to throw Vayhawk off but could not dislodge him.

His eyes were glazing over and faint wheezing sounds were coming from his constricted throat.

Senea shuddered. She could not bear watching it and tried to turn her head but could not.

Landry made a weak gesture of surrender, a wave of the hand that asked for quarter. A humiliating thing.

Vayhawk released him and stood up.

Chest rising and falling as he struggled to regain his wind, Landry rolled over, coughed a couple of times, and spat phlegm onto the ground.

There was silence. Then there was a thunderous cheer from the compound.

Vayhawk gathered up the knives and broke them, first one, then the other, tossing them to the ground. Then he turned and his eyes found Senea.

Roskel took her by the elbow and drew her in front of him. Vayhawk was coming toward her, and the entire Held was watching.

Then Roskel moved and went out to the center of the clearing where Landry was gathering himself slowly to his feet.

"Vayhawk is still Heldlan!" Roskel called out, and was met by a boisterous cheer. When it finally died away he said, "The Games are over! The heldii have earned their gold!" Another cheer went up that took longer to die. "The heldii and their trainers will stay here until the gold is presented." Another cheer interrupted him. He waited patiently until it was through. "The rest of you . . . back to your patrols!" This time the crowd broke out in loud boo's, but they began to disperse.

Senea stood silently, her back cold, her fingers nervously tracing the seam of her knife sheath. She looked up at Vayhawk and felt a thrill go through her. Roskel came up to them and handed Vayhawk his knife belt without a word. Then with an expressionless glance to Senea, he turned and strode away.

"Come, heldan," Vayhawk said. "Let's go get your gold."

Senea hesitated. He looked at her puzzled.

"Am I not still heldii?" she asked.

His hand had grasped hers. There was a very slight reaction to that question.

"Do I not yet have to get to your knife before you do?"

He was silent a moment. Then, "Do you think you can?" His voice was soft.

She considered, then lifted her chin in sudden mischievous defiance. "Do you think I can't?"

Vayhawk did not move, his eyes on her face. A corner of his mouth quirked in amusement. "Okay, heldii." He emphasized that. "You're on. When this is over, we'll see just how fast you are."

His hand moved up her arm, grasping it firmly. There was no effort to mask the look in his dark eyes, amusement that played around the edges of another darker look, a smoldering gaze that had nothing to do with humor. Senea's heart stopped beating for an instant and a flush went over her skin.

"Come," he said finally. "Let's go get your gold."

She let him guide her across the compound to the other heldii. Vayhawk left her there and strode to where the arm bands were being made and marked. She watched him as he spoke to the helden that were marking the gold, the light of the early afternoon sun shining bright on his head and shoulders. Long minutes passed while he supervised the making of her arm band.

Senea watched as the heldii next to her received her arm band. The heldan who had been her trainer put it on her arm and then bent to kiss her cheek. That shook Senea, and she looked around and saw others doing the same. She ran a hand up to where her own arm band was going to be, the arm that had escaped injury, and she swallowed nervously.

She saw then that Vayhawk was coming toward her, the afternoon sun reflecting off the gold band in his hand. She watched him approach and her heart began to beat very fast. Apprehension filled her, and on another level it was raw fear. She knew that he was going to tighten the ties that held her to him, that he was going to make them forever unbreakable, even as he gave her the symbol of her freedom; and she could do nothing to stop him. She very suddenly wanted to run. But she forced herself to remain where she was, knowing it would do no good. He'd just come after her.

He stopped before her, and she looked up at him. His eyes searched her face and a silence came between them, a silence in which the rest of the Held seemed to disappear. Wordlessly he took her wrist in his hand, slipped the gold band over her fingers, and moved it up her arm where he clasped the seam together. Then he took her shoulders in his hands, leaned forward, and kissed her cheek. The touch of his lips on her skin startled her.

He started to draw back, but stopped.

His breath fluttered over her cheek, warm against her.

Then his lips were on hers in a gentle possession that took her breath away, the shock of it ripping through her like fire and ice, setting her head to spinning. The strength drained from her. His kiss moved across her lips, a caress of infinite gentleness that surprised her. Then his mouth left hers, the withdrawing of it so slow it ached like pain. She looked up at him and found him gazing down at her, his face only inches from hers.

"Welcome to the Held, Senea," he said. His words were barely above a whisper, and they shivered along her spine.

Her heart was beating so fast that she could only cling to him, afraid that her legs were going to collapse under her. She knew that if he let go of her she would not be able to stand.

"Vayhawk . . ." she whispered, about to protest that there would be repercussions, that they would lose everything they had gained that day.

"Sh, sh," he silenced her, a breath against her skin that had no sound. The warmth of his body pressed lightly against her, and he drew her slowly but irresistibly closer, barely touching her lips with his. It was a gentle evocative touch that sent a shaft of lightning through her. He raised his eyes to hers, and there was a dark, fathomless look in them that sent her heart hammering hard at her ribs, beating like a wild thing trying to escape.

"Senea!" A voice startled her, and hands pulled at her arm. She tore her gaze from Vayhawk and saw Mara beside her. She looked back to Vayhawk again. Her body felt oddly chilled, as if its source of warmth had been taken away.

"You made it, girl!" Mara cried. "You made it!"

"Yes," Senea murmured, nodding, unable to pull her eyes

away from Vayhawk. He was regarding her with a contemplation that reminded her of that first day when she had come into the Held.

"Come," Mara said, pulling at her. "We have to celebrate."

"What?" Senea said absently. He was smiling faintly at her, sending a shock of a thrill lancing through her.

"My bunkmates and I are going to help you celebrate."

"Celebrate?" Senea echoed. Vayhawk nodded imperceptibly for her to go with them.

"Yes. Come on before there are no tables left in the eating hall." Hands pulled at her, and Senea nodded, her eyes still on Vayhawk.

"All right," she said, and let Mara lead her away. Vayhawk turned then and walked across the compound. She watched him go.

Then she saw Sky out of the corner of her eye. She looked suddenly and narrowly at him. He smiled at her across the compound, a cold and cynical gesture that told her he had seen everything. Senea's blood turned to ice. He turned and walked to where a door led through the Held to the plain. No one spoke to him. Treyna was not with him. Senea's eyes stayed fixed on him, and she knew that he would not let what he had seen go unchallenged.

CHAPTER
NINETEEN

They had dinner in a corner near one of the fires.

The afternoon had still been young when they left the bath and went to the eating hall. Mara settled in the chair nearest the fire and folded her arms, extending her legs before her. Her face quirked into an engaging smile. Slowly, Senea sank into the chair in the corner where she could look across the crowded room to the door. One of Mara's bunkmates had taken a seat across from her. Another sat down next to her.

Senea still did not know who was who; her mind was too preoccupied to concentrate on putting names with faces. But she thought that these two were paired together. She looked at them and wondered where the other one was. Probably on patrol, she thought . . . where she herself would rather be.

She suddenly realized that she wouldn't be going out on patrol with Vayhawk very much anymore. There were still things that he had to teach her; she didn't know half the knife and wrestling routines that he did, but she was considered heldan now even though for a long while yet he would be teaching her. As the other helden would be teaching their heldii who were now considered helden.

She'd have to go to Roskel for her patrol assignments instead of following where Vayhawk took her. She thought of the aloneness of the plain, thought of the emptiness that there would be without the sound of his tread, without his presence watching her every move. She thought what it would be to be paired to another heldan for life, without the nearness of Vayhawk as she walked the troughs of dried streambeds and crested the hills to see what lay beyond. Suddenly she was left with a strange feeling of desolation.

She felt the unaccustomed weight of the gold band on her arm. On it was inscribed the double-ring symbol of the Held. Beside that was her rank. Ninth.

The memory of Vayhawk sliding the band up her arm was still vivid in her flesh, the tracing of his fingers on her skin, the pressing of his lips on her cheek . . . and on her mouth . . . For a moment a shiver raced like ice through her.

"Well, I don't know about you," Mara said, drawing Senea out of her thoughts, "but I'm famished." She stood up and went over to a neighboring hearth where a large pot was steaming over some coals. Quickly she returned, bearing a large and laden tray. "You'll have to get your own," she told her bunkmates. "Senea's the only guest of honor here." She sat down and handed Senea a bowl of stew and gave her a twisted smile. "I'm not serving them, too."

"No one asked you to!" one of them said, the blonde—Cora, Senea seemed to remember, but wasn't sure.

Mara grinned back at them, and they stood up together and went after their own meals. When they had gone, Mara's face went sober. "How does it feel to out-rank almost everybody in the Held?" Her voice dropped low and there was an ominous sound in her words.

Senea thought about it. "All right, I suppose," she said.

"You out-rank Sky."

Senea frowned over that. She hadn't clearly thought it out. When she had won against him, she took his rank while he dropped one.

"He dropped three ranks during these Games because of you," Mara added. Senea had been realizing that fact at the very moment that Mara had voiced it. "He's not going to like it."

Senea blinked, no more than that. It was the truth. She understood.

Mara reached and pressed Senea's hand. "Always watch your back."

"I will."

Mara leaned back in her seat, relaxing. "Good."

There was a movement, and Mara and Senea looked up together. The third of Mara's bunkmates was coming swiftly toward them.

"Kariana," Mara said, pleased, a sudden smile coming to her face.

"I'm here!" Kariana cried. "It took forever to find Roskel." She collapsed into a chair breathlessly.

"Where are you and Jaron assigned?"

"The Deijoi borders." Her nose wrinkled with disgust. She sat up and took a slice of bread off the tray, then slumped back and said sadly, "Ten days."

Mara shook her head. "Hard luck. But at least it's far away from the Ja'sid." She began to eat. "Who are you going with?"

"I think Layna and Strat."

"Good team."

Kariana nodded.

Cora and Elene came back then and sat down. Mara looked up and waved a spoon at them. "These two have the week off. As if they really needed it."

Elene, the heldan with the black hair and blue eyes, looked at Mara with a puzzled frown. But Cora grinned mischievously.

"We deserve it."

Mara didn't pause in her eating, but threw Cora a look of suspicion as if she thought the heldan might not be entirely right in the head.

Cora laughed. "You haven't been easy to be around lately. You've been as nervous as a sandbeetle. You'd think that it was *your* heldii who had to fight in the Games." She heaved a greatly exaggerated sigh. "We all need a rest."

Mara's eyes moved silently from one heldan to the other, finally resting on Senea.

Senea played with her food, stirring the stew with an idle spoon, too nervous to eat.

"It's a good thing Tason and I have to leave on patrol in the morning," Mara said to Cora, "or I'd *really* make your life miserable."

Cora went quiet at that, but the smile did not leave her face. Kariana chuckled. Senea turned her eyes to watch Mara shove another spoonful of stew into her mouth and follow it with a bite of grain-bread. She suddenly understood something that she had not thought on before. Mara was her friend—a very good friend—the best she'd ever had, and she had been from the beginning. She only realized it now as she looked at Mara and saw how deep that friendship went, helping her to learn the ways of the Held; even standing up to Vayhawk in her behalf.

Suddenly there was a disturbance at the door, a movement that caught Senea's attention. Mara and her bunkmates turned to look, also.

It was Vayhawk, his hand still holding the door open. His eyes searched the room until he found Senea. He looked at her, waiting—so obviously waiting that those at her table were hushed, as if no one dared breathe. Senea remained silent and motionless in her chair, hearing the loud noise of the rest of the room. Her eyes flickered over to Mara and found the heldan watching her. Mara gently took her hand, which had been clutching her spoon on the table, and smiled, giving her a small wink.

Senea looked back to Vayhawk. He lifted his chin slightly, staring straight at her while he let the door swing closed. *Come here,* that meant. Senea stood and started around the table.

"Where are you going?" Cora asked suddenly. "You're not heldii anymore."

The question threw her off balance, and without thinking Senea told her the truth. "I have one more test to pass."

"What test?"

"Shut up, Cora . . ." Mara said behind her as Senea moved away. She heard nothing more of what Mara said as she threaded her way across the room toward Vayhawk.

He turned and pushed through the door before she reached him. She followed and found him standing in the hall where the light from the compound shone through a door on him. He just stood there looking at her, then nodded his head finally toward his room. He wanted her hand, holding his out. She hesitated a moment before placing her fingers into his. She was very aware of the warmth of his skin next to hers as his hand closed.

He took her down the hall, to his room, then held his door open, letting her in first. The door shut behind them, leaving only darkness. He moved around her in the gloom, his hand trailing across her waist, went to the table, struck a flame, and lit the lamp. The light flickered, then burst into yellow and blue flame, brightening the room and sending long shadows bouncing off the walls. He drew his knife, the lamplight gleaming on the long blade, strode to the center of the room, dropped to his heels, and stabbed the knife hard into the floor.

His eyes raised to her where she stood by the door.

Her fingers brushed the wooden door behind her. She understood the silent order. Clenching her hand, she studied the expression on his face for a moment, then went forward. She knelt in front of him without speaking. Vayhawk settled to his knees, the knife between them; Senea's heart lurched, so near he was. He looked into her face. His eyes burned with dark, smoldering fires.

"Go for it," he said softly.

She started to say something, but let it die in her throat. There was nothing but for her to try. Mara's words suddenly began to sound in her head: *The reason he's Heldlan is because no one can do anything faster or better than he can.* She flexed her hand. *You'll stay heldii forever if that's the test he's given you.* She grabbed at the knife.

Vayhawk's hand slapped around her wrist.

She met his eyes and said nothing. There was nothing to say.

He bent forward, his face coming close to hers, his breath on her lips.

"Not fast enough." There was a glimmer of humor in his eyes. He raised his other hand and touched her cheek, brushing his fingertips toward her mouth.

Senea drew in a breath. "Did you intend that I ever be?" She kept her voice steady.

Eyebrows shot up at this.

"Mara says that I will always be heldii to you." Senea continued, unsure why she was saying these things. "That I can never win. The test is an unfair one."

The brows came down into an instant frown. Senea's heart thudded in dismay. She regretted her words at once and wished that she could take them back. He released her wrist and sat back, a withdrawal that was more than a putting of distance between them.

"That's easily solved." His voice was toneless, his eyes veiled and distant.

Senea's breath turned painful in her throat when she saw that lack of warmth on his face.

"Do it again."

She stared at him.

He made an impatient, challenging gesture. "Do it again." The tone of that chilled the flesh. He folded his arms and watched her expressionlessly.

Senea pressed her hands together to keep them from betraying her. She had been completely unprepared for his reaction and knew that this time he would not stop her from reaching the knife. His face was untouched by any emotion, cold as stone. She stared down at the knife, her stomach curling into knots. She could not touch it. She clenched her fingers together with a slight shake of her head.

"No," she choked, and she was up on her feet.

A blink of the dark eyes.

She turned and escaped to the dark corner by the table, her heart beating so strongly she hurt. She almost forgot to breathe when she looked around and saw that he was watching her closely.

He raised back up so that he sat on his heels again and crouched there a moment, arms across his knees. Then he reached out and pulled the knife out of the floor with a strong tug. He glanced at her without speaking, thrust the knife into its sheath, then rose to his feet with an effortless unfolding and came to her.

She watched him, unable to move, until she was caught between the wall and his solid body. Before she could speak, his arms were around her and his mouth was on hers. There was a sense of shock as if her heart suddenly stopped beating. It seemed to her at that moment that the world held nothing but the fire of his lips and the strength of his arms, and she did not have the will to resist. Then as suddenly as he was kissing her, he was not.

She gasped, and adrenaline drained away, leaving her legs shaking under her. His hands were warm against the chill of her skin, his touch moving slowly over her arms. He was looking down on her with a faint smile.

"Are you all right?" he asked, his voice quiet.

She nodded, unable to speak. He brushed her shoulder with a caress. He bent his head and grazed her lips with his, the nebulous touch sending a tremor through her like wildfire. For a moment she let his lips trail over to the point below her ear. Closing her eyes as she yielded to him, her breath whispered from her body as he drew her into his arms again. Then she remembered the Maiden's eye that Mara had given her, and she pulled back suddenly and came up against the wall, her eyes flying open.

"Vayhawk . . . don't . . ." she gasped. There was a lack of strength in her voice.

His brows drew together as he looked at her. "What's the matter?"

She could only shake her head. No words would come.

"Senea." The tone of his voice stopped her cold. Then he drew in a long breath through his nostrils while his eyes moved slowly over her face.

"All right," he said finally, impatience barely under control at the edge of his voice. "It's up to you. You decide if this goes any further or not."

Senea looked up at him and slowly took his meaning.

"It's your decision," he said. "It will end right here, if you say so." His hands left her and raised to the wall on either side of her. He leaned his weight on them, his eyes watching her with cold detachment.

And that sent an understanding through her, that this was her last chance; that if she wanted to, she could walk out the door and he would let her go. He'd never come after her again. Never again would he approach her in any way other than as Heldlan. It would be final—irrevocable—unrepentable. She would have to go to Mara for anything else that she did not know, for he would not teach her anything more.

A heavy silence fell between them, and Senea could hear her heart beating, thudding painfully against her ribs. The blood was rushing through her in a way that took the last remaining strength from her. She suddenly had the dual sense of being both trapped and exhilarated. She looked at him, at his dark eyes that bored into hers, and looked at his mouth. The memory of it was still on her, burning and lingering. She thought what it would mean to never feel it again and thought what it would be to want that touch in vain. A brief moment of desolation came on her at that possibility.

There was only one decision possible. For her there was no other. The ties with which he had set out to bind her were unbreakable, and she could only surrender to him.

Trembling so that it threatened to consume her, she reached up and touched a kiss to his lips, feeling the unyielding smoothness of his mouth. Her heart lurched even as she did it. Half a breath she thought he rejected her. There was no response at all in him.

Then his mouth molded to hers, and he drew her kiss with a gentleness that sent a cold fire of joy racing through her. It was like a sip of water, intoxicatingly sweet and sensual, after a journey in a dry-parched desert. She leaned to him knowing that there was no undoing of it.

His hands left the wall and went to her face, holding her kiss firmly against his, while his lips coaxed and caressed her until she couldn't breathe. Then his arms went around her with a fierceness that startled her, crushing her against the hardness of his body. His mouth forced her lips apart, and suddenly he was kissing her in a way that she had never imagined, shock ripping through her like a knife.

She was powerless and utterly helpless against his strength, and she could do nothing but give way to him and become a part of him, letting him possess her, making no attempt to stop him because she knew it would be utterly useless.

His hand moved from behind her and took hers to draw it up between them. Releasing her mouth he turned his head to press his lips into her palm. Then he put her hand to his chest, holding it there with his own. The rapid beat of his heart was a fever-heat against her palm. Then, as if some magnetism compelled her against her will, her eyes were slowly drawn to his and met a look that was dark with restrained fire.

"From the moment I first saw you," he said, "I knew it would be like this." He raised a hand to her face. His thumb moved over her bottom lip. "When I saw you standing there, I knew you were important. I couldn't let you go to another.

"I knew that together we would be able to get a hold on this power of the Ja'sid's. With you as my heldii, I knew that we would be able to find it. I'm certain that the closer the relationship is between two helden, the stronger the power is. I had to find out. The only way was to be paired to you. And it had to be you; not any other." His hand moved down over her throat, and his mouth came very near to hers.

"Not just because of this Ja'sid power, either. I saw instantly that there would be something between us. I saw it in your face. I could have taken you right there, had I wanted to . . . in front of Aldived, in front of Roskel and the entire Held. You wouldn't have done anything to stop me.

"I will not let you go now that I have you." His words whispered over her. His hand tightened slightly on her throat.

"Understand that, Senea. We are confederates now. Closer than heldii and heldan. Closer than man and wife. For the rest of our lives. Do you understand that?"

Senea's heart was beating very fast. "Yes."

He moved his hand delicately, his fingers tracing her jaw. "Good." After a moment he continued, "There were three in my dream."

"Dream?"

"I dreamed about you before you ever came into the Held. That's how I recognized you. There were three helden in my dream that would play important roles in this struggle with the Ja'sid."

"Who are they?"

"You and me, my dear. The third, I'm not ready to say, yet."

"But you know who it is."

Vayhawk nodded. "I wasn't certain, for a while, but I'm getting a pretty good idea. The third is the antagonist."

Senea looked at what she could see of him, his throat and chin, wondering about what he was saying. She had never thought of dreams as something one paid attention to. That there was a power in them, a dreaming of truth, was as foreign an idea to her as the Ja'sid power had been when Vayhawk had first told her about it. But she had felt the reality of that Ja'sid power. Now she had no choice but to accept what he said again.

"Is the third heldan Sky?" she asked.

"No. He doesn't figure in this very much, other than what he thinks he does. But enough talk."

And his mouth moved and closed over hers, and he kissed her with a slow, exploring caress, seeking and possessing so that she could only flow with it. His hand took hers and moved it up his chest, pressing it to him until she was trembling. Underneath her hand, a warm force was gathering. And where his hand covered her, the warmth ran down her fingers and up her arm.

At that moment there came a knock at the door. The sound was startling, a sudden intrusion. Vayhawk drew back, his smoldering gaze on Senea's mouth, then rising to her eyes. She slid her hand down his chest, feeling suddenly cold. For a moment neither one of them moved. Then he bent his head and kissed her once more. The knock sounded on the door again.

This time he stepped away, turning to the table. "Come," he said, raising his voice only slightly, and Senea was amazed at his control.

She leaned against the wall fearing that her legs would not hold her.

Roskel came in, stopping just within the room. "Aldived wants to see you." His gaze swung from Vayhawk to Senea where she was in the partial shadow and slowly took in her flushed face and trembling hands and sized up the situation exactly. He looked back to Vayhawk, his face expressionless.

"When?" Vayhawk asked.

"Right away."

Vayhawk expelled a breath and made an impatient gesture. "Very well."

Roskel looked at Senea again, the directness of his gaze bringing heat to her face. Then nodding wordlessly to Vayhawk, he turned and left.

Senea drew in a breath. "What's he going to do?"

"Do?" Vayhawk came to her.

"He knows."

"Of course he knows."

"But won't he object?"

He laughed as if that question surprised him, and Senea made a helpless shrug.

"You don't need to worry about Roskel." He put his hand to her face and bent down to touch his lips to hers. "Come with me." And he turned to the door, drawing her after him.

CHAPTER
TWENTY

Tired to the bone, Senea stood swaying in the center of the entry hall where the glare from the late afternoon sun fell through the open window and across the tiled floor in a white-gold blaze to the opposite door. Vayhawk had left her in this uncomfortable, hot place while he went to talk to Aldived.

And now that she was alone in the silence of the Tribelord's place, a deep weariness was starting to descend on her. It was a heaviness that settled into her bones and a pain that slid into every bruise that Sky had given her.

Looking around she saw a bench in a corner out of the glare of the sun. Going to it she sat down, leaned her head against the wall, and slept.

Images were in her dreams: Vayhawk pulling his knife from the floor, sliding it into its sheath, him coming toward her, his arms going around her; Sky holding her prisoner against a dark doorway, the point of his knife pressed against her throat, the heat of his breath against her face.

She came awake, a cold sweat on her face. She wiped at it with her hand and drew in a breath. Slowly the pounding of her heart resumed its normal pace and she relaxed against the wall, stretched her legs out in front of her, and closed her eyes again.

After a time a sound intruded onto her attention, a quiet closing of a door that brought her eyes open. She heard approaching footsteps, and somehow she knew who it was. She quickly turned, blood draining cold to her middle.

Sky and Yunab.

She rose to her feet, a careful straightening.

Yunab was looking at her like a scavenger, watchful and challenging.

She glanced to Sky, and his mouth quirked to a one-sided smile, something glittering in the depths of his eyes, something dark. There was too much humor in that dark green gaze, and it made her uneasy.

"Yunab," she greeted with a slight nod of the head, looking from one to the other warily.

"Heldan," Yunab returned. There was a faint mocking tone to that.

She looked back to Sky, and he inclined his head to her, a salute that was an insolent acknowledgment of her new rank over him. She stared at him, her breath going chill in her throat. She saw for the first time the swollen bruise on the side of his face where she had struck him with her knife and saw the black jagged cut above it where she had hit him with the chair leg.

Unconsciously, she took a step backward, the side of her leg brushing along the bench. A slow, threatening smile moved across his lips, and Sky stepped up to her, effectively cutting her off from any exit.

"Well, heldan. What are you going to do now that you're no longer Vayhawk's heldii?" he asked her, the tone of his voice saying that he didn't need to ask. He had seen what he had seen on the compound and had guessed the rest. There was something in his eyes that she did not recognize, but she realized that it made him even more dangerous than before.

It struck her like a hammer blow, and she could not answer him for a moment. She could not summon the words that would deny what he thought he knew. Heat leapt to her face as she met his smoldering gaze. Then swallowing, she said lamely, "I don't know what you're talking about." She kept her voice carefully steady.

His hand came against her shoulder, pushed her back against the wall. "You know exactly what I'm talking about. Let's be honest, heldan."

She looked at him squarely, fighting down a growing anger, quickly and effectively removed his hand. "Touch me again and you'll lose it!"

She had to quell her reaction at the sudden anger on his face.

"Come, come," Yunab said, stepping forward and putting a

restraining hand on Sky's shoulder, moving him back. "We did not come here for hostilities."

"Then why are you here?" Senea asked, switching her glare to him.

"Come sit by me," he bade her, motioning to the bench. "Let's talk."

Senea stared at him with suspicion, knowing that there was some hidden motive to this, recalling the last time she had been in this place and Yunab had talked to her. The counselor looked at her in his turn, with no hint of insolence. His face was a perfect mask. There was no clue at all to tell her what he was up to. She was tense and alert for any trick.

"Come. Sit." He took her hand in his, put his arm about her shoulders, and drew her unwillingly down to the bench with him. "There's no reason for us to be enemies. What harm could a little talk do?" He smiled at her. There was no change in his eyes.

Senea drew in a breath, forced herself to look to Sky, and found him regarding her with that watchful waiting of his.

"I want to congratulate you on your success in the Games," Yunab said. There was a slight flicker in Sky's eyes, but it was quickly gone. Senea pulled her gaze from him and turned back to Yunab, enduring his touch with an iron patience.

"You surprised everyone," he said, and shrugged. "A lot of bets were lost. Heldii don't very often rise to the first ten their first Games. Of course, Vayhawk did, as I recall. And he was a mere boy. But then he's an exceptional individual. I guess it's understandable that his heldii would provide a similar performance. Quite an astounding feat. Of course, you realize that puts you within reach of becoming Heldlan yourself." His voice trailed off with meaning.

Her pulse sped. She thought about it a moment, then shrugged, suddenly wary.

"I'm hoping that we can put an end to this unpleasantness between us. It's unfortunate that it happened in the first place. I can't see any reason for it to continue. Can you?"

Senea considered him and cautiously chose her words. "I haven't been aware of any unpleasantness between us, Counselor."

The black eyes bore into hers. "There's no reason to deny it, heldan. It's very regrettable, but it has happened. I'm hoping that we can come to some sort of understanding . . . now that you're no longer heldii."

The tone of that chilled the flesh. She restrained an involuntary shudder.

"Hostility is not going to get us anywhere," he continued. "Besides, you may decide to press your advantage now."

Advantage?

What advantage?

Then she made herself look at that hateful face, suddenly understanding what he meant.

Betrayal.

Indignant anger came on her that he'd even think she'd consider it, but caution kept her still, and she glanced to Sky where he stood with his arms crossed watching her. The expression on his face was unreadable, but she found it unnerving that he watched her so closely.

"And what then?" she asked, looking back to Yunab, her voice sounding to herself like it belonged to someone else.

"What then?" the counselor echoed.

"After I . . . press my advantage?"

Yunab's lips compacted into a narrow grimace something like a smile. "Well, that all depends on the arrangements made."

"Arrangements?"

"Certainly. Something like this can't be accomplished alone."

"Meaning that I would have help."

"If you should decide to rise to Heldlan, there would be obstacles to overcome. Some assistance would be necessary."

"Coming from you and Sky."

"Well, Sky has been heldan much longer than you; he knows things about the Held that you do not. And I . . . have Aldived's ear. Together we could accomplish a great deal. I'm confident that we can work something out . . . if you decide to ally yourself to us."

Senea frowned, perceiving she was being pressed, that Yunab was choosing the direction he pushed her. She drew a long breath, let it go again. "I see. And once I am Heldlan . . ."

"I will be there to advise you."

"Because I haven't been in the Held very long."

"Unfortunately. But you will gain experience, and in time

you may no longer need anyone in an advisory position. But only time can tell that for certain."

Senea glanced to Sky. Still, she could not see anything on his face that could tell her what was going on inside.

"How do you feel about this?" she asked him. "Do you want me to become Heldlan?"

There was a flutter of something in his eyes that was gone almost before she saw it.

"Sky wants what is best for the Held," Yunab answered for him.

But Senea saw Sky look to the counselor, an imperceptible glance of dislike that Yunab did not see, but it told her that the counselor did not know Sky's mind on this. She wondered what sort of trap was being closed around her. Yunab with his plans. Sky with his own. And of the two, Sky's would be the most deadly. And she saw the certainty of it on his face as he studied her, waiting to see what she was going to do.

"You don't want to be Heldlan yourself?" she asked, doggedly forcing the issue, realizing even as she did that she was inviting repercussions that she could learn to regret.

Suddenly there was tension in the room, close and dark. Sky's moss-dark eyes went to Yunab, lingered there a moment, then turned back to her, his face revealing nothing.

Yunab's voice broke the silence. "The Games changed that. Sky knows this, and he has agreed."

"To be Held-second?" she asked, forcing herself to meet Sky's gaze steadily. "Do you think that is wise? There is no friendship between us; what's to keep him from pressing *his* advantage?"

Sky's stare became guarded.

"I don't think you'll need to worry about that," Yunab said. "These things can be worked out."

"Don't you think that there will be blood between us?"

"I'm sure that Sky can be persuaded to loyalty, given the right conditions."

"Loyalty?" Senea almost laughed out loud. She looked at Yunab incredulously.

The counselor smiled at her. "Everybody wants something, heldan. You do. I do. Sky does. It's just a matter of working out a way to make everyone happy."

"And you know what Sky wants." She suddenly realized the trap that Yunab was trying to maneuver her into.

"I think I do." His words fell on a deadly quiet.

Senea found herself staring at Sky, his dark gaze on her, challenging and defiant, turning into a black smoldering that swept over her, causing her breath to stop in her throat. She looked back to Yunab in outraged disbelief. His eyes were veiled, but the slight curve of his lips showed amusement.

He was playing them against each other, heldan against heldan, opponent against opponent, enemy against enemy, a cunning game in which he hoped to be the winner. She clenched her hand where it was hidden beside her until her nails dug into her palm, her grip tightening fiercely.

She drew a long breath and let it go again. "Sorry," she said. "Not interested."

There was silence after that; she had destroyed all the pretenses. The false smile on Yunab's face vanished and so did the casual tone. Menace was now on his lips.

"You'll regret that decision." His hand crushed hers.

She flinched from it, pulled away.

He narrowed his eyes and locked them with hers. "Vayhawk's days as Heldlord are not many, I promise you that. It makes no difference to me if it takes one dead heldan or two. The choice is yours." He rose to his feet and smiled, but there was malice in the deep grooves of his gaunt face, and in his eyes as well.

"I'm not done with you, heldan," Yunab said, fixing her with his stare. "There are things I know . . ." His voice sank to the faintest of whispers. "Things I know that are life and death to you . . . and to your Heldlan. You can't remain paired to him now. You know that, don't you?"

Senea looked sharply from him to Sky and knew at once that he had told Yunab what had happened on the compound. The dark challenging fire of his gaze that had been leveled on her only moments before was gone. In its place was an icy stillness. He regarded her now with a faint smile.

She hated him, for that moment, thoroughly, and she knew that he saw it. A dangerous glint came to his eyes.

"You better watch your step from now on," Yunab said, bringing her attention back to him. His voice was soft, but it boded ill. And that was all. He left; Senea stared after him through the door and trembled in every muscle. Whether it was from anger or fear she did not know.

She found her hands sweating, not sure whether it was because of the insufferable heat in the room or the hammering of her heart. She rose to her feet. That made Sky turn to her.

"Stay put," he said, and took a step toward her.

For an instant she hesitated, not knowing what he might do; but he just stood regarding her.

He drew in a breath finally and said, "You can't hold out forever, you know."

She bit at her dry lips. "I can try."

"You will go down with him, Senea. You know what he's done; what he's doing. Do you want to be a part of that?"

Senea thought about that in sudden caution. That was a question posed hunter-style, flatly, an attempt to draw a kind of confession out of her. She let go her breath, a slow hiss.

"Better than going down with you . . . as my Held-second."

Sky caught that sarcasm. He gave her a long and penetrating look. "Don't worry. It won't happen." His voice was cold, cold. Then he closed the distance between them. "You listen to me. There's a point past which anyone can be pushed. There always is. And, heldan, I'm going to push. You can count on it. Yunab might have his plans for you . . . but I have my own. And I'm going to push until you break."

Senea lifted her chin defiantly. "I'm not afraid of you, Sky."

He went stone-faced. "Then you're stupid. I never promise what I can't deliver."

"This is pointless," she said with disgust, and tried to shoulder past him.

He stood in her way. "When I get through with you, you'll wish that Yunab had gotten to you first."

"Get away from me, Sky."

He smiled at her, a slow move across his mouth that sent rage through her. "You can't keep running away."

"Can't I?"

"It won't do you any good." He reached out to touch her, but she pulled back, came up against the wall. The smile on his face twitched, became something sinister, and he lifted his hands in mock surrender. "I can wait, Senea. It doesn't matter to me. Now or later, it's all the same."

"Get out of my way!"

"I'm a patient man." His voice became deathly quiet. "But I'll not wait forever." He stepped up to her so that she was trapped against the wall and the bench. "I'm coming after you. I swear it!" He looked down on her with shadow-darkened eyes. "And when I'm through with you, it won't matter if Yunab tells Aldived about your little indiscretion with Vayhawk or the breaking of heldcode. There's more to this than that, anyway."

"What are you talking about?"

His face took on a careful look. "Let's just say there is, umm?"

It was outrageous. He walked the perimeters of open accusation and yet stopped just short of saying it. It was enough! She clenched her teeth together and shoved her way past him. "I don't have to listen to this!"

"Senea." It was a whipcrack bringing her around to face him. There was rage and something else. "You'll listen to whatever I have to say!"

"I don't have to do anything where you're concerned. I outrank you, heldan!" The words were out before she could stop them. But they were said, and she had to play it out. She turned on her heel to leave.

He caught her tightly just above the elbow, wrenching her around to face him. "I'm not asking you, Senea." His eyes blazed into hers. "You may out-rank me, but I know enough about you to take you to Roskel. And I'm not talking about a little flirtatious breaking of heldcode by meeting with enemy helden. I'm talking about conspiracy; I'm talking about treachery; and I'm talking about taking heldcode and destroying it."

"I don't know what you mean!"

"Our forerunners devised heldcode in order to do away with the power that the Ja'sid are now using against us. Vayhawk wants to bring it all back. He will destroy the heldcode and the Held to do it."

Senea felt the hairs on the nape of her neck bristle. "And you absolutely honor the heldcode."

"I do what has to be done."

"Like using this Ja'sid power against me whenever you are able to control it," Senea said, knowing that that was what he was planning.

Sky pulled her closer. "Heldan, Yunab will have complete control of the Held before long. He already has Aldived in his control, and he has several helden. Soon he will have disposed of Vayhawk and Roskel, and that in turn means disposing of you. Unfortunately, Yunab's plans are not my plans. So I do what I have to do."

"What are you talking about?"

"*You* showed this power to me. *You* showed me how to use it. And Vayhawk's interest in it makes it of interest to me. As I have said, Yunab's plans are not my plans. So I do what I have to do. What Vayhawk uses, I use. And you owe me."

"Owe you?"

"Owe me. For keeping quiet. For keeping Yunab quiet. For giving you an out the day you followed me back to the Held to keep an eye on me."

His hand tightened savagely on her arm. She winced. "I don't know what you are talking about!"

"I lied to Yunab. I told him that heldcode required two witnesses to bring charges against the Heldlan. But that was not true. There's no such code. Of course, Yunab knew that, but he couldn't be absolutely sure, so he let it go." The pressure on her arm increased.

"Pull that rank stuff on me again, and I'll haul you to Roskel so fast you won't be able to think about it."

Afraid her voice would betray her pain, she silently shook her head.

"Then you better pay attention to me, because someday I'm going to find you out there alone. Nobody to stop me. And then, heldan, I'm going to do to you what I did not have the chance to do at the Games. The things I'm going to do to you, girl, you haven't even dreamed of yet." He pulled her hard against him, jarring the breath out of her.

"Trust it," he whispered, gripping her arm, making her wince against the searing pain in her wound. "Maybe tomorrow . . . maybe next week . . . you'll never know when I'm going to be there." Hard fingers slid up her other arm in a painful caress and touched her face with an intimacy that shook her. His dark eyes burned down into hers with hatred and that something else that was always there, threatening and unidentifiable.

"Then you'll know what it means to have an enemy." His breath fluttered across her skin and she shivered, tried to meet his gaze without flinching. "I'm going to break you."

He looked to her mouth and smiled. For a moment she thought he was going to do something more, that he was going to force her closer, pull her up to him and . . .

She steeled herself, ready to shove him away and more if

she needed to. But he just raised his eyes back up to hers and looked at her, a mocking turn across his lips.

He was laughing at her. He had seen that thought on her face and was laughing at her.

She pulled angrily at the grip he had wrapped around her arm, but his hold on her was tight. His other hand went around her and crushed her painfully to him, pinning her against him with a brutal strength, his body hard and unyielding.

"Let go of me!"

The smile died on his face and his fingers dug into her. "What's the matter, Senea? Afraid you're going to like it?" His words grazed over her, slithered down to rest in the middle of her.

"Afraid you won't want to stop me?" His mouth came very close to hers, and she strained in anger to break free. His savage grip that was around her arm moved around her to where his other hand held her against him, forcing the breath from her lungs. "Or that you won't be able to?" He held her so tightly she couldn't move, couldn't breathe, couldn't even gasp for air. Then he lowered his head that tiny bit and kissed her violently and roughly, fingers digging into her as his mouth bruised hers with a savage intensity.

She struggled, but vainly, fighting for breath against a force she had never known before. Then she was left reeling when he tore his lips from hers.

"Stay close to that Heldlan of yours." He released her abruptly. "You're going to need him." His voice was low, edged, cruel.

She staggered back a step and came up against the bench.

There was rage on his face, and he looked at her with a strange, bitter regret. Then he spread his hands in a gesture that was almost like surrender, an acknowledgment of failure that chilled her beyond belief. Suddenly she knew that this had been her last chance. Whatever he had wanted from her, he would never give her another. There would be no more words, no more threats ... The next time they met, there would be blood.

Without another word he turned on his heel, strode to the door, and closed it behind him. His footsteps retreated down the hall.

Senea rubbed her sore arm. Her legs shook under her; adrenaline drained away. She sank down with her hand pressed against her mouth, staring at the door and trying to think what to do now.

Several minutes later the door opened, and Vayhawk came in. His expression was drawn.

She rose to meet him. "What's wrong?"

He came to her and took her hands. "I want you to go to Roskel and have him assign you to patrol."

"Why? What's happened?" Then in the next breath she knew. "You have to go back to the northern border. Another meeting."

"I want you to talk to him tonight." He turned her and drew her with him toward the opposite door.

"Sky and Yunab will be watching you even closer than ever now," she protested. She almost told him what Sky and Yunab had said and done just minutes before. "If they find you out there . . ."

"Yunab already knows where I'm going."

She looked up at him in dismay. If Yunab knew, then Sky knew, and that knowledge filled her with foreboding.

"It's a trap," she said.

"Of course."

"And you're still going?"

He looked sidelong at her and opened the door. "You know heldcode, Senea."

"But . . ."

His look silenced her. "I have to do this."

"Then let me go with you."

He shook his head. "No. You go talk to Roskel."

"I can watch for you."

"Do as I say, Senea," he said, reading what was on her face. "I don't want you anywhere near that northern border." His hand at her back took her through the door.

There was tense silence while she walked beside him. The brightness of the setting sun was an orange ache to the eyes. Suddenly it seemed to sink into the ground far out on the plain. Great shadows fell across the hills, and the ridge behind the held-tribe stood in an isolated light of the last of the sun's rays as it sank out of sight. The windshift began to hiss over the dry grass, and a night bird twittered overhead as it darted toward the plain.

It would be of no use to ask Vayhawk again to let her go.

He would not change his mind. Senea knew that he would not tolerate her following him this time.

Then she saw movement at the corner of the Held, a figure approaching them from the direction of the held-tribe. She watched it disinterestedly a moment. Then she caught her breath in a half sob. Her heart stopped beating for an instant.

Coming toward her was her sister Melina, here, where she should not have been, and Senea just stared in shock and felt a hollowness in her stomach that had not come when she had faced Sky. But now she glanced to Vayhawk for help.

He looked from Melina to her. He knew. He raised his head and blinked in the fading light, watching Melina come ...

She stopped short, a few feet away. A change had come about in her. She was with child and had a hard-eyed look that had not been there before. The sight disturbed Senea; it hit her like a blow to the stomach. Melina stood fixed, her eyes moving back and forth from Senea to Vayhawk.

Senea was transfixed, unable to say anything.

Melina gave her a long, hard look, took in the knife at her side, the gold on her arm, the heldan dress, and turned a curious gaze on Vayhawk.

He nodded slightly to her. "You should not be here ... Melina?"

Senea looked up at him, surprised that he remembered the name. She had told him only once about her family, on that first day when she had become his heldii.

His hand came up and went lightly around her arm, a slight touch of reassurance that drew her closer to him. Melina caught the movement and looked to his hand, to his face, to Senea. Her expression was unreadable.

"Why have you come here?" Vayhawk asked her. When she didn't respond, he said, "It's all right. You can speak." His voice held a note of impatience.

Melina nodded very slightly. "I did not think to find Senea here. I only wished to leave word at the gate."

"What word?"

Melina's eyes flicked aside to Senea, back to him. "Our mother has died."

Senea gasped, but managed not to show any other sign of her shock. Sudden grief washed over her in a flood of pain. She clenched her hand at her side and felt Vayhawk's grip on her arm tighten slightly, reminding her to keep her composure. It was hard. Extremely hard.

"What has that to do with Senea?" Vayhawk asked Melina, his tone cold and impassive.

"I thought perhaps she would want to know."

"Why?"

There was a long silence in which Melina looked at him uncertainly. "She is my sister . . ."

"She is heldan." His words stopped her. "Do you know what that means?"

She shook her head.

"It means that she has no family. No mother. No father. No sisters. Nothing but the Held."

"And no responsibility to family anymore?" Melina asked angrily.

"It is a hard code that we helden live by. But it is a necessary one. It is what keeps you safe."

Melina looked from him to Senea, visibly fighting down resentment and anger. "And what about us? When our situations change, and we need her back?"

"To you, she is dead."

"But she is not." Melina stared pointedly at Senea, then spoke to her. "We need you to come home. Loran needs someone to take care of her. I can't do it."

Senea was too surprised to answer and would not have been permitted to even if she had had the words. She was shocked that Melina had even made such a suggestion, and she couldn't believe that she had heard right.

"Do you not know held-law?" Vayhawk's voice was incredulous and cold.

"You can let one heldan go. Loran needs her much more than the Held does. She hasn't been the same since Senea left. She won't talk. She won't play. She won't do anything. And I'm not going to take care of her. I can't."

Vayhawk was silent for a long minute, measuring Melina with a slow, deliberate gaze that caused her to pale and step back.

"It is well," he finally said, "that you were not the one taken by held-law. You would not have made half the heldan that your sister is."

Melina stared at him and broke contact after a moment and looked to Senea. "Come home. We need you."

Senea shook her head. Vayhawk's grip on her arm tightened, a reminder that she could not acknowledge Melina as kin. She turned an imploring gaze on him. "Vayhawk, please."

He drew in a breath and then let it go. "All right, Senea. But make it to the point."

Nodding, she turned back to Melina. When she tried to speak, her voice was no more than a whisper. "I never thought I'd see you again. I've missed you terribly. I miss our father and Loran. I will mourn our mother." Her voice broke, but she went on. "I can't go home with you, Melina. I'm heldan. I live by heldcode, and if I tried to go home, someone would come for me."

"We would just send them away."

"No." Senea hesitated. "You don't understand. Heldcode is very strict. If I left the Held, it would be desertion. Punishment would be death."

Melina's eyes flickered with startlement.

"I'm sorry, but that's the way it is. You'll have to take care of Loran yourself; I can't help you. I thought my leaving would make things better for you. I really hoped that it would. I'm sorry that it did not."

Melina stared at her in mute stubbornness. Her hand at her side closed into an angry fist. Her eyes narrowed and became hard and dark and filled with hatred. Then without a word she turned and walked away. Senea looked up at Vayhawk and made a pained, helpless gesture. His dark eyes were on her, then raised to the retreating girl.

"Melina," he said.

The crack of authority was in his voice. Senea winced at it. Her sister turned, startled.

"Your sister has already faced death for you. Was just about killed for you. Think on that when you go home. Think on what she is doing so that you can have your child in peace." His hand moved down Senea's arm to take her hand. "And know this, she ranks nine in the Held and has been paired with the Heldlord these past months." It was a vindication that sent a flood of fierce gratitude through Senea. He gave her hand a squeeze.

Melina lifted herself from her shocked silence. Her eyes went to Senea and back to Vayhawk, then looked at how close they stood together, his hand around hers, the way he stood— confident with the authority that rested on him. Comprehension came to her face. She glanced at Senea, surprised and impressed, and then she frowned at Vayhawk as if she were comparing him to the boy she had wed and found her own state sadly wanting. She looked at Senea finally, fierce envy on her face, hatred spilling from her eyes.

"Heldan witch," she hissed, her voice hoarse from suppressed rage.

Senea stared at her. All the spit seemed to have gone out of her mouth. Her hand came up and touched her throat.

Melina turned then and walked away. It was all she had left herself to do.

Vayhawk put his arm about Senea's shoulders, and Senea clenched her arms about her. She tried to conceal her disappointment. She wanted desperately, fiercely to ignore it, but the hurt was too painful. She shook her head to dispel it. Her movement was injudicious. It caught Vayhawk's attention. His hand moved soothingly down her arm.

"Why did you tell her all of that?" she was finally able to ask.

"She needed to know what the helden are . . . what you are."

Senea suddenly felt too weak to stand and leaned against him, stricken. A deep loneliness and sense of loss swept over her, leaving her devoid of anything but pain. It had been a long, bad day, and she was suddenly very weary.

Gently Vayhawk drew her away, directing her back to the Held. She looked back from time to time to the retreating figure of her sister until she couldn't see her anymore. Then she wept. She did not know it until the windshift turned the tears on her face cold.

CHAPTER
TWENTY-ONE

Senea lay awake for a long time, staring at the darkness of the bunk overhead. To her left, the soft, rhythmic breathing of Treyna in her own bunk was the only sound that Senea could hear. The Held had lapsed into a deep silence in the aftermath of the Games. It was a subdued quiet that almost felt like rest after the unrestrained excitement that had resonated in the corridors and on the compound for two days. The comings and goings of the helden along the corridor had long since ceased.

She had slept—some—but sleep was gone from her now as thoughts of Vayhawk going back to the northern border assailed her. It was a trap; she could feel it with every instinct she had. It was a trap set by Yunab to further his ambitions to take over the Held.

He meant to have Vayhawk dead.

And Sky in his place.

She thought of her mother because she could no longer keep it away. Profound grief came over her, and she tried to silence deep wrenching sobs that came. Her mother, the mother of her childhood, the mother she had not denied even though she had come to the Held, the mother who had cared for her, loved her, consoled her, and in the end who had wept for her, was dead. Gone. And she didn't even know how it had happened. Melina hadn't said. Her sister was so changed, so full of bitterness, so unloving, so uncaring. How had she come to that? How had she, in getting what she wanted, not become happy?

Senea sat up in agitation, trying to stem the thoughts that raced through her. She was heldan and had no kin. She could see the wisdom of that now. There was nothing that she could do about Melina, or Loran, or her mother, or her father. It was better not to know.

Suddenly she was unable to remain on her bunk. She drove herself to her feet and went out into the dimly lit corridor. An unaccustomed predawn chill was coming into the Held from the open doors to the compound, and she shivered as she went barefooted along the hall to Vayhawk's door. There she paused. He might already be gone, and she was too late. She knocked once, softly.

At that moment she heard her name spoken low, behind her.

She turned and saw Vayhawk coming toward her from the direction of the eating hall and the baths. His bow quiver was in hand. Crossing her arms in front of her almost guiltily she walked forward to meet him. When she reached him, she looked up at him in the dim light.

"Tired of sleeping, again?" There was mischievous humor at the corner of his mouth, a sly reminder of the time when he found her in the corridor after she had been wounded, when she should have been in her bunk.

Senea regarded him wryly. "No."

"Come," he said, taking her arm. "Walk with me."

She let him draw her with him back the way he had come. There was silence for a little space. She held her tongue, reluctant to say anything in the quiet that came between them. It was almost as it was in the first days, almost as if they were strangers again.

The memory of his hand on the small of her back, pulling her tightly against him, came to her. Every nerve could still feel the strength and the heat of him.

She cast a glance at him. His hand left her arm and checked his knife at his hip. Then he asked her, "Have you gone to Roskel?"

"Yes."

His gaze brushed over her. "Good."

"I wish you would let me go with you."

"No. I want you on patrol."

Senea did not answer. He wanted her far away from the northern border. It was in his voice.

"And I don't want you following me."

She shook her head. "I won't."

He stopped and took hold of her arm, his face stern. "If you do, you will put us both in danger."

"I won't follow, Vayhawk. I promise."

He studied her a moment, his dark eyes seeming to search for confirmation of her words. Then drawing in a breath, he turned and resumed walking in silence, his hand on her arm, keeping her at his side.

There was the lure of him, the warmth of him drawing at her, working on her with a strength she found difficult to resist. Almost she pulled away from him, the attraction of him causing her a dismay and apprehension that she did not feel before. His hand was hot on her cold skin, and in a sudden shift of mood she wanted him to slide his arm around her and pull her close.

She wanted desperately to lean into his strength and let everything go on without either of them. But she held herself apart, and then they were at the held-door.

"Wish me luck," he said, turning to her.

She looked up at him, her heart constricted in apprehension.

"You do wish me luck, don't you?" His dark eyes rested on her.

"Yes." She was surprised at how odd her voice sounded.

"Then say it." His voice was still, soft and thrust like a shaft into her.

She swallowed at a tightness caused by a foreboding in her throat and forced the words out.

He smiled briefly, bent, and gave her a kiss, just a whisper of a touch that turned her insides to havoc. His lips were soft on hers, lingering, pulling away slowly. Then he was gone—out into the darkness. Senea stared after him with a heavy prescience that death would be the result of his going.

There was a sound behind her. She whirled around, suddenly aware that she was not alone. Sky—standing in the dim light of the corridor, the smallest hint of a smile parting his lips. He knew where Vayhawk was going. He had been waiting for him to go and had seen everything.

Senea stepped back from him instinctively.

He crossed the short distance between them and stood a moment looking down at her, his gaze moving slowly over her face. It was in his eyes that the confrontation he had promised her was being postponed this once. It would come. The certainty of it lurked at the corner of his mouth. It would come, though not just now.

But next time ... Next time.

Sky's lips twitched, and a mocking smile moved across them. He went around her to the held-door that still stood open. He stopped on the threshold and looked back at her.

"I have him, now," he said. He held up a hand, fingers spread, and closed his fist with a slow intimation of power, to show that he meant to crush Vayhawk—for his own reason ... not for what Yunab had sent him to do, but for what he planned to do. Because of Senea. She understood that as clearly as he wanted her to. Because of her.

The outcome would be the same, although the reason was not the same. She was the reason.

She held herself silent and watched him walk away into the darkness. The heldan standing guard at the door looked at her, puzzled. She ignored him.

Powerless to act for a long terrible moment, alarm warred within her. Thoughts assailed her from a hundred different directions. She ran across the compound to her bunkroom, where she grabbed her weapons, strapped them on, hurriedly put on her sandals, then ran along the corridor in search of Mara.

Sky had to be stopped!

She had to go after him and prevent him from finding Vayhawk. She had to do anything she could to keep him away from the northern border.

But she could not do it alone. She needed a witness to say why she killed him.

Then she recalled that Mara had patrol. She clenched her hands in desperate hope that the heldan hadn't left yet. She pushed into the bath, and cast about anxiously in the close, humid gloom, but did not see her. Turning, she shouldered back out into the corridor to go look for her in the eating hall. Then she heard Mara's voice in the washroom. Laughter and a murmured joke.

She crossed to the washroom and saw Mara draping some washed clothing over the wooden rod that ran the length of the room. Another heldan was wringing water out of her own clothing into a bin on the opposite wall. A momentary lull in their conversation cloaked the room in a silence that almost brought Senea up short. She almost turned away without talking to Mara at all. But she needed the heldan's help, so she forced herself to enter the room.

Mara looked up as she approached and greeted her. "Going on patrol, too?"

Senea shook her head. "No." She stopped beside Mara and turned her back on the other heldan so she could talk low. "I've got to talk to you."

"Sure. You don't mind if I finish this, do you?"

Senea glanced apprehensively over her shoulder at the other heldan, who had turned around and was looking at them curiously. "Alone," she murmured. "I haven't much time."

Mara saw Senea's glance and frowned. She waved the other heldan out of the room, and when she had gone, Mara turned to Senea with concern. "What's wrong?"

"You've got to come with me. Sky has left the Held to find Vayhawk and kill him. And he's going to do it this time. We've got to go after him and stop him. I can't do it by myself . . . I have to have a witness . . ."

"Wait. Wait a minute. What are you talking about? What makes you think that Sky is going to kill Vayhawk?"

"Because Vayhawk is going to meet . . ." She broke off quickly. Almost the secret had escaped on a traitorous tongue. She swore in frustration. How was she going to explain this? She stared at Mara.

The only way was by betrayal.

Tightening her heart against the surge of guilt, she told Mara everything: the meetings with the Wuepoah helden, the meetings with Aldived, the conflicts with Sky and Yunab, and everything about the Ja'sid power and the heldcode. When she was finished she felt dirty.

Mara turned, walked to the front of the room, walked back again. "Do you know . . ." Her voice was no more than a whisper. "Do you understand what you're into?"

Senea made a gesture with her hand. There was nothing more she could say. Time was too short for discussion. She had to go now, with or without Mara. She shook her head when Mara laid an imploring hand on her arm.

"I have to go. I can't wait any longer. Will you come? I need you to witness."

Mara's eyes were quick with worry. "You would be wise to stay out of it."

"I can't!" She shook off Mara's hand and turned to leave.

"Wait," Mara said. "I will come." It was not enthusiasm, but willingness.

Senea drew in a breath of relief.

"I'll have to get my weapons."

Senea nodded. "I'll wait for you outside." She turned then and quickly left the bath. Long anxious minutes she waited outside the Held watching the sky. Dawn was coming. Fast. Too fast.

Finally the door opened. Mara came to her. "Let's go," she said.

Hours later, Senea wiped a hand over her brow to keep the perspiration out of her eyes while she searched the ground for signs that she could follow. The sun that had been so benevolent that morning now beat down with a terrible intensity that sapped the strength from her legs and made her head ache. She raised her face and squinted at the westering orb, trying to estimate how long until sundown. She was tempted to find some shade where Mara and she could wait out the heat. Her body cried out for her to do so, but urgency kept her moving, not stopping, not resting.

"Over here," Mara called to her from the bottom of a depression they had been following. Senea veered in that direction to look at the scuff mark that her inexperienced eyes would have missed. She nodded wordlessly and followed where Mara led.

Still north. Always north. Toward Vayhawk.

She would not have been able to track Sky as surely as Mara did. Mara could find even the smallest sign, a pebble that had been moved at the passing of a light step, grass that had parted at the gentlest of brushings. Alone, Senea would have lost him. She would never have found him in the vastness of the plain, although she would have tried even after it was too late, if only to kill him.

She slipped a hand around the handle of her knife in its sheath at her hip. The feel of it was no comfort at all. She recalled how close Sky had come to killing her at the Games. If Vayhawk hadn't stopped him, he would have succeeded. The next time they met he just might succeed. Her skills were not tried and seasoned as his were. Behind him was a fierceness that she did not possess. He would not hold his hand against her the next time.

Well, neither would she hold her hand back against him!

She ran her hand up to where he had caught her arm with

his knife. Her arm had been stiff all day. The ache flared into pain whenever she had to move it. As the day had worn on, the ache became more acute and unpleasant. Finally, she had to hold her arm close to her side to avoid jarring it.

Well, what she was going to do to him was going to hurt a lot worse.

The sun began to lower in the west, and the light of the late afternoon was on the land as she followed Mara up a rise and down the other side. The shadow of a distant butte was long and thin across their path. And as the sun slowly dipped to the horizon, the western sky became striped with color, dusty purple, gold, red, almost as sultry as a dying fire.

They stopped in a narrow, wooded valley where a small trickle of water wound its way along the dry course of a much larger stream. Senea rested against a tree, eased her arm onto her leg, and watched as Mara filled a skin bag from the slow-moving water.

The heldan had been unusually quiet, saying very little, only indicating where Sky's spoor lay, and nothing at all about what she was thinking. The heldan straightened, lifted the bag to her mouth, and drank, then stood for a long, silent moment looking at the fading colors of the sky.

The light was almost gone, dying in the sky and in the reflection on the water. Night was moving in on them as the last of the sunlight slipped from view. One by one white stars sprang out as the sky faded. The moon, like a pale violet shadow, hung high and full.

Senea thought, as she sat there, how the plain at night was amazingly beautiful. Placid and still, the grasses shone softly in the moonlight, and the hills and swells took on a glow and radiance they concealed during the day. But night was also a more deadly time. It was then that the wolfhounds came out from their dens, then that the yellow snake and the golden spiders slithered and crawled from dark holes to prowl for prey under the soft glow of starlight.

Mara came to her and sat down, handing her the skin bag. Senea drank, then drank again.

"We're not far behind," Mara said. "The signs are getting fresher."

"Do you think we'll find him tonight?"

"I don't know." She fell silent for a long time, just staring into the dark and tapping her toe repeatedly against a rock.

Senea wished that she'd say something . . . anything . . . about what she was thinking. Then she said, "We'd better go, or we'll lose him." She rose to her feet and waited for Senea.

Senea stood, slung the strap of the bag over her head, and held the swollen skin to her side with her sore arm.

"Watch every shadow," Mara said, as she turned to cross the streambed.

Senea followed Mara across the valley, climbed up away from the trees to the level of the plain, slid down a moonlit ridge in a white powdering of dust, and crossed the long slope to lower ground.

Late morning the next day found them still following the trail north without having seen Sky anywhere. They had crossed a long expanse of flat plain and now were skirting around hills and cliffs that were the beginnings of the lands to the northwest, a vast area of canyons and long retreats into a new level of the plains. In those canyons and farther beyond were the Ja'sid.

Here the sands were red, beginning with the cliffs, in contrast to the pale plain that they had just crossed, and the red hills were banded at times with white and a darker red that approached purple.

A rare morning wind moaned a dreary tune under the overhanging coves, among the holes in the rock, and through the sunburnt scrubs. The sky was an ocher yellow, but the air in the relatively sheltered place among the rocks was still clear. A few birds darted about, gray flycatchers, golden sand birds. In the dust and on the sand Senea could read the passage of other creatures, from the big track of a wolfhound to the tiny prints of mice, beetles, and sandworms. Optimistically, she looked for sign of Sky but found none.

She looked up and up, where a ridge shadowed them from the morning sun, scrub trees clinging even to that purchase.

"Mara. What about up there? Good vantage point." She looked at the heldan. Mara gave agreement with a gesture. Laboriously they climbed the sharp slope and halted for a moment halfway. Then they climbed again.

Senea was gasping and sweating by the time she reached the top of the ridge. She stood there leaning over, her hands on her knees, getting her breath and scanning the plain that stretched out below them. She looked to the canyons on her left, but knew Sky would not have turned aside into them. She crouched in a prolonged silence behind a large upthrusting to avoid making a silhouette against the sky, and squinted against the yellow haze that was settling over the plain underneath the oppressive heat of the sun.

Then Mara pointed. "Over there."

Senea searched in the direction where Mara was pointing. There was nothing. For long minutes she looked for movement in that monochromatic brown and tan landscape, but still saw nothing.

Mara made a pursing of her lips, her eyes very much alert. "I think we've been spotted."

Senea turned. "Sky?"

"I don't know."

Senea said nothing, but looked down across that space.

Everything seemed to be withering in the heat, blasted and shrunken under the furnace of the sun. The distant buttes and hills began to bend and undulate, seeming to melt into one another, merging like cloud forms stirred by a draft of air, so that the profile of one could not be distinguished from that of another. In the foreground the rocks and scrubs wavered like moss under water.

The air seemed to suck moisture from every pore, and Senea was beginning to feel just how hungry, tired, and thirsty she really was.

Then she saw it, but could not tell at first if it was a trick of the heat. A movement that could have been the shimmering illusion of a rock bobbed up and down as if in a stretch of water.

She stared intently at the spot. Sweat trickled down her back. She ignored it and waited. Just as she was beginning to think she had been mistaken, she saw it again.

A figure darting from one rock to another.

Sky was doubling back on them.

"There," she said to Mara, pointing. "He knows we're here."

Mara nodded.

Senea watched the spot where he had disappeared and knew intuitively that the confrontation he had promised her was about to come. He had left off hunting Vayhawk to turn back for her.

She turned and slid down the slope, Mara behind her. She would not wait for him to come to her. Nor would she run.

She had to take the offensive to him on her own terms—meet him and make an end of it.

She staggered when she hit the bottom, caught her balance, and threw herself around an outcropping of rock. Then she sprinted across several yards of open space for cover behind a sand dune.

She lay against the side of the dune, her hand pressed to her side, trying to keep her breathing normal, and heard the movements of Mara to her right. She saw the heldan disappear over another dune, leaving only the depressions of her footprints in the sand. Then there was silence.

Slipping her bow out of the quiver on her back, she strung it, nocked an arrow, and went crouching around the crescent arm of an adjacent dune.

Something urged at her hearing. She kept her eyes to the tops of the dunes and the troughs in between.

A rapid sound of footsteps followed her track through the sand. She reckoned it for Mara, and she glanced over her shoulder.

A shadow flowed between the dunes.

She turned, bringing the bow up as the shadow fell across her. It was Sky who had come up behind her.

He hissed softly between his teeth.

For half a breath she hesitated, taken aback by the intense look of regret in his eyes. It was not what she had expected, pain on his face at what he was going to do. The surprise of it held her motionless for the length of a heartbeat. Then she realized that it was not going to stop him. She drew back on the bow, but her hesitation had given him the time he needed to reach her, and he blocked that attempt with brutal force, knocking the bow out of her hands.

Then he was on her, the force of his attack throwing her to the ground.

She fought back, clawing and scratching at his face. This time she knew she was fighting for her life.

He bared his teeth and struck her across the face. Once. Twice. Pain exploded in her head, and she slumped, momentarily stunned.

Hands were on her then, dragging her to her feet. A black fuzz obscured her vision. She blinked furiously and felt an arm around her throat, pinning her back against a hard chest. Labored breathing was in her ear.

"You could not leave it alone," Sky whispered, a rusty sound like something long unused. "You had to force it."

Her legs buckled under her, and his other arm went around her waist to hold her up.

"You could have let it go." His arm tightened. "You could have let it go."

Senea's head began to clear. She did not know what he was talking about, but she could hear the same regret in his voice that had been on his face.

Then she heard footsteps coming toward them. Fast.

Mara!

She opened her mouth to shout a warning, but Sky's arm tightened savagely around her throat, choking off any sound.

"Not one word," he said. "If you want to live, not one word."

She clutched at his arm, struggling for breath, trying to pull out of his grasp until she realized that he could kill her that way. It would require no effort at all to strangle her. She went suddenly limp against him.

"That's better," his voice said in her ear.

Mara came skidding around a dune and stopped. Her hand whipped her knife out. "Turn her loose, Sky."

He laughed, a low sound in Senea's ear. "I don't think so. Not just yet."

Senea reached down to take hold of her own knife, moving slowly so that he wouldn't notice. But his arm moved from around her waist, and his hand clamped around hers on the hilt of her knife.

"Not another step," he said to Mara. "I'll kill you if you come any closer."

Mara smiled chillingly. Her eyes took in how he stood with Senea pulled against him, one arm around her throat, the other hand at her knife. Clearly she did not think he could make good on his threat. She strode up to him and said, "Turn her loose!"

But before Senea realized his intention, Sky pulled her knife free of its sheath and thrust it full up under Mara's ribs.

For a shocking moment no one moved, and it was possible to hear the flycatchers flitting between the dunes.

Senea stared at the knife. Her hand was still on it. Sky's grip was painful around hers. Her lungs burned; there was the sharp edge of blood in the air she breathed. Thick red spilled out onto her fingers, warm and wet, covered them completely, and dripped off her knuckles in a rapidly growing stream.

The blade began to flicker. Not a flickering of light, but a feeling of darkness that seemed to pulsate in her hand. And where her hand and Mara's blood both touched the knife there was a strong pulling that Senea could feel through her skin.

There was a flicker again of darkness. Something hard and heavy struck at her through that triple-fold contact. She suddenly realized it was Mara's life-force being pulled out of her with a strength and swiftness that was terrifying.

Senea instantly and desperately pushed at the power, trying to fling it away. But it didn't move. She tried again and still nothing. It was too strong.

Mara suddenly doubled over the knife as if in terrible pain, her hands raised as if to protect herself.

Senea pushed again at the power, but felt Sky using his strength against her. He was stopping her attempt to seize hold of the power.

Another surge of heavy darkness struck at them, and Mara's hand clawed blindly in Senea's direction, a plea for help which she couldn't voice. Senea watched in horror, breathing stridently, struggling not to be sick. If she didn't do something, Mara didn't have a chance.

She kept up the struggle, hunting for any leverage, anything that would stop it, but Mara was already done. Her bubbling breath was hoarse in Senea's ear as the last of her strength was jerked away.

She looked up to Mara's face in horror. The heldan had gone white. Then she was falling, and Senea reached out with a cry to catch her.

Sky's arm tightened around her, preventing her. She gasped for breath and began to fight him. "Let me go!" she choked.

Mara was on the ground motionless, and the blood of the wound was running copiously into the sand.

"Let me go!" she cried against the pain in her throat, pulling at his arm.

Sky sniffed, jerked her against his chest, and flung her free all in two quick motions. She stumbled to her knees and touched Mara's shoulder fearfully. Then turning her over she obtained a faint movement, a gasp for breath, a flutter of the eyes. The wound in her midsection continued to bleed freely and Senea knew she'd be dead in a few moments. She thought to try to stop the flow, but she could not touch it. It was pointless. She pressed her hands together to keep them from trembling. Then Mara gave a couple of quick sighs and a long final one. Then nothing.

Senea let go a shuddering breath, and the tears in her eyes spilled over. She stared at her hands covered with Mara's blood and knew that that contact had helped to kill her.

Her mind struggled for balance; disbelief and appalled horror battled for dominance. Grief threatened to consume her. There was a dreamlike slowness to it all, the aching of her heart, the tightness of her lungs, the burning of her eyes. There was a nightmarish quality about it all that was so unreal it almost convinced her that it was a lie. But it was no lie. It was very real indeed. Mara, who was her friend, her only friend, was dead.

As the realization of it burned like a chill thing through her, she wept, long and bitterly. And slowly the pain of it turned to cold fury. This should not have happened! Not between helden of the same Held. It was a violation of heldcode, a violation of loyalty! A violation of trust!

She looked up, outraged, and saw that the knife still rested in Sky's hand. His eyes were fixed on her, an expression in them of mocking amusement. If he felt regret at what he had done, he did not show it.

She rose to her feet and faced him. "You're going to pay for this!"

He didn't reply but continued to stare mockingly at her.

Then she said with an edge of utter bitterness, "It was a cowardly thing to do!"

It hit to the mark. The green eyes shifted from hers, and she realized with faint surprise that he was stung by her words. A flicker of anger showed in his face and as swiftly disappeared. She looked at him, suddenly wary, every sense alert.

He stepped to her and caught her wrist and pressed the knife into her palm. "I was not the only one with my hand on the knife." His voice was hoarse. His eyes bored directly into hers. "And my hand was not the only hand that pulled the life out of her."

Senea could not look away. "No! This was not my doing!"

"No?" he said low, his face hard.

She stood defiant, forcing herself to ignore the numbness

that was creeping up her fingers from the pain of his grip around her wrist.

A shout echoed from above.

She turned. Helden were sliding down the dune behind her, the sand cascading before them in a growing wave. She looked back to Sky. His hand tightened on her wrist.

"My companions," he said ominously, and smiled faintly at her, threat in the curve of his lips. For an instant his gaze filled with such venom that she recoiled.

"What are you going to do?" she asked, and there was a sudden coldness in his eyes.

The sound of footsteps came up from behind. The wind whispered along the sand, the beginnings of the winds that brought the wet season. Helden surrounded them, and eyes were on her, questioning. Treyna stood next to Sky, her face hard. Senea looked from one to the other knowing that she was surrounded by enemies.

"You can see what has happened," Sky said then, his gaze unwaveringly on her. "I heard quarreling, and on investigation I found this heldan here with this." He lifted the blood-covered hand that he had been holding captive. "Mara was dead. I could do nothing."

There was silence, stark silence.

Senea stared at him, not in the least surprised.

The others were looking at her, at Mara on the ground, coming to conclusions that were only too obvious. What they saw was one of their own dead. The knife was in her hand, blood drying on its blade and on her flesh in silent conviction. Savagely, struggling against the threat of blind rage, she forced her muscles to obey her and turned her head. Landry was standing next to her. She looked up and found him glowering down at her.

"No. I didn't do it. Sky . . ." Quite abruptly she stopped, knowing it was pointless. Landry merely raised his brows. She looked down at her hand, so tightly clasped in Sky's grip the knuckles showed white through Mara's blood.

She tried to swallow and found her throat achingly dry. She looked up at Sky. If ever in her life she would have attacked one of her own with intent to kill it would have been then, under that very steady stare. Her heart slammed against her ribs so hard it affected her breathing.

Landry deftly reached and relieved her of her knife belt,

took the quiver of arrows, and handed them to another heldan on the left.

"Search her," he said.

She pulled back at Sky's grip, but to no avail. His fingers were like a vise. Hands were on her then, quick and brutal. Her straight back never betrayed her fury. Sky was watching her with an expression that she could not read, his eyes sweeping her from head to foot. Her steadiness might be mistaken by the others for self-control. But Sky knew it for what it was. A bead of sweat ran down her temple.

"There is heldcode to be carried out," Landry said, not saying what everyone was thinking. The death penalty to be invoked.

There was another silence, deep and long.

Sky sucked at his lips. Senea's gaze switched from him to Landry, then back again. The seconds crawled into hours.

"No," Sky said finally. "Not yet. This heldan can lead us directly to Vayhawk. It is obvious that she is protecting his back . . ." He let his voice trail off meaningfully. "A few minutes alone with her, and I'll find out what we need to know."

"And you can do it in your own way," Treyna spoke up icily.

Sky threw a black look at her. Their eyes met, clashed, and held. Treyna returned his stare unflinchingly.

Senea watched the exchange with sudden interest. Treyna had implied far more than she was saying. She knew from experience what Sky was capable of. She had been his heldii for months and had been at his mercy for that same time. She had been driven relentlessly by him and had felt his wrath. It was he who had made her what she was. But something had recently changed her. Senea could see it, now that she studied the heldan. There was a difference in the hardness that had become Treyna. It was no longer single-focused on her, but for some reason was also aimed at Sky, an icy fury that seethed under a deceptively quiet exterior.

"Do I need to remind you of your rank?" Sky's voice was quiet.

Treyna's back went stiff. "No."

"Good." Then he motioned with his head. "Go keep watch."

Treyna glared at him, then dipped her head in salute. "But remember," she said, pausing for emphasis, her voice barely above a whisper. "I know you." And she turned away, pushing through the helden behind her.

Senea watched her stride across the sand and wondered if she could be turned into a temporary ally. Landry had edged closer. A heavy hand descended on her shoulder. She winced under the clutch of the strong fingers.

Sky looked back to Landry and gestured impatiently. "Leave me alone with her. It will only take a short time."

Landry drew back, his hand leaving her shoulder. "She's yours."

Sky smiled slightly. There was no humor in that upturning of lips.

"Come, heldan," he said to her, stepping around so that he could grip her arms from behind, his steel-like fingers digging painfully into her muscles. Searing pain sliced in the aching wound on her arm.

"We have much to talk about," he continued.

It was delivered very softly, with the same undertone that he had used during the Games. It promised—she had no idea what.

"I didn't kill Mara!" Senea snarled. "He did!"

Sky's arms went painfully around her, held her up. "Shut up!" he said.

"No!" She kicked at him, struggling to get away. "You can't do this to me! I didn't kill her, and you know it!"

Sky's arms tightened, threatening to crush her. Senea's eyes fell on Landry.

"He'll kill me."

Landry shrugged. "It's heldcode."

"But I didn't do it!"

He shrugged again. He didn't believe her. Sky had been too convincing. She glared at him in anger when he turned away, motioning the others to go with him.

Sky dragged her over to a dune and threw her to the sand. "You're a fool," he said. "I'm what's keeping you alive!"

"And I'm what's going to be your death." A tremor had started in her arms, exhaustion, and pain in her chest.

His eyes darkened.

It was a mistake. Senea looked into that gaze and knew it. She did not care.

He dropped to one knee in the sand and took hold of her shoulders and jerked her up so that her face was close to his,

his breath hot on her mouth. His eyes were almost black with hatred.

"I'm going to tear you to pieces."

For one long instant her whole world narrowed to the dark flame of his eyes and to his breath that was ragged on her. "If you kill me, you'll never know where Vayhawk is." She spoke with slow deliberation.

He straightened back, letting her to the sand, as if he had not expected that. He laughed coldly. "Are you offering?" He was up on his feet, breathing heavily, trying to control his anger. "You will take me to him?" His mouth twisted briefly as if his own words had reminded him of some private and none-too-pleasant joke.

Suddenly he lunged forward and grabbed her shoulders and yanked her to her feet, shaking her violently. For a moment she thought he was going to strangle her. Then abruptly his grip loosened, and he turned away.

"I already know where he is." He looked sideways at her, his eyes burning with dark, smoldering fires. "I don't need you. You offered too late."

"I was making no offer," she said. "I would never lead you to him. Never."

He turned on her with a cold rage so terrible that her words froze on her lips. He flung an arm northward. "I'm going to kill this man. This man that you protect so foolheartedly and are so willing to die for. I'll kill him just as surely as I stand here breathing. You think, you *think* on that, Senea." Suddenly his eyes were filled with such angry regret, it shook her. "What," he said then, in a quiet, quiet voice, "what will you do then?"

His question took her by surprise, and to her amazement she discovered she was unable to answer, but could only stare at that angry sadness that was unwavering on his face.

His hand fell when she did not respond and even then the expression did not vary. "This is pointless."

He took a cord out of his side pouch and strode to her. She tried to back away from him, unable to get firm footing in the shifting sand. She swung at him and turned to run. He caught her and held her so she faced him and couldn't move.

"Where do you think you're going?" He smiled at her, a

cold and cynical gesture. "You wouldn't get very far with my people out there."

For all the warmth of the day, the wind was chill, but the cold she felt had nothing to do with the wind.

His mouth compressed into a grim line, and his gaze moved slowly over her face, causing the blood to rise to her cheeks. Her heart was beating very fast, and her legs ached. She felt herself falling, falling, an illusion born of hatred as she stared at him.

Sky's lips twitched, and a mocking smile moved across them, a silent laughter that jolted Senea back to herself.

She had been staring at him, reliving the moment when his mouth had savagely crushed hers while he kissed her, a kiss so vicious that it had left her stunned. The recalling of it was as vivid as when it had happened. He saw that memory on her face, saw it in the way she stared at him. A dangerous glint darkened his green eyes, and he raised his hand to her face, lightly tracing his finger toward her mouth.

He looked back up to her eyes. The fire in his gaze angered her, and she pulled back at his grip but could not pull free. He leaned close so that his breath was on her mouth. And she pulled again at the viselike hand that held her.

"Go with me," he said, "when I go to find Vayhawk. Go with me and we can put an end to this." He gently ran his fingers over her lips that were so close to his own. "Senea . . ." It was almost like a prayer the way he said it. "Go with me."

She realized with astonishment what he was offering her. Protection. Life. Amnesty. And in some strange way, forgiveness.

He was offering her life with him. It was in the way he touched her, in the way he spoke her name. It had been in the way he had always approached her, threatening, frightening, possessive. Go with him or die. And sentencing Vayhawk to death no matter what she did.

Immediately an inner voice said, vehemently, *No!* She couldn't do it . . .

He saw it on her face. His eyes narrowed abruptly.

"You're more of a fool than I thought you." His voice was deathly quiet. He raked her with a searing glance in which she saw the echoes of regreat that would never be there again.

She felt herself hollow, centered with a different kind of

emptiness than she had ever felt before. She knew the enormity of what she had done, and had time to realize it clearly.

Bending to retrieve the cord he had dropped, he dragged her down to her knees in the sand. "You'll be there to watch it," he said, and pulled her arms painfully behind her. "He'll die in such a way to make your blood cold. And then," he breathed in her ear as he bound her, "it will be your turn." He yanked on the cord so that she cried out in pain. Then he lashed her feet together.

"Sky," she said. "Don't do this."

He hissed between his teeth and stood. Stepping around to stand in front of her, he looked down with contempt.

"Let me go." She tried to move and found that he had bound her hands and feet together so that she couldn't stand.

He laughed, short and soft.

"Untie me." Her voice trembled with rage.

"I'm sorry, Senea. I can't do that." He turned then and walked away.

"Sky!" She struggled to rise, only to fall back with a curse.

He stopped and looked back at her. After a moment of consideration he recrossed the distance between them and settled down to his heels in front of her. She watched him as he reached out and wiped the sweat off her cheeks, a gentle gesture.

"Let me go, Sky," she said, searching for a sign of softening in him.

He shook his head ever so slightly. "No." He looked at his hand and rubbed the moisture of her sweat between finger and thumb.

"You can't do this to me. It's breaking heldcode."

He put his hand to the side of her face and gently ran his fingers over her lips. "Heldcode is with me on this one, my dear."

"Don't be a fool." The wrong thing to say. She knew it, but it could not be unsaid.

His eyes hardened then, and he rose to his feet. She tried to call after him as he walked away, but the words died on her tongue. His footsteps whispered in the sand. The last she saw of him was a tan shadow that moments later disappeared around a dune.

There was a movement at her side, and Treyna dropped to her heels next to her. "He walked off, did he?" she asked.

Senea looked at her angrily. She saw, not her bunkmate, but a face now become alien to her.

"You're going to let him get away with this," she said, accusing her.

Treyna shrugged. "No one crosses Sky," she said, rubbing her knee. "Not even me."

Bitterly Senea wondered about the truth of that. "I didn't kill Mara. Sky did."

"Yes. I know. You defend Vayhawk and the Held. Sky kills."

Senea looked narrowly at her. She still had that look of quiet anger on her. It strained at her mouth and the lines in her face.

"Treyna," Senea ventured warily, "would you cut me loose, let me warn Vayhawk?"

The eyes shot up to lock on hers, abrupt and invasive, seeming to read her clear to her soul. She spat, half a laugh. "You're asking for my help? After what you did to me?" She laughed again, which was no laughter.

Senea's heart thudded. "That old quarrel," she said in a still voice. "Can't we put that behind us? It is not right that this is happening. It was not right that that happened then. Help me put a stop to it."

Treyna eyed her slowly; on her side was lack of trust, dead silence.

"Please."

Treyna shook her head then. "No. I live by one simple code, only: I am extremely cautious what I do around Sky."

Senea drew in a deep breath and looked away. "Then you won't help me." Her voice was harsh and she fought to make it even again. "It is not right what he is doing to you."

"He has some small cause, do you not think?" Treyna asked quietly.

Senea looked at her again. "What . . . that you lost at the Games? That is cause?" With difficulty she forced a friendly note into her voice. "How can that justify . . ." She stopped, found herself almost trembling with anger, a violence in which she could kill. "Let me go," she said hoarsely. "He has to be stopped."

Treyna turned to her and said harshly, "You have taken something from him, Senea. What do you expect him to do about it?"

Senea stared at her. "You can't mean that."

Treyna looked away.

Senea seized eagerly on the sign of weakening. "You *don't* mean that."

Treyna turned back to her. "I don't mean anything, heldan. I saw how he was with you. I saw how he reacted every time your name or Vayhawk's came up. But especially yours. And I'm telling you that I don't want to have him coming after me if I let you loose."

Senea studied her face with a sinking heart. Treyna met her gaze with a dark glower, then she looked away, an avoidance of Senea's eyes. She pushed up angrily to her feet and climbed back up the dune from where she came. Senea watched her go, failure knotting in her stomach.

She turned and looked for the first time on the corpse of Mara lying where she had been left. Senea sat, rocking with the emotion that welled up in her, and mourned. Her mourning confounded itself with her rage. She clenched her hands behind her. She wept, and then she tried to feel nothing; that was easier than trying to deal with the impotent anger that boiled in her. She lay down, easing her shoulder into the sand, finding a strange comfort in it. She heard Sky's helden come, heard their movings about the scene; their stirrings that told her they were taking Mara away. She lay still a moment, listening, her eyes useless from her vantage point, as if divorced from it all. She ached. And time was unimportant. That she lay exposed to the blazing sun was a long, long nightmare. She slept.

A hand took hold of her arm. Her eyes started open. Treyna laid her hand on Senea's mouth, her eyes warning.

"I'm going to get you out of here," she said. "Can you run?"

Senea nodded. Treyna reached over her and cut the cord and pulled it free. Senea groaned and closed her eyes as she clasped her arms together in front of her. There was pain in her muscles that she had not expected.

"Here," Treyna said, pushing a water bag in her hands. "I've left your weapons over there." She indicated a nearby dune with her chin. "They're burying Mara, so you don't have much time."

"Why are you doing this?"

"I don't know. I must be crazy."

Senea clasped her hand in gratitude. "Thank you."

Treyna shrugged, not displeased, but uncomfortable.

"What will they do to you when they find I'm gone?"

"Don't worry. I'll handle it. Now go."

Senea nodded and stumbled away. Then she turned back. There was one final thing. "You have to go tell Roskel. And Aldived. Fast. They can stop this. Aldived knows what Vayhawk is doing. He sent him."

Treyna frowned.

"Please."

"I don't know. Maybe."

"It's the only way."

"Aldived could never make it out here."

"But Roskel can. And he'll bring others."

"I'll think about it. Now get out of here."

Senea drew in a breath and backed away. Treyna turned and began to climb the dune again. Senea clenched her hands and forced herself to look away and stagger to where Treyna had left her weapons. She bent to pick them up.

"Hey," someone said, and she started, whirling to her knees and half to her feet, like something wild. But there was no one there, an echo from over the dunes. She quickly strapped her knife belt on, forcing herself to ignore the fact that that knife had been the death of her best friend. Slipping the quiver strap over her head she settled the quiver on her back. Then with her bow in her hand she took a few steps forward away from the dunes, then a few steps more. She didn't see or hear anybody.

Then she was running, running.

CHAPTER
TWENTY-TWO

She ran until her lungs hurt, ran until she thought she was going to die.

Her legs burned, her sides ached, and she couldn't breathe in the oppressive heat. The smell of the plain came to her, odors of dry, burnt grasses, acrid soil blasted by the sun, her own sweat, the smell of dust kicked up by her feet.

Knowing that Sky would soon discover that she had escaped drove her. He'd be after her, if he wasn't already, with murderous rage. If he caught up to her . . . he would not hesitate even a moment to vent that fury on her. The certainty of it beat with a growing urgency in her, driving her to the very edge of endurance.

Finally, she looked back when she came to the top of a long, long rise. She turned to survey the plain over which she had come, the view a sprawling perspective of the land. It was a desolation in which no human movement disturbed the stillness. But just because she couldn't see him didn't mean that Sky wasn't out there somewhere.

He'd be tracking her with a relentless determination and with a skill that would be far better than Mara's.

She saw a way to work down a long rock slope in front of her, around some low rocks and a sandy shelf, and soon enter the area of shallow ravines that eventually turned into deep, narrow canyons that bordered on the lands of the Ja'sid. She drank from the skin Treyna had given her, then began that descent. The rocky depression held the heat like a closed fist.

At the bottom she began to run again, pushing past dead brush, careless now because of fatigue. All night she followed

273

the ravine, catching her feet on loose slabs of rock and boulders that she did not see.

By the time she came to the head of the ravine, dawn was in the sky. She was running with a slow shuffling limp. She looked in dismay at the sharp slope that was in front of her and on both sides. The only way out of the ravine was to climb it, or to retrace her steps.

For a moment she just stared at the slope, unable even to find the energy to move. Then she forced herself to climb through the brush, making noise, breaking branches as she struggled to each upward level, not able to take care that she might be heard. Dead brush raked her; she fended with her good arm, kept the other to her side. Close to the top she stumbled, skidded, and came to a jolting stop against a projecting boulder. Pain shot through her arm. The binding came loose. The wound began to ooze, moisture soaking the loose binding, trickling down to her elbow. She felt it and brought away reddened fingers. She wiped a smear on the rock that had stopped her, fingers trembling. She kept climbing.

She came to the top, gasping for breath; she caught a mouthful of air, sat down in the shade of a large rock, and slept.

The sun was in her face when she woke. It was hot, and she was thirsty. Taking a pull from the water skin she decided that it was still early afternoon.

Finally she stood and looked around her. She was disappointed. It had looked flat up here from the ravine below, but she was still a long way from the crest of the hill.

She climbed the rest of the way, but when she reached the top, she saw the land was not plateau as she had expected. The land was cut with canyons and ravines and she began to think she was lost. This was no place to cross, but she had no choice.

She looked for a higher ridge and headed for it. At the top she looked back. It was a very long way down to where she had been that morning. And down there, at the bottom of the ravine, was a shadow that moved.

Senea's eyes jerked back to it, straining upon that one spot. There was nothing. She did not move, just stared, letting the weariness in her body rest. She almost forgot to breathe whenever her eyes would deceive her into believing that she had seen movement below.

Then she did see it, a dark movement at the base of the slope she had climbed. Then another. Her heart beat very fast. Sky and his helden were very close on her trail. She thought of the blood on the rock where she had wiped it and knew that Sky would find it. There was very little time in which to find Vayhawk.

And then, because there was no other option, she turned around and began running across the vast stretch of plain in front of her, knowing that she would only be halfway across it when Sky reached the top of that slope. Her flight would be easily seen then. She felt the pursuit behind her like an oncoming weight of darkness.

She slowed finally, out of breath, and walked dizzily until she could run again. The shadows among the hills were where they hadn't been before. She stopped running long after she had spent her breath and slumped down amongst the rock and grasses. She wiped sweat from her eyes, first the left, and then the right, and took stock of herself. Her tunic was hanging over her knife, and she put it to rights with trembling hands, belt over and low at the hip. She sat there against the rock with tears of exhaustion tugging at her, and she fought the tears off with swipes of her hand.

Then with a slow dawning she realized where she likely was, near white rocks that followed a dried streambed, a mounding hill that she tried to recognize from this angle, hoping that it was the one from which she had watched Vayhawk with the Wuepoah helden so long ago.

She rose, and uncertainty was in her mind—wondering how she was going to explain all this when she found him. She heard something and knew with her ears when it was coming across the plain behind her. She was going to be too late.

She began to climb the hill, running and stumbling, clutching her bow in her hand. Someone whistled, far and lonely up the hill where there were flycatchers darting and soaring. It was a human sound. One of the watchers had seen her.

The important thing now was not to startle him into violence.

She had climbed halfway to the top of the hill. Now she stopped, holding her hands out away from her body, unstrung bow clenched tightly in her fist. There was nothing else to do.

Soon there was a heldan dressed in brown, with silver on his arm, coming down the hill toward her. She stood silently watching him closely, her back against the open plain where Sky would be able to see her as he closed the distance between them, knowing that he was watching her even as she stood there.

The Wuepoah stopped a few feet from her, a frown drawing deep lines between his black brows, his hand resting on his knife at his side.

Senea swallowed and ducked her head in salute, then looked up. "I have a message for Vayhawk." Her voice was hoarse.

The heldan looked on her, and it struck Senea like a blow upon a wound that she was now as guilty as Vayhawk, talking to an enemy heldan. She clenched and unclenched her free hand, telling herself that this was not an enemy heldan, but was an ally. She held her tongue while he studied her. There was fire in her arm where the wound was seeping again.

The heldan lifted his head only slightly, a gesture she took for a summons.

It was a matter of minutes then; she inwardly prayed it would be enough. She did not look back as she started up the hill behind the Wuepoah. Sky was there behind her, very near the hill now. She did not need to see him to feel his presence, his gaze on her back.

The Wuepoah waited for her at the crest of the hill, then walked beside her as she started down the slope. She felt the short hairs on the back of her neck rise, as she gazed at last from the long white ridge and saw the helden below sitting together in conference. Her eyes searched for and found Vayhawk in the center of the circle; he had not yet looked up. The very air seemed alive with his presence, and her heart beat with an emotion she could not identify. Fear closed and knotted in the vicinity of her stomach. Her hand was clenched so tightly around the belt that secured the knife at her hip that the heavy leather was doubled.

The helden around Vayhawk grew quiet as she approached with her escort. They rose, looking at her with quizzical eyes, a strange silence following her as she made her way among them. They disturbed her with their strangeness, and she felt the blood drain from her face to her stomach, understanding why they looked at her with such suspicious caution. She tried to ignore them, respectful of their right to be here.

"Messenger, Heldlan," her escort announced quietly when they reached Vayhawk and the heldan he was talking to.

The heldan from the north turned his eyes on her, and Senea realized with surprise that this was the Heldlan her escort had spoken to. She squinted in the westering sun at him and touched a tongue to her dry lips. She had to be careful. Tension was like a physical force in the air.

"You're the messenger?" the Wuepoah Heldlan asked her directly.

"Yes, sir," she said, and realized with a sudden flush that it might not be proper for her to defer to this heldan. She was not Wuepoah.

She looked apprehensively to Vayhawk. He crouched there a moment, arms flung across his knees. The anger in his eyes chilled her, and she drew in a deep breath. He rose, looked at her from beneath lowered lids. No one moved.

"Did Roskel send you?" he asked.

She shook her head very faintly, knowing even as she did it that Vayhawk had already guessed.

"But I had to come," she said. "Sky followed you. He has Treyna and Landry with him. And there are many others. He knew where you were going. Mara and I tried to stop him. But . . ." Her voice faltered. Her body hurt. Her head hurt. Her arm was on fire, and she was tired.

"Sky killed Mara. If Treyna hadn't helped me . . . He is only a few minutes behind me. I had to warn you."

There was a blink of the dark eyes. The faces about her were suddenly stark with apprehension, palpable dismay in the gathering. Vayhawk returned her gaze but said nothing for a long moment.

They were cut off from the wind by the ridge behind, and the air was still and stuffy. Senea wiped the sweat from her eyes and glanced left. As she did so, she noticed the Wuepoah Heldlan glancing slowly around his men, scrutinizing each one.

"He's behind you?" Vayhawk said in that tone that meant business, that could frighten others into listening to whatever he wanted to say. "How far?"

"Not far." She swung to her left, for the sense of danger issued from that direction. It was too late. They had been found. A whistle caught her ear, above her on the rim; she looked up at a figure that appeared over the crest of the ridge, light hair blowing on the wind up there. For a moment she did not breathe, did not move. Three others showed.

"He is an enemy, this Sky?" the Wuepoah Heldlan asked quietly.

"A renegade."

Senea looked at Vayhawk when he said that.

He took her arm. "Move."

The helden scattered. Vayhawk pulled Senea with him behind a stand of rocks. She slumped down to the ground and wiped the beads of perspiration from her face with her hand. Her clothes were drenched with sweat. She trembled from exhaustion.

Vayhawk leaned against a rock, a grim expression on his face. He studied her intently before he asked, "Senea, did you lead him to us?" It was tense and to the point.

There was silence during which Senea tried to decide whether he believed that of her. She could see uneasy movement on the hill and knew there was going to be more blood spilt this day.

"No," she said, her voice exhibiting more certainty than she felt. "He already knew where you were." She turned to meet his eyes. "He would have dragged me here bound and gagged if Treyna hadn't . . ."

Vayhawk put a finger to her lips to keep her from speaking further, then pointed his hand to the hill. She wiped at her cheek and looked over the rocks, feeling him next to her. It was all she could do to keep from huddling against him and trying to become invisible. Exhaustion was a pain in her, and all she wanted to do was escape into his warmth. He shifted his weight and laid a hand gently against her face and brushed her hair back.

"I would like," he said softly, "one question answered."

She nodded.

"Do you know what you have gotten yourself into?" His eyes searched her face slowly. "We both could die because of this."

The sun was hot on her back. Her muscles soaked up the heat. Her arm throbbed. Her hand upon the haft of her knife grew sticky, and she drew the hand away, wiping it on her leg.

"You don't know what he's threatened to do."

"I can imagine. I've known him for a long time."

For some reason that touched her deeply, and she felt a

surge of gratitude. He drew in a soft breath and pulled her close while he looked over the rocks, his eyes sweeping the breadth of the hill.

"Can you fight?" he asked, the faint vibration in his voice running over her.

She nodded.

"Good." He took her by the arm then and put her gently from him. "You stay here." And that was all. He left, and Senea stared after him.

The sun dropped westward, and the hill seemed to burn with some interior light. Then she heard it, the first sounds of fighting. She looked over the rocks and saw two helden struggling in the dirt, the sun shining off gold and silver arm bands.

It was irrevocable. Nothing would stop it now.

She could hear fighting elsewhere, cries of pain and anger. Somewhere in the back of her mind, she knew she should check on other danger points.

Then she sensed someone waiting to pounce on her, and she forced herself to turn around and started to rise. A dark body hurled into her—hands gripping. She sprawled, went down, the body upon her.

Tearing her knife from its sheath, she stabbed upward. Too late, the heldan saw his mistake and tried to twist away from the blade, but it sank into his side just below the ribs and went to the hilt. The light eyes that stared at her were astonished. At the same time, Senea could feel her strength ebbing away while the heldan momentarily seemed fiercer than ever. Then the blood flowed down the blade to her fingers, and she felt his life-force pulled out of him over her skin and onto the ground.

The body tightened over her, then relaxed.

She thrust him away, appalled. She had not only killed a heldan from her own Held, but had used the Ja'sid power to do it.

She broke out of the brush into the light, saw movement, and looked aside to see Vayhawk smash Landry in the face a blow that knocked the heldan double. A blow from behind at Vayhawk's legs staggered him, and two helden moved all at once as Landry tackled him and weighed him down. He twisted, struck where he had a moment's leverage, and almost flung himself up. But Landry dropped flat on him, circling his neck with his arm while he wrapped his leg over so that

Vayhawk could not lift his knee to brace himself. It took four of them to hold him.

The Wuepoah Heldlan was stretched out on the ground a short distance away. Others were dead in the brush.

Senea tore her eyes from it and looked up the hill where Sky was visible, silhouetted against the beginnings of sunset. She imagined that his face was a study of swiftly suppressed emotions, the glint of triumph dominant.

A heldan came up behind her like a black wall. She spun, facing him. He was tall and reedy, all muscle and no fat, and had a tanned stern face with a pair of keen gray eyes. The gold of her own Held was on his arm.

"It would be a grave mistake," he said, "if you made any kind of move."

That was polite. The tone surprised her. For a pulse beat, she wondered if he was going to help her. She clutched her knife and looked at him warily. Then she recognized the challenge in his eyes and the edge of his voice—a threat that was very real. He smiled thinly.

She stepped back instinctively, prepared to defend herself. He shook his head. She stopped.

"Give it up." He raised a hand, wanting her knife.

Every instinct warned her against handing it over. She held the knife out, did not even argue the point. He took it and stepped up to her and gripped her arm with fingers that bit into the flesh. Then at last, with a last effort, Senea threw off the inertia that had a hold of her. She twisted as he tried to catch her arm again and pull her back.

"Heldan . . . you're finished," he said. "Surrender with some grace." He was being civil. But there was no softness under that voice.

Senea stopped. She glanced over toward where Vayhawk was being hauled to his feet. Her heart was beating more than fast and she felt the color draining from her face. She looked back to the heldan.

"You've all fallen for Sky's lies, you know."

His hand tightened on her arm imperceptibly. "Over there," he said, motioning with his head and turning her with an impatient move.

She went where he steered her, sat down next to Vayhawk. The heldan took her quiver of arrows and then strode away.

She met Vayhawk's eyes with reluctance. He was bound, arms behind his back, legs in front, so that he could not rise.

"Are you hurt?" His voice was a comforting murmur in the madness that was all about them.

She shook her head wordlessly.

A Wuepoah heldan was brought and pushed down beside Vayhawk.

Then the helden began to settle to their heels around them, one by one, all but Landry, who stood there with his face expressionless and his hands caught in his belt. Senea watched, apprehension flooding through her.

"Just be calm," Vayhawk whispered.

She tried to smile at him, but failed. She wiped her face, trying to summon at least some anger to face what was to come next.

The sun had touched the rim of a distant ridge, sitting on the crest like a small, intense globe of molten metal, as if the ridge itself were burning.

The tension in the air seemed almost unreal.

Senea looked up in a sudden silence and saw Sky there, in a place beside Landry—arriving like an apparition, and on his face was a slight twist of lips that might have been a smile.

"Well done," he said, then snapped his fingers and pointed at the Wuepoah. "Kill that one."

The Wuepoah started. A knife was in his back the next instant. He slumped backward, slouched to the ground while Senea stared and suddenly found the anger that she wanted.

"Now you see how it is," Sky said, squatting down, face to face with her. "It is as I promised. I have you." He looked to Vayhawk. "And I have him."

Senea sat still, the adrenaline going hot and cold through her limbs.

"You're a fool," Vayhawk said quietly. His tone expressed utmost disdain.

Sky's face went hard. For a moment he said nothing at all. Then his eyes hooded. "What you think of me is unimportant. You are a traitor, and that's what matters here."

"You're a liar," Vayhawk murmured softly. "You know it, and you're a fool."

Sky said nothing, but his eyes were cold—cold, with suppressed rage. He stood up again and looked round him at Landry. "Take care of them." He turned neatly on his heel and walked away, silent, disrespectful. There was silence behind him.

The sun had been throwing its last orange light into the sky and sank in that moment, casting twilight before the ridge. The windshift was sighing over the ground causing the brush to whisper. Senea couldn't help staring at Landry as he came to her with a cord in his hands. An odd brooding smile curved his lips, a chilling light on a face unused to such exercise. He dropped to his heels and roughly began to lash her feet together.

"This is a mistake," she said to him. "What was going on here wasn't what you think. You don't understand."

Landry stopped and regarded her dispassionately. "Indeed," he said.

"Don't, Senea," Vayhawk said. "Let it go."

Landry turned his head. The Heldlan looked at him with contemptuous hostility. Landry failed to flinch. The eyes remained steady and silence hung there.

Guilty, was the thought that then came to Senea, watching him. He knew the lies. And chose not to do anything about them. He was backing Sky up on this—all the way. Even in murder, if it came to it.

She stared at him a long moment. He pulled her hands forward and bound them tightly with the same cord that was around her legs so that she had to sit with her knees drawn up. She could not move. The pain in her arm had lessened from searing pain to one of throbbing waves.

A fire was started, and Landry withdrew, sending a couple of helden to take care of the dead.

"Senea," Vayhawk's low voice spoke beside her. "Are you going to talk to me now?"

She looked up at him not knowing what he meant. It was not the question; it was the silence that went after it.

Comprehension slowly dawned as she met the stab of that dark gaze.

"You know," she breathed. Of course he knew! How could she think he would not know? Very slowly she drew a breath.

"I think it's time you tell me, don't you? About Sky?"

"I didn't want you to know."

Again there was a stab of those dark, fathomless eyes.

"All right," she said. A quiet all right. She dropped her gaze to the ground for a brief moment, looking at nothing in particular.

Then she told him everything.

He listened wordlessly until she was through, his eyes on her unvarying, virtually unblinking. His nearness was an intoxicating force and she wanted to lean into it, but she held herself apart, uncertain at how he was receiving what she told him.

"Watch him, Vayhawk. He means to kill you."

"If he can." His mouth was set hard, the firelight etching his face into dark lines and creases that showed his tightly controlled anger. "I shall have to make sure that I kill him instead," he said.

Senea said nothing. There was nothing to say. Her fingers felt numb. A lot of her did, and she put her head to her knees. Sounds from the fire came to her, laughter, murmuring voices, the cracking of the wood in the flames.

She tried to believe that Vayhawk could change things. But she had looked Sky in the eyes.

"I'm sorry, Vayhawk," she said then. "I should have told you before it came to this."

"I will forgive you," he answered, looking into her eyes with a gaze that missed nothing, "so long as you have regard for me." He inclined his body slightly to her so that his voice was soft against her. "Do you?"

The breath went out of her and she stared into his eyes. His face was so close she could feel his breath on her lips. And somehow she knew everything hinged on that question.

"Yes," she whispered, surprised at the depths from which that answer came.

"Good," he said, and his lips touched hers in a kiss so gentle it almost tore her soul from her.

A dark figure separated from the firelight and came toward them. Two more followed.

"On your feet, Heldlan." It was Landry, bending to slice through the knot that secured the cord around Vayhawk's legs.

"What are you getting out of this, Landry?" Vayhawk asked with an icy edge to his voice. "Held-second?"

The stare was cold.

Hands pulled him roughly to his feet.

"Where are you taking him?" Senea demanded.

Landry observed her disdainfully for a moment, then no longer paid any heed.

"Vayhawk?" Her voice dropped to an anxious whisper. She was suddenly desperately afraid for him.

He glanced at her without speaking, a wordless persuasion for restraint that was like a knife-thrust to her. The pain of it left her reeling. She had to clamp her teeth together to keep from raging at them all. She sat there and watched as he let himself be led away. Tears threatened to break through to the surface. She forced them back ferociously and took an angry grip on herself. She couldn't afford to show signs of weakness.

She held herself silent and followed the distant figure with her eyes. She thought that they were going to kill him now. And she marveled at his self-control.

A weight settled beside her—Sky sinking to sit cross-legged on the ground.

"Go away," she said very softly.

He looked at her coldly—almost with contempt, it seemed to her. He was silent.

"It won't be long now." He actually smiled, a gesture that made his mouth the tighter.

Senea made a slight move of her head to the dark where Vayhawk had disappeared. "Where are they taking him?"

"Why the concern?" He leaned back leisurely on an elbow with unconcealed arrogance, his other hand negligently resting on his drawn-up knee.

"What are they going to do to him?"

He just stared at her, his hand resting on his knee, jaw set, eyes hard.

"You're not going to get away with this."

"I already have." Sky's hand left his knee and drew his knife from its sheath, then lifted it up for her to see. Firelight reflected with a cold gleam along the length of its blade. With utter calmness, he stabbed it into the ground between them. Senea winced because of the unspoken intent in that move.

"How can you do this?" she asked him. "You know, as well as I do, what Vayhawk was doing here. How can you lie to these helden like this?"

He reached out across his body and traced a finger along her jaw. Then his hand dropped. "Who's to say who's lying?" He shrugged. "It could be the Heldlan who has lied."

She fixed him with a glare. "You know that he hasn't."

"Do I?"

"Yes. You do."

Sky sneered. "This loyalty of yours is touching."

She said nothing to that. She just looked at him, repulsed by him.

The dark eyes rested on her, traveled the length of her, and redirected to her face. "You could have had it all," he said. "You know that." She flushed. He had that satisfaction. "You don't take that seriously, do you." He smiled, a move of the lips, not the rest of his face. "That's too bad."

"You're crazy," she said. "You're outright crazy."

He considered her slowly. "Perhaps."

She hissed between her teeth in derision.

"Let me tell you something, heldan." He leaned forward and jabbed a forefinger at her. "This needn't have gone this far. It lies on you that it has."

"That's ridiculous," she heard herself say vehemently. "This is your doing and no one else's. And when Treyna reaches the Held . . ." She caught herself too late.

Suddenly his hand shot out and gripped her arm painfully. "You'd better explain that."

She was silent.

"Answer!" he snarled and shook at her arm, his fingers digging painfully into the muscle. "What about Treyna?"

Senea cursed herself. Instinct said silence; common sense said it was not going to work.

"You should not have treated her the way that you did." She smiled at him. "You have turned her into an enemy. She's gone for Roskel. And to talk to Aldived."

A strange tense look crossed Sky's face. He lifted his right hand so that it drew her attention, and she stared at his fist that was barely held in check.

"You're going to die before this is through, Senea." His voice was tight with fury. "And I will be sorry."

He thrust himself to his feet then, pulled his knife from the ground, and slammed it into its sheath. Then he turned on his heel and strode away.

He meant it. Senea realized it with a shock. He didn't want it to be this way either. But he wasn't going to change it.

She waited until the sound of his footsteps proved he had really gone. Then she attempted to work her bindings loose, but to no avail. She rubbed her wrists raw, but it did no good.

A heldan brought her some roasted meat and held it while she ate. She didn't want it, but instinct told her that the strength her body would draw from the food would be essential. Afterward she sat with her knees to her chest, her arms wrapped around them where they were bound, clamped her teeth together, and stared at the fire.

The dried leaves of the brush behind her sent a faint, spicy fragrance into the air; the golden grasses and the bayonets of the spear plants were dull and vague in the firelight. The moon floated cold and distant, and the plain was shrouded in shadow.

Senea sat, for a long time, tired but unable to close her eyes. She was worried about Vayhawk, anxious about where he was and what was happening to him. She sat, and the night deepened.

Finally she was able to sleep, curled up on the ground, despite the numbness of her wrists and feet from the too-tight bindings.

She was awakened suddenly by a hand clamped tightly across her mouth. Her startled cry was muffled.

"No," came a whisper in her ear. "Don't."

Her mind was numbed by sleep and at first she thought she was imagining the voice. But someone was kneeling over her with a hand covering her mouth hard. She struggled, her vision clearing. She knew the face that leaned over her and knew the voice. She tried to twist her face away from his hand.

"Stop it!" Sky shook at her.

Senea fought him harder.

Sky cursed and slammed his fist into the side of her head. She dropped to the ground. When she got her breath back, she was lying on her side, half-stunned.

"Do not make a sound or I will kill you," Sky said quietly.

She managed a nod.

"All right," he whispered hoarsely. "Not one sound. Sit up."

She felt her arm taken and was pulled forward. She sat there, numb. He leaned over her, his chest hard against her back, and suddenly her legs were free. She saw his knife move and sever the cord around her hands. She gasped in pain at the rush of blood that surged through her fingers. Then he was dragging her to her feet.

Her arms were pulled behind her, and her wrists lashed together. Then a rope was passed around her throat and tied behind her so that if she moved her arms it would be pulled painfully tight, and only Sky could loosen it again. Senea knew how effective it was, because Vayhawk had taught it to her. If she tried in any way to break free of the ropes she would be strangled to death.

"Move," Sky said harshly into her ear.

Senea staggered, and Sky grabbed her around her waist.

"I said, move," he growled.

She stumbled where he pulled her, catching herself on the uneven ground. The jolt sent shards of pain up her legs, and before she could stifle it, a cry was torn out of her.

Sky stopped, his arm tightening savagely around her. He stood still for a long time and listened.

There was silence but for the ceaseless whisper of the night's breeze. It was the cold, chill hour before the first stir of dawn, and the moon was low. Senea shivered in the tight circle of Sky's arm.

Finally, he seemed satisfied with the silence and forced her on into the night.

CHAPTER TWENTY-THREE

To the east, under the spreading sunrise, there were mesas and canyons, league on league of red cliff and arid tablelands, extending through purple distances over the bulging lift of the land. The air lay dead and still upon the long, dry slope; no breath of air stirred among the red and brown rocks. A haze covered the sky, seeming to gather and intensify the heat as the sun rose, making every breath an effort.

Sky was silent, his hand tight on Senea's arm, taking her relentlessly into that alien land. He seemed deep in brooding, his silence a heavy thing between them, grim and almost angry. Senea did not break into his reflections, sensing that he was in a dangerous mood. She went where he directed her and set herself to ignore the occasional rough going when she'd jar her whole body. Her legs began to ache, but somehow she managed to pace on and keep the rope from tightening around her throat.

They came to a hill and climbed it. The crest was far wider than it seemed from below, and to Senea's surprise she saw that a few scrubs and trees stood well concealed by boulders. There was even some weedy, yellow grass.

"Rest," Sky said, pushing her underneath a short, scraggly tree. He wiped at the sweat that gathered on his upper lip and looked out across the desert.

Senea was glad to sit down. Her knees were weak, and her feet hurt. She leaned back against the rough bark with a sigh. A hot wind swirled among the rocks and rattled the sun-scorched leaves overhead. Salt burned into her eyes, impairing her sight.

"Can I have water?" she asked. Her voice cracked from a dry throat.

He lifted his water skin over his head, uncorked it, and held it while she drank. When she was finished, he turned to scout back the way they had come with his eyes. He thought they were being followed, she realized. She saw then the tension and animal intensity in the way he moved and in the way he studied the desert.

Sky lifted up the skin. Swallowing a mouthful, he twisted the cork tightly in place and slung the strap over his head, settling the bag against his hip with an unconscious hand.

"On your feet."

Senea rose stiffly, struggling for balance without her hands, but apparently she moved too slowly for his liking. He seized her elbow and hurried her.

The rope tightened painfully around her throat when he yanked her to her feet. Gagging, she pulled back at his hand. Wordlessly, he loosened the rope, then directed her forward, deeper into the desert.

By midmorning the wind began to pick up. Sand swirled and at times it was almost impossible to see. By sunset the sun hung swollen and bloody, just above the western edge of the desert. The wind had finally settled, dust hanging in the air turning the western sky into a blazing swath of flame. Windshift would not come now in the beginning approach of wet season, and the silence was eerie, the air stilled and quiet. Off to the west stood another grim range of mesas easily as high and as treacherous as those Senea had seen in the east that morning.

They had been climbing a gradual rise in the land for some time, finding little shelter in the desolate landscape. The cracked soil was harder than fire-baked stone. And then, just as the sun was slipping past the horizon, they came to a ridge of rock that extended like a single finger into the vast stretch of emptiness. The cliff, where the wind had worn at the sandstone, was undercut with shallow grottoes and caves.

Sky steered Senea to one of the closest and thrust her down against the back wall. For a moment she just sat there. She was sweating freely, breathing heavily, and her heart was pounding in a labored manner. She was tired, very tired. Shaking off a creeping lethargy that was already threatening to take possession, she pulled her knees up and leaned against the rock wall, trying to ignore the throbbing pains of her body, especially the fire in her arm. She watched Sky as he moved about inspecting the cave.

He came to her, dropping to his heels in front of her.

"Lean forward," he said, drawing out his knife. When she just stared at him, he sighed, reached out, and pulled her toward him by the arm. He reached around and cut the rope. Then he pulled it free.

Motioning with his hand, he said, "Take off your sandals."

"What?"

"Take them off, or do I assist you?" he asked with no patience at all.

She glared at him defiantly, then she unlaced them, first one and then the other, thrusting them at him. He dropped them out of her reach.

Taking her hands and binding them again, he lashed the two ends of the cord around her legs several times, securing it with a knot under her feet where she could not reach it. He tied her sandals together and slung them over his shoulder.

"I'm going to get us something to eat. Don't go anywhere." He smiled wryly, and then he was gone.

Senea stared after him into the dying sunset. The sky was changing from a bloodred to plum, outlining the distant horizon of buttes and canyons in dark relief. She could not hear the heldan as he left, guessing that he was going along the base of the cliff.

She shivered. The night was going to be cold. She leaned her head back against the rock, eyes shut, listening as the night insects began their chorus. She was beginning to feel uncomfortable in the growing chill, but she was too tired to do anything more than acknowledge it.

A hand came out and rocked her shoulder, pressing with strong fingers. She opened her eyes with a start. Sky was kneeling beside her, looking down at her. The sunset behind him was gone; points of stars glimmered against the now-black horizon. A small fire was burning in a corner of the cave, hidden behind some rocks, an enticing aroma of cooking meat filling the air.

She was suddenly ravenously hungry.

He untied the cord, pulled it free of her legs and hands, then stood up and pulled her from the rock to her feet. "Over here, where it's warm."

Senea followed him, limping on stiffened legs.

"Sit down," he said.

She did so, close to the fire, and leaned into the heat of the small blaze. She savored the moment as long as she dared, letting the warmth burn the chill out of her flesh.

Sky sat down on a broad flat rock and turned the spit on which a snake was impaled. Juices dropped into the fire, sizzling and snapping.

Senea noticed for the first time how strong and sure his hands were. She just stared, crossing her arms in front of her, wincing slightly at the painful stiffness of her wound.

"If I had been a Wuepoah, you would be dead." He spoke so abruptly that she jumped. He looked at her, apparently amused.

Senea recognized the challenge in his eyes and in his voice; his attention put her on the defensive. "Little I could have done about it, if you had been."

Sky's laughter grated unpleasantly. He moved his right hand, a flippant gesture that was a satire of himself. "It would have been interesting to see what one would have done, finding you all trussed up like that."

Senea shrugged. "Probably would have stuck around to find out who had trussed me up."

Sky's smile faded. "Yes," he murmured. Then he sat there in silence. He understood. She read it in his eyes as well as in the grim tightness at the corners of his mouth. If she had been found, they would both be dead. She looked back to the fire, feeling far from comfortable under the stare of those keen eyes.

The spit turned again, and juices spattered against the glowing wood in the depths of the fire. The skin of the snake was beginning to turn from golden-yellow to brown, splitting in places between the scales revealing the white flesh underneath. Senea's mouth watered, and her stomach twisted in complaint. She couldn't even remember the last time she had eaten. She couldn't even remember eating trail rations with Mara, although she must have.

Thinking of Mara brought a stab of pain, but she thrust away her thoughts to think of Treyna.

Treyna would only just be reaching the Held by now. But by the time she talked to Roskel and Aldived and got back to Vayhawk with help, Sky would have taken her so far north that no one would be able to find them. That is, *if* Treyna had decided to go to Roskel at all. Senea thought on that with a growing dread and uncertainty.

She glanced in Sky's direction. He was watching the snake as he slowly turned the spit, a figure that belonged in firelight, dusty yellow and gray clad, his face lit by the light and smoke, his eyes dark with an inner smoldering.

"Where are we going?" Senea asked.

A shadow passed over Sky's face to be replaced by a somewhat cynical smile. He stretched out his hand and swept it at all the horizon. "We have the whole of the desert and beyond from which we may choose." Senea found herself staring into the moss-green of his eyes. "Do you have a preference?" His smile became one-sided. "Barring going back the way we came, of course."

She shook her head mutely. His flippant attitude irritated her, and she looked at him warily. He was aware of the effect he had produced, and it amused him. "Where did you think we were going?"

"I don't know," she said, shrugging.

He chuckled low, then sobered. "There is no place we *can* go." He turned to test the snake with an experienced pinch and quickly wiped his fingers on his knee. "But we can go anywhere. The whole world is ours . . . if you want it."

He lifted the spit off the forked tree branches he had been using and held it out to her. "Take what you need."

She took it from his grasp and held it, unwilling to eat while he watched her. He frowned and made an impatient gesture.

"You can go hungry if you want to. But you might not get any more for quite a while."

Senea controlled the quick annoyance that came at once and started to pull the crisp skin off in long strips, tossing the pieces into the fire. Steaming juices welled out of the white meat and dripped onto the ground. The aroma hit her nostrils, and suddenly she could not stave off her hunger any longer. She ate, tearing the flesh off the spit and bones with her teeth, swallowing almost without chewing.

Sky lounged back against a rock and watched her in a long silence. Drawing his knife, he began to turn it idly from hand to hand, light flashing off the blade, bright and cold and hard. Then he reached down and tossed his water skin to her. It landed next to her feet. Senea looked at it with surprise; it was full, the outside beaded with moisture.

"I found a small spring," he said. "You can have all you want."

His manner confused her; and she looked at him wondering what new game he was playing. There was an absence of anger in the way he leaned against the rock and watched her. There was no sign of threat on his face. It must be her imagination, she thought. The mind played all manner of tricks when a person was as tired and as exhausted as she was. She shifted uncomfortably and pulled the water skin closer.

"Why are you doing this?" she asked of him. "Why are we going so deep into Wuepoah territory?"

Sky sat there in silence for a long moment. Then he shrugged. "Why not?"

Senea frowned at him.

He laughed shortly and softly, and the sound gave back a peculiar echo that might almost have been another, alien voice. Then he leaned forward and looked into her eyes. "Is there anywhere more remote?" He smiled, though coldly.

His eyes were locked on hers, and she was unable to look away. The blood pounded in her veins and his words came back to her, *I'm going to find you out there alone. Where there won't be anyone to help you. Nobody to take my knife. Nobody to stop me. And then, heldan, I'm going to do to you what I didn't have a chance to do ...*

"You're going to kill me," she said at last, answering her own question.

Sky was silent a moment, his dark green eyes on her face. Then he shrugged. "Maybe not."

The quiet denial shot through her. She was too surprised to answer.

He moved to sit cross-legged, and like a man idly passing the time in the presence of a friend, he leaned his elbows on his knees and began to heat the point of his knife in the dying fire.

"It's entirely up to you, of course."

"Up to me?"

"Of course."

"How is it up to me?" she asked, unable to keep the irritation out of her voice.

His head turned a little to the right so that he could look

sidelong at her. His eyes flickered with a dark, smoldering flame.

She stopped, seeing that look.

"It has always been up to you," he said.

"I don't see how!"

He looked away and went on turning the point of the knife in the flame, pulling it out before it started to turn color from the heat. "But you must do as you think fit," he said quietly.

Senea sat back in angry silence. She stared at the spit in her hand and realized that she had forgotten to eat. She started to bite into the meat only to find that she was no longer hungry. Leaning the spit against the rock wall she took up the water skin, took a drink, and twisted the cork back in place.

She cast a sidelong look at Sky and watched as he methodically lifted small glowing embers from a smoldering piece of wood and flicked them, one after the other, to the edge of the fire where they quickly died. She was going to have to get away from him. She knew that. And she knew she had to do it now. She took another long drink from the water skin, keeping a wary eye on Sky.

He turned his face to her then, his eyes dark and thoughtful. He was silent a long time, turning his knife over and over in his fingers. Finally he arose, sliding the knife back into its sheath.

"Come," he said. "It is time for sleep."

Senea hesitated a moment, thinking she hadn't heard him right. Then anger swept through her. "What do you mean?" she demanded.

She straightened up defiantly as he approached and came up against the wall of rock behind her. Her hand was reaching sideways to grab the spit and partially eaten snake to defend herself with.

Sky frowned, puzzled for a moment. Then when comprehension came, he laughed outright at her.

"What did you think I meant?" he asked. His eyes flashed, his lips parted in a terrible smile.

Senea glared at him, anger quickly becoming fury, and she refused to answer.

But he knew.

He was looking at her with an intensity that was almost alarming. "You know," he said, ever so softly, "it's going to come to that sooner or later."

"No," she countered fiercely.

A dark expression crossed his face, and he took a half step forward, so menacingly that Senea steeled herself for a blow. But before she knew what he was about, the heldan had grabbed her by the arm and pulled her away from the cave wall. He took the cord up from where he had left it and sank to his heels to bind her hands.

"I can be patient a little while longer." He did not see Senea's hand close around the spit beside her.

Bringing it up, she swung it hard. There was a sickening wet sound when it hit. The snake came apart, and pieces of meat flew through the air, striking the rock wall and rolling over the sand.

Meat juices mingling with blood ran down Sky's face. Surprise instantly replaced by rage darkened his eyes. His hand shot up to grab at her, but she struck with the spit again, scrambling back away from him.

He rounded on her with a snarl that was almost a growl and lunged. Skidding on his elbow through the sand, he drove her up against the rock wall with jarring force.

The air rushed out of her lungs at the impact, the weight of Sky on her an excruciating pain.

Sky grabbed her savagely and yanked her up to a sitting position. He looped the cord painfully around her wrists, secured it with a knot, whipped the remaining lengths around her legs, and tied the ends roughly under her feet. Then he leaned forward to one knee and gripped her chin with angry fingers, his thumb passing over her lower lip.

"My patience is nearly at an end, Senea." His fingers went to the pounding pulse-beat in her throat, the span of his hand reaching from ear to ear, tightening.

"When it is . . ." He let that trail off to silence a moment. "There will be no stopping it."

Senea drew in an agonizing breath. "I'll kill you first," she croaked.

His smile was slow and chill. "If you can."

"You know I can."

He shook his head. "I don't think so."

The high-pitched wail of a wolfhound sounded out in the night, echoing back and forth through the dark.

Without relinquishing his hold on her, Sky looked over his shoulder into the gloom beyond the glowing embers of the fire.

Something else moved out there, rattling loose pebbles over the stretch of rock that extended beyond the mouth of the cave. Sky whirled, his hand automatically closing on his knife hilt. He moved swiftly and buried the smoldering coals with two large scoops of sand and then disappeared into the darkness.

Senea sat tensely, listening anxiously at the silence, wondering if the Wuepoah had found them, knowing that if they had she would end up dead very quickly. Then there was a dark movement, and Sky came quietly back into the cave.

"Just a desert fox," he said, dropping to his heels beside her. He gazed out into the dark a long time, the light from the moon falling white on his face.

Senea eyed him warily until he turned to look at her. "Get some sleep."

She shook her head slightly. "No."

He made a sound that might have been irritation or amusement. "Senea, you're so tired you are shaking. Get some sleep, and I'll keep watch."

"But who'll keep a watch on you?"

His eyebrows drew together into an instant frown. He snapped his jaws together with exasperation. She knew his answer before he uttered it.

"I'm not going to hurt you!"

"But you said you were going to do to me things I hadn't even dreamed of yet," she reminded him doggedly. She had deliberately used the phrase that he had used on her, noticing with satisfaction that it had stung his memory. The look he turned on her was almost savage.

"All right, Senea. Do as you please. Sleep ... don't sleep. Whatever you wish." Then he shifted suddenly to lean forward close to her.

"Dreams *can* be good." There was a controlled undertone of anger in his voice.

Senea's heart lurched and she glared back at him. "Not any dream that has you in it."

He raised an eyebrow.

"Let us be honest between ourselves, Senea. It doesn't have to be this way. You know that."

She shook her head in disbelief as she stared at the dark shadow of his eyes. "You can't really believe that."

His slight smile was secretive. "Can't I?"

"It will never be any other way! Not as long as I'm alive."

He looked at her a long moment before he shrugged. "We'll see." He raised his hand to her face and ran his fingers over her mouth. "It really would be smart if you got some sleep. Tomorrow is going to be a long day."

Senea returned his gaze defiantly. And when she didn't answer him, he shrugged again.

"It's really up to you." He rose to his feet. "But I would advise it."

Senea watched him as he walked away and disappeared into the darkness. With an effort, she forced herself to relax. He was right in one thing. If she rested, her strength would return. She leaned her head back against the rock and gradually gave herself to sleep. At one point she was aware of Sky sitting beside her in warm proximity.

There were dreams born of exhaustion, and one of them was a shadow that was close and strong.

It seized her and held her tightly, and she struggled and cried out, trying to free her arms. But she had no strength to move them. The grasp closed around her hand held her still, and for a time there was only a heartbeat for reality, a throbbing against her ear, and a dull sense of arms about her drawing her close into a warmth that had no end.

She woke up and groaned softly. The nightmare was gone, but the memory was still all too current and all too vivid, filling her with a sense of dread. It was several moments before she found enough will to open her eyes. The starry black sky was touched with a hint of indigo as it reflected the dawn from the eastern horizon. She stirred slightly and found that she was held in strong arms. The steady beating of a heart was in her ear. Abruptly she realized what had happened and recalled the presence that had pulled her close to calm her in her dream.

She pulled away from Sky, angry that she had been so vulnerable. He let her go so easily she knew he had not been sleeping.

"I'm all right now," she announced in a tight voice, her face averted from his eyes.

He was quiet so long that she turned to look at him.

"Senea," he replied finally, in a low voice, "you are most welcome."

Senea felt herself color, and she grew doubly angry. "If you think I'm going to thank you for . . ." Her tone was disbelieving.

Sky interrupted her, speaking very softly. "It wasn't anything other than a matter of necessity. You were making enough noise to bring three patrols down on us. I did what had to be done, short of knocking you senseless." He began to untie her, pulling the cord away from her feet and legs.

Senea snapped her teeth shut.

"I knew you would object to anything more." His eyes glinted at her. She glared at him. "Besides . . . Did I hurt you?" His fingers lightly touched her as he loosened the cord around her wrists.

"No!"

"Then let it be." He pulled the cord free and began to loop it around his hand. "We have more important things to think about anyway." He caught her eye. "The Wuepoah will have more patrols the farther into their lands we go. They could already be on our trail. We'll know soon enough." He turned his head thoughtfully to look out on the desert, an unpleasant smile touching the corner of his mouth.

"Then we shouldn't be out here going farther into their lands."

Senea's sarcasm hit home, and Sky gave her an angry glance. He said nothing, and his continued silence as he stuffed the cord back into his pouch began to unnerve her. She rubbed her palms on her thighs as she eyed him. Dawn was growing in the sky, and the desert was covered with gray light. He turned to hand her her sandals, and she took them, putting them on, lacing and tieing them securely.

Then before he could turn again, she threw herself at him, fingers reaching for his eyes, her other hand groping for his knife. But she found herself countered immediately.

The weight of his body wrapped itself around her, his arm going around her throat, yanking her back hard against him. His voice was harsh in her ear.

"You're going to make this difficult, aren't you?"

She struggled. His arm tightened instantly around her throat, cutting off her air.

"Think it over, heldan. Do you really want to do this?"

Senea struggled harder, trying to kick him with her heels, her hands pulling at his arm.

He growled and slammed her into the rock wall, half stunning her. She tried to turn to fight him. But his body held her tightly against the white sandstone while he got the cord around her throat, tightening it painfully. He wrenched her arms one at a time behind her, lashing them together so that she could not move them without strangling herself.

Then he jerked her around, thrusting his arm through the strap of his quiver to settle it on his back.

"Let's go." There was a blackness about him now that had not been there before; it was a brooding sort of patience. He looked at her, feet slightly apart, head high, eyes flashing. His casual pose was gone.

Sky took hold of her arm, but she pulled it free, ignoring the slight tightening of the rope around her throat.

"I can walk on my own," she said.

He swore under his breath, then paused. In that pause, Senea felt the sudden tension in him. She held down an impulse to say something that would antagonize him further. Smiling a tight, chilly smile, he gestured for her to lead the way. Silence enveloped them, and she walked. Sky went behind her.

They descended a steep scarp that flattened into deeply eroded country, carved by the constant wind and scouring gray sand. Senea caught glimpses of weird humps of pale rock on either side, and shuddered as the wind moaned a dreary tune under the overhanging caves and among the holes in the rock. She descended into a dry streambed, wondering how the Wuepoah could survive in such a forbidding country.

And then, it happened.

Sky had worked his way around in front of her, and there he stopped so abruptly that Senea, hard on his heels, nearly collided with him. He cut off her complaint with an abrupt gesture.

"Patrol," he warned.

She had heard nothing.

He turned his head, listening, and swept her up with his hand going around her arm. "Come on."

He took her, running, out of the streambed and across a wide-open space on the farther side. He headed for a clump of white rocks, pulling her with him. Once behind them he released her.

"Down," he said, crouching and turning to glance back the way they had come. And, as she hesitated, he said again, "Down!"

She shrank back against a rock, and for a moment she stood breathing hard in the shadow. His pulling on her arm and the running had tightened the rope uncomfortably around her throat.

With a yank that tore a gasp from her, the heldan pulled her to the ground. She grimaced at the sharp pull on the rope. He turned to peer around the rock. His knife gleamed like a cold blue shadow in his hand. There was no sound, though Senea held her breath and strained to hear. She crouched against the rock and tried to move her arms behind her so that the tension would ease up on the rope.

"Shh," Sky said softly, his hand touching her to get her attention.

A moment later there was an abrupt move.

He launched himself forward, hit a brown-clad heldan, throwing him to the ground, and the Wuepoah was dead in the same instant. Sky came to his feet, his knife glistening with wet running streaks, then whirled as he was hit from behind.

Senea stared, unconsciously backing away from the struggle. She was tied and had no way to defend herself—that fact burned like a white brand into her mind. And then she stopped.

This was her chance to get away. She probably would not get another, and she had to do it now. Clenching her hands behind her into determined fists, she moved toward the back of the rocks, glancing over her shoulder. Sky was locked in a death hold under the Wuepoah.

She ran. And she did not look back.

She was out of the rocks, sprinting for cover a distance away. She reached the edge of the open space and bolted for some low rocks, surprised that she apparently had not been seen. She gasped for air at the tight rope around her throat and changed directions, darting round the rocks and running with all the strength she had remaining. Then making a quick choice, she headed for the hills, hide-and-seek in the rocks, the high places, as she worked her way south.

The sun rose high above the desert, blazing white, and its hot breath burned her neck and arms. The land around her lay empty, the shadows slowly growing shorter as she forced herself to keep going. The heat from the sun made her head ache, and the glare from the white sand and rocks made her eyes water.

Her arms screamed in pain from being held in a position that prevented the cord from tightening again into a stranglehold.

She stopped after a while in a narrow strip of shade, sitting on a boulder, trying to figure how to free herself and wishing that she had Sky's water skin. The hot, dry wind that had been surging out of the west had left her feeling parched.

A strange kind of lethargy was on her, and she almost lacked the strength to push herself up from where she sat. Slowly she climbed a long ridge, forcing each foot in front of the other. She had to stop frequently to catch her breath and to clear the numbing haze out of her head. Each time it was doubly hard to move again. Instinct told her that she had to get out of the sun, but her eyes could not distinguish the features of the ridge to find shade where she could rest. Time seemed to stand still even though the sun moved from the zenith and began to lower in the west.

She came at last to the top and stood precariously on the edge of the other side, trying to suck the suffocating air past the rope into her lungs. The heat seemed to stricture her and she had to gulp at each breath.

Then balance failed her. She moved, too late, to save herself, and that move led to the next step and the next. She slid, rocks ripping at her arm, tearing her wound open again, pulling roughly at the rope, catching at her clothing, crumbling away under her in a landslide that carried her uncontrollably to an outcropping of boulders. She hit them hip-high, her leg betraying her as she twisted in an attempt to avoid the impact. Grunting in pain and choking at the strangling rope, she braced herself, and kept moving downhill, no other direction possible.

Her body kept moving with its own logic, heedless of dangers, as she was carried along, stumbling and tripping. The late afternoon sun was a smear of white in the immensity of blue, and it blasted its strength down on her relentlessly, taking her strength.

At last she sprawled full length, and this impact tightened the rope mercilessly. She rolled over and struggled to her feet, leaning against one of the pillars of earth for support while she fought for air. Black threatened around the edges of her sight.

Gulping and choking, she blinked her eyes trying to clear them and heard rocks shift and rattle above her, stones that she had not stirred.

Something crashed down on her.

A hand grabbed her hair and pulled back so hard she thought her neck was going to snap. A flash of sunlight off a blade in front of her face temporarily blinded her and she knew she was going to die.

Then, just as suddenly as it had come, the weight was gone.

She struggled into a kneeling posture. The rope around her throat had loosened some, and she gasped at the little bit of air she could get in. Then she turned to see Sky dragging a Wuepoah to his feet.

For half a breath they faced each other, the Wuepoah empty-handed, his knife lying several feet away.

Sky swung, ramming his knife to the hilt in the Wuepoah's midsection, twisting it brutally as the heldan staggered against him. The knife was yanked free, and when the Wuepoah did not fall, Sky drove the knife into his belly again. The heldan toppled to the ground, and Sky hit him yet another time.

Senea watched as she fought for breath, her mind reeling with the fact that Sky was alive when she had thought that he was dead.

He drew himself up and turned full to her. His expression was vindictive, his voice low and tense. "Get up!"

She hesitated, still unable to fully get her bearings.

He stepped forward and caught her arm, swiftly cutting the rope with his knife. And if she thought to resist, she thought better of it with the edge of his knife near her face. She struggled up to her feet and went where she was compelled to go.

He urged her up the slope of the ridge, toward where she had been only moments before, and in sudden desperation she refused, bolted out of his grasp, and ran down among the brush at the right, breaking twigs and thorns, shielding her face with her arms.

She heard his roar of rage as he came after her.

She crashed through the brush to the other side, scrambling up the slope toward a low cliff.

She reached it just as he caught her, spun her around, and backhanded her across the face. She fell back against the rock wall, crying out at the impact, then moved in pain to get away as he reached for her.

But it was too late. He slammed her against the rock.

She cried out and closed her eyes against the pain.

His body was on hers, pinning her to the cliff, his breath hot in her face. She opened her eyes and stared into his fury-blackened eyes and knew that she was dead. Whatever emotion had been there before was gone. The only thing that was there now was rage.

And then, before she realized what she was doing, or even why she was doing it, she was kissing him—fiercely—almost angrily, instinct guiding her out of desperation.

He hesitated a moment in surprise and started to pull away, but then with a groan that sounded like it came from a deep emptiness within his soul, his arms went around her, crushing her to him. His mouth bruised hers with a demanding hunger that alarmed her.

His mouth was hard on hers, cruel and possessive. She had a sense of suffocation, of being overwhelmed, of being taken by force. She wanted to cry out, wanted to struggle against him, but she leaned into him instead. She wanted it to seem as if he had conquered her and was making her utterly subservient to his will so that she had no power left of her own.

Then she let herself go suddenly limp, and as Sky bent to pull her back to him, she brought her knee up—hard—shoved him back and ran.

She heard him gasp and then she heard nothing.

Stumbling over low, dry brush she hurled herself from rock to rock, scrambling from one winding turn to the next, fending off dead branches of the scrub brush with her hand.

Coming to another cliff she cast about and saw that to the left the ground rose along the wall. It was a climb through soft dirt that would slow her down, and to the right there was a sharp drop to another creekbed, dry and strewn with dead brush and boulders. It was an impossible jump.

She could not remember the decision, but she faced the climb. Using hands as well as feet, she slipped, then gained a body's length, then another.

Then suddenly she was being dragged back.

She turned, snarling as Sky's hand clutched at her ankle. Sliding down into him, she kicked at him repeatedly.

He caught her arm with fingers like iron bands and yanked her to the foot of the climb, where unexpectedly he lost his hold, and she sprawled onto the ground.

He grabbed her by the shoulders and pulled her up to her feet.

"Heldan," he whispered savagely in her ear, and all but

threw her against the cliff wall where the hardness of the rock knocked the wind out of her. "I'm going to tear you to pieces."

She had a split second of the view overhead, the cliff rising up to a wind-weathered curl, a scraggled brush growing out of a crack twenty feet overhead. A crevice wide enough to crawl into was five feet higher than that, but there was no way to get to it.

His face was next to hers, and she could see beyond him at the periphery of her vision the rise of the canyon and the cliff wall above it. The sun was just behind it, a sliver of glare that hurt her eyes. It was going to be dark soon.

His hands grasped her arms with vise-fingered coercion, and she could tell by the stilted way he moved that he was still in pain. He had come after her in spite of it.

"Sky, you're insane," she said. "Roskel and Vayhawk are going to find us. You know they will."

Incredibly Sky began to laugh, startling, the echoes of his voice sounding weirdly off the cliff rocks.

"They'll hunt us until they find us. No matter how long it takes."

Sky's laughter suddenly doubled. He threw back his head and laughed outright, his hand clutching her.

"You think it's funny?" His reaction frightened her and she felt cold bafflement creep over her.

Sky's laughter subsided to a chuckle that shook his body as he tried to control it.

"That's going to be a little difficult," he said in an uneven voice.

"Why?" She was beginning to feel alarm.

"Because Vayhawk's dead. And when Roskel finds him, he's going to be dead, too. I left Landry to take care of him."

There was a moment of shocked silence.

A cold chill went through her. "That's—that's impossible!"

"I should know, Senea. I killed the Heldian myself."

Senea felt the world around her begin to spin. It was hard to breathe.

"A knife in the ribs," he whispered, leaning close so that his words shivered over her mouth.

It hit her like a blow. The blood began to roar in her ears so fiercely that she couldn't hear anything else.

"No!" she spat at him through bared teeth. It was a word full of anguish and hatred that erupted from the depths of her bowels. She struck at him in blind fury. She growled through her teeth as she dug at his face with her nails. He was going to die; it was the only thought in her screaming brain. Piece by piece, inch by inch, she was going to spread him around the desert, until no one would ever be able to find him again.

And somewhere in the background of her murderous rage there was an anguished cry that threatened to break through.

"Senea!" Sky seized her wrists, fighting her hands away from his face. "Listen to me!"

She wrenched at his arms, and he jerked her hands down. His body leaned against hers, pinning her to the rock. "Listen to me!" His face was close to hers. "The only life you have now is with me." His voice was hard. "You have nowhere to go. The *only* place you have is with me."

She fought at his grasp. His hand tightened warningly on her until his fingers pressed tendon to bone, and she winced at the pain. The dark shadow of his face loomed before her.

"Senea, don't you dare oppose me in this." His voice dropped to an intense, icy whisper, shaking with anger. "Don't make me have to do to you what I did to Vayhawk. Don't!" He caught her to him and angrily fought her clenched hand between them. Spreading apart the fisted fingers, he kissed the open palm. Looking back up at her, he bit out, "Don't force me to it."

Senea was barely able to keep herself from spitting in his face. The sheer magnitude of what he had done, the treachery of it, sliced through her like a white-hot knife. In her was an almost-uncontrollable desire to kill, to take revenge. Vayhawk was dead, and she felt like dying; the pain of it was more than she could bear. But she was going to take Sky with her!

There was a faint sound, coming from a distant place. It was the sound of bitter weeping as if a heart had been broken, and in the back of her mind, Senea knew that the weeping was hers.

Then she flung herself to Sky, tearing her hands out of his grip, reaching up like a wild animal clawing at his eyes.

His response was explosive. He slammed her back against the wall of the cliff and struck her openhanded across the jaw. A crack of light split through her head.

"I can be gentle or behave like a savage," he said in a tight whisper, his teeth bared. "Which is it to be?"

She struck out with her right fist and caught him alongside

his face, thrust at him, trying to twist away. His hand snaked up and seized her hair, pulling back her head so that she thought her neck would break.

"Stop fighting me," he said with hoarse rage.

"Never." Her lips were dry, her voice choked. Her hand closed around his knife and jerked it free. Swinging upward with it, she drove for his neck.

He caught her hand with equal swiftness. His fingers were murderous, and he twisted her arm until the knife fell out of her grasp.

Then a blow to the side of the head swept her along the cliff face. Her brow and shoulder struck hard against the rock. Falling to the ground, she lay stunned.

CHAPTER
TWENTY-FOUR

She was still alive.

She discovered this slowly.

With great effort she rolled over on her back and stared up at the white that showed through some dried branches. Her breath came in labored, shallow gasps.

A muted sound came to her ears, and she stopped. Straining, she listened. It was a slight sound, the scrape of a step against loose shale.

She turned her head as Sky's hand clutched at her.

"Move!" he said. He pushed her harshly back into the grass, crouching down so that he could twist her around and slide his hand over her mouth. He held her in a viselike grip.

"Lie flat and still!" he whispered. He pulled her farther back into the shade of the brush.

Senea looked around with her eyes, wondering how they had gotten to the stand of scrub brush. Sky must have dragged her or carried her there.

Just then Senea's slow senses picked up a faint sound coming toward them, footsteps coming up the hill. There was a low murmur of voices just beyond the scrubs, indistinguishable, half whispered; a small patrol tracking them. Senea froze beside Sky, instinct against another Held suddenly allying her with him again.

A figure loomed nearby, facing away from where she lay in Sky's arms. Tan-colored hair gleamed in the sunlight, and she knew who it was.

Shock tore the breath from her.

Vayhawk!

She would have risen, but Sky held her with a grip of steel. "Stay where you are!" he said in a harsh whisper.

Senea stared at Vayhawk's back, stunned beyond thought.

She slowly became aware of the pain of her heart thudding with hard jarring strokes, and of her hand clenching Sky's arm so tightly her nails were drawing blood, and of the tidal force of the blood surging in her ears, very much like a high wind before an oncoming storm.

Sky had lied! And she had believed him!

Sky held her still and silent, his arm crushing her to him, his other hand clamped tightly over her mouth. She watched as Vayhawk turned to move away.

She was furious with herself. How could she have believed Sky so easily? She hadn't even doubted. Angry tears trickled down her face.

There was a taut moment of silence.

"So, I lied," Sky whispered in her ear. His hand slid away from her mouth and intimately down her throat.

"Lied?" she demanded angrily, and swore at herself that her voice had no sound.

"Be careful, little girl," he whispered. "You'll lead him to us. And I guarantee you that he will not like what he will find . . ." His fingers moved to grip her tunic at the shoulder. "One sound, one tiny move, and it will be very convincing. Vayhawk's heldii in the arms of another heldan," he said softly. "I will make it extremely convincing. Too final to be a pretense."

His hand twisted in the fabric of her tunic, and Senea knew that he would have it off her with very little trouble if she so much as breathed too hard.

"What will you do then?" he whispered mockingly. "Will you welcome him with open arms? Will you embrace him? Kiss him the way you kissed me?" He leaned down and brushed her ear with his lips. "Do you think he'll let you?"

Then he released her. "I'm going to see if he's gone. Don't—you—move!"

Senea turned to look at him. His eyes rested meaningfully on hers. She could only stare back with loathing.

Sky pulled his knife from its sheath as he slid forward. Slowly he inched through the brush, then poked his head through a gap in the undergrowth, and he lay still within grabbing distance. Senea watched breathlessly as he lay still for several long minutes. She did not dare move or cry out because Sky was still close enough that he'd be on her with a single lunge. So she lay still with her hand pressed to her mouth and her heart pounding so hard she thought that Sky might hear it.

She watched him closely. As soon as he was far enough away, she'd make a run for it.

But then, he carefully slid backward through the brush, rearranging the grass and branches as he moved. He lay very still, gripping his knife and thinking.

Then he looked at Senea. "He's still there. Trying to find our trail. I have no choice but to take him."

Before she could even move, he seized her, pulling and twisting her until she was back against him. The point of his knife pressed to her neck. "Call him!" It was a harsh whisper in her ear. The knife slithered up to her jaw.

Her blood pounded through her veins. "What?"

The knife pressed harder. "Call him!"

"No!"

Senea's heart began to thud as the force of power shivered through the violence of their contact. It was a fire that moved from Sky to her, binding them together, and would go on forever as long as they touched. There was a strange, distant thunder that came from deep within herself. An answering of that power that was equal in strength and energy.

"You call him," Sky said, "or I will make sure he finds us in a very compromising circumstance." His arm about her waist moved so that his hand spread on her stomach and then he gathered up her tunic in a slow closing of fingers. She felt the fabric strain and pull at her back. "Don't think that I won't." He pulled the fabric much tighter and the strain became a harsh rip.

Senea couldn't move or struggle—the grip of the force was too strong. She grew alarmed. If this rising power within her met that which was coming from Sky, there would be no controlling it. She would be lost to it and to Sky. And so would Vayhawk.

"All right," she said angrily to him. She called out to Vayhawk.

"Louder," Sky snarled.

Senea closed her eyes with a tight intake of breath and called again.

"I said, louder!" He twisted the tunic and there was another sharp rip. In a few more moments he'd have it off her.

"Vayhawk!" she shouted. "Vayhawk! Over here!" And heard a few seconds later the unmistakable approach of a masculine stride.

Sky pushed her away so violently that she gasped and crashed into the brush.

"Senea?" It was Vayhawk's voice, anxious, hoarse.

Then, suddenly, he was there.

She stared up at him, her heart beating so hard she had the sensation that it might leap into her throat and choke her.

She rose to her feet, and the world seemed to whirl around her, shadow and light breaking up into a symmetric pattern. With an audible intake of air, she reached out with one hand and gripped the rough trunk of a scrub.

She could only stare at him while a rising tide of emotions swirled inside her. Her eyes drank in the strength of him, the lift of his head, the rolling liquid stride, the minute movements of his shoulders and upper arms, the extreme danger leashed tightly inside him.

Unconsciously, her fingers rose to her cheek to brush away the dirt and dust.

His face was strained, the shadows of the lack of sleep around his eyes, yet she felt the intensity of his gaze. His eyes locked onto hers, and for an unfathomable instant Senea felt suspended in time and space.

"Are you all right?" His slightly textured voice seemed unreal to her. Only minutes before, she had thought that he was dead.

"Yes," she answered, almost without any sound to her voice. A look of relief passed over his face.

Then there was another presence . . . Roskel coming silently from the brush and stopping next to Vayhawk, his hand resting on his knife.

"Heldlan," a harsh voice said from behind them.

Vayhawk swung around, the sun reflecting off the blade in his hand.

"Greetings, Vayhawk," Sky said, looking at him with a taunting smile on his face. "I thought we had seen the last of you."

"Did you?"

"Somehow, we had gotten the idea that you were dead. A knife in the ribs."

"You were mistaken."

"I can see that. A shame. Things were going so well." There was a suggestive tone in his voice. He glanced at Senea, his smile deepening ... that smile not going unnoticed by Vayhawk. "So very well."

Then Sky shrugged, grimacing sheepishly as he continued. "I think we were making progress. I trust we were, anyway." His eyes shifted from Vayhawk to Senea again, an adder about to strike. "At least a little while ago."

There was a terrible silence. Vayhawk turned to look at her, his eyes silently searching. Senea's breath burned in her lungs as if the air had been forced through a fire, and she wanted to strike out at Sky and tear off his face. Sky laughed, and the sound meant that he was going to attempt to bury her deeper.

"Tell him or not, as you please, Senea—it makes no difference. You cannot deny how you kissed me."

She flinched inwardly at the truth in his words that somehow he had turned into a lie. Looking up and meeting Vayhawk's penetrating brown-black gaze, she knew that there was no need to deny it. He would know the difference if she did.

"I caught him off guard," she said. The corner of her mouth quirked. "I got away for a while."

Suddenly her legs buckled, the last of her strength draining away. Vayhawk's quick grip on her arm let her gently to the ground, and he sank to his heels in front of her.

"I should have killed him instead. He told me he had killed you."

Vayhawk reached out and touched her cheek lightly with his fingertips, then lowered his hand. Breath hissed, and his hand curled up into a fist. A strange, almost cruel expression narrowed his eyes. He uncoiled, like some lethal animal.

"Hold her," he told Roskel as he turned to Sky.

Senea looked at Roskel. She had forgotten him. His light brown eyes went to the heart of her and peeled away the layers. She watched him warily as he strode to her. This was one man from whom the truth would never be hidden. He reached down and helped her to her feet.

"Come with me," he ordered her as he encircled her and pulled her back into the brush.

Then as she was looking through the dry branches, she saw Vayhawk attack Sky with such blinding speed and ferocity that she literally jumped. They skidded across the ground, crashing through brush, coming up hard against the cliff.

Sky twisted free to wrench his knife out of its sheath. His eyes flashed, and his lips curled in a snarl as he struck at Vayhawk in a single, rapid movement.

The Heldlan tackled him low; low enough to avoid the knife. It swung well over his head, and Sky was falling backward and down. They wrestled there on the ground until Vayhawk rolled over twice, breaking through low brush as Sky's knife missed him by inches, driven up to its hilt in the dry ground.

Vayhawk exploded onto both feet, his knife held up in his hand. Sky wrenched his own weapon out of the ground. He feinted, testing the Heldlan for weakness or indiscretion. The two crouched, facing each other across six feet of space, knife hands weaving.

"Roskel," Senea said. "Do something."

"No," came his voice in her ear. "I can't . . ."

Senea twisted in his arms, but stopped when she looked up at him, the force of will behind his eyes so powerful it caused her words of protest to die in her throat.

"This is a heldcode matter, Senea."

She drew in a tight breath and let her head rest forward on his chest. She nodded, feeling the knot in her stomach tighten, and understood. Vayhawk could die, because of her. She exhaled and forced herself to watch, leaning against Roskel for support.

"Give it up, Sky," Vayhawk was saying, his voice deathly quiet.

"And if I won't?"

"You know the answer to that!"

Sky laughed. "Pretty sure of yourself."

A slight shake of the head. "Give it up, Sky. It's over."

"Over?" He laughed a low, chilling sound. "You think it's over? Where's your pride, Heldlan?" He looked scornful. "It may be over for me, but it will *never* be over for you, believe me. What did she tell you just now . . . ? That she tricked me? Are you satisfied with that? How are you ever going to be sure?" He smiled cold, cold. "It's going to be a very empty victory."

"So you have your revenge. What good does it do you?"

"You take me for a fool, Heldlan. Who said anything about revenge?" he asked, his face growing furious.

"Love?" Vayhawk's voice spat out the word. "Is that how you describe it?"

Sky smiled slowly. "Describe it however you want. The point is, I took her from you. In more ways than one."

"All right," Vayhawk whispered savagely. "I see there's no point to this. Let's end it. Right now."

Sky nodded and beckoned him with his knife. "Let's go for it." His face held such an expression of finality that it filled Senea with foreboding. She heard the note of weariness in his voice. He was not going to make it through this. He knew it, and Senea knew it.

"Roskel, you've got to stop this!"

"Vayhawk will take care of it," the Held-second told her.

Senea turned around abruptly to plead with Vayhawk. Her movement caught Sky's attention, and for just the slightest instant, he became more focused on her than he was on Vayhawk. It was a fatal mistake. Senea watched as Vayhawk translated motionlessness into motion.

With the power of a wolfhound's attack, Vayhawk hurled Sky off his feet, and he crashed against the cliff. Sky swore, leapt with a lateral strike, which Vayhawk neatly blocked sliding to the right, feinting, then lunged. Sky pivoted to meet him. His left arm jerked up as he snared his knife in Vayhawk's tunic. For a second the blade caught in the tough lining, then he twisted it free and jumped back. Hissing wickedly, Vayhawk's return strike skimmed the front of Sky's own tunic.

Sky scrambled to his feet then froze, regarding Vayhawk with disbelief. The Heldlan had hit him, drawing a line of blood that welled under the sliced-open tunic.

Again Sky pounced, and this time he twisted to the right where Vayhawk had been dodging.

Instead of faking back and out, Vayhawk met the man's knife hand on the point of his own blade, drawing blood again.

He attacked, and the heldan gave ground slowly before Vayhawk's advance. Sandals scuffled over the hard-baked soil. Senea heard Sky's breathing, and could smell sweat and a faint odor of blood on the air. There was the clatter of weapons hitting the cliff when Sky was forced up against it.

With a frustrated growl, he drove his knife forward and sprang at Vayhawk, steel flashing. He caught the Heldlan's hand. The blade flew out of it as he twisted, and Vayhawk went crashing down. Sky's face was sweating in the sunlight, his eyes shining with sparks.

Vayhawk drove and dodged and stumbled to his knees again.

Knowing she had to do something, Senea reached out desperately for the Ja'sid power. Silence fell around her. A kind of blackness came. She sensed rather than saw the presence of the two fighting helden beyond.

In her anxiousness for Vayhawk, she felt the power rise in her, touching her with its strength, first her head and then her back. It mounted: heat upon heat upon heat . . . upon heat.

She took a deep breath. There was a pain, sharp and clear and contrastingly cold to the heat of the power, a knife of ice slipping in and out of her lungs. She focused on the only heldan she could direct it against and pushed at it, thrusting it at him. She felt it hit him full force.

She saw naked fear and shock wipe Sky's face clear of triumph, and she watched as he got himself under control. A malevolent sneer replaced surprise at this new threat.

A blow from Vayhawk at his legs staggered him.

Senea pulled the force away, then slid it home again without thinking about where it was going when Vayhawk struck Sky full with his knife.

There was instant answering agony in Senea's body. Sky disengaged himself from Vayhawk, staggered backward. Senea felt a pain like a dart of poisoned ice pierce her left shoulder.

She saw Sky stagger blindly, and Vayhawk caught him in his arms. The heldan stared wildly around. Senea was aware of his shock.

A deadly chill was spreading from her shoulder to her arm and side. She blurred it so the pain was not so intense.

"Use all your strength now!" Vayhawk called to her.

Sky had slumped where he sat, collapsed with his head fallen against the rock wall, one arm hanging limp on the ground.

Senea thrust the power at him one last time, twisting it as

she felt it enter him. And alongside her force, she felt Vayhawk's presence, dark and hot, adding strength to the shaft of power that lanced to the heart of the heldan.

It was several moments before Senea saw that Vayhawk's arm was extended out, his knife blade gleaming.

It was already on its course. As if slicing butter, the blade went in along Sky's right side, high up under the ribs. Vayhawk twisted the knife and answering pain tore through Senea. She felt the blood wash over her hand even as it did over Vayhawk's.

The heat of Sky's life-force crawled up her arm. The knife fell from his grip, and he groaned.

His eyes fell on Senea. He knew what had been done to him, and he knew how it had been done. Utter hatred was plain on his face, replacing the haunted regretful anger that had been there.

The blood had drained from his face, leaving him ashen and sweating, and his breathing became heavy. She stared at him. She could feel the death that was in him.

Then he seemed to crumple, and he collapsed back to the ground. Blood seeped into the shale from his wound.

Vayhawk bent over him and felt for his pulse.

Senea watched as if through a haze. She was shaking, very much aware of what she had done—of what Vayhawk and she had done together. She leaned against Roskel, trying to cope with the sickness in the depths of her.

It wasn't the killing. It was the using of the Ja'sid power to do it, the finding that Vayhawk's instincts had been right. If two helden were close enough emotionally, they did not need to be physically touching for the power to work.

And it was reaction to all that had taken place, finding that Vayhawk was alive, and the killing of Sky.

For a moment she found it difficult to believe that it had actually been done. It had sapped what was left of her strength and drained her energy. Her body ached in every joint and muscle. And in her was an infinite sadness for the death of a fellow heldan.

Bitter tears stood in her eyes.

"Enough," Roskel whispered. "Enough."

She looked up at him in surprise. He was watching her narrowly.

"Forget him," he advised sharply. How uncannily he could

guess at her thoughts! "Vayhawk has been half out of his mind with worry for you. Don't give him anything else to worry about. Don't."

"I won't," she said, and brushed at her face.

"I'm glad to hear it." A flicker of impatience appeared in his eyes, and as quickly disappeared.

Senea swallowed. "I didn't . . ." She felt indignation start. She didn't want to finish the sentence, but his compelling eyes forced her to continue.

"It wasn't as he tried to make it seem."

Roskel's brows drew together. Then he said, "That's good."

"You don't believe it?"

"Of course I believe it. You say so."

It was on his face, and Senea thought it would have been easy enough for him to wring the truth out of her had she lied. She felt his presence close and warm next to her.

"Here," he said, and held a water skin to her lips, forcing her to drink. The warm liquid rolled over her tongue and trickled down her sore throat. A fit of coughing left her gasping and weak. Roskel helped her to the ground.

"Don't take very much," he said.

She took a long, slow, deep breath and reached for the skin, but her hands were shaking so much that she couldn't get it to her lips. He steadied it for her.

There was movement through the brush, and Vayhawk approached and sank wearily to his heels beside Roskel. He looked sidelong at her, then looked away, but before he did Senea saw something in his eyes that she could only interpret as regret. Her heart did a painful lurch of dismay.

Roskel's eyes were full of compassion, and with a rare demonstration of affection, he gripped the Heldlan's shoulder tightly.

"It had to be done," he said. "I'm sorry."

Vayhawk looked at him. His eyes had a bruised look, and his lips were tight. He reached for the water skin.

"I just need to get some water down my throat." His hand shook violently as he poured the water into his mouth.

There was a silence. Senea looked at Vayhawk beneath her lashes. He was staring at her.

"I'll go take care of the body," Roskel said, releasing Senea and rising to his feet.

Vayhawk nodded, and Roskel left.

For long moments he looked at her, his thumb moving restlessly over the neck of the water skin. Her gaze faltered before his, and she clenched her fingers together.

"Won't you please say something?" she said at last, lifting her eyes to his. "Anything." Then all sound left her under the force of his gaze.

"Did he hurt you?" he asked, a question that warmed her heart with a warmth that surprised her and brought the sting of tears to her eyes. She fought them down.

"Only a little," she lied, and saw that he knew it.

Their eyes met, his clouded with pain for her.

She took a deep breath, torn between conflicting pulls of grief, guilt, and relief. "You killed him," she said softly.

"It was heldcode."

She nodded and looked down. "Do you want me to go?" It was out before she had a chance to snatch it back. She needed him now more than she had ever needed anyone in her life. But she knew that it had been guilt at Sky's death that had pulled the words out of her. She watched him.

There was a frown drawing deep lines between his brows as he looked at her. "I was worried about you." It was a whisper, reaching out to her across the chasm that Sky had eroded between them.

He shifted to his knees, so close she could feel his heat. He stared into her eyes. "I'll make a deal with you."

"A deal?"

"We won't discuss this any further, and you come back with me."

"That's a deal?"

"The only one I'm going to offer."

"But what Sky said . . ."

"Shh." His fingers came up and covered her lips. "He said nothing."

"But . . ."

"No," he whispered, shaking his head. "Whatever happened, didn't." His fingers moved around to caress her jaw.

She stared at him, not knowing what to say, and he smiled. How many hundreds of years had it been since she had seen him smile? It seemed so long ago. His eyes watched her closely as she tried to comprehend what he was saying.

At that moment, Roskel appeared beside him. "Heldlan."

Vayhawk turned and Roskel held a knife sheath out to him. "I thought you'd want this."

Vayhawk met Roskel's expressionless gaze and then took the knife with a nod. Roskel turned and strode away.

Senea stared at the knife and a morbid shiver took her. Weapons of the dead. Always retrieved. Always.

Vayhawk turned his gaze on her, silent for a long minute. Then he held out the sheathed knife, and she saw that it was her own. The handle was milk-white with the cobweb of bloodred veins curling around it in delicate lacing.

She drew in a breath and took it from him, clasping it tightly in her hand. "I don't know what to say."

"Say you love me." His voice was so low she almost didn't hear him.

She looked up in surprise. "What?"

He leaned forward, his lips almost on hers. "Say you love me."

"What about Roskel?"

"His being here does not prohibit you from saying it. Besides, I'm sending him to the Wuepoah with Aldived's regrets on the death of their Heldlan."

Senea shook her head. "None of this would have happened if . . ."

"Shh." He bent so that his lips touched hers, stopping her. "Just say you love me. Nothing else matters."

Senea closed her eyes; his hand touched her cheek and slid around to the nape of her neck. Her breath deserted her and her heart raced. "You know I do."

"Then say it."

The touch of his lips on hers was making her head spin, and she clutched at his arm, afraid she was going to lose her balance. His breath was warm across her mouth, and he held back, only just letting his lips barely brush against hers until she was dizzy with anticipation.

"Vayhawk . . ." she protested breathlessly.

"No." His lips withdrew from hers and her heart crashed. "It can't be so hard to say."

His hand entwined in her hair, holding her prisoner right where she was. And she knew he would not let her go until she had said what he wanted to hear. For a perverse moment, she thought of not saying anything so that he'd have to hold her forever. But then she swallowed at the beating of her heart and drew a breath.

"I love you," she whispered. "I always will."

She heard him exhale in relief, and she looked at him in surprise. He hadn't been sure.

He pulled her to him, his arms going around her, drawing her up to him until his lips were on hers, gentle at first, lingering, tasting, and caressing until she was clinging against him. It was warm and surprisingly sweet until his mouth became more possessive, and his kiss deepened and lengthened until she was out of breath. Then he lifted his head and looked into her eyes. His hand came up to her cheek, his fingers moving slowly to the point below her ear, his thumb caressing her lower lip.

"Do we have a deal?"

"A deal?"

"Will you come back with me? I do not ever intend to let you get away from me again."

"But I didn't—"

"Do we have a deal, Senea?"

She looked at him and then nodded. "Yes." Then mischievously, she asked, "What do I get out of this deal?"

He lifted his eyes to hers in surprise, a slight frown between his brows. "What do you want?"

She lowered her gaze. "Nothing much, really." She hesitated, smiling to herself. "Just for you to say you love me." She looked up at him sheepishly.

His eyes glinted in appreciative amusement and he laughed, pulling her close. "Yes, Senea. I love you."

She sighed and closed her eyes, feeling the heat of him against her cheek, heard the strong beat of his heart, and she slid her hand up his chest, delighting in the maleness of him.

"Then we have a deal."

CHAPTER
TWENTY-FIVE

Windshift had begun, that which each evening attended the cooling of the land, and Senea tucked her hands close to her as she rested on her heels, scanning the vast reaches before her, taking her breath after her long walking.

The chasms below her girdled the earth, separating the boundary of her held-tribe's land from the Ja'sid's greater and expanded lands. The Ja'sid had been advancing for two cycles of seasons now. Two wet seasons had come and gone. The Games were coming up again soon, and Senea thought on that for a moment before turning her attention again to the landscape in front of her.

The sun was stretched across the western horizon in a brilliant elliptical half globe and lit the canyons to the north in a vast maze of lights and darks, blue-black shadows, orange and pink highlights. The silence, except for the whisper of the windshift through the grass, was absolute. She watched as the shadows drifted, the light in the canyons passing to amber twilight, while the sun stained the rocks higher and higher as it sank behind the hazy distance, going down over the far, invisible rim as if it vanished in midair, drawing out shadows.

She looked eastward. At the mid of the hill was Treyna. She need not have worried. Treyna would come.

They had both advanced in rank, the last Games, she to fifth, Treyna to tenth. They were paired, an unlikely pairing, but one that worked. Roskel assigned them to patrol the Ja'sid borders often. Senea had watched Treyna become quiet and withdrawn since Sky's death, a hardness that was colder and fiercer than before. She had been in love with Sky, Senea had come to realize, and watched as that loss turned her into a silent shadow that came and went among the helden, preferring to keep to herself. And for some reason Senea preferred it that way, having no other, besides Vayhawk, at her side.

No other could defend the borders with the ferocity that had become the trademark of their unusual alliance.

It was not a friendship, nothing like what had been between Mara and herself, a closeness that she missed painfully at times.

But an unspoken thing was between them, a mutual agreement that neither voiced or tried to break. And together they had become a formidable team that no Ja'sid had yet prevailed against.

There were other changes at the Held. Yunab was dead, killed by the hand of Aldived in a show of strength and resolve that had stunned the entire Held. Now he was proving to all that the disinterest and ineptitude of his had been a ruse to pull out the disrupting influences within the Held. He took care of those helden with a finality and swiftness that none but Vayhawk and Roskel had thought him capable of. The Held was becoming more disciplined because of it.

And it was time to put Vayhawk's plan into motion.

Treyna arrived, in her own time, and paused on the slope below the rocks—she began, slowly, to climb up to Senea. When she had done so, she sank down on the flat stone beside where Senea sat, arms draped loosely over her knees.

"Anything?" Senea asked, even though she knew the answer was negative.

"A couple of wolfhounds."

"Vayhawk?"

"Not yet."

Senea looked out, and in the darkening north, there was the first sparkling of stars. "We'll wait."

Treyna nodded. "Always we wait. He always comes late, this Heldlan of ours."

"Treyna," Senea objected.

"He travels too far. He does not need to come."

Senea said nothing, but gathered up a stone and rolled it between her fingers. Treyna simply rested. It was a conversation that never got finished, an unspoken understanding between them to never discuss Vayhawk.

Senea tossed the stone away with a flick and looked in the twilight over her shoulder, seeing nothing but the dark rise of the hill behind them. She turned back, noting Treyna's shadowed gaze on her. She ignored it and picked up another stone.

"When the time comes," Treyna finally said, "I will do the deed."

Senea crumbled the soft stone in her hand. "There will be no need. Vayhawk will be with us." She knew without having to see it that there was an instant scowl on the heldan's face.

"Roskel said nothing to me."

Senea let the crumbled rock sift through her fingers. "He said it to me."

"He knew I would not come."

"Yes."

"Roskel is too clever. I'll go back."

"No." Then Senea added, "Don't. We need you."

Treyna snorted softly. "You don't need me. You are only going after one man."

"But there is all the Ja'sid between."

"Yes," she conceded. "And a long way. The chances are not good."

"No."

"We might not make it."

Senea accepted that "we" in silence. She draped her arms around her knees, resting her chin there.

"I have no love for him," Treyna said after a while. "He knows it."

There was a long silence. Senea did not answer.

"If I challenged him out there, he would kill me."

"There are the Games."

"No. No Games."

Senea turned her head, but could not see Treyna's face in the dark. "Don't do it," she said.

There was a long pause in which Treyna stared out into the night. Then she said, "No. I won't."

That left silence then. They sat still, staring alike at the dark land. The moon came up and slowly rose into the sky.

Treyna stirred. "I'll go take another look." There was movement, and she was gone.

Senea stretched her back and looked after her into the dark. There was no sound of her going, and it was just as if she hadn't been there.

The soft sound of a pebble rolling over stone brought her head around. At first she saw nothing, only a blacker darkness where the rocks were silhouetted against the stars. Then a shadow detached itself and came silently toward her. She tensed for just a moment until she was certain of the identity, the signal of pebble on stone telling her who it was before she had even known he was there. But caution was a thing that was part of her now, as much as her knife and her bow.

She sat still and let him come to her, felt his warmth as he settled beside her, his arm pressing lightly against hers.

"I waited until she was gone," he said, his textured voice quiet.

The desert magnetism of him settled on her with an intimacy that was like a touch of his hand. She drew in a breath. "There was no need."

"I know . . . I waited all the same."

Senea did not answer, letting the closeness of him encircle her and draw her, felt his arm move against hers as he drew his knees up.

"She wants a quarrel, that one."

"She won't."

"Perhaps not."

"Vayhawk . . ." she said. "Please . . . bear with her."

"I do," he said. "For your sake."

She regarded him, the animal strength of him, the familiar gold that shone softly on his arm.

He looked at her, his face not discernible in the dark. "I asked for her to be with us on this."

"Yes, I know."

"It is a dangerous thing that we have set for ourselves. I will not tolerate dissent. You know this."

"Yes."

"If she gives me trouble I will not hesitate to deal with it. You know this?"

"Yes."

"If it comes to heldcode—you would abide by it?"

The question stopped her cold. Her heart clenched. "Yes," she said after a moment.

"You could not be mistaken?"

"No."

"If it comes to that, I will decide as it has always been decided. The heldan way. Do you hear me?"

"I hear you." She lowered her voice in midbreath at

Vayhawk's touch, made a gesture of helpless appeal. "Only give her a little—I ask this."

He reached up a hand to her face, a caressing move from her cheek to her hairline, and his face came close to hers. "Only a very little."

She shut her eyes an instant and caught the essence of him, a quiet thing and determined.

"But dealing with the Ja'sid Tribelord and putting an end to this Ja'sid aggression against us will be my first consideration, Senea. I want you to understand this."

"Yes. I understand."

"Good." He bent then and touched his lips to hers in a slow, caressing kiss that caused her heart to leap against her ribs with hard jarring strokes. His hand went around to the nape of her neck, his thumb moving along her jawline, holding her to him for a moment. Then he withdrew a little and his thumb ran slowly down the length of her throat.

"I missed you," he said, a whisper like a knife's slash. "I'd like to take you back to the Held instead of out onto the Ja'sid desert."

He was silent for a long moment, his fingers moving slowly over her skin.

"But it's time," he said. Then his hand dropped and he sat back a little. "It's time to put this Ja'sid thing to the test."

Senea looked reluctantly down out to the darkness of the desert. "Yes, I know. That is why Treyna is here."

"Yes."

"It is a hard thing that we will do to her."

"She is heldan. She will bear it."

Senea turned back to Vayhawk. "This will work? This is what you dreamed?" She asked only to reassure herself. He had been over this with her many times already.

"Yes," he answered.

Senea drew in a breath, thinking of the ordeal that waited ahead of them.

His plan had been teaching Treyna the Ja'sid power and using her hatred for Vayhawk as the emotion to make it potent. If Vayhawk was right, the Ja'sid would be stopped dead where they were. The clash between love and hatred with Vayhawk as the focal point should make the power so strong that none of the Ja'sid would escape.

Vayhawk sat back. He released her and rose to his feet. "It's time to go."

Senea nodded. She picked up the bow that lay beside her and stood with a single effortless motion. As she turned to follow him, he stopped her, taking hold of her hand.

"When we get through with this . . ." he said, his hand traveling intimately up her arm. But he didn't finish what he was going to say.

Senea understood. When this whole thing was over and he had her back at the Held, he was going to challenge heldcode and the prohibition against having kin-ties. He wanted to marry her.

He turned then, his hand momentarily around her arm as he descended the rocks.

The slope ran down into deeper shadows that lay among the rocks and knobs of stone, wind-smoothed in places, deep recesses in others. A breath of air moved along the ground, a sigh that dissipated and faded up the hill. And there was a darkness that was nearest of all, a shadow not cast by stone against moonlight.

It acquired substance.

The slope straightened, and a woman appeared, heldan clad, hand at knife hilt, silent and waiting where Senea knew that she would be. If not here then some other place farther on— Treyna's way to retreat whenever Vayhawk came to them on their patrol.

She fell into step beside Senea, a shielded silence that was like a wall of blackness, sullen and defiant.

"Treyna," Vayhawk said, acknowledging her presence.

Treyna did not answer for a moment but gazed at Senea, at him, a stubborn tilt to her head.

Senea held her breath while waiting for Treyna to say something, fully expecting her to be insolent, and exhaled softly when she merely inclined her head and murmured, "Heldlan."

Senea looked to Vayhawk and saw him watching Treyna with a sober measuring assessment, the soft light of the moon shining on his face. His eyes slid to hers and she knew, in that way of silent understanding that was between them, that this was exactly what he had expected from her. His hand brushed lightly against hers, and Senea moved up beside him, felt the closeness of him like an enveloping embrace.

She looked back at Treyna, who had fallen behind a couple of paces, her face shadowed in the dark.

The Ja-sid had no chance, she thought to herself. Treyna would surprise them all.

DEL REY DISCOVERY

**Experience the wonder of Discovery
with Del Rey's newest authors!**

...Because something new is always worth the risk!

Coming in July
to your local bookstore...

MISTWALKER
by Denise Lopes Heald

"Quite an adventure tale, a love story, and
a damned good ecological drama!"
—Anne McCaffrey

Published by Del Rey Books.